THE
SEARCHER

ALSO BY TANA FRENCH
Available from Random House Large Print

The Witch Elm

THE
SEARCHER

Tana French

Copyright © 2020 by Tana French

All rights reserved.
Published in the United States of America by
Random House Large Print in association with Viking,
an imprint of Penguin Random House LLC.

Cover design Darren Haggar
Cover photograph Matt Anderson Photography/Getty Images

The Library of Congress has established a
Cataloging-in-Publication record for this title.

ISBN: 978-0-593-34250-3

www.penguinrandomhouse.com/large-print-format-books

FIRST LARGE PRINT EDITION

Printed in the United States of America

10   9   8   7   6   5   4   3

This Large Print edition published in accord with
the standards of the N.A.V.H.

For Ann-Marie

THE
SEARCHER

ONE

When Cal comes out of the house, the rooks have got hold of something. Six of them are clustered on the back lawn, amid the long wet grass and the yellow-flowered weeds, jabbing and hopping. Whatever the thing is, it's on the small side and still moving.

Cal sets down his garbage bag of wallpaper. He considers getting his hunting knife and putting the creature out of its suffering, but the rooks have been here a lot longer than he has. It would be pretty impertinent of him to waltz in and start interfering with their ways. Instead he eases himself down to sit on the mossy step next to the trash bag.

He likes the rooks. He read somewhere that they're smart as hell; they can get to know you, bring you presents even. For three months now he's been trying to butter them up with scraps left on the big stump towards the bottom of the garden. They watch him trudge up and down through the grass, from the ivy-loaded oak where they have their colony, and as soon as he's a safe distance away they swoop down to squabble and comment raucously over the scraps; but they keep a cynical eye on Cal, and if he tries to move closer they're gone, back into the oak to jeer down at him and drop twigs on his head. Yesterday afternoon he was in his living room, stripping away the mildewed wallpaper, and a sleek mid-sized rook landed on the sill of the open window, yelled what was obviously an insult, and then flapped off laughing.

The thing on the lawn twists wildly, shaking the long grass. A big daddy rook jumps closer, aims one neat ferocious stab of his beak, and the thing goes still.

Rabbit, maybe. Cal has seen them out there in the early mornings, nibbling and dashing in the dew. Their holes are somewhere in his back field, down by the broad copse of hazels and rowans. Once his firearm license comes through, he's planning to see if he remembers what his grandpa taught him about skinning game, and if the mule-tempered broadband will deign to find him a recipe for rabbit stew. The rooks crowd in, pecking hard and bracing their feet to jerk out bites of flesh, more of them zooming down from the tree to jostle in on the action.

Cal watches them for a while, stretching out his legs and rolling one shoulder in circles. Working on the house is using muscles he'd forgotten he had. He finds new aches every morning, although some of that is likely from sleeping on a cheap mattress on the floor. Cal is too old and too big for that, but there's no point in bringing good furniture into the dust and damp and mold. He'll buy that stuff once he has the house in shape, and once he figures out where you buy it—all that was Donna's department. Meanwhile, he doesn't mind the aches. They satisfy him. Along with the blisters and thickening calluses, they're solid, earned proof of what his life is now.

It's headed into the long cool September stretch of evening, but cloudy enough that there's no trace of a sunset. The sky, dappled in subtle gradations of gray, goes on forever; so do the fields, coded in shades of green by their different uses, divided up by sprawling hedges, dry-stone walls and the odd narrow back road. Away to the north, a line of low mountains rolls along the horizon. Cal's eyes are still getting used to looking this far, after all those years of city blocks. Landscape is one of the few things he knows of where the reality doesn't let you down. The West of Ireland looked beautiful on the internet; from right smack in the middle of it, it looks even better. The air is rich as fruitcake, like you should do more with it than just breathe it; bite off a big mouthful, maybe, or rub handfuls of it over your face.

After a while the rooks slow down, getting towards the end of their meal. Cal stands up and picks up the trash bag again. The rooks cock smart, instant glances at him and, when he starts down the garden, heave themselves into the air and flap their full bellies back to their tree. He hauls the bag down to a corner beside the creeper-covered tumbledown stone shed, pausing along the way to check out the rooks' dinner. Rabbit, all right, a young one, although barely recognizable now.

He leaves the trash bag with the rest and heads back to the house. He's almost there when the rooks kick off, jostling leaves and yelling cuss words at something. Cal doesn't turn around or break stride. He says very softly through his teeth, as he closes the back door behind him, "Mother**fucker.**"

For the last week and a half, someone has been watching Cal. Probably longer, but he had his mind on his own business and he took for granted, like anyone would have a right to do amid all this empty space, that he was alone. His mental alarm systems were switched off, the way he wanted them. Then one night he was cooking dinner—frying a hamburger on the rust-pocked stove's one working burner, Steve Earle good and loud on the iPod speaker, Cal adding in the occasional crash of air drums—when the back of his neck flared.

The back of Cal's neck got trained over twenty-five years in the Chicago PD. He takes it seriously. He ambled casually across the kitchen, nodding along to the music and examining the counters like he was missing something, and then made a sudden lunge to the window: no one outside. He turned off the burner and headed for the door fast, but the garden was empty. He walked the perimeter, under a million savage stars and a howler's moon, fields laid out white all around him and owls yelping: nothing.

Some animal noise, Cal told himself, drowned out by the music so that only his subconscious picked it up. The dark is busy around here. He's sat out on his step well past midnight, a few times, drinking a couple of beers and getting the hang of the nighttime. He's seen hedgehogs bustling across the garden, a sleek fox stopping on its route to give him a challenge of a stare. One time a badger, bigger and more muscular than Cal would have expected, trundled along the hedge and disappeared into it; a minute later there was one high shriek, and then the rustle of the badger moving off. Anything could have been going about its business out there.

Before Cal went to bed that night, he stacked his two mugs and two plates on the bedroom windowsill and dragged an old desk up against the bedroom door. Then he called himself a dumbass and put them away.

A couple of mornings later he was stripping wallpaper, window open to let out the dust, when the rooks exploded up out of their tree, shouting at something underneath. The fast trail of rustles heading away behind the hedge was too big and noisy for a hedgehog or a fox, too big even for a badger. By the time Cal got out there, he was too late again.

Probably bored kids spying on the newcomer. Not much else to do around here, with the village no bigger than the little end of nothing, and the closest two-horse town fifteen miles away. Cal feels dumb for even considering anything else. Mart, his nearest neighbor up the road, doesn't even lock his door except at night. When Cal raised an eyebrow at that, Mart's high-boned face creased up and he laughed till he wheezed. "The state of that there," he said, pointing towards Cal's house. "What would anyone rob off you? And who'd rob it? Am I going to sneak in some morning and go through your washing, looking for something to spruce up my fashion sense?" And Cal laughed too and told him he could do with it, and Mart informed him that his own wardrobe would do him grand, seeing as he had no plans to go courting, and started explaining why not.

But there have been things. No big deal, just stuff that flicks at the edges of Cal's cop sense. Engines revving, three a.m. down faraway back roads, deep-chested bubbling snarls. A huddle of guys in the back corner of the pub some nights, too young and dressed wrong, talking too loud and too fast in accents that don't fit in; the snap of their heads towards the door when Cal walks in, the stares that last a second too long. He's been careful not to tell anyone what he used to do, but just being a stranger could be plenty, depending.

Dumb, Cal tells himself, turning on the burner under his frying pan and looking out the kitchen window at the dimming green fields, Mart's dog trotting beside the sheep as they plod peacefully towards their pen. Too many years on the beat in bad hoods, now farmhands look like gangbangers.

Bored kids, ten to one. All the same, Cal has started keeping his music down so he won't miss anything, he's thinking about getting an alarm system, and this pisses him off. Years of Donna lunging for the volume knob, **Cal, that baby next door is trying to sleep! Cal, Mrs. Scapanski just had surgery, you think she needs that blowing her eardrums? Cal, what are the neighbors gonna think, we're savages?** He wanted land partly so he could blast Steve Earle loud enough to knock squirrels out of the trees, and he wanted buttfuck nowhere partly so he wouldn't have to set alarms any more. He feels like he can't even, for example, adjust his balls without looking over his shoulder, which is something a man ought to be able to do in his own kitchen. Kids or not, he needs this put to bed.

At home he would have solved this with a couple of good, discreet cameras that uploaded straight to the cloud. Here, even if his Wi-Fi could handle that, which he doubts, the idea of taking his footage down to the nearest station doesn't sit well. He doesn't know what he might start: neighbor feud, or the watcher could be the officer's cousin, or who knows what.

He's considered tripwires. These are presumably illegal, but Cal is pretty sure this in itself wouldn't be a big deal: Mart has already offered twice to sell him an unregistered shotgun that he's got lying around, and everyone drives home from the pub. The problem is, again, that Cal is in the dark on what he might set in motion.

Or what he might have set in motion already. Listening to Mart, Cal has started to get an inkling of how tangled up things get around here, and how carefully you have to watch where you put your feet. Noreen, who runs the shop in the brief double line of buildings that counts as Ardnakelty village, won't order the cookies Mart likes because of a complicated saga that took place in the 1980s and involved her uncles, Mart's father and grazing rights; Mart doesn't speak to an unpronounceable farmer on the other side of the mountains because the guy bought a pup that was sired by Mart's dog when it somehow shouldn't have been. There are other stories like that, although Cal doesn't have them all straight, because Mart talks in big sweeping loops and because Cal doesn't fully have the hang of the local accent. He likes it—rich as the air, with a needle-fine point that makes him think of cold river water or mountain wind—but chunks of the conversation go right over his head, and he gets distracted listening to the rhythms and misses more. But he's gathered enough to know that he could have sat on someone's stool in the pub, or cut across the wrong piece of land on one of his walks, and that that could mean something.

When he arrived here, he was ready for closed ranks against the stranger. He was OK with that, as long as no one set his place on fire; he wasn't looking for golf buddies and dinner parties. But it didn't turn out that way. People were neighborly. The day Cal arrived and started hauling stuff into and out of the house, Mart wandered down to lean on the gate and probe for information, and ended up bringing over an old mini-fridge and recommending a good building supplies store. Noreen explained who was what kind of cousin to who and how to get onto the group water scheme, and—later, once Cal had made her laugh a few times—started offering, only half-way joking, to set Cal up with her widowed sister. The old guys who apparently live in the pub have moved from nods to weather comments to passion-ate explanations of a sport called hurling, which to Cal looks like what you might get if you kept the speed, dexterity and ferocity of ice hockey but took away the ice and most of the protective equipment. Up until last week he felt that he had been, if not exactly welcomed with open arms, at least accepted as a mildly interesting natural phenomenon, like maybe a seal that had taken up residence in the river. Obviously he was always going to be an outsider, but he was getting the feeling that that wasn't a big deal. He's no longer so sure.

So, four days ago, Cal drove into town and bought a big bag of garden soil. He's aware of the irony of buying more dirt, when he just spent most of his sav-ings on ten acres of it, but his personal dirt is rough and chunky, shot through with grass roots and small sharp rocks. For this he needed fine, moist, even stuff. The next day he got up before dawn and spread a layer of it by the outside wall of his house, under each of the windows. He had to pull weeds and creepers and scrape back pebbles to get a decent surface. The air was cold right down to the bottom of his lungs. Slowly the fields lightened around him;

the rooks woke up and started bickering. When the sky got bright and he heard Mart's faint peremptory whistle to his sheepdog, Cal crumpled up the soil bag to stuff at the bottom of the trash, and went inside to make breakfast.

Next morning, nothing; morning after that, nothing. He must have got closer than he thought, the last time, must have given them a scare. He went about his business and kept his eyes off the windows and the hedges.

This morning, footprints, in the dirt under his living-room window. Sneakers, going by the fragments of tread, but the prints were too scuffed up and overlapped to tell how big or how many.

The frying pan is hot. Cal throws in four slices of bacon, meatier and tastier than what he's used to, and once the fat sizzles cracks in two eggs. He goes over to his iPod, which lives on the same left-behind wooden table where he eats his meals—the sum total of Cal's current furniture is that table, a left-behind wooden desk with a busted side, two scrawny left-behind Formica chairs, and a fat green armchair that Mart's cousin was throwing out—and puts on some Johnny Cash, not too loud.

If he's done something that pissed someone off, the prime candidate has got to be buying this house. He picked it off a website, on the basis that it came with some land, there was good fishing nearby, the roof looked sound, and he wanted to check out the papers sticking out of that old desk. It had been a long time since Cal had got a wild hare like that and chased after it, which seemed like an extra reason for doing it. The estate agents were asking thirty-five K. Cal offered thirty, cash. They about bit his hand off.

It didn't occur to him at the time that anyone else might want the place. It's a low, gray, undistinguished house built sometime in the 1930s, five hundred and some square feet, slate-roofed and sash-windowed; only the big cornerstones and the broad stone fireplace give it a touch of grace. Going by the website photos, it had been abandoned for years, probably decades: paint peeling in big streaks and mottles, rooms strewn with upended dark-brown furniture and rotting flowered curtains, saplings springing up in front of the door and creepers trailing in at a broken window. But he's learned enough since then to understand that someone else might in fact have wanted this place, even if the reasons aren't immediately apparent, and that anyone who felt they had a claim on it was likely to take that seriously.

Cal scoops his food onto a couple of thick slices of bread, adds ketchup, gets a beer out of the mini-fridge and takes his meal to the table. Donna would give him shit about the way he's been eating, which doesn't include a whole lot of fiber and fresh vegetables, but the fact is that even living out of a frying pan and a microwave he's dropped a few pounds, maybe more than a few. He can feel it, not just in his waistband but in his movements: everything he does has a surprising new lightness to it. That was unsettling at first, like he had come unhitched from gravity, but it's growing on him.

The exercise is what's doing it. Just about every day Cal goes walking for an hour or two, nowhere particular, just following his nose and getting the lay of his new land. A lot of days it rains on him, but this is OK: he has a big wax jacket and the rain is like nothing he's felt before, a fine soft haze that seems to hang motionless in the air. Mostly he leaves his hood down just so he can feel that haze against his face. As well as seeing farther than he's used to, he can hear farther: the occasional sheep's bleat or cow's bawl, or farmer's shout, comes to him from what seems like miles away, thinned and gentled by the distance. Sometimes he sees one of the farmers, going about his business away across the fields, or chugging down a narrow lane in a tractor so that Cal has to press back into the unruly hedge as he goes past lifting a hand in greeting. He's passed strong-built women hauling heavy things around cluttered farmyards, red-cheeked toddlers staring at him through gates and sucking on the bars while the rangy dogs bark up a storm at him. Sometimes a bird calls a wild high streak above his head, or a pheasant explodes out of the undergrowth as he comes close. He gets back to the house feeling like he made the right call, throwing everything up in the air and coming here.

In between walks, with nothing else to call on his attention, Cal pretty much works on the house from morning till night. The first thing he did when he arrived was sweep away the thick cocoon of cobwebs and dust and dead bugs and what-have-you that was patiently working to fill every inch of the place. Next he put new glass in the windows, and replaced the toilet and the bath—both of which had been smashed up pretty good by someone with a lump hammer and a deep-seated grudge against bath-room fixtures—so he could stop shitting in a hole in the ground and washing out of a bucket. Cal is no plumber, but he's always been handy and he has YouTube how-to videos, when the internet doesn't crap out on him; it worked out OK.

After that he spent a while going through the left-behind stuff that littered the rooms, taking his time, giving each piece his full attention. Whoever lived here last was serious about religion: they had pic-tures of Saint Bernadette, a disappointed-looking Virgin Mary, and someone called Padre Pio, all in thin cheap frames and all left to yellow in corners by less devout heirs. They liked condensed milk, of which there were five cans in the kitchen cup-board, all of them fifteen years out of date. They had pink-printed china cups, rusted-out saucepans, rolled-up oilcloth tablecloths, a figurine of a kid in a red robe and crown with the head glued back on, and a shoebox holding a pair of old-fashioned men's dress shoes, worn to creases and polished to a shine that still showed. Cal was a little surprised to find no evidence of teenage occupation, no empty beer cans or cigarette butts or used condoms, no graffiti.

He figured this place must be too remote for them. At the time, that seemed like a good thing. Now he's less sure. The possibility of teenagers checking on their old hangout is something he'd prefer to have on the menu.

The papers in the desk turned out to be nothing much: articles torn out of newspapers and magazines, folded into neat rectangles. Cal tried to find some unifying thread among the articles, but failed: they involved, among other things, the history of the Boy Scouts, how to grow sweet peas, tin whistle tunes, the Irish peacekeeping forces in Lebanon, and a recipe for something called Welsh rarebit. Cal kept them, seeing as they were in a way the thing that had brought him here. He tossed most of the other stuff, including the curtains, which now seems like a bad call. He's considered digging them back out of the heap of trash bags that's growing behind the shed, but some animal has probably either chewed them up or pissed on them by now.

He's replaced gutters and downpipes, climbed up on his roof to evict a sturdy crop of yellow-flowered weeds from his chimney, sanded and polished the old oak floorboards, and these days he's working on the walls. The last inhabitant had surprisingly unconventional tastes in decoration, that or a few buckets of cheap paint. Cal's bedroom used to be a deep, rich indigo, till the damp mottled it with streaks of mold and pale patches of bare plaster. The smaller bedroom was a light minty green. The living-room part of the front room was rusty red-brown, slapped on top of layers of buckling wallpaper. It's unclear what exactly was going on in the kitchen area, which looks like someone might have been aiming to tile it and then got sidetracked, and nobody made even that much effort with the bathroom: it's a tiny tacked-on cube at the back of the house, with plaster walls and a remnant of green carpet more or less covering the raw floorboards, like it was made by aliens who had heard about this thing called a bathroom but weren't exactly clear on the details. Cal, at six foot four, has to squeeze himself into the bath with his knees practically under his chin. Once he's tiled the room he'll put in a shower fixture, but that can wait. He wants to get the painting done while the weather is good enough that he can leave the windows open. Already there have been days, just one or two of them, with the sky a dense gray and the cold rising up from the ground and the wind riding straight across hundreds of miles and through his house like it's not there, to warn him of what winter's going to be. Nothing approaching the snowbanks and subzero of Chicago winters—he knows that from the internet—but something in its own right, something steely and intractable, with a tricky side.

Cal takes a look at his day's work while he eats. The wallpaper melded into the wall in places over the years, which makes this slow going, but he's got more than half the room stripped to bare plaster; the wall around the chunky stone arch of the fireplace is still a scuffed red-brown. An unexpected part of him likes the room this way. It implies things. Cal is no artist, but if he was, he'd be inclined to leave it like this for a while, paint a few pictures.

He's halfway through his food and still considering this when the back of his neck flares again. This time he even hears the signal that triggered it: a small, clumsy scramble, almost instantly cut off, like someone started to trip into the undergrowth outside the window and then caught themselves.

Cal takes another big, leisurely mouthful of sandwich, washes it down with a long gulp of beer, and wipes foam off his tache. Then he grimaces and leans forwards, with a belch, to put his plate on the table. He pulls himself out of the chair, cracks his neck and heads for the john, already fumbling at his belt buckle.

The bathroom window opens as smoothly and silently as if it's been sprayed with WD-40, which it has. Cal has also practiced the climb onto the toilet cistern and out the window, and he manages it a lot more deftly than anyone could expect of someone his size, but that doesn't change the fact that one reason he quit being a beat cop was because he had had it with climbing unreasonable objects in pursuit of mopes doing gratuitous crap, and he had no plans to go back to that. He lands on the ground outside with his heart speeding in the old familiar hunting rhythm, his ass scraped up by the window frame, and a rising sense of aggravation.

The best he's got is a piece of pipe, left over from the bathroom work and stashed in a bush. Even holding it, he feels empty-handed and too light, without his gun. He stands still for a minute, letting his eyes adjust and listening, but the night is speckled all over with small noises and he can't pick out any one that seems more relevant than the others. It's got dark; the moon is up, a sharp slice chased over by ragged clouds, casting only a faint unreliable light and too many shadows. Cal adjusts his grip on the pipe and moves, with the old practiced compromise between speed and silence, towards the corner of the house.

Below the living-room window a huddle of denser darkness crouches, motionless, head just high enough to peer over the sill. Cal scans carefully, as best he can, but the grass all around is clear: looks like just the one. In the spill of light from the window he catches a buzz cut and a smudge of red.

Cal drops the pipe and charges. He's going for a full tackle, planning on flattening the guy and figuring out the rest from there, but his foot turns on a rock. In the second while he's flailing for his balance, the guy leaps up and away. Cal lunges into the near-darkness, grabs hold of an arm and hauls with all his might.

The guy flies towards him too easily, and the arm

is small enough that his hand wraps right around it. It's a kid. The realization loosens Cal's grip a notch. The kid twists like a bobcat, with a hiss of breath, and sinks his teeth into Cal's hand.

Cal roars. The kid yanks free and takes off across the garden like a rocket, feet almost noiseless on the grass. Cal starts after him, but in seconds he's disappeared into the scribble of shadow by the roadside hedge, and by the time Cal reaches it, he's gone. Cal shoves his way through the hedge and looks up and down the road, narrowed to a faint ribbon by the moon-shadows of the hedges crowding in. Nothing. He tosses a couple of stones into the bushes in various directions, trying to flush the kid out: no.

He doubts the kid had reinforcements—he would have yelled out, either for help or to warn them— but he jogs a circle around the garden just in case. The rooks are asleep, undisturbed. New footprints in the soil below the living-room window, same tread as last time; nowhere else. Cal backs himself up in the heavy shadow of the shed and waits for a long time, trying to quiet his panting, but there's no rustle in any hedge and no shadow sneaking away across any field. Just the one, and just a kid. And not coming back, at least not tonight.

Inside, he takes a look at his hand. The kid got him good: three teeth broke the skin, and one place is bleeding. Cal got bit once before, on the job, which led to a maelstrom of paperwork, interviews, blood tests, legal wrangling, pills and court appearances that went on for months, till Cal got fed up keeping track of what was for what and just handed over his arm or his signature on request. He finds his first-aid kit and soaks his hand in disinfectant for a while, then sticks on a Band-Aid.

His food has gone cold. He nukes it up and takes it back to the table. Johnny Cash is still going, mourning his lost Rose and his lost boy, in a deep broken quaver like he's already a ghost.

Cal isn't feeling the way he would have expected. Kids spying on the new guy were the thing he was hoping to find, the best-case scenario. He figured he would shout vague threats after them while they zoomed away yelling and laughing and calling insults over their shoulders, and then he would shake his head and go back indoors bitching about kids nowadays like some old geezer, and that would be the end of that. Maybe they would come back for another round, every now and then, but Cal was basically OK with that. Meanwhile, he could return to doing his renovation and playing his music loud and adjusting his balls whenever he damn well pleased, with his police sense put back to bed where it belongs.

Except he doesn't feel like that was the end of that, and his police sense isn't going back to sleep. Kids screwing with the stranger for kicks should have come in a bunch, and they should have been rowdy, hopped up on their own daring like it was caffeine. He thinks of this kid's stillness under the window,

his silence when Cal grabbed him, the snake-strike
ferocity of his bite. This kid wasn't having fun. He
was here for a purpose. He'll be back.

Cal finishes his food and does the dishes. He nails
up a drop sheet over the bathroom window and takes
a fast bath. Then he lies on his mattress in the dark
with his hands behind his head, looking out the window at the cloud-patched stars and listening to foxes
fighting somewhere out across the fields.

TWO

The busted-up desk, when Cal gets it outside and takes a good look at it, is older than he thought and better quality: dark-stained oak, with delicate curls carved into the rail above the drop front and along the bottoms of the drawers, and a dozen little cubbyholes nested inside the drop. He had it stashed away in the smaller bedroom, since he wasn't planning on getting to it for a while, but it seems like it might come in useful today. He's hauled it out to the bottom of the garden, a carefully judged distance from the hedge and the rooks' tree, along with his table to act as a work surface, and his toolbox. That toolbox is one of the bare handful of things he shipped over here. Most of those tools were his grandpa's. They're scuffed, nicked, paint-splattered, but they still work better than the crap you pick up in hardware stores these days.

The main thing wrong with the desk is a big splintered dent in one side, like whoever went over the bathroom with a lump hammer took a swing at this on his way out. Cal is leaving that for last, once he gets his hand back in. He's planning on starting with the drawer runners. Two of them are plain gone, and the other two are warped and split till the drawer won't go out or in without a fight. He takes both drawers out, lays the desk on its back and starts drawing pencil outlines around the remaining runners.

The weather is on his side: it's a mild, sunny day with just a light breeze, little birds in the hedges and bees in the wildflowers, the kind of day where a man might naturally feel like taking some work outside. It's mid-morning on a school day, but judging by the other incidents, Cal doesn't reckon this necessarily means he's wasting his time. Even if nothing happens straightaway, he's got plenty here to keep him busy till school lets out. He whistles his grandpa's old folk songs through his teeth, and sings a few of the words when he remembers them.

When he hears the swish of feet in grass, a ways off, he keeps whistling and keeps his head down over the desk. After a minute, though, he hears a messy scramble through the hedge, and a wet nose shoves under his elbow: Kojak, Mart's raggedy black-and-white sheepdog. Cal straightens his back and gives Mart a wave.

"How's she cuttin'?" Mart inquires, over the side fence. Kojak lopes off to check out what's been in Cal's hedge since he was here last.

"Not too bad," Cal says. " 'Bout you?"

"Sound as a pound on the ground," Mart says. Mart is short, maybe five foot seven, wiry and lined; he has fluffy gray hair, a nose that got broken once or twice along the way, and a wide selection of hats.

Today he's wearing a flat tweed cap that looks like it's been chewed by some farm animal or other. "What're you at with that yoke?"

"Gonna fix it up," Cal says. He's trying to bump the second runner free, but it's holding fast; this desk was made right, way back whenever.

"Wasting your time," Mart tells him. "Have a look on one of them adverts websites. You'll pick up half a dozen of them for nothing."

"I only need one," Cal says. "And I've got one."

Mart clearly considers arguing the point, but he decides to drop it in favor of something more rewarding. "You're looking well," he says, eyeing Cal up and down. Mart was predisposed to approve of Cal from the start. He loves conversation, and over his sixty-one years he's sucked all the juice out of everyone around here. Cal is, from Mart's point of view, Christmas.

"Thanks," Cal says. "You too."

"I'm serious, man. Very slender. That belly's melting offa you." And when Cal, patiently rocking the drawer runner back and forth, doesn't answer: "D'you know what's doing that?"

"This," Cal says, nodding backwards at the house. "Instead of sitting on my ass at a desk all day."

Mart is shaking his head vigorously. "Not at all. I'll tell you what it is. It's the meat you're ating. Them sausages and rashers you get off Noreen. They're local; so fresh they'd hop off the plate and snort at you. They're doing you a power of good."

"I like you better than my old doctor," Cal says.

"Listen, would you. That American meat you were ating back home, that's chock fulla hormones. They pump those into the cattle to fatten them up. So what d'you think they do to human beings?"

He waits for an answer. "Can't be good," Cal says.

"They'll swell you up like a balloon and put tits on you like Dolly Parton. Mad yokes. The EU has them all banned, over here. That's what put the weight on you to begin with. Now that you're ating dacent Irish meat, it'll fall off you again. We'll have you looking like Gene Kelly in no time."

Mart has apparently picked up that Cal has something on his mind today and is determined to talk him out of it, either from a sense of neighborly duty or because he likes the challenge. "You oughta market that," Cal says. "Mart's Miracle Diet Bacon. The more you eat, the more you lose."

Mart chuckles, apparently satisfied. "Saw you heading into town there yesterday," he mentions, just in passing. He squints across the garden at Kojak, who is getting serious about a clump of bushes, scrabbling hard to jam his whole front end in there.

"Yeah," Cal says, straightening up. He knows what Mart is after. "Hold on." He goes inside and comes back out with a pack of cookies. "Don't eat 'em all at once," he says.

"You're a gentleman," Mart says happily, accepting the cookies over the fence. "Did you try them yet?"

Mart's cookies are elaborate constructions of pink

fluffy marshmallow, jam and coconut that, to Cal, look like something you would use to bribe a five-year-old in a great big hair bow into quitting her tantrum. "Not yet," he says.

"Dip them, man. In the tay. The marshmallow goes soft and the jam melts on your tongue. Nothing like it." Mart stashes the cookies in the pocket of his green wax jacket. He doesn't offer to pay for them. The first time, Mart presented the cookie run as a once-off, a favor that would make a poor old farmer's day, and Cal wasn't about to demand a handful of change from his brand-new neighbor. After that Mart treated it as a long-established tradition. The amused slide of his eyes at Cal whenever he takes the cookies says he's testing.

"I'm a coffee man," Cal says. "It wouldn't be the same."

"Don't be telling Noreen about these, now," Mart warns him. "She'd only find something else to take off me. She likes to think she's got the upper hand."

"Speaking of Noreen," Cal says. "If you're heading that way, can you pick me up some ham? I forgot."

Mart gives a long whistle. "Are you after getting yourself into Noreen's bad books? Bad move there, bucko. Look where that landed me. Whatever it is you done, get you down there with a bunch of flowers and make your apologies."

The fact is, Cal wants to stick around home today. "Nah," he says. "She keeps trying to set me up with her sister."

Mart's eyebrows shoot up. "What sister?"

"Helena, I think she said."

"God almighty, man, then away you go. I thought there you meant Fionnuala, but Noreen must like the cut of you. Lena's got a good head on her shoulders. And her husband was tight as a duck's arse and he'd drink the river dry, God rest him, so she's not suffering from high standards. She won't go mad if you bring your muddy boots inside or fart in the bed."

"Sounds like my kind of woman," Cal says. "If I was looking."

"And she's a fine strapping lass, too, not one of them scrawny young ones that you'd lose if they turned sideways. A woman needs a bit of meat on her. Ah, now"—pointing a finger at Cal, who has started to laugh—"that's your filthy mind, that is. I'm not talking about the riding. Did I say anything about the riding?"

Cal shakes his head, still laughing.

"I did not. What I'm saying"—Mart settles his forearms on the top bar of the fence, getting comfortable to expand on this—"what I'm saying to you is, if you're going to have a woman in the house, you want one that fills a bit of space. It's no good having some skin-and-bones scrap of a girl with a mousy wee voice on her and not a word out of her from one day to the next. You wouldn't be getting your money's worth. When you walk into the house, you want to be seeing your woman, and hearing her. You need to know she's there, or what's the point in having her at all?"

"No point," Cal says, grinning. "So Lena's loud, huh?"

"You'd know she was there. Away with you and get your own ham slices, and ask Noreen to set up that date. Give yourself a good wash, shave that wookiee off your face, put on a fancy shirt. Bring her into town, now, to a restaurant; don't be bringing her down the pub to be stared at by all them reprobates."

"You should take her out," Cal says.

Mart snorts. "I've never been married."

"Well, exactly," Cal says. "Wouldn't be right for me to take up more than my share of loud women."

Mart is shaking his head vigorously. "Ah no no no. You've it all arseways, so you do. What age are you? Forty-five?"

"Forty-eight."

"You look well on it. Them meat hormones must keep you young."

"Thanks."

"Either way, but. By the time he's forty, a man's either in the habit of being married or he's not. Women have ideas, and I'm not accustomed to anyone's ideas but my own. You are." Mart extracted this and other key vital statistics from Cal on their first meeting, with such near-invisible expertise that Cal felt like the amateur.

"You lived with your brother," Cal points out.

Mart is at least reciprocal with information: Cal has heard all about his brother, who preferred custard cream cookies, was an awful gom but a great hand at the lambing, gave Mart that broken nose by hitting him with a spanner in an argument over the TV remote, and died of a stroke four years ago.

"He'd no ideas," Mart says, with the air of someone scoring a point. "Thick as pig shite. I couldn't have some wan bringing her ideas into my house. Wanting a chandelier, maybe, or a poodle, or me to do yoga classes."

"You could find a dumb one," Cal offers.

Mart dismisses that with a puff of air. "I'd enough of that with the brother. But d'you know Dumbo Gannon? On that farm there?" He points across the fields at a long, low, red-roofed building.

"Yeah," Cal says, making an educated guess. One of the old guys in the pub is a little runt with a set of jug ears you could pick him up by.

"Dumbo's on his third missus. You wouldn't credit it, the head on him and the price of spuds, but I'm telling you. One of the women died and the other one ran off on him, but both times Dumbo had himself a new one inside the year. The same as I'd get a new dog if Kojak died on me, or a new telly if mine went, Dumbo goes out and gets himself a new missus. Because he's in the habit of someone bringing in ideas. If there's no woman in it, he doesn't know what to have for the dinner, or what to watch on the telly. And with no woman in it, you won't know what colors to paint the chambers in that mansion over there."

"I'm gonna go for white," Cal says.

"And what?"

"And white."

"See what I'm telling you?" Mart says triumphantly. "Only in the heel of the hunt, you won't. You're in the habit of having someone bringing in ideas. You'll go looking."

"I can get in an interiors guy," Cal says. "Fancy hipster who'll paint it chartreuse and puce."

"Where are you planning on finding one of them around here?"

"I'll import him from Dublin. He gonna need a work visa?"

"You'll do the same as Dumbo," Mart informs him. "Whether you plan on it or not. I'm only trying to make sure you do it right, before some skinny bitta fluff gets her hooks into you and makes your life a misery."

Cal can't tell if Mart actually believes any of this or is just spinning it on the fly, hoping for an argument. Mart loves arguing like he loves his cookies. Sometimes Cal goes along with it, in a spirit of neighborliness, but today he has a few specific questions and then he wants Mart to leave the coast clear. "Maybe in a few months," he says. "I'm not gonna start anything with any woman right now. Not till I get this place fixed up enough that I can let her see it."

Mart squints over at the house and nods, acknowledging the validity of this. "Don't be leaving it too long, now. Lena could have her pick, around here."

"It's been falling apart for a while," Cal says. "Gonna take me a while to put it back together. You got any idea how long it's been empty?"

"Fifteen year, must be. Maybe twenty."

"Looks like more," Cal says. "Who was living here?"

"Marie O'Shea," Mart says. "Now, she never got herself another man after Paudge died, but women do be different. They get in the habit of marrying, same as men, but the women do like a rest in between. Marie was only widowed the year before she died; she hadn't had a chance to catch her breath. If Paudge had gone ten year earlier—"

"Her kids didn't want the place?"

"They're gone, sure. Two in Australia, one in Canada. No harm to your estate, but it's not the kind that'd bring them running home."

Kojak has given up on the bushes and trotted over to Cal, tail wagging. Cal rubs behind his ear. "How come they just sold it now? They fight over what to do with it?"

"From what I heard, they hung on to it at first because prices were going up. Good land going to waste, because them fools thought it would make them millionaires. And then"—Mart's face splits into a grin of unholy glee—"didn't the crash come, and they were stuck hanging on to it because no one would give them sixpence for it."

"Huh," Cal says. That could raise some bad blood, one way or another. "Did anyone want to buy it?"

"My brother did," Mart says promptly. "The eejit. We'd enough on our plates. He watched too much **Dallas,** that fella. Fancied himself a cattle baron."

"Thought you said he had no ideas," Cal says.

"That wasn't an idea, that was a notion. I nipped it in the bud. There's no nipping women's ideas. Cut them down one place, they grow up another. You wouldn't know where you'd be."

Kojak is leaning up against Cal's leg, eyes half closed in bliss, butting Cal's hand whenever he forgets to rub. Cal has been planning on getting a dog; he was going to wait till he had the house in better shape, but it looks like sooner might be a good idea. "Any relations of the O'Sheas around here?" he asks. "I found some stuff they might want."

"If they wanted it," Mart points out logically, "they had twenty year to take it. What class of stuff?"

"Papers," Cal says vaguely. "Pictures. Figured I might as well check before I throw it out."

Mart is grinning. "There's Paudge's niece Annie, a few mile up the road beyond Moneyscully. If you fancy taking that stuff to her, I'll bring you, just to see the look on Annie's face. Her mammy and Paudge couldn't stand the sight of each other."

"Think I'll pass," Cal says. "She have any kids who might want mementoes of their great-uncle?"

"They're all gone off, sure. Dublin or England. Use them papers to light your fire. Or sell them on the internet, to some other Yank that wants a bit of heritage."

Cal isn't sure whether this is a jab or not. With Mart, he can't always tell, which he knows is half the fun of it. "I might do that," he says. "This isn't my heritage, anyway. My family's not Irish, so far as I know."

"You've all got a bit of Irish in ye over there," Mart says, with supreme confidence. "One way or another."

"Guess I oughta hang on to that stuff, then," Cal says, giving Kojak a final pat and turning back to his toolbox. Annie doesn't sound like she's sending kids round to scope out the ancestral home. Cal would love a lead on who the kid might be—he thought he had a fair handle on all his near neighbors, but he isn't aware of any kids—but being a middle-aged male stranger asking questions about the local little boys seems like a good route to a hiding and a couple of bricks through your windows, and he has enough going on as it is. He rummages through the toolbox for his chisel.

"Good luck with that yoke there," Mart says, straightening up off the fence with a grimace. A lifetime of farm labor has ground Mart's joints to rubble; he has trouble with his knee, his shoulder, and everything in between. "I'll take the firewood off your hands when you're done with it."

"Ham," Cal reminds him.

"You'll have to face Noreen sooner or later. You

can't be hiding away up here hoping she'll forget. Like I told you, bucko: once a woman gets an idea, it's going nowhere."

"You can be my best man," Cal says, working the chisel under the runner.

"Them ham slices is two euros fifty," Mart tells him.

"Huh," Cal says. "So're those cookies."

Mart wheezes with laughter and slaps the fence, making it bounce and rattle alarmingly. Then he whistles to Kojak and they head off.

Cal goes back to the desk, shaking his head and grinning. He sometimes suspects that Mart is putting on the gift-of-the-gab yokel act, either for shits and giggles or in order to make Cal more amenable to the cookie run and whatever else he has in mind. **Betcha,** Donna would've said, back when they used to love coming up with stuff to make each other laugh, **betcha when you're not around he wears a tux and talks like the queen of England. That or else he's in his Yeezys, busting a move to Kanye.** Cal doesn't think about Donna constantly, the way he did at first—it took months of dogged work, blasting music or reciting football lineups out loud like a loon every time she came into his head, but he got there in the end. She still crops up from time to time, though, mostly when he runs across something that would make her smile. He always loved Donna's smile, quick and complete, sending every line of her face flying upwards.

From having seen his buddies go through this

process, he expected that getting drunk would give him the urge to call her, so he stayed away from booze for a while, but it didn't turn out to work that way. After a few beers Donna feels a million miles away, in some other dimension, like no phone could reach her. When he goes weak is when she takes him by surprise like this, on an innocent fall morning, blooming right across his mind so fresh and vivid that he can almost smell her. He can't remember why he shouldn't pull out his phone, **Hey, baby, listen to this.** Probably he should delete her number, but they might need to talk about Alyssa sometime, and anyway he knows it by heart.

The drawer runner finally comes free, and Cal pulls out the old rusted nails with a pair of pliers. He measures the runner and scribbles the measurements on it. First time he was in the building suppliers he picked up a few bits of lumber, different sizes, because he had that toolbox and because you never know. One long piece of pine is just about the right width for the new runners, too thick but not by much. Cal clamps it to the table and starts planing it down.

Back home his plan would have been to grab the kid again, in a better hold this time, and deliver a fear-of-God speech about trespassing, assault and battery, juvie, and what happens to kids who fuck with cops, maybe finished off with a slap upside the head and a good hard shove off his property. Here, where he's not a cop and where that feeling of not knowing what he might set in motion is settling in deeper, not one bit of that is an option. Anything he does, he needs to keep it smart and careful, and do it with a light touch.

He gets the wood planed to the right thickness, rules two lines down it and saws along each of them, a quarter-inch deep. A part of him wondered if he would still know what to do with these tools, but his hands remember: the tools fit like they're still warm from his last grip and move smoothly through the wood. It feels good. He's whistling again, not bothering with tunes this time, just tossing out amiable little trills and riffs to the birds.

The day warms up till Cal has to stop and take off his sweatshirt. He starts chiseling out the strip of wood between the two sawn lines, taking his time. He's in no hurry. The kid, whoever he is, wants something. Cal is offering him the opportunity to come and get it.

The first time he hears a sound, off behind the hedge, it's blurred by his whistling and the slide of the chisel, and he's not sure. He doesn't look up. He finds his tape measure and checks the groove he's making: long enough for one runner. When he moves around the table to get his saw, he hears it again: a sharp rattle of twigs, someone ducking or dodging.

Cal glances up at the hedge as he stoops for the

saw. "If you're gonna watch," he says, "you might as well get a good view. Come over here and gimme a hand with this."

The silence from behind the hedge is absolute. Cal can feel it thrumming.

He saws off the runner, blows away the dust and measures it against the old one. Then he tosses it, underhand and easily, towards the hedge, and follows it with a sheet of sandpaper. "Here," he says to the hedge. "Get that sanded down."

He picks up his chisel and hammer and goes back to cutting the groove. The silence lasts long enough that he thinks he's struck out. Then he hears the rustle of someone easing, slowly and warily, through the hedge.

Cal keeps working. In the corner of his eye he sees a flash of red. After a long time he hears the rasp of sanding, clumsy and inexpert, with gaps between the strokes.

"Doesn't need to be a work of art," he says. "It's going inside the desk, no one's gonna see it. Just get the splinters gone. Go along the grain, not across it."

A pause. More sanding.

"What we're making here," he says, "is drawer runners. You know what those are?"

He glances up. It's the kid from last night, all right, standing on the grass about a dozen feet away and staring at Cal, with every muscle poised to run if he needs to. Mousy buzz cut, too-big faded red hoodie, ratty jeans. He's maybe twelve.

He shakes his head, one quick jerk.

"The part that holds the drawer in place. Makes it run in and out nice and smooth. That groove, there's a piece on the drawer that'll fit into it." Cal leans over towards the desk, good and slow, to point. The kid's eyes follow his every move. "The old ones were falling apart."

He goes back to his chiseling. "Easiest thing would be to use a router for this, or a table saw," he says, "but I don't have those handy. Lucky for me, my grandpa liked carpentry. He showed me how to do this by hand, when I was about your size. You ever done any carpentry?"

He takes another glance. The kid shakes his head again. He's built wiry, the type who's as fast as he looks and stronger, both of which Cal already knew from last night. In the face he's ordinary: a little of the baby softness left, not strong-featured or fine-featured, or good-looking or ugly; the only things that stand out are a stubborn chin and a pair of gray eyes fixed on Cal like they're running him through some CIA-level computer check.

"Well," Cal says, "now you have. Drawers nowadays, they've got metal runners, but this is an old desk. I can't tell you how old, exactly; that's not my area. I'd love to think we've got ourselves some **Antiques Roadshow** material here, but more'n likely it's just a piece of old crap. I've taken a shine to it, though. I want to see if I can get it up and running."

He's talking like he would to a stray dog in his

yard, steady and even, not bothering much about the actual words. The kid's sanding is getting faster and more confident, as he gets the hang of it.

Cal measures his groove and saws off the next runner. "That should be done enough by now," he says. "Lemme see."

"If it's for a drawer," the kid says, "it oughta be real smooth. Or it'll stick."

His voice is clear and blunt, not broken yet, and his accent is almost as thick as Mart's. And he's not stupid. "True," Cal says. "Go ahead and take your time."

He angles himself so he can see the kid out of the corner of his eye while he chisels. The kid is taking this seriously, checking each surface and edge with a careful finger, going back over it again and again till he's satisfied. Finally he looks up and throws Cal the runner.

Cal catches it. "Good job," he says, testing with his thumb. "Look." He fits it over the tenon at the side of the drawer and slides it back and forth. The kid cranes his neck to watch, but he doesn't move nearer.

"Smooth as butter," Cal says. "We'll wax it up later on, just for a little extra slide, but it hardly even needs that. Have another one."

When he reaches for the second runner, the kid's eyes go to the Band-Aid on his hand.

"Yeah," Cal says. He holds up the hand so the kid can get a good look. "This gets infected, I'm gonna be real pissed off with you."

The kid's eyes snap wide and his muscles snap tight. He's on the verge of flight, toes barely touching the grass.

"You've been keeping a pretty good eye on me," Cal says. "Any reason for that?"

After a moment the kid shakes his head. He's still ready to run, eyes fixed on Cal to catch the first signs of a lunge.

"There something you want to know? Because if you do, now would be a real good time to go ahead and ask straight out like a man."

The kid shakes his head again.

"Got any problems with me?"

Another head-shake, this one more vehement.

"You planning on robbing me? 'Cause that would be a bad idea. Plus, unless this turns out to be **Antiques Roadshow** stuff after all, I got nothing worth stealing."

Hard head-shake.

"Someone send you?"

Incredulous grimace, like Cal just said something bizarre. "Nah."

"You do this as a regular thing? Watch people?"

"No!"

"Then what?"

After a moment the kid shrugs.

Cal waits, but no further information is forthcoming. "OK," he says, in the end. "I don't much care why you were doing it. But that shit stops now. From now on, you get the urge to watch me, you do it like this. Face-to-face. This is the only warning I'm gonna give you. We clear?"

The kid says, "Yeah."

"Good," Cal says. "You got a name?"

The kid has relaxed a notch or two, now that he knows he's not going to need to run. "Trey."

"Trey," Cal says. "I'm Cal." The kid nods, once, like this confirms what he already knew. "You always this chatty?"

The kid shrugs.

"I gotta get some coffee inside me," Cal says. "And a cookie or something. You want a cookie?"

If the kid's been trained in stranger danger, this is a bad move, but Cal doesn't get the sense he's been trained in much of anything. Sure enough, he nods.

"You've earned it," Cal says. "Back in a minute. You sand this down meanwhile." He tosses Trey the second runner and heads up the garden without looking back.

Inside, he makes himself a big mug of instant coffee and finds his pack of chocolate chip cookies. Maybe those will get Trey talking, although Cal doubts it. He can't get a handle on this kid. He might have been lying, in one or more places, or he might not. All Cal gets off him is urgency, so concentrated that it shimmers the air around him like heat coming off a road.

When Cal goes back outside, Kojak is snuffling in the undergrowth at the base of the shed, and Mart is leaning on the fence with a packet of ham slices dangling from one hand. "Well, begod," he says, inspecting the desk, "it's still alive. I'll have to wait for my firewood."

The half-sanded runner and the sandpaper are lying on the grass. The kid called Trey is gone, like he was never there.

THREE

Over the next few days there's no sign of Trey. Cal doesn't take this to mean that the matter is concluded. The kid struck him as a wild creature, even more than most, and wild creatures often need some time to percolate an unexpected encounter before they decide on their next step.

It rains day and night, mildly but uncompromisingly, so Cal takes the desk inside and goes back to his wallpaper. He enjoys this rain. It has no aggression to it; its steady rhythm and the scents it brings in through the windows gentle the house's shabbiness, giving it a homey feel. He's learned to see the landscape changing under it, greens turning richer and wildflowers rising. It feels like an ally, rather than the annoyance it is in the city.

Cal is reasonably certain that the kid isn't going to screw with his place while he's out, certain enough that on Saturday night, when the rain finally clears, he heads down to the village pub. It's a two-mile walk, enough to keep him at home in bad weather. Mart and the old guys in the pub find his insistence on walking hilarious, to the point of driving home alongside him calling out encouragement or making herding noises. Cal feels that his car, a loud, grumpy, geriatric red Mitsubishi Pajero, is noticeable enough to attract the attention of any bored officer who might be tooling around, and that it would be a bad idea to score himself a DUI while he's still waiting for his firearm license, which can be denied if he's known to be of intemperate habits.

"Sure, they oughtn't to give you a gun anyway," Barty the barman told him, when he pointed this out.

"Why not?"

"Because you're American. Ye're all mental with the guns, over there. Shooting them off at the drop of a hat. Blowing some fella away because he bought the last packet of Twinkies in the shop. The rest of us wouldn't be safe."

"What would you know about Twinkies?" Mart demanded, from the corner where he and his two buddies were ensconced with their pints. Mart feels a responsibility, as Cal's neighbor, to defend him against a certain amount of the ribbing he gets. "It's far from Twinkies you were reared."

"Didn't I spend two year on the cranes in New York? I've et Twinkies. Horrible fuckin' yokes."

"And did anyone shoot you?"

"They did not. They'd better sense."

"Should've done," one of Mart's buddies said. "Then we might have a barman who could put a dacent head on a pint."

"You're barred," Barty told him. "And I'd've liked to see them try."

"There you are, then," Mart said triumphantly.

"And Noreen doesn't stock Twinkies anyhow. So let this fella have his rifle, and give him his pint."

The pub, identified as Seán Óg's by lopsided Celtic letters above the door, is in the same down-at-heel cream-colored building as the shop. During the day people wander back and forth, buying cigarettes to take back to the pub or bringing their pints into the shop so they can lean on the counter and chat with Noreen, but at night the connecting door is locked, unless Barty needs bread and ham to make someone a sandwich. The pub is small and low-ceilinged; it has a red linoleum floor with the occasional fraying piece of carpet positioned apparently at random, an eclectic assortment of battered bar stools, splitting green PVC banquettes around rocky wooden tables, a wide variety of beer-themed bunting, a plaque mounted with a rubber fish that sings "I Will Survive," and a cobwebby fishing net draped from the ceiling. Whoever put up the net distributed a few glass balls artistically inside it, as a finishing touch. Over the years patrons have added multiple coasters, a rubber boot and a Superman figure missing one arm.

Seán Óg's is, by its own standards, buzzing tonight. Mart and a couple of his buddies are in their corner, playing cards with two unprepossessing young guys in tracksuits whom they've acquired somehow. The first time Cal saw Mart and his homies bring out the cards, he expected poker, but their game is something called Fifty-Five, which they play with a speed and ferocity out of all proportion to the small piles of coins accumulating on the table. Apparently the game flows best with four or five, and when no one else is available, they try to rope Cal in; Cal, knowing when he's outclassed, stays clear. The young guys are going to lose their wages, if they have wages, which looks unlikely to Cal.

A parallel group of guys is sitting at the bar, arguing. A third group is in another corner, listening to one play the tin whistle, a fast spiraling tune that makes the others tap their hands on their knees. A woman called Deirdre is sitting on a banquette on her own, holding a small glass in both hands and staring into space. Cal is unsure what exactly Deirdre's deal is, although he gets the general gist. She's somewhere in her forties, a dumpy woman with depressing dresses and an unsettlingly vague stare in her large droopy eyes. Occasionally one or another of the old guys will buy her a double whiskey, they'll sit side by side and drink without saying a word to each other, and then they'll leave together, still in silence. Cal has no intention of inquiring about any of this.

He sits at the bar, orders a pint of Smithwick's from Barty and listens to the music for a while. He doesn't have the names in here straight yet, although he has most of the faces, and the gist of the personalities and relationships. This is excusable, given that Seán Óg's clientele is a shifting bunch of clean-shaven white guys over forty, all wearing more or less the same hardy trousers and padded vests and ancient sweaters, and most of them looking like cousins; but the truth is that, after twenty-five years of maintaining an intricate mental database of everyone he met on the job, Cal enjoys the lackadaisical feeling of not bothering to remember whether Sonny is the one with the big laugh or the one with the cauliflower ear. He has a good handle on who he should avoid or seek out, depending on whether he's in the mood for talk and what kind, and he figures that's plenty to keep him going.

Tonight he plans to listen to the music. Cal had never encountered a tin whistle till he moved here. He is unconvinced that he would enjoy the sound at, say, a school concert or a police bar in downtown Chicago, but here it seems fitting: it sits right with the warm, uncompromising raggedness of the pub, and makes him keenly aware of the quiet expanse spreading in every direction outside these four walls. When the grasshopper-skinny old musician brings it out, a few times a month, Cal sits a couple of stools away from the talkers and listens.

This means he's halfway through his second pint before he tunes in to the argument going on down the bar. It catches his ear because it sounds unusual. Mostly the arguments in here are the well-worn kind that can be made to stretch for years or decades, resurfacing periodically when there's nothing fresh to discuss. They involve farming methods, the relative uselessness of various local and national politicians, whether the wall on the western side of the Strokestown road should be replaced by fencing, and whether Tommy Moynihan's fancy conservatory is a nice touch of modern glamour or an example of jumped-up notions. Everyone already knows everyone else's stance on the issues—except Mart's, since he tends to switch sides regularly to keep things interesting—and is eager for Cal's input to mix the conversation up a little.

This argument has a different ring to it, louder and messier, like it's one they haven't practiced. "There's no dog could do that," the guy at the end of the bar is saying stubbornly. He's little and round, with a little round head perched on top, and he tends to wind up on the wrong end of jokes; generally he seems OK with this, but this time he's turning red in the face with vehemence and outrage. "Did you even look at them cuts? It wasn't teeth that done that."

"Then what d'you think done it?" demands the big bald slab of a guy nearest to Cal. "The fairies?"

"Feck off. I'm only saying, it was no animal."

"Not them fecking aliens again," says the third guy, raising his eyes from his pint. He's a long gloomy streak with his cap pulled down close over his face. Cal has heard him say a total of about five sentences.

"Don't mock," the little guy orders him. "You're saying that because you're uninformed. If you ever paid any notice to what's going on right above your thick head—"

"A crow would shite in my eye."

"We'll ask him," the big guy says, pointing his thumb at Cal. "Neutral party."

"Sure, what would he know about it?"

The big guy—Cal is pretty sure his name is Senan, and he mostly gets the last word—ignores this. "Come here," he says, shifting his bulk around on the bar stool to face Cal. "Listen to this. Night before last, something kilt one of Bobby's sheep. Took out its throat, its tongue, its eyes and its arse; left the rest."

"**Sliced** out," Bobby says.

Senan ignores this. "What would you say done it, hah?"

"Not my area," Cal says.

"I'm not asking for an expert scientific opinion. I'm only asking for common sense. What done it?"

"If I was a gambling man," Cal says, "my money'd be on an animal."

"What animal?" Bobby demands. "We've no coyotes or mountain lions here. A fox won't touch a grown ewe. A rogue dog would've ripped her to bits."

Cal shrugs. "Maybe a dog took out the throat, then got scared off. Birds did the rest."

That gets a moment's pause, and a raised eyebrow from Senan. They had him pegged as a city boy, which is only partly true. They're re-evaluating.

"There you go," Senan says to Bobby. "And you making a holy show of us with your aliens. He'll take that back to America now, and they'll be left thinking we're a bunch of muck savages that'd believe anything."

"They've got aliens in America as well," Bobby says defensively. "They've more than anyone, sure."

"**Nowhere** has fuckin' aliens."

"Half a dozen people seen them lights last spring. What d'you think that was? The fairies?"

"That was Malachy Dwyer's poteen. A few sups of that and I see lights too. One night walking home from Malachy's, I seen a white horse wearing a bowler hat cross the road in front of me."

"Did it kill your sheep?"

"Damn near kilt me. I jumped so high I went arse over tip into the ditch."

Cal is comfortable on his stool, drinking his beer and appreciating this. These guys remind him of his grandpa and his porch buddies, who enjoyed each other's company in the same way, by giving each other shit; or of the squad room, before a quicksand layer of real viciousness seeped in under the pretend stuff, or maybe just before he started noticing it.

"My grandpa and three of his buddies saw a UFO one time," he says, just to feed the conversation a little bit. "They were out hunting, one evening about dusk, and a big black triangle with green lights on the corners came along and hovered over their heads for a while. Didn't make a sound. My grandpa said they about shit themselves."

"Ah, holy God," Senan says in disgust. "Now

you're starting. Is there no one in here with a titter of sense?"

"Now," Bobby says triumphantly. "D'you hear that? And you getting the vapors about what the Yank might think of us at all."

"Cop yourself on, would you. He's only humoring you."

"My grandpa swore blind," Cal says, grinning.

"Did your grandpa know any moonshiners, did he?"

"A few."

"I'd say he knew them well. Think about this," Senan says, turning back to Bobby and pointing his glass at him. This argument is well on its way to joining the permanent repertoire. "We'll say there's aliens out there. We'll say they've put in the time and the technology to come all them light-years from Mars or what-have-you, all the way to Earth. They could find themselves a whole herd of zebras to do their experiments on, or a fine strapping rhinoceros, or head down to Australia and pick up a shower of kangaroos and koalas and mad yokes, for the crack. But instead of that"—he raises his voice over Bobby, who is objecting—"instead of that, hah, they come all this way and settle for one of your ewes. Are they all loopy, up on Mars? Are they soft in the head?"

Bobby is swelling up again. "There's nothing wrong with my ewes. They're better than feckin' **koalas.** Better than your scrawny, limpy—"

Cal has stopped paying attention. The quality of the talk from Mart's table has changed. "I bid twenty," one of the young guys is saying, in a tone that Cal recognizes. It's the aggrieved tone of a guy who's going to insist, to the point of making everyone's evening considerably messier than it needed to be, that he has no idea how that crack pipe got in his pants pocket.

"Get outa that," one of Mart's buddies says. "You bid twenty-five."

"You calling me a cheater?"

The guy is in his mid-twenties, too soft and too pale for a farmer; short, with greasy little dark bangs and something that has ambitions to be a mustache someday. Cal has registered him before, a couple of times, in the back corner with the huddle of other young guys who stare for a second too long. Without ever having spoken to the guy, he would be pretty confident listing a number of facts about him.

"I'm calling you nothing if you put that pot back," Mart's buddy says.

"I fucking won it. Fair and square."

Behind Cal, the argument has stopped; so has the tin whistle. The realization that he's unarmed hits Cal with a vivid shot of adrenaline. This guy is the type who would carry a Glock to make him feel like a badass gangster, and would have no clue how to handle it. It takes him a moment to remember that this is unlikely to be an issue here.

"You heard me say twenty," the chubby guy says to his pal. "Go on and tell them."

The pal is lanky and big-footed, with buckteeth that keep his long jaw hanging and a general air of being the last person to figure out what just happened. "I wasn't listening right," he says, blinking. "Sure, it's only a couple of quid, Donie."

"Nobody calls me a cheater," Donie says. He's getting a bull-eyed stare that Cal doesn't like.

"I do," Mart informs him. "You're a cheater, and d'you know what's even worse, you're fecking useless at it. A babby'd do a better job."

Donie shoves his stool back from the table and spreads his arms, beckoning Mart. "I'll take you. Come on."

Deirdre lets out a halfhearted yelp. Cal has no idea what to do, and this fact baffles him further. At home this is the point where he would have stood up, after which Donie would have either settled down or left, one way or another. Here, that doesn't seem like an option—not because he's short his gun and his badge, but because he doesn't know how things are done in these parts, or whether he has a right to do anything at all. That feeling of lightness overtakes him again, like he's perched on the edge of his stool like a bird. He finds himself wanting Donie to go for Mart, just so he'll know what to do.

"Donie," Barty says from behind the bar, pointing at the young guy with a glass-cloth. "Out."

"I did nothing. This prick called me—"

"Out."

Donie folds his arms and slumps down on his stool, bottom lip jutting, staring mulishly into space.

"Ah, for fuck's sake," Barty says in disgust. He throws down his cloth and comes out from behind the bar. "Give us a hand," he says to Cal, on his way.

Barty is a few years younger than Cal and not much smaller. Between them they pick Donie up by the armpits and maneuver him the length of the pub, dodging stools and tables, towards the door. Most of the old guys are grinning; Deirdre's mouth hangs open. Donie goes limp and makes himself into dead weight, his feet dragging on the linoleum.

"Stand up like a man," Barty orders him, wrestling with the door.

"I've a full pint back there," Donie says, outraged. "Ow!" as Barty semi-accidentally whacks his shoulder off the door frame.

On the sidewalk, Barty hauls Donie backwards for maximum momentum, then gives him a hefty swing forwards and lets go. Donie flies staggering across the road, arms flailing. His tracksuit pants come down and he falls over them.

Barty and Cal watch, getting their breath back, while he scrambles to his feet and hauls at his pants. He's wearing tighty whities. "Next time get your mammy to buy you big-boy underpants," Barty calls across to him.

"I'll burn you out of it," Donie yells, without much conviction.

"Go home and pull your lad, Donie," Barty calls back. "That's all you're fit for."

Donie casts around and spots a discarded cigarette packet, which he hurls at Barty. It falls six feet short. He spits in Barty's direction and stamps off up the road.

There are no streetlights, and only a couple of lights are on in the houses lining the road; half of them are empty. He's invisible in seconds. His footsteps take longer, echoing off the buildings away into the dark.

"Thanks," Barty says. "On my own I'd've put my back out. Fat little fucker."

The lanky guy comes out of the pub and stands on the step, silhouetted against the yellow light, scratching his back. "Where's Donie?" he asks.

"Gone home," Barty says. "You go on, too, J.P. You're done here for tonight."

J.P. thinks this over. "I've got his jacket," he says.

"Then bring it to him. Go on."

J.P. lopes obediently off into the darkness. "That guy make trouble often?" Cal asks.

"Donie McGrath," Barty says, and spits on the sidewalk. "Fuckin' latchico."

Cal has no idea what this means, although the tone implies something akin to a bum. "I've seen him in here before."

"Now and again. The young lads mostly go into town, looking for the ride, but if they haven't the money for that, then they come in here. He'll stay away for a while, anyway. Then he'll swan in with his pals, pretending it never happened."

"He actually gonna try and burn you down?"

Barty snorts. "Jaysus, no. Donie hasn't the guts of a louse. And that'd be too much like hard work."

"You reckon he's harmless?"

"He's pure fucking useless," Barty says with finality. Behind him the tin whistle starts up again, neat and jaunty. He dusts Donie off his hands and heads back into the pub.

Nobody else seems particularly unnerved by the incident, either. Mart and his buddies have reshuffled and started a new round of Fifty-Five; the argument at the bar has shifted to the merits of this year's hurling team. Barty gives Cal a free pint. Deirdre finishes her drink, casts a long hopeless look around the pub, and drifts out when nobody meets her eye.

All the same, Cal hangs around, making his freebie last, till Mart and his buddies finish up their game and start gathering their things. Mart was the one who called Donie a cheat. When he offers Cal a ride home—which he does every time, purely for the pleasure of ribbing Cal when he turns it down—Cal says yes.

Mart is moderately drunk, enough that he drops his keys in the footwell of the car and has to get out again to fumble around for them. "Don't be worrying," he says with a grin, reading Cal's expression and giving a slap to the side of his car, a decrepit blue Skoda covered in mud splatters and smelling strongly of wet dog. "This yoke knows her way home from the pub, even if I fall asleep at the wheel. She's done it before."

"Great," Cal says, retrieving the keys and handing them over. "I feel better now."

"What happened to your hand?" Mart inquires, clambering painstakingly back into the car.

Cal's hand is healing up fine, but he still has that Band-Aid on so no one can see the tooth marks. "Caught myself with a saw," he says.

"That's what you get," Mart says. "Next time you'll listen to me and go to them websites." He fires up the car, which coughs, shudders and springs off up the road at an alarming pace. "What was that big lump Senan going on about? Was it Bobby's ewe?"

"Yeah. Bobby figures it was aliens. Senan doesn't agree."

Mart wheezes with laughter. "I'd say you think Bobby's mad as a brush, do you?"

"Nah. I told him about the time my grandpa saw a UFO."

"You made him a happy man, so," Mart says, turning off the main road and shifting gears with a nasty crunching noise. "Bobby's not mad. All that's wrong with him is he spends too much time at the farm work. It's grand work, but unless a man's pure thick, it can leave his mind restless. Most of us have something to look after that: the family, or the cards, or the drink, or what-have-you. But Bobby's a bachelor, he's got no head for the drink, and he's that bad at cards we won't have him in our game. When his mind does get restless, he's got no option but to head up the hills hunting UFOs. The lads want to buy him a harmonica, give him something else to occupy him, but I'd rather listen to him go on about aliens any day."

Cal considers this. It seems to him that aliens are probably a healthier antidote to restlessness of the mind than some of the others on Mart's list. The way Mart is driving supports this theory.

"You don't reckon the aliens got his sheep?" he asks, just to yank Mart's chain.

"Arrah, fuck off, would you."

"He says there's nothing round here that would do it."

"Bobby doesn't know everything that's round here," Mart says.

Cal waits, but he doesn't elaborate. The car bumps over potholes. The headlights illuminate a narrow streak of road and waving branches on either side; a pair of luminous eyes flare suddenly, low to the ground, and are gone.

"There you go," Mart says, slamming to a stop in front of Cal's gate. "Safe and sound. Just like I told you."

"You can drop me up at your place," Cal says. "Just in case you've got a welcoming committee."

Mart stares at him for a second and then laughs so hard he doubles over coughing, slapping the steering wheel. "Well, begod," he says, when he recovers. "I've got my own knight in shining armor to escort me home. Surely to God you're not worrying about that little scut Donie McGrath? And you from the big bad city."

"We get guys like him in the city, too," Cal says. "I don't like them there either."

"Donie wouldn't come next nor near me," Mart says. The last of the laugh is still creasing his face, but there's a flat note to his voice that startles Cal. "He knows better."

"Humor me," Cal says.

Mart giggles, shaking his head, and starts the car again. "Go on, so," he says. "As long as you're not expecting a good-night kiss."

"In your dreams," Cal says.

"Save them for Lena," Mart tells him, and he laughs all the way up the road.

At Mart's place—a long white cottage with undersized windows, set well back from the road amid neglected grass—the porch light is on and Kojak is there to greet him when he opens the door. Cal lifts a hand and waits while Mart tips his tweed cap in the doorway, and while the inside lights go on. When nothing else happens, he heads for home. Even if Donie McGrath shows an uncharacteristic flash of initiative, Kojak is pretty good backup. But something about the sight of Mart in his doorway, at ease amid the fields and the huge wind-roamed dark, Kojak wagging beside him, has left Cal feeling slightly ridiculous, although not in a bad way.

His gate is about a quarter-mile from Mart's. The sky is clear and the moon is big enough to keep him on the road with no need for his flashlight, although once or twice when the tree shadows crowd in he gets addled and feels one foot sink into the deep grass of the verge. He keeps an eye out for whatever crossed in front of the car, but it's either gone or turned cautious. The mountains on the horizon look like someone took a pocketknife and sliced neat curves out of the star-thick sky, leaving empty blackness. Here and there, spread out, are the yellow rectangles of windows, tiny and valiant.

Cal likes the nights here. The ones back in Chicago were overcrowded and fractious, always a raucous party somewhere and an argument getting loud somewhere else and a baby howling on and on, and he knew too much about what was going on in the hidden corners and might spill out at any moment, demanding his attention. Here, he has the soothing knowledge that the things happening in the night aren't his problem. Most of them are self-contained: small wild hunts and battles and matings that require nothing from human beings except that they stay away. Even if there is anything going on, under this great mess of stars, that needs a police officer, Cal is irrelevant. It belongs to the local guys, up in that two-horse town, who presumably would also prefer him to stay away. Cal can do that; is, in fact, savoring it. The kid called Trey, by making night-time back into a place that required vigilance and action, brought home to him just how little he had missed those. It's occurred to him that he might have an undiscovered talent for letting things be.

His place is as undisturbed as Mart's. He cracks open a beer from the mini-fridge and sits out on his back step to drink it. Somewhere down the line he's going to build himself a back porch and get a big-ass chair to go on it, but for now, the step does fine. He leaves his jacket on; the air has a bite to it that says autumn is here for real, no more playing.

An owl calls, out over Mart's land. Cal watches for a while and catches a glimpse of it, just a scrap of denser shadow floating leisurely between trees. He wonders whether, if events had gone differently, he might have been this all along: a guy who fixed things and sat on his porch with a beer, watching for owls and letting the rest of the world take care of itself. He's not sure how he feels about that. It makes him uneasy, in ways he doesn't fully understand.

To get away from the sudden restlessness that's come down on him like a cloud of mosquitoes, Cal pulls his phone out of his pocket and calls Alyssa. He calls her every weekend. Mostly she answers. When she doesn't, she sends him a WhatsApp later on, usually at three or four in the morning his time: **Sorry I missed you, was in the middle of something! Catch you later!**

This time she picks up. "Hey, Dad. How're you doing?"

Her voice is brisk and blurred at the edges, like she's got the phone caught under her jaw, doing something else at the same time. "Hey," Cal says. "You busy?"

"No, it's fine. Just cleaning up some stuff."

He listens, trying to figure out what, but all he can catch is random rustles and thumps. He tries to picture her: tall and athletic, her face a miraculous blend of him and Donna—Cal's blue eyes and level eyebrows, Donna's mobile upswept features—that blows him away. The problem is that he still sees her running around in cutoff jeans and a big sweatshirt, her hair caught up in a glossy brown ponytail, and he has no way of knowing whether any of this still touches the reality at any point. Last time he saw her was Christmas. She could have chopped her hair short, dyed it blond, bought suits, put on twenty pounds and started wearing a faceful of makeup.

"How you doing?" he says. "You get rid of that flu yet?"

"That was just a cold. It's gone."

"How's work?" Alyssa works for a nonprofit in Seattle, something to do with at-risk teenagers. Cal missed the ins and outs of it when she first told him she was applying for the job—she applied for a lot of jobs, and work and Donna were taking up most of his mind around then—and it's gotten too late to ask.

"Work's good. We got our grant—big relief—so that should keep the show on the road for another while."

"How about that kid you were worried about? Shawn, DeShawn?"

"Shawn. I mean, he's still coming, which is the main thing. I still think things are pretty bad for him at home, like really bad, but he freezes up whenever I try to ask. So . . ."

She trails off. Cal would love to come out with something useful, but most of his techniques for making people open up were designed for situations that don't have much in common with this one. "Give him time," he says in the end. "You'll do fine."

"Right," Alyssa says, after a moment. She sounds tired all of a sudden. "I hope."

"How's Ben doing?" Cal asks. Ben is Alyssa's boyfriend, has been since college. He seems like an OK guy, a little earnest and a little talky when it comes to his opinions on society and the things everyone should be doing to improve it, but then Cal is sure he himself was a pain in the ass at twenty-five, one way or another.

"He's OK. He's going nuts in that job, but he's got an interview next week, so fingers crossed."

Ben's current job is in Starbucks or somewhere. "Tell him good luck from me," Cal says. He's always had the sense Ben isn't crazy about him. At first he didn't give a damn, but at this point it seems like he should try to do something about it.

"I will. Thanks."

"You hear anything from your mom?"

"Yeah, she's good. How about you? How's the house going?"

"Getting there," Cal says. He knows Alyssa doesn't want to talk to him about Donna, but sometimes he can't help it. "Slowly, but hey, I got time."

"I got those pictures. The bathroom looks great."

"Well. I wouldn't go that far. But at least these days it doesn't look like I've been holed up in there fighting off zombies."

That gets Alyssa to laugh. Even as a little kid she had that great laugh, big and rich, an outdoors laugh. It makes Cal catch his breath.

"You should come visit," he says. "It's beautiful here. You'd like it."

"Yeah, I bet. I should. Just, getting time off work, you know?"

"Yeah," Cal says. And after a second: "Anyway, you should probably wait till I get the place in shape. Or at least till I have furniture."

"Right," Alyssa says. Cal can't tell if he's imagining the touch of relief in her voice. "Let me know."

"Yeah, I will. Soon."

Away across the fields, a tiny lit window extinguishes itself. The owl is still calling, cool and relentless. Cal wants to say something else, to keep her on the line a while longer, but he can't think of anything to say.

"You should get some sleep," Alyssa says. "What time even is it over there?"

When Cal hangs up he has the same empty feeling he always gets after talking to Alyssa these days, a sense that somehow, in spite of having been on the phone for all that time, they haven't had a conversation at all; the whole thing was made of air and tumbleweed, nothing solid there. When she was a little kid she would trot along holding his hand and tell him everything, good and bad, it all poured straight from her heart to her mouth. He can't remember when that changed.

The cloud of restlessness hasn't cleared. Cal gets himself another beer and brings it back to the step. He wishes Alyssa would send him pictures of her apartment. He asked once, she said she would, and then she never did. He hopes this is because she never got around to it, rather than because her place is a shithole.

In the hedge at the bottom of the garden, a twig cracks.

"Kid," Cal says wearily, raising his voice to carry across the grass. "Not tonight. Go home."

After a pause, a fox steps delicately out of the hedge and stands staring at him, something small and limp hanging from its mouth, its unfathomable eyes glinting in the moonlight. Then it dismisses him as immaterial and trots off along its route.

FOUR

Two days later, the kid comes back. Since the day has brightened up after a rainy start, Cal and his desk are back out in the garden. He finished off the drawer runners last time, so he's moving on to the nest of cubbyholes inside the drop front. The pieces of wood that make them up are delicate, dadoed together in an intricate jigsaw, and several of them are broken. Cal lays the desk on its back on a drop sheet and takes photos of the whole contraption on his phone before he carefully works the broken pieces free, loosening old glue with a scalpel blade, and starts measuring them for replacements.

He's finishing up the first one, chiseling the last of the dado that will slot it snugly into place, when he hears twigs cracking. This time he doesn't need to play any games. The kid pushes through the hedge and stands there watching, hands in the pockets of his hoodie.

"Morning," Cal says.

The kid nods.

"Here," Cal says, holding out the piece of wood and a sheet of sandpaper.

The kid comes over and takes them out of his hand without hesitation. He seems to have refiled

Cal from Dangerous Unknown to Nonthreatening Known since they last saw each other, the way a dog will, based on some mysterious judgment process of his own. His jeans are damp to the shins from walking through wet grass.

"This part's gonna be visible," Cal says, "so we're gonna be a little bit pickier about it. When you've finished with that sandpaper, I'll give you a finer one."

Trey examines the piece of wood he's holding, then the splintered original on the table. Cal points to its gap among the cubbyholes. "Goes here."

"Wrong color."

"We'll stain it to match. That comes later."

Trey nods. He squats on the grass, a few feet from the drop sheet, and gets to work.

Cal starts penciling out the next piece of wood, positioning himself so he can look the kid over, in glances. The hoodie is clearly a hand-me-down, and one big toe is poking out through a hole in his sneaker. He's poor. It's more than that, though. Cal has seen plenty of kids poorer than this one who were ferociously well cared for, but nobody has been checking that this kid's neck is scrubbed clean or patching his worn-out knees. He appears to get fed, more or less, but not a lot beyond that.

Leftover raindrops tick in the hedges; small birds hop and peck in the grass. Cal saws, measures, chisels out dadoes and grooves, and gives Trey the fine sandpaper when he's done with the coarse one. He can feel the kid glancing at him, the same way he was glancing at the kid, assessing. He whistles softly to himself, here and there, but this time he doesn't talk. It's the kid's turn.

He appears to have picked the wrong kid for that: Trey has no problem with silence. He finishes the shelf to his satisfaction, brings it over to Cal and holds it out.

"Good," Cal says. "Have another. I'm gonna wax this one up here and here, see? and then fit it in where it belongs."

Trey hovers for a minute or two, watching Cal rub wax along the dadoes, and then drifts back to his spot and starts sanding again. The rhythm has changed, though, got faster and less neat. The first shelf was to prove himself. Now that that's done, there's something else moving around in his mind, looking for an exit.

Cal ignores that. He kneels by the desk, lines up the shelf and starts gently hammer-tapping it into its grooves.

Trey says, behind him, "I heard you're a cop."

Cal nearly hammers his thumb. He's been careful to keep that piece of information to himself, going off his experience with the people around his grandpa's place in backwoods North Carolina, to whom being a cop as well as a stranger would not have been a big plus. He has no idea how anyone could have found out. "Who said that?"

Trey shrugs, sanding.

"Maybe next time don't listen to them."

"Are you?"

"I look like a cop to you?"

Trey surveys him, squinting against the light. Cal looks back. He knows the answer is no. That was one of the points of the beard, and the overgrown hair: no more looking like a cop, and no more feeling like a cop. **More like Sasquatch,** Donna would have said, grinning, twisting a lock around her finger to tug it.

"Nah," Trey says.

"Well then."

"You are, but."

By now Cal has made up his mind: no point playing games if people already know. He considers a deal—you tell me where you heard, I'll answer your questions—but he decides it wouldn't fly. The kid is curious, but not enough to rat on his own. Deals need to wait a while longer. "Was," he says. "Not any more."

"Why not?"

"Retired."

Trey examines him. "You're not that old."

"Thanks."

The kid doesn't smile. Apparently he doesn't do sarcasm. "Why'd you retire, so?"

Cal goes back to the desk. "Things just got shittier. Or seems like."

He wonders too late about cussing, but the kid doesn't seem shocked, or even startled. He just waits.

"People got mad. Seemed like just about everyone was mad."

"About what?"

Cal considers this, tapping at the corner of the shelf. "Black people got mad about being treated like crap. Bad cops got mad 'cause they were getting called on their shit all of a sudden. Good cops got mad 'cause they were the bad guys when they hadn't done anything."

"Were you a good cop or a bad cop?"

"I aimed to be a good one," Cal says. "But everyone would say that."

Trey nods. "Did you get mad?"

"I got weary," Cal says. "Bone-weary." He did. Every morning got to be like waking up with the flu, knowing he had to trek miles up a mountain.

"So you retired."

"Yeah."

The kid runs his finger along the wood, checking, and goes back to sanding. "Why'd you come here?"

"Why not?"

"No one ever moves here," Trey says, like he's pointing out the obvious to a moron. "Only away."

Cal jiggles the shelf a quarter-inch farther in; it's a tight fit, which is good. "I was sick of shitty weather. You guys don't get snow or heat, not what we'd call, anyway. And I'd had enough of cities. Round here is cheap. And good fishing."

Trey watches him, unblinking gray eyes, skeptical.

"I heard you got fired 'cause you shot someone. On the job, like. And you were going to get arrested. So you ran."

Cal did not see this one coming. "Who said that?"

Shrug.

Cal considers his options. "I never shot anyone," he says, truthfully, in the end.

"Ever?"

"Ever. You watch too much TV."

Trey keeps watching him. The kid doesn't blink enough. Cal is starting to fear for his corneal health.

"You don't believe me, Google me. Something like that, it'd be all over the internet."

"Don't have a computer."

"Phone?"

The corner of Trey's mouth twists: nah.

Cal takes his phone out of his pocket, unlocks it and tosses it onto the grass in front of Trey. "Here. Calvin John Hooper. The signal is shit, but it'll get there in the end."

Trey doesn't pick up the phone.

"What?"

"Might not be your real name."

"Jesus, kid," Cal says. He leans over for the phone and puts it back in his pocket. "Believe what you want. You gonna sand that, or not?"

Trey goes back to sanding, but Cal can tell from the rhythm that he's not done. Sure enough, after a minute he asks, "Were you any good?"

"Pretty good. I got the job done."

"Were you a detective?"

"Yeah. The last while."

"What kind?"

"Property crime. Burglary, mostly." He gets the sense, from Trey's look, that this is a letdown. "And fugitive apprehension, for a while. Tracking down people who were trying to hide from us."

That gets a swift flash of a glance. Apparently Cal's stock has gone back up. "How?"

"Bunch of ways. Talk to their relatives, buddies, girlfriends, boyfriends, whatever they've got. Watch their homes, the places they like to hang out. Check if their bank cards get used anywhere. Tap some phones, maybe. Depends."

Trey is still watching him intently. His hand has stopped moving.

It's occurred to Cal that he may have found his explanation for what the kid is doing here. "You want to be a detective?"

Trey gives him the moron look. Cal gets a kick out of this look, which is the kind you would give the idiot kid in your class who just fell for the rubber cookie yet again. "Me?"

"No, your great-gramma. Yeah, you."

Trey says, "What time is it?"

Cal checks his watch. "Almost one." And when the kid keeps looking at him: "You hungry?"

Trey nods. "Lemme see what I've got," Cal says, putting down the hammer and getting to his feet. His knees crack. He feels like forty-eight shouldn't be old enough for your body to make noises at you. "You allergic to anything?"

The kid gives him a blank look, like he was speaking Spanish, and shrugs.

"You eat peanut butter sandwiches?"

Nod.

"Good," Cal says. "That's about as fancy as I get. Finish that off meanwhile."

He half-expects the kid to be gone when he comes back out with the food, but he's still there. He glances up and holds out the piece of wood for Cal's inspection.

"Looking good," Cal says. He passes the kid a plate, and pulls a carton of orange juice from under his arm and his mugs from the pockets of his hoodie. Probably he should be giving a growing kid milk, but he drinks his coffee black, so he doesn't have any.

They sit on the grass and eat in silence. The sky is a dense cool blue; yellow leaves are starting to come off the trees, lying lightly on the grass. Off over Dumbo Gannon's farm, a cloud of birds swoops through impossible, shifting geometries.

Trey eats in big wolfish bites, with an intentness that makes Cal glad he fixed him two sandwiches. When he's done, he downs his juice without pausing for breath.

"You want some more?" Cal asks.

Trey shakes his head. "I have to go," he says. He puts down the glass and wipes his mouth on his sleeve. "Can I come back tomorrow?"

Cal says, "Shouldn't you be in school?"

"Nah."

"Yeah you should. How old are you?"

"Sixteen."

"Bullshit."

The kid evaluates him for a moment. "Thirteen," he says.

"Then yeah you should."

Trey shrugs.

"Whatever," Cal says, as it suddenly occurs to him. "Not my problem. You want to skip school, knock yourself out."

When he looks over, Trey is smiling, just a little bit. It's the first time Cal has seen him do that, and it's as startling as catching a baby's first smile, seeing an unsuspected new person breaking through.

"What?" he asks.

"A cop's not supposed to say that."

"Like I told you. I'm not a cop any more. I don't get paid to hassle you."

"But," Trey says, the smile vanishing. "Can I come here? I'll help with this. And the staining. All of it."

Cal looks at him. That urgency is back in his body, poorly concealed, hunching his shoulders forwards and pinching his face.

"What for?"

After a moment Trey says, " 'Cause. I wanta learn how."

"I'm not gonna pay you." The kid could clearly use some cash, but even if Cal had any to spare, he doesn't plan on being the stranger who hands out money to young boys.

"Don't care."

Cal considers the possible ramifications. He reckons that if he says no, Trey will go back to lurking. Cal prefers him visible, at least until he works out what the kid wants. "Why not," he says. "I could use a hand."

Trey lets out his breath and nods. "OK," he says, getting to his feet. "See you tomorrow."

He brushes off his jeans and heads for the road with a long, spring-kneed woodsman's lope. On his way past the rookery he tosses a rock up into the branches, with a hard wrist-whip from a pretty good arm, and tilts his head back to watch as the rooks explode in all directions and cuss him to hell and back again.

———

After Cal washes up the lunch things, he heads for the village. Noreen knows everything and talks a blue streak—Cal figures these are two of the real reasons why she doesn't get along with Mart, who likes to have a monopoly in those areas. If he can aim her in the right direction, she might give him an idea where Trey popped up from.

Noreen's shop packs a lot into a little space. It's floor-to-ceiling with shelves crammed with the essentials of life—tea bags, eggs, chocolate bars, scratch cards, dish soap, baked beans, batteries, jam, tinfoil, ketchup, firelighters, painkillers, sardines—and a variety of things, like golden syrup and Angel Delight, that Cal doesn't understand but has ambitions to try if he can work out what to do with them. It has a little fridge for milk and meat, a basket of depressed-looking fruit, and a ladder so Noreen, who's about five foot one, can reach the high shelves. The shop smells of all those things, with a strong underlay of some uncompromising disinfectant straight out of 1950.

When Cal pushes open the door with a cheerful bell-ding, Noreen is up the ladder, dusting jars and humming along to some cheesy young guy on the radio aiming for a hoedown feel. Noreen favors tops with explosive flowers and has short brown hair set in such tight curls that it looks like a helmet.

"Wipe your boots, I'm only after washing the floor," she orders. Then, noticing Cal properly: "Ah, 'tis yourself! I was hoping you'd call in today. I've that cheese in that you like. I've been keeping a packet back for you, because Bobby Feeney does like it as well, and he'd buy the lot on me and leave you with nothing. He'd eat it like a chocolate bar, that fella. He'll have himself a heart attack one of these days."

Cal wipes his boots obediently. Noreen comes down the ladder, pretty nimbly for a round woman. "And come here to me," she says, waving her dust cloth at Cal, "I've a surprise for you. There's someone I want you to meet." She calls through the door into the back room: "Lena! Come out here!"

After a moment a woman's voice, husky and firm, calls back, "I'm making the tea."

"Leave the tea and come here. Bring that cheese out of the fridge, the one in the black packet. Do I have to come in and get you?"

There's a pause, in which Cal thinks he catches an exasperated sigh. Then there's movement in the back room, and a woman comes out holding a packet of cheddar.

"Now," Noreen says triumphantly. "This is my sister Lena. Lena, this is Cal Hooper that's after moving in up at O'Shea's place."

Lena isn't what Cal expected. From what Mart said, he was picturing a beefy, raw-red six-footer with a voice like a cow's bellow, brandishing a frying pan menacingly. Lena is tall, all right, and she has meat on her bones, but in a way that makes Cal picture her hillwalking, rather than hitting someone upside the head. She's a couple of years younger than him, with a thick fair ponytail and a broad-cheekboned, blue-eyed face. She's wearing old jeans and a loose blue sweater.

"Pleasure," Cal says, offering his hand.

"Cal the cheddar fan," Lena says. She has a firm shake. "I've heard plenty about you."

She gives him a quick wry grin and hands over the cheese. He grins back. "Same here."

"I'd say you have, all right. How're you getting on in O'Shea's? Keeping you busy?"

"I'm doing OK," Cal says. "But I can see why nobody else wanted to take it on."

"There's not a lot of people looking to buy houses, round here. Most of the young people take off for the city as soon as they can. They only stay if they're working the family farm, or if they like the country."

Noreen has her arms folded under her bosom and is watching the two of them with a maternal approval that makes Cal itchy. Lena, hands in her jeans pockets and one hip leaned up against the counter, doesn't appear to give a damn. She has an unforced stillness to her, and a direct gaze, that are hard to look away from. Mart was right about this much: you would know she was there.

"You stuck around, huh?" Cal says. "You in farming?"

Lena shakes her head. "I was. I sold the farm when my husband died, just kept the house. I'd had enough."

"So you just like the country."

"I do, yeah. The city wouldn't suit me. Hearing other people's noise all day and all night."

"Cal was in Chicago, before," Noreen puts in.

"I know," Lena says, with an amused tilt to her eyebrow. "So what are you doing here?"

Part of Cal is tugging him to pay for his cheese and take off, before Noreen calls in a priest to marry them on the spot. On the other hand, he came here today for a purpose, besides which he's out of a bunch of stuff. Complicating this is the fact that he can't remember the last time he was in a room with a woman he liked the idea of talking to, and he's unsure whether this is a point in favor of sticking around or of getting the hell out of Dodge.

"Guess I just like the country too," he says.

Lena still has the amused look. "A lot of people think they do, till they go full-time. Come back to me after a winter here."

"Well," Cal says, "I'm not exactly a tenderfoot. I lived out in the backwoods off and on, when I was a kid. I figured I'd settle right back in, but looks like I've been in the city longer than I thought."

"What's getting you? Not enough to do? Or not enough people to do it with?"

"Nope," Cal says, grinning a little sheepishly. "I've got no problem with either one of those. But I've gotta admit, I get a little jumpy at night, with no one close enough to notice if any trouble came calling."

Lena laughs. She has a good laugh, forthright and throaty. Noreen snorts. "Ah, God love you. You'll be used to all them armed robberies and mass shootings." The beady glance confirms for Cal that she knows about his job, not that he doubted her. "We've none of that round here."

"Well, I didn't reckon you would have," Cal says. "What I had in mind was more like bored kids looking for entertainment. There was a crew of us that used to mess with the neighbors: prop up trash cans full of water against someone's door and then knock and run, or else fill up a big potato-chip bag with shaving cream and slide the open end under the door, and then stomp on it. Dumb stuff like that." Lena is laughing again. "I figured a stranger might get a little bit of that treatment. But I guess, like you said, the young people don't stick around. Seems like I'm the only person under fifty for miles. Present company excepted."

Noreen jumps right on that. "Will you listen to him, making us out to be God's waiting room! Sure, this townland's got plenty of young people. I've four myself—but they don't be going out making trouble, they know I'd redden their arses if they did. And Senan and Angela have four as well, and the Moynihans have their young lad, and the O'Connors have three, but they're all grand young people, not a bother out of them—"

"And Sheila Reddy's got six," Lena says. "Most of them still at home. That enough for you?"

Noreen's mouth pinches up. "If you did have any trouble," she tells Cal, "it'd be from that lot."

"Yeah?" Cal says. He scans the shelves and picks himself out a can of corn. "They bad news?"

"Sheila's poor," Lena says. "Is all."

"It costs nothing to teach a child manners," Noreen snaps, "or get it to school. And every time those childer do come in here, there's something missing after. Sheila says I can't prove it, but I know what's in my own shop, and—" She remembers Cal, who is peacefully comparing chocolate bars, and stops. "Sheila'd want to get her head on straight," she says.

"Sheila does what she can with what she's got," Lena says. "Like the rest of us." To Cal she says, "I used to pal around with her, in school. We were wild then. Getting out our windows at night to go drinking in fields with the lads. Hitching lifts into town to the discos."

"Sounds like you were the teenagers I worry about," Cal says.

That gets another laugh from her. "Ah, no. We never did any damage to anyone except ourselves."

"Sheila did herself damage, all right," Noreen says. "Look what she got out of all that messing. Johnny Reddy and six just like him."

"Johnny was a fine thing, back then," Lena says, with a lift at the corner of her mouth. "I shifted him once or twice myself."

Noreen tuts. "At least you'd more sense than to marry him."

Cal decides on a Mint Crisp bar and puts it on the counter. "The Reddys live near enough to me that I oughta keep an eye out?" he asks.

"Depends," Lena says. "How much of a worrier are you?"

"Depends. How close is the trouble?"

"You're grand. They're a few miles beyond you, up in the mountains."

"Sounds good to me," Cal says. "Johnny a farmer, or what?"

"Who knows what Johnny is," Lena says. "He went off to London a year or two back."

"Left Sheila high and dry," Noreen says, with a mix of condemnation and satisfaction. "Some pal of his over there had a business idea that was going to make the pair of them millionaires, or so he said. I'm not holding my breath, and I hope Sheila's not either."

"Johnny was always a great man for the ideas," Lena says. "Not so great for making them happen. You can relax. Any child of his, a crisp packet full of shaving foam would be more than they could organize."

"Good to know," Cal says. He has a feeling that one, at least, of Johnny Reddy's kids may not take after his daddy.

"Now, Cal," Noreen says, struck by a thought and pointing her dust cloth at him. "Weren't you telling me only the other day, you were thinking of getting a dog? And wouldn't that be the perfect way to put your mind at ease? Listen to me now: Lena's dog'll be whelping any day, and she'll be wanting homes for the pups. Let you go with her now and have a look."

"She hasn't whelped yet," Lena says. "It won't do him much good staring at her belly."

"He can see if he likes the cut of her. Go on."

"Ah, no," Lena says pleasantly. "I need my cup of tea." Before Noreen can open her mouth again, she nods to Cal, says, "Nice to meet you," and is gone into the back room.

"You'll stay and have a cup of tea with us," Noreen orders Cal.

"Appreciate it," Cal says, "but I oughta be getting home. I didn't take the car, and it looks like rain."

Noreen gives an offended sniff, turns the radio louder and goes back to dusting, but Cal can tell from the occasional glance she shoots his way that she hasn't given up that easy. He grabs groceries fast and more or less at random, before she can come up with a fresh scheme. At the last minute, when Noreen is already adding up his bill on the noisy old manual cash register, he throws in a carton of milk.

FIVE

Trey does come back the next day, and the ones after that. Sometimes he shows up around mid-morning; sometimes it's mid-afternoon, which gives Cal the comforting impression that he does occasionally go to school, although he's aware that this may be deliberate. The kid sticks around for an hour, or a couple, and mostly for some food. Then—in response to some mysterious inner alarm clock, or maybe just when he gets bored—he says, "Haveta go," and leaves, tramping up the garden with his hands deep in his hoodie pockets, not looking back.

The first rainy day, Cal doesn't expect to see him. He's stripping wallpaper and singing the odd half line along with Otis Redding when a shadow crosses the light, and when he looks around, there Trey is at the window, watching him from inside a disreputable wax jacket a couple of sizes too small. Cal is momentarily dubious about inviting him in, but with rain dripping off the kid's hood and the end of his nose, he doesn't feel like he has much choice. He hangs the kid's jacket on a chair to dry and gives him a scraper.

On sunny days they go back to the desk, but

sunny days are getting scarcer as September runs itself down. More and more often, rain whips the house, and wind packs sodden leaves at the bases of walls and hedges. The squirrels are in a hoarding frenzy. Mart announces that this means a bastard of a winter ahead, and provides dramatic accounts of years when the townland was cut off for weeks and people froze to death in their own homes, although Cal fails to be properly impressed. "I'm used to Chicago," he reminds Mart. "We don't call it cold till our eyelashes freeze."

"Different kind of cold," Mart informs him. "This one's sneaky. You wouldn't feel it coming, not till it's got you."

Mart's opinion of the Reddys turns out to match Noreen's, only with more flourishes. Sheila Brady was a lovely girl from a decent family, with a fine pair of legs on her; she was planning to move to Galway and train as a nurse, except before she could get that far she fell for Johnny Reddy. He could talk the cross off an ass and never held a job for more than three months in his life, because nothing that would take him was good enough for him: "no kind of worker," Mart says, with a depth of scorn that Cal and his squad reserved for granny-muggers. Sheila and Johnny had six kids, lived on benefits in some relative's dilapidated cottage up in the hills—Mart does explain the relationship, in detail, but Cal loses track after three or four degrees—and now Johnny has fecked off, Sheila's people have all died or moved away, and the family is as close as this place gets to trailer trash. Mart agrees with Noreen and Lena that the kids are unlikely to be above a little petty crime, but equally unlikely to have the capacity for anything high-level. "Holy God," he says, amused, when Cal gives him the worried-city-boy spiel, "you've too much time on your hands. Get yourself a woman, like I told you. Then you'll know what worry is."

In fact Cal has more or less ruled out the possibility that the kid is planning on robbing him, given that he would be going about it in the dumbest possible way, and from what Cal can tell he appears to be far from dumb. Now that he knows a little bit about Trey's probable family, other, more likely scenarios present themselves: the kid is getting picked on and needs protection, the kid is being abused one way or another and wants to tell someone, the kid's mom is a drunk or on drugs or getting beat up by a boyfriend and he wants to tell someone, the kid wants Cal to track down his wayward daddy, or the kid is looking to establish some kind of alibi for something he shouldn't be doing. Cal feels that the locals, biased by Johnny Reddy's fecklessness, may be underrating his son's abilities in that department. And, while he has every reason to know that kids can on occasion rise above a shitty family, he also has every reason to know that on most occasions it doesn't turn out that way.

He pokes around the subject of Johnny Reddy a little, giving Trey an opening if that's where he's headed, but Trey shuts that down right quick. "Yeah, we can use this," Cal says, examining his first attempt at chiseling out a groove. "You're pretty handy, kid. You help out your dad with stuff like this?"

"Nah," Trey says. He takes back the shelf and gives one end of the groove a few extra taps, squinting low over the wood. He likes things done right. Stuff that Cal would be fine with, Trey shakes his head and goes back over it two or three times before he's satisfied.

"So what do you do with him?"

"Nothing. He went off."

"Where to?"

"London. He rings us sometimes."

This pretty much confirms Trey as a Reddy, unless London is a common destination for the local deadbeat dads. "My dad went off a lot," Cal says. He's aiming for rapport, but Trey seems unimpressed. "You miss him?"

Trey shrugs. Cal is getting the hang of Trey's shrugs, which are many and nuanced. This one means the subject is closed due to lack of interest.

This leaves Cal with two main possibilities: Trey is doing something bad, or something bad is being done to him. So far he hasn't come up with a good way to broach either of those. He's aware that, if he fucks it up, Trey will be gone for good. This is fine by Cal if Trey is the one making the trouble, but his newfound talent for letting things be doesn't stretch to an abused kid. So he's dealing with Trey the same way he did at the start: going about his own business, and letting the kid come closer in his own time.

His own time turns out to be around two weeks. It's a rainy morning, cool and soft, with a small breeze that wanders in the open windows smelling of pasture. Cal and Trey between them have finished sanding the living-room walls smooth, they've painted primer along the edges, and they're taking a break before they get started on the main job. They sit at the table eating chocolate sandwich cookies, Trey's contribution—he's taken to showing up with cookies some days, or one time an apple pie. Cal is pretty sure where this stuff comes from, and he feels a mild twinge of guilt about eating it anyway, but he figures things will be more peaceful if he doesn't get into that.

Trey is working his way, methodically and with intent, through the cookies. Cal is trying to knead a knot out of his neck. It's from the mattress; his muscle aches and pains have mostly faded. His body is getting accustomed to the work, and Cal likes that, the same way he liked the aches to begin with. At first he wondered if he might be too old to get accustomed to it at all, but his body has come through for him. He feels younger than he did six months ago.

"Squirrel," he says, pointing out the window to the garden. "One of these days I'll shoot me a few of them and make us a squirrel stew."

Trey considers this, watching the squirrel scrabble under the hedge. "What's it taste like?"

"Pretty good. Gamey. Stronger'n chicken."

"Squirrel bit my sister once," Trey says. "On the finger. I'd eat 'em."

"When I was about ten," Cal says, "I was staying with my granddaddy, and me and three of my buddies, we used to camp out in the woods back of his place. The first time we did it, my granddaddy told us we oughta be careful, because there was a thing called a squatt living out in those woods. Cross between a squirrel and a cat, but bigger'n either one, and fiercer. It had great big claws and fangs, and orange fur, and it'd go either for your throat, if you were sitting down, or for your balls if you were standing up. You could tell it was getting ready to attack because you'd hear it making this weird noise. Like growling mixed with chattering."

He demonstrates. Trey listens, watching him and scraping the filling out of a cookie with his teeth. Cal has gotten into the habit of telling Trey whatever comes into his head, purely for companionability, without paying much heed to whether or not he gets a response.

"We camped out anyway," he says, "but we made ourselves a big pile of rocks in the tent, just in case. Late at night, we were just getting comfortable in our sleeping bags, we heard a noise outside." He makes the noise again. "We about shit ourselves. We snuck out of the sleeping bags, got ourselves a big handful of rocks each, and came out of the tent firing. Got in a few good hits before we heard my granddaddy yelling for us to stop. Someone got him right in the face, split his lip open."

"It was him," Trey says. "Making the noise."

"Sure was. No such thing as a squatt."

"What'd he do? He beat you?"

"Nah. Laughed his ass off, cleaned up the blood, brought us out a big bag of marshmallows."

Trey digests this. "How come he did that? Pretended?"

"I guess he wanted to see what we'd do," Cal says, "if a bad situation came up. Seeing as he was letting us stay out there all by ourselves. The day after that, he started teaching me how to shoot a rifle. Said if I was gonna go fighting things that scared me, I might as well do it right, and I better know how to be damn sure what I was shooting at before I pulled the trigger."

Trey considers this. "Can you teach me?"

"I don't have a gun here yet. When I get one, then maybe."

Apparently this is good enough: Trey nods and finishes his cookie. "Bobby Feeney says he seen aliens up the mountains," he says, out of some train of thought of his own. "I heard in school."

"You planning on shooting an alien?"

Trey gives Cal his idiot look. "There's no aliens."

"What, you figure Bobby made it up to mess with people, like my granddaddy?"

"Nah."

Cal grins, drinking his coffee. "Then what'd he see?"

Trey shrugs, a one-shouldered twitch that means he doesn't want to discuss this. "You don't believe in aliens," he says, watching Cal to check.

"Probably not," Cal says. "I like to keep an open mind, and I figure they might be somewhere out there, but I haven't seen anything that would make me think they're coming visiting."

"Have you got brothers and sisters?" Trey demands, out of nowhere. The kid hasn't mastered the art of small talk. Every question comes out sounding like part of an interrogation.

"Three," Cal says. "Two sisters, one brother. 'Bout you?"

"Three sisters. Two brothers."

"That's a lot of kids," Cal says. "You got a big house?"

Trey blows air derisively out of the side of his mouth. "Nah."

"Where're you? Oldest? Youngest?"

"Third. What're you?"

"Oldest."

"Are you close to the others?"

This is the most personal Trey has ever got. Cal risks a glance at him, but he's focused on taking another cookie apart. He has a fresh buzz cut, but it looks like maybe he did it himself: a patch towards the back of his head got missed.

"Close enough," Cal says. In fact his are half siblings, he's never met any of them more than a couple of times, and there could well be more out there somewhere, but none of this information seems like it would be useful here. "How 'bout you?"

"Some of them," Trey says. He shoves the cookie abruptly into his mouth and stands up: break is, apparently, over.

"Drink your milk," Cal says.

"Don't like milk."

"I bought it. You drink it."

Trey throws back the milk, grimaces, and slams the mug down on the table like he's just taken a shot. "OK," Cal says, amused. "Let's do this. Hold on."

He goes into his bedroom, comes back with an old plaid shirt and tosses it to Trey. "Here."

Trey catches it and looks at it blankly. "What for?"

"You go home covered in paint, your mama's not gonna be happy."

"She won't notice."

"If she does, she's gonna know you weren't in school."

"She won't care."

"Your call," Cal says. He sets about levering the lid back off the primer can with a screwdriver.

Trey examines the shirt, turning it over in his hands. Then he puts it on. He turns to Cal, holding up his hands and grinning: the cuffs flap, the shirt comes down past his knees, and it's wide enough to fit about three of him.

"Looking good," Cal says, grinning back. "Hand me those there."

He's pointing to the paint trays and rollers, in a corner. He bought two sets; they were cheap, and he figured they would come in handy even if the kid quit showing up. Trey has clearly never seen contraptions like these before. He inspects them and gives Cal a question-mark look, brows pulled down.

"Watch," Cal says. He pours primer, dips the roller and rolls off the extra on the grid, then gives a patch of wall a fast going-over. "Got it?"

Trey nods and copies him, exactly, down to the little angled shake to get any drips off the roller's edge. "Good," Cal says. "Don't get too much paint on there. We're gonna do a few coats; we don't need them to be thick. I'll start here and do the top half, you do the bottom from over there. Meet you in the middle."

They work easily together, by now; they know each other's rhythm, and how to make the right space for it. The rain has eased off. The cries of geese limbering up for their long journey come to them from high up in the sky; far below, in the grass outside the window, the small birds hop and dart after worms. They've been painting for about twenty minutes when Trey says, out of the clear blue sky, "My brother's gone missing."

Cal manages to freeze only for half a second before his roller starts moving again. He would know from the tone, even if he hadn't heard the words: this is why Trey is here.

"Yeah?" he says. "When?"

"March." Trey is still rollering his patch of wall, meticulously, not looking at Cal. "Twenty-first."

"OK," Cal says. "How old is he?"

"Nineteen. His name's Brendan."

Cal is feeling his way, toe by toe. "What'd the police say?"

"Didn't tell them."

"How come?"

"Mam wouldn't. She said he went off, and he's old enough if he wants."

"But you don't think so."

Trey's face, when he stops painting and looks at Cal at last, has a terrible, tight-wound misery. He shakes his head for a long time.

"So what do you think happened?"

Trey says, low, "Think someone's got him."

"Like, kidnapped him?"

Nod.

"OK," Cal says carefully. "You got any idea who?"

Every cell in Trey's body is focused on Cal. He says, "You could find out."

There's a moment of silence.

"Kid," Cal says gently. "More than likely, your mama's right. From what everyone tells me, people mostly do take off from here, soon as they're old enough."

"He'd've told me."

"Your brother's still a teenager. They do dumb shit

like that. I know it's gotta hurt, if you guys are close, but sooner or later he'll grow up a little bit and realize it was a crappy thing to do. He'll get in touch then."

That stubborn chin has hardened. "He didn't go off."

"Any reason you're so sure?"

"I **know.** He didn't."

"If you're worried about him," Cal says, "you oughta go to the police. I know your mama doesn't want to, but you can do it yourself. They can take a report from a minor. They can't make him come home till he's ready, but they'll look into it, put your mind at ease."

Trey is looking at him like he can't believe anyone this dumb is still breathing. "What?" Cal says.

"Guards won't do anything."

"Sure they will. It's their job."

"They're fucking useless. You do it. You investigate. You'll see: he didn't go off."

"I can't investigate, kid," Cal says, even more gently. "I'm not a cop any more."

"Do it anyway." Trey's voice is rising. "Do the stuff you said, for finding people. Talk to his mates. Watch their houses."

"I could do that stuff because I had a badge. Now that I don't, no one's gotta answer my questions. I stake out someone's house, I'm the one who's gonna get arrested."

Trey isn't even hearing him. He's holding the roller

high in a clenched fist, like a weapon. "Tap their **phones.** Check his **bank** card."

"**Kid.** Even when I was a cop, it wasn't around here. I don't have buddies where I can call in favors."

"Then **you** do it."

"Does this place look like I have the technology to—"

"Then do something else. **Do something.**"

"I'm retired, kid," Cal says, still gently, but with finality. He's not going to leave the kid hoping. "There's nothing I could do, even if I wanted to."

Trey throws his roller across the room. He rips off Cal's old shirt, buttons popping, and stuffs it deep in the can of primer. Then he whips round and smashes the dripping shirt into the cubbyholes of the desk, with all his weight behind it. The desk goes over backwards. Trey runs.

———

The desk is a mess. Cal straightens it up and uses the shirt—which is a write-off anyway; no laundromat is going to deal with that—to wipe away the bigger globs of primer. Then he wets a cloth and cleans off the rest. Luckily it's water-based, but it's got right into half the joints, where no cloth can reach it. Cal goes at it with his toothbrush, calling Trey a little bastard under his breath.

In fact, he's finding it hard to actually get mad.

First the kid's daddy, then his big brother; no wonder he wants an answer that would bring one of them home and wouldn't involve him deliberately walking out without a backwards glance. Cal just wishes he had come out with this earlier, instead of building his hopes in secret all this time.

What he is, he realizes, more than mad, is unsettled. He doesn't like the feeling, or the fact that he recognizes it and understands it perfectly; it's as familiar to him as hunger or thirst. Cal never could stand to leave a case unresolved. Mainly this was a good thing, making him into a dogged, patient worker who got solves long after most guys would have given up, but on occasion it was also a failing: hammering on and on at something that's never going to break gets a man nothing but tired and sore. Cal scrubs harder at the desk and tries to recapture the light-headed freedom of not caring if Trey plays hooky. He reminds himself that this isn't his case, and in fact is almost certainly not a case at all. The unsettled feeling doesn't budge.

In his head Donna says, **Jesus, Cal, not again.** Her face isn't laughing this time; it's weary, dragged into downward lines that don't fit there.

A scrawny young rook has flapped down onto the windowsill and is eyeing the room speculatively, considering both the cookie packet and the toolbox. Cal has finally been making progress with the rooks: he's got them as far as settling on the stump to eat his scraps while he watches from the back step, although they eyefuck him and make dirty jokes about his mama while they do it. Right now, though, he's not in the mood. "Keep moving," he tells this one. The rook makes a noise that sounds like a raspberry, and stays put.

Cal gives up on the rook, and the desk. He wants, suddenly and powerfully, to be out of the house. The only thing he can think of that seems like it might settle his mind is catching his own dinner, but he doesn't feel like sitting on a riverbank all day getting his ass damp on the off chance of catching a perch or two, and his damn firearm license still hasn't come through. In general, taking into account some of the people he's known to own guns and the fact that Donie McGrath didn't have the option of whipping out a Glock in the pub, he can see the reasoning behind the restrictions in these parts, but today they piss him off. He could have got married or bought a house quicker, both, in Cal's opinion, undertakings considerably more hazardous than owning a hunting rifle.

He decides to head into town and see if the guy at the station can give him an update on that license. He can hit the laundromat while he's at it, and buy himself a new toothbrush, as well as a heater so Mart's sneaky cold doesn't get him. On his way out of the house with his trash bag of clothes, he locks the door.

The rain has picked up again, long curtains of it sweeping the windshield. Cal catches himself keeping an eye out for Trey. A few miles up into the hills, Lena said, which would be a long walk in this weather. But the road is deserted, just the odd cluster of cows sheltering against low stone walls and sheep dotted around the fields grazing, unperturbed. Branches droop low and swish along the sides of the Pajero. The mountains are dim and ghostly under a heavy veil of rain.

Kilcarrow town is old and comfortable, with rows of creamy-colored houses fanning out around a market square, and a hilltop view over fields and the twisting river. It has a couple of thousand people, which, factoring in the satellite villages, adds up to enough traffic for stuff like a hardware store and a laundromat. Cal hands in his clothes and makes for the police station with his head tucked down against the rain.

The station is in what looks like an oversized shed, sandwiched between two houses and painted white with a neat blue trim. It's open a few hours here and a few hours there. In the back room, several people on the radio are talking over each other about potholes. At the desk out front, a uniform is reading the undersized local paper and scratching his armpit with real dedication.

"Afternoon," Cal says, wiping rain off his beard. "Some weather out there."

"Ah, sure, it's a grand soft day," the uniform says comfortably, putting his paper away and leaning back in his chair. He's a few years younger than Cal, with a round face, a belly under construction and an air of having been scrubbed shiny-clean all over. Someone has mended a rip in his shirt pocket with tiny, careful stitches. "What can I do for you?"

"I applied for a firearm license, couple of months back. Seeing as I'm in town, figured I'd check if there was any update on that."

"You should receive a letter within three months of the application date, one way or the other," the uniform tells him. "If you don't, that means you've been refused, officially. But sure, sometimes they do get a bit behind. Even if you don't hear anything, you could be grand. I'd give it an extra month before you start worrying. Two, maybe."

Cal has met this guy before, in various forms. He's out in the boondocks not because he's a dud or a troublemaker, or a wannabe detective chafing with frustrated ambition, but because he's happy here. He likes his days unhurried and unsurprising, his faces familiar, and his mind unclouded when he goes home to his wife and kids. He's the cop who Cal, in some or possibly most ways, wishes he had decided to be.

"Well, I don't guess I have much right to complain," Cal says. "When I was on the job, paperwork went straight to the bottom of the pile and stayed there. You're not gonna mess around with some guy's dog license when you've got actual police work to do."

This has the uniform's attention. "You were on the

job?" he asks, making sure he has things straight. "On the force, like?"

"Twenty-five years. Chicago PD." Cal grins and holds out his hand. "Cal Hooper. Pleased to meet you."

"Garda Dennis O'Malley," the uniform says, shaking his hand. Cal was betting on him not being the type who would see this as a dick-measuring contest, and he bet right: O'Malley looks genuinely delighted. "Chicago, hah? I'd say you saw some action there."

"Some action and a lotta paperwork," Cal says. "Same as everywhere. This seems like a good post."

"I wouldn't swap it," O'Malley says. Cal can tell from his accent that he's not from round here, but he's from somewhere not too different: that rich, leisured rhythm didn't come out of any city. "It wouldn't suit everyone, now, but it suits me."

"What kind of stuff do you get?"

"A lot of it'd be motor vehicles," O'Malley explains. "They do be hoors for the speeding, round here. And for the drink-driving. Three young fellas went into a ditch coming home from the pub, Saturday night, up beyond Gorteen. None of them made it to hospital."

"I heard about that," Cal says. Noreen's cousin's friend's husband was the poor bastard who came across the aftermath. "That's a damn shame."

"That'd be about the worst we get, now. There's not much other crime. Oil does get robbed, now and again." At Cal's uncomprehending look: "Heating oil, out of the tanks. And farm equipment. And we'd get a bitta drugs—sure, they're everywhere, nowadays. Nothing like what you got in Chicago, I'd say." He gives Cal a shy grin.

"We got plenty of MVAs," Cal says, "and drugs. Not a whole lot of farm-equipment theft, though." And then, before he knows he's going to say it: "Mostly I worked Missing Persons. I don't guess you've got much call for that around here."

O'Malley laughs. "Ah, Jaysus, no. I'm here twelve years, and we've had two people go missing. One fella came up in the river a few days later. The other was a young one that had a row with her mammy and flounced off to stay with her cousin in Dublin."

"Well, I can see why you wouldn't swap this place," Cal says. "Thought I heard a guy did go missing on you this spring, though. Did I hear wrong?"

This startles O'Malley into sitting upright. "Who's that, then?"

"Brendan something. Reddy?"

"Reddys from up by Ardnakelty?"

"Yeah."

"Ach, them," O'Malley says, relaxing back into his chair. "What one's Brendan?"

"Nineteen."

"Sure, no surprise there, then. And, being honest with you, no loss."

"They trouble?"

"Ah, no. Wasters, just. A few domestics, but himself went off to England a coupla years back, and that put a stop to that. I know them because the childer won't go to school. The teacher doesn't want to be calling in child protection, so she rings me. I go out there and have a word with the mammy, put the fear of God into the childer about juvenile homes. They shape up for a month or two, and then we're back where we began."

"Know the type," Cal says. He doesn't need to ask why the teacher won't call child protective services for anything short of broken bones, or why O'Malley doesn't do it himself. Some things are the same out here as they were in his childhood backwoods. No one wants the government sending down city boys in suits to make things worse. Business gets handled as close to home as possible. "Their mama can't make them go, or she won't?"

O'Malley shrugs. "She's a bit . . . you know. Not mental or anything, like. Just not up to much."

"Huh," Cal says. "So you reckon Brendan's not missing?"

O'Malley snorts. "God, no. He's a young fella. He's got sick of living up the hills with his mammy, gone off to kip on some pal's floor in Galway or Athlone, where he can go to the discos and meet the young ones. Natural enough, sure. Who said he was missing?"

"Well," Cal says, scratching the back of his neck meditatively, "some guy in the pub was saying he was gone. I musta got the wrong end of the stick. Guess I spent too many years in Missing Persons, now I'm seeing 'em everywhere."

"Not here," O'Malley says cheerfully. "Brendan'll be back when he gets tired of doing his own washing. Unless he finds himself a young one who'll do it for him."

"We could all do with one of those," Cal says, grinning. "Well, I wasn't aiming to use that rifle for self-defense anyway, but it's nice to know there won't be any need around here."

"Ah, God, no. Hang on a minute there," O'Malley says, extracting himself bit by bit from his chair, "and I'll have a look on the system for that license. What gun are you getting?"

"Got a deposit down on a nice Henry twenty-two. I like 'em old-fashioned."

"That's a beauty," O'Malley says. "I've a Winchester myself. I'm not great with it, now, but I took down an aul' rat in my garden the other week. Big fella, looking at me bold as brass. Felt like Rambo, so I did. You wait there, now."

He ambles off into the back room. Cal looks around the warm little foyer, reads the raggedy posters on the walls—SEAT BELTS SAVE LIVES, WALK FOR SUICIDE PREVENTION, TEN FARM SAFETY TIPS—and listens to O'Malley singing along to a bread-ad jingle on the radio. The place smells of tea and potato chips.

"Now," O'Malley says triumphantly, coming back out front. "That's marked in the system as approved—and sure, why wouldn't it be. You should have your letter any day now. You can take it into the post office and pay the fee there."

"Much appreciated," Cal says. "And nice to meet you."

"Likewise. Call in another day when we're closing up, sure; we'll bring you for a pint, welcome you to the Wild West."

"I'd be honored," Cal says. The rain is still coming down hard. He pulls up his hood and heads out into it, before O'Malley thinks of inviting him to stick around for a cup of tea.

While he waits for his laundry, Cal finds a pub and gets himself a toasted ham-and-cheese sandwich and a pint of Smithwick's. This pub is an entirely different species from Seán Óg's: big and bright, smelling of hot savory food, with a shine on the wooden furniture and a wide selection of taps at the bar. A bunch of women in their thirties are having lunch and a laugh in one corner.

The sandwich is good and so is the beer, but Cal doesn't enjoy them the way he ought to. His chat with O'Malley, which should have settled his mind, has only stirred it up worse. Not that he believes for a minute that Brendan Reddy has been kidnapped by persons unknown. If anything, O'Malley confirmed what Cal thought from the start: Brendan had every reason to take off, and not many reasons to stick around.

What's bothering him is the fact that Trey was right about one thing: the Guards are, for his purposes anyway, fucking useless. Once O'Malley heard the name Reddy, he was done. So is everyone else.

Cal thinks of those rain-blurred hills, and a mother who's not up to much. A kid that age shouldn't be left with nowhere to turn.

The restlessness is still biting. Cal finishes his pint faster than he meant to, and heads back out into the rain.

He picks up an oil heater and a new can of primer in the hardware store, and a bunch of supplies including a new toothbrush at the supermarket. He doesn't bother with milk. He's pretty sure the kid won't be coming back.

SIX

The next morning is all soft mist, dreamy and innocent, pretending yesterday never happened. As soon as he finishes his breakfast, Cal packs up his fishing gear and heads for the river, two miles away. On the slim chance that Trey does come back, he'll take the empty house as an extra kick in the teeth, but Cal figures this is a good thing. Better let the kid be upset now than let him build up another head of false hope.

This is only the second time Cal has fished this river. He's regularly gone to bed intending on fishing the next day, but the house always had more of a welcome pull on him: this needed getting under way, he wanted to see how that turned out, the fish could wait. Today that pull just feels like nagging. He wants the house far away, with his back turned on it.

At first the river feels like what he needs. It's narrow enough that the massive old trees touch across it, rocky enough to make the water swirl and whiten; the banks are speckled orange-gold with fallen leaves. Cal finds himself a clear stretch and a big mossy beech tree, and takes his time picking a lure. Birds flip and sass each other between branches, paying no attention to him, and the smell of the water is so strong and sweet he can feel it against his skin.

After a couple of hours, though, the romance is wearing off. Last time Cal was out here, he caught himself a perch dinner in half an hour flat. This time, he can see the fish right there, picking bugs neatly off the surface, but not one of them has worked up the interest even to nibble at his lure. And he's starting to discover what Mart meant about the sneaky cold: what seemed like a nice cool day has seeped right up through his ass to chill him from the bones out. He digs a few worms out of the rich mulch under the layers of wet leaves beside him. The fish ignore those too.

The day he planned on teaching Alyssa to fish turned out like this. She was maybe nine; they were on a log-cabin vacation in some place Donna found whose name escapes him now. The two of them sat by a lake for three hours with nothing biting but midges, but Alyssa had promised her mama she would bring home dinner, and she wasn't leaving without it. In the end Cal looked at her red, miserable, stubborn little face and told her he had a plan. They swung by the store and bought a bag of frozen fish sticks, hooked it onto Alyssa's rod, and came in the cabin door yelling, "We got a big one!" Donna took one look and told them that fish was still alive and she was going to keep it for a pet. All three of them were giggling like idiots. When Donna dumped the bag in a bowl of water and named it Bert, Alyssa laughed so hard she fell over.

Cal feels like, if just one damn fish would give him a good fight and then a good dinner, all the things rattling around loose inside his head would shake themselves back into place. The fish, uninterested in his emotional requirements, keep right on playing tag around his hook.

After a full half day of nothing, Cal is starting to think that the river's reputation is a tourist-board scam and last time's perch dinner was a fluke. He packs up his gear and starts walking home, in no hurry to get there. On the off chance that Trey does show up for another try, he needs to shoot that down without biting the kid's head off.

Halfway home he runs into Lena, walking the other way at a good pace, with a dog rummaging in the hedges ahead of her. "Afternoon," she says, calling the dog back with a snap of her fingers. She's wearing a big russet wool jacket and a blue knit beanie pulled down low, so only a few strands of fair hair show. "Any fish?"

"Plenty," Cal says. "All of 'em smarter'n me."

Lena laughs. "That river's temperamental. Give it another go tomorrow, you'll catch more than you can keep."

"I might do that," Cal says. "This the mama dog?"

"Ah, no. She only whelped last week; she's at home with the pups. That's her sister."

The dog, a smart-looking young tan-and-black beagle, is quivering and huffing with eagerness to check Cal out. "OK if I say hi?" Cal asks.

"Go on. She's a lover, not a fighter, that one."

He holds out a hand. The dog snuffles over every inch of him she can reach, her whole rear end wagging. "She's a good dog," Cal says, rubbing her neck. "How's the mama and babies?"

"Grand. Five pups. I thought at first one of them might not make it, but now he's fat as a fool and pushing all the others out of the way to get what he's after. D'you fancy a look, if you're in the market?"

Lena catches the second it takes Cal to collect his thoughts on this. "Don't be minding Noreen," she says, amused. "You can come see a few pups without me taking it as a proposal. Cross my heart."

"Well, I don't doubt that," Cal says, embarrassed. "I was just wondering if I oughta leave it till a day when I'm not carrying all this stuff. I don't know how far your place is."

"About a mile and a half over that way. Up to you."

He says, only partly to make her amused look go away, "I reckon I can manage that. Appreciate the invitation."

Lena nods and turns around, and they head up the narrow road, hedges of yellow-flowered gorse swaying at them on either side. Cal slows his pace automatically—he's accustomed to Donna, five foot four in shoes—before he realizes there's no need:

Lena can keep up with him just fine. She has a countrywoman's long, easy stride, like she could keep walking all day.

"How're you getting on with the house?" she asks.

"Not too bad," Cal says. "I've started painting. My neighbor Mart keeps giving me flak because I'm sticking to plain old white, but Mart doesn't seem like the best place to get advice on interior decoration."

Part of him is expecting Lena to come out with suggestions for color schemes—Mart's talk must have got into his head. Instead she says, "Mart Lavin," with a wry twist of her mouth. "You wouldn't want to listen to that fella. Nellie," she says sharply to the dog, which is dragging something dark and sodden out of the ditch. "Leave it."

The dog reluctantly drops the object and trots off to find something else. "And the land?" Lena says. "What have you planned for it?"

Ironically, Mart regularly asks Cal that same question, not bothering to hide the fact that he's trying to pry out Cal's long-term intentions. Cal is a little hazy on those himself. Right now he can't imagine a time when he'll want to do anything more than fix up his house, fish for perch and listen to Noreen explain Clodagh Moynihan's dental history. He recognizes that that time might come around someday. If it does, he figures he can do a little bit of traipsing around Europe, before he gets too old, and then come back here when he's scratched the itch out of his feet. There's nowhere else he needs to be.

"Well," he says, "I haven't rightly decided. I've got that piece of woodland, I'm gonna leave that the way it is; it's about half hazel trees, and I'd eat hazelnuts all day long. I might add in a couple of apple trees, give me something sweet to go with the nuts in a few years' time. And I was thinking of planting out another piece with vegetables."

"Oh, God," Lena says. "You're not one of them off-the-grid types, are you?"

Cal grins. "Nah. Just been sitting at a desk for too long, feel like spending some time outdoors."

"Thank God."

"You get a lot of off-the-grid types round here?"

"Now and again. Notions about getting back to the land, and they think this is the place to do it. It looks the part, I suppose." She nods to the mountains ahead, hunch-shouldered and tawny, shawled here and there with rags of mist. "Most of them don't know one end of a spade from the other. They last about six months."

"I'm OK with doing my hunting and gathering mainly out of your sister's store," Cal says. "I gotta admit Noreen scares me a little bit, but not enough to make me want to grow my own bacon."

"Noreen's all right," Lena says. "I would say ignore her and in the end she'll leave you alone, but she won't. Noreen can't see anything without wanting to put it to use. You just have to let it roll off you."

"She's backing the wrong horse here," Cal says. "I'm not that useful to anyone, right now."

"Nothing wrong with that. And don't let Noreen convince you different."

They walk in silence, but an easy silence. There are blackberry brambles mixed in with the gorse; a couple of thickset, tufty ponies in a field are nibbling at them, and every now and then Lena pulls a blackberry off a hedge and eats it. Cal follows her lead. The berries are dark and full, still with a tart edge to them. "I'll get a rake of them, one of these days, and make jam," Lena says. "If there's a day when I can be arsed."

She turns off the road, down a long dirt lane. The fields on either side are pasture, thick with long grass and the smells of cows. A man examining a cow's leg lifts his head at Lena's call and waves, shouting back something Cal doesn't catch. "Ciaran Maloney," Lena says. "Bought the land off me." Cal can picture her out in those fields, in rubber boots and muddy pants, neatly outmaneuvering a frisky colt.

Her house is a long white bungalow, freshly painted, with boxes of geraniums on the windowsills. She doesn't invite Cal in; instead she leads him round the side of the house, towards a low, rugged stone building. "I tried to get the dog to whelp inside," she says, "but she was having none of it. It was the cattle byre she wanted. In the end I thought, what harm. The walls on it are thick enough to keep out the cold, and if she does get chilly, she knows where to come."

"That what you and your husband farmed? Cattle?"

"We did, yeah. Dairy. They weren't kept here, but. This is the old byre, from a century or two back. We used it mostly for storing feed."

The byre is dim, lit only through small high windows, and Lena was right about the walls: it's warmer in there than Cal expected. The dog is in the end stall. They squat on their haunches, while Nellie keeps a respectful distance, and peer in.

The mama dog is tan and white, curled up in a big wooden box around a squeaking mass of pups wriggling over each other to get in close. "That's a fine-looking litter," Cal says.

"This here's the runt I was telling you about," Lena says, reaching in and scooping up a fat pup mottled in black, tan and white. "Look at the size of him now."

Cal reaches to take the pup, but the mama dog half-rises, a low growl starting in her chest. The other pups, disturbed, squeak furiously. "Give her a minute," Lena says. "She's not as well trained as Nellie. I've only had her a few weeks, haven't had a chance to put manners on her. Once she sees her sister doesn't mind you, she'll be grand."

Cal turns his shoulder to the litter and makes a big fuss of Nellie, who soaks it up joyfully, licking and wriggling. Sure enough, the mama dog sinks back down among her pups and, when Cal turns back, allows him to take the runt from Lena with only a lift of her lip.

The pup's eyes are closed tight and his head wobbles on his neck. He gnaws at Cal's fingertip with tiny toothless gums, looking for milk. He has a tan face and black ears, with a white blaze running up his nose; the black patch on his tan back is the shape of a ragged flag flying. Cal strokes his soft floppy ears.

"Been a while since I got a chance to do this," he says.

"They're nice to have about, all right," Lena says. "I'd no wish for puppies—or for two dogs, come to that. I fancied having the one, so I got Nellie out of a shelter, after the pair of them were left on the side of a road. The people that took Daisy didn't bother spaying her; when she came up pregnant, they dropped her back to the shelter. The shelter rang me. At first I said no, but in the end I thought, why not?" She reaches into the basket to tickle a pup's forehead with one finger; the pup nuzzles blindly into her hand. "You take what comes your way, I suppose."

"Mostly doesn't seem like there's much choice," Cal agrees.

"And of course the pups are some mad mix. God knows who'll want them."

Cal likes the angle of her next to him: not tilted towards him like a woman who wants him or wants him to want her, off balance as if he might have to catch her any minute, but planted solid on her feet and shoulder-to-shoulder with him, like a partner. The byre smells of cattle feed, sweet and nutty, and the floor is scattered with strawy golden dust. The riverbank cold is starting to thaw out of his bones.

"Some retriever in there, I'd guess," he says. "And that one at the end's got a little terrier around the ears."

"Pure mutt, I'd say. No way to know if they'd be any good for hunting. And beagles are no use as guard dogs. You'd get more savagery out of a hamster."

"They any good as watchdogs?"

"They'll let you know if someone's on your land, all right. They notice everything, and they want to tell you about it. But the worst they'll do to him is lick him to pieces."

"I wouldn't ask a dog to do my dirty work for me," Cal says. "But I'd want one that'd let me know if something needs doing."

"You've a good way with them," Lena says. "If you want one, you can have one."

Cal wasn't aware, till that moment, that he was being evaluated. "I'll take a week or two to think it over," he says. "If that's all right."

Lena, her face turned to him, has that amused look again. "Did I give you a fright, with all that talk about the blow-ins packing it in after one winter?"

"It's not that," Cal says, a little taken aback.

"I told you, most of them last six months. You're

here, what now, four? Don't worry, you won't be setting any records if you cut and run."

"I want to be sure I'll do a dog justice," Cal says. "It's a responsibility."

Lena nods. "True enough," she says. There's a slight lift to her eyebrow; he can't tell whether she believes him. "Let me know whenever you make your mind up, so. Is there one that takes your fancy? You're the first person I've offered; you can have your pick."

"Well," Cal says, running a finger down the runt's back, "I like the looks of this one right here. He's already proved he's no quitter."

"I'll tell people he's spoken for," Lena says. "If anyone asks. If you want to come up and see how he's growing, give me a ring first to make sure I'm about—I'll give you my number. I work odd hours, some days."

"Where do you work at?"

"In a stable the other side of Boyle. I do the books, but sometimes I give a hand with the horses as well."

"Did you use to have those? As well as the cattle?"

"Not of our own. We boarded a few."

"Sounds like you had a pretty serious operation here," Cal says. The runt has rolled over in his palm; he tickles its tummy. "This must be a big change."

He's not expecting her swift curl of a grin. "You've got it in your head I'm a poor lonesome widow woman devastated by losing the farm where she and her man worked their fingers to the bone. Haven't you?"

"Something like that," Cal admits, grinning back. He always did have a weakness for women who were a step ahead of him, although look where that got him.

"Not a bit of it," Lena says cheerfully. "I was only delighted to be rid of the bastard. We worked our fingers to the bone, all right, and Sean never stopped worrying that we'd go bankrupt, and then he started drinking to ease the worry. The three things between them gave him the heart attack."

"Noreen told me he died. I'm sorry for your loss."

"It was almost three years back. I'm getting used to it, bit by bit." She rubs behind the mama dog's ear; the dog narrows her eyes in bliss. "But I held it against the farm. Couldn't wait to get the place off my hands."

"Huh," Cal says. It occurs to him that Lena is talking pretty freely to someone she's hardly met, and that most people he's known to do that were either crazy or looking to lower his guard for their own purposes, but from her it doesn't make him wary. He's aware that, however revealing this conversation might appear to be, the vast majority of her is held so far apart as to be imperceptible. "Your husband wouldn't leave it, huh?"

"Not a chance. Sean needed the freedom. He couldn't stick the thought of working for some other man. For me"—she tilts her head at her surroundings—"this is freedom. Not the other. When I walk out of work, I'm done. No being dragged out of bed at three in the morning because a calving's going wrong. I like the horses, but I like them even better now that I can leave them at the end of the day."

"Makes plenty of sense to me," Cal says. "And it worked out that simple?"

She shrugs. "More or less. Sean's sisters were bulling: the family farm, sold away before he was even cold in the ground, that kind of thing. They wanted me to let their sons work it, then leave it to them when I die. I decided I could live without them better than I could live with this place still on my back. I never liked them much anyway."

Cal laughs, and after a moment Lena does too. "They think I'm a cold bitch," she says. "Maybe they're right. But there's ways I'm happier now than I've ever been." She nods at the runt, who's flipped himself right side up and is squeaking furiously enough that his mama's ears prick up. "Will you look at that fella. I don't know where he's going to put it, but he's looking for more."

"I'll let you all go back to business," Cal says, sliding the pup gently back into the box, where he squirms in among his brothers and sisters, heading for food. "And I'll get back to you about this little guy."

Lena doesn't invite him in for a cup of tea, or walk him to the main road. She nods good-bye outside her front door and goes inside, Nellie bouncing after her, without even waving him off. All the same, Cal leaves her place feeling more cheerful than he has all day.

This mood lasts until he gets home, when he discovers that someone has let the air out of all four of his tires.

"Kid!" he yells, at the top of his lungs. "Get out here!"

The garden is silent, except for the rooks jeering back at him.

"Kid! **Now!**"

Nothing moves.

Cal cusses and digs his jump-starter, which has a built-in tire inflator, out of the back of his car. By the time he has the damn thing set up and working, and the first tire back in shape, he's calmed down enough that something occurs to him. It would have been quicker and easier to slash the tires than to let the air out. If Trey bothered to do this instead, it's because he wasn't aiming to do real damage. He was aiming to make a point. Cal isn't clear on what that point is—**I'm going to hassle you till you do what I need,** possibly, or maybe just **You're a dick**—but then communication never has been Trey's strong suit.

He's moving on to the second tire when Mart and Kojak show up. "What're you at with the prize pony?" Mart inquires, nodding at the Pajero. Mart, having come upon Cal waxing it one day, feels that

Cal's attitude to it is altogether too precious and citi-
fied for a back-country beater. "Putting ribbons in
her mane?"

"More or less," Cal says, giving Kojak's head a rub
as Kojak checks out the evidence of Lena's dogs on
his pants. "Topping up the air."

Luckily Mart has more important things on his
mind than the fact that Cal's tires are flat as a witch's
tit. "A young lad's after hanging himself," he informs
Cal. "Darragh Flaherty, from over the river. His father went out this morning to do the milking and
found him hanging from a tree."

"That's a damn shame," Cal says. "Give my re-
spects to his family."

"I will. Only twenty years of age."

"That's when they do it," Cal says. For a second
he sees Trey's tense face: **He didn't go off.** He goes
back to screwing the inflator onto the valve stem.

"I knew that lad wasn't right, the last while,"
Mart says. "I seen him at mass in town three times
this summer. I said it to his father, to be keeping
an eye on him, but sure you can't watch them day
and night."

"Why shouldn't he go to church?" Cal asks.

"Church," Mart tells him, pulling his tobacco
pouch out of a jacket pocket and finding an undersized rollie, "is for women. The spinsters, mostly; they
do like to get themselves in a tizzy over whose turn it
is to do the second reading, or the altar flowers. And

the mammies bringing in the childer so they won't grow up heathens, and the aul' ones showing off that they're not dead yet. If a young lad starts going to mass, it's a bad sign. Something's not sitting right, in his life or in his head."

"You go to mass," Cal points out. "That's where you saw him."

"I do," Mart acknowledges, "now and again. There's great chats at Folan's, after, and the carvery dinner. I get a fancy sometimes to have my dinner cooked by someone else. And if I'm looking to buy or sell stock, I'd go to mass all right. There's many a deal done in Folan's after noon mass."

"Here I had you down as just a prayerful kinda guy," Cal says, grinning.

Mart laughs till he chokes on smoke. "Sure, I've no need for that carry-on at my age. What sins would I commit, an aul' lad like me? I haven't even got the broadband."

"There's gotta be a few sins available in these parts," Cal says. "How 'bout Malachy Whatshisname's poteen?"

"That's no kind of sin," Mart says. "There's what's against the law, and then there's what's against the church. Sometimes they do be the same, and sometimes they don't. Did they never teach you that, in your church?"

"Might've done," Cal says. His mind isn't entirely on Mart. He would be happier if he had a clearer sense both of Trey's capabilities and of his boundaries.

He has a feeling that both are flexible, determined almost entirely by context and need. "Been a while since I was a churchgoing man."

"We wouldn't meet your requirements, I suppose. Ye've all them churches where they play with the snakes and speak in tongues. We wouldn't be able to offer you any of that round here."

"That darn Saint Patrick," Cal says. "Chasing away our equipment."

"He couldn't foresee Yanks arriving in on us. Sure, ye weren't even invented back then."

"And now look at us," Cal says, checking the tire pressure gauge. "Getting everywhere."

"And welcome. Sure, wasn't Saint Patrick a blow-in himself? Ye're the ones that keep our lives interesting." Mart crushes the end of his rollie under his boot. "Tell us now, how've you been getting on with that aul' wreck of a desk?"

Cal glances up sharply from the gauge. Just for a second, he thought there was a slant to Mart's voice that put more into the question. Sections of Mart's land have a perfect view of Cal's backyard.

Mart cocks his head inquisitively, guileless as a kid.

"Doin' OK," Cal says. "Some staining and varnishing, and it'll be back on the road."

"Fair play to you," Mart says. "If you ever need the extra few bob, you can set up as a carpenter: have your workshop in that shed there, find yourself an apprentice to give you a hand. Just make sure you pick a good one." And when Cal looks up again: "Did I see you heading into town there, yesterday afternoon?"

Cal fetches Mart's cookies and shoots the shit with him till Mart gets bored, whistles for Kojak and heads off up the field. The tires are back in shape, for the time being, anyhow. Cal packs away his jumpstarter and goes inside. At least the house is undamaged, as far as he can see.

The sandwiches he brought to the river seem like they were a long time ago, but he doesn't feel like cooking. Yesterday's restlessness has built itself into outright worry, the sharp buzzing kind he can't pin down, let alone crush.

It's still early in Seattle, but he can't make himself wait. He goes out back, where the reception is less crappy, and phones Alyssa.

She answers, but she sounds blurry and breathless. "Dad? Is everything OK?"

"Yeah. Sorry. I had a minute, so I figured I'd go ahead and call now. Didn't mean to scare you."

"Oh. No, it's fine."

"How 'bout you? You doing OK?"

"Yeah, everything's good. Listen, Dad, I'm at work, so . . ."

"Sure," Cal says. "No problem. You sure you're OK? That flu didn't come back?"

"No, I'm fine. Just got a lot on my plate. Talk to you later, OK?"

Cal hangs up with that worry getting bigger and

more fractious, gathering speed as it prowls his mind. He could probably use a shot or two of Jim Beam, but he can't make himself do it. He can't shake the feeling that some emergency is heading towards him, someone is in danger, and he needs to keep all his wits about him to have a chance of fixing things. He reminds himself that anyone else's danger isn't his problem, but it doesn't take.

He bets the damn kid is watching him from somewhere, but Mart is out in his field doing something with his sheep; if Cal shouts, he'll hear. Cal walks the perimeter of his garden, tramps his back field and circles his patch of woodland, without finding anything but a couple of rabbit holes. When he replays that phone call in his head, Alyssa's voice sounds wrong, worn and beaten down, worse every time.

Before he believes that he's actually going to do it, he's phoned Donna.

The phone rings for a long time. He's on the verge of giving up when she answers.

"Cal," she says. "What's up?"

Cal almost hangs up right there. Her voice is absolutely, totally neutral; he doesn't know how to respond to that voice coming out of Donna. But hanging up would make him feel like such a damn fool that instead he says, "Hey. I'm not gonna hassle you. Just wanted to ask you something."

"OK. Go ahead."

He can't tell where she is or what she's doing; the

background noise sounds like wind, but it could just be the reception. He tries to figure out what time it is in Chicago: noon, maybe? "Have you seen Alyssa lately?"

There's a slight pause. Every conversation he's had with Donna since the split has been peppered with these pauses, while she evaluates whether answering his question would fall within the new rules she's single-handedly established for their relationship. She hasn't communicated these rules to Cal, so he has no idea what they are, but he sometimes catches himself deliberately trying to break them anyway, like some shitty little kid.

Apparently this question is allowed. Donna says, "I went out to them for a couple of weeks in July."

"Have you been talking to her?"

"Yeah. Every few days."

"She seem OK to you?"

The pause is longer this time. "Why?"

Cal feels aggravation rising. He keeps it out of his voice. "She doesn't sound too good to me. I can't tell what it is, if she's just overworked or what, but I'm worried about her. Is she sick or something? Is that Ben guy treating her OK?"

"What are you asking me for?" Donna is fighting hard to keep that neutral voice, but she's losing, which gives Cal a tiny bit of satisfaction. "It's not my job to be you guys' go-between any more. You want to know how Alyssa is, ask her yourself."

"I did. She says she's fine."

"Well there you go."

"Is she . . . Come on, Donna, give me a break. Is she getting shaky again? Did something happen?"

"You ask her that?"

"No."

"Then go ahead and ask."

The heaviness seeping through Cal's bones is so familiar it makes him tired. He and Donna had so many of these fights, the year before she left, fights that went on forever without ever getting anywhere or even having any clear direction, like those dreams where you run as hard as you can but your legs will barely move.

"Would you tell me?" he asks. "If there was something wrong?"

"Hell no. Anything Alyssa doesn't tell you, she doesn't want you to know. That's her choice. Even if there was something, what are you gonna do about it from there?"

"I could come over. Should I come over?"

Donna makes an explosive noise of sheer exasperation. Donna always loved words and used plenty of them, enough to compensate for Cal's shortages, but they never were enough to contain what she was feeling; she needed her hands too, and her face, and a mockingbird's array of noises. "You are unbelievable, you know that? For a smart guy, my God . . . You know what, I'm not doing this. I don't do your thinking any more. I gotta go."

"Sure, you do that," Cal says, his voice rising. "And

give my love to Whatshisname," but she's already hung up, which is probably a good thing.

Cal stands there in his back field for a while, with the phone in his hand. He wants to punch something, but he knows that would do nothing but bust his knuckles. Having that much sense makes him feel old.

Evening is filtering into the air; there are streaks of cold yellow above the mountains, and in the oak tree the rooks are having their evening conference. Cal goes back to the house and puts some Emmylou Harris on the iPod. He needs someone to be sweet to him, just for a little while.

He takes that bottle of Jim Beam out onto the back steps after all. He can't see any reason not to. Even if someone is in some kind of danger, it seems the last thing they want is any help from him.

He also can't see any reason not to let himself sit there and think about Donna, seeing as he already fucked up and called her. Cal never had much time for nostalgia, but thinking about Donna seems like an important thing to do every now and then. He sometimes gets the feeling that Donna has methodically erased all their good times from her memory, so that she can move on into her shiny new life without ripping herself up. If he doesn't keep them in his, they'll be gone like they never happened.

What he thinks about is the morning they found out Alyssa was coming. He can remember clear as day how Donna felt when he hugged her, her skin hotter than normal like some engine was firing on new cylinders, the stunning gravitational pull of her and the mystery inside her. He sits on his back steps, watching green fields turn gray with evening and listening to Emmylou's sad gentle voice drift out his door, and tries to work out how on earth he got from that day to this one.

SEVEN

Cal wakes up next morning with that bad feeling still running round his gut. His last year or two on the job, he woke up every day like this, with this same thick knotted certainty that something bad was rolling towards him, something unpreventable and implacable, like a hurricane or a mass shooting. It made him jumpy as a rookie; people noticed, and gave him shit about it. When Donna walked out, he thought that must be it, the bomb he had been waiting for. Only the feeling was still there in his gut, hulking and surly as ever. Then he figured it must be the hazards of the job catching him in some new middle-aged awareness of mortality, but when he put in his papers and walked away, still it stayed. It only started to loosen its grip when he signed the papers on this place, and it only finally left him the day he walked through his overgrown grass to his peeling front door. And now here it is again, like it just took a little while to sniff him out, all these miles away, and track him down.

He deals with it the way he did on the job, which is by trying to work it to death. After breakfast he gets back to painting the living room, as hard and fast as he can and whether he wants to or not. This works as well as it ever did, which is to say not particularly, but at least he gets shit done along the way. By dinnertime he has the primer put on, walls and ceiling, and most of the first coat of paint. He's still skittish as a wild horse. The day is windy, which means all kinds of noises inside and outside and up the chimney, and Cal jumps at every one of them even though he knows they're nothing but leaves and window frames. Or, possibly, the kid. Cal wishes the kid's mama had decided to send him to military school when he first started playing hooky.

The days are shortening. By the time Cal knocks off work it's dark, an edgy, blustery dark that makes his plan to walk off the rest of the feeling seem a lot less attractive. He's eating a hamburger and trying to firm up his resolve when something smashes against his front door. Not the wind, this time; something solid.

Cal puts down his hamburger, goes quietly out the back and edges around the side of the house. There's only a sliver of moon; the shadows are thick enough to hide even a guy his size. From out over Mart's land floats the imperturbable call of an owl.

The front lawn is empty, wind yanking the grass this way and that. Cal waits. After a minute, something small comes whizzing out of the hedge and smacks into the wall of the house. This time, with the juicy crack and splatter it makes against the stone, Cal gets it. The damn kid is egging his house.

Cal goes back indoors and stands in his living

room, evaluating the situation and listening hard. The same applies to the eggs as to the tires: a couple of rocks would have been easier to come by, and would have done a lot more damage. The kid isn't attacking Cal; he's demanding him.

Another egg splats against the front door. Before he knows he's going to do it, Cal gives up. He can hold out against this kid and he can hold out against his own intractable unsettled places, but not both at the same time.

He goes to the sink, fills up the plastic tub where he does his dishes, and finds an old dish towel. Then he takes them both to the door and flings it wide open.

"Kid!" he calls, good and loud, to the hedge. "Get out here."

Silence. Then a flying egg misses Cal by inches and splatters against the wall.

"Kid! I changed my mind. Knock that shit off before I change it back again."

There's another silence, this one longer. Then Trey, egg box in hand and egg in the other, steps out of the hedge and stands waiting, ready to run or throw. The V of light from the doorway stretches his shadow behind him, turning him elongated and narrow, a dark figure materialized in headlight beams on a deserted road.

"I'll look into your brother," Cal says. "I'm not promising you anything, but I'll see what I can do."

Trey is staring at him with pure, feral suspicion. "Why?" he demands.

"Like I said. I changed my mind."

"Why?"

"None of your beeswax," Cal says. "Not because of you pulling this dumb crap, tell you that much. You still want me to do this, or not?"

Trey nods.

"OK," Cal says. "Then first off, you clean up all this shit. When you're done, come inside and we'll talk." He dumps the towel and the bucket on the doorstep, goes back inside and slams the door behind him.

He's finishing up the last of his burger when he hears the door open and the wind comes charging in, looking for things to grab. Trey stands in the doorway.

"You done?" Cal asks.

Trey nods.

Cal doesn't need to check whether he did it right. "OK," he says. "Sit down."

Trey doesn't move. It takes Cal a minute to realize: he's scared he's being lured inside for a beating.

"Jesus, kid," he says. "I'm not gonna hit you. If you cleaned up, we're square."

Trey's eyes go to the desk, in a corner.

"Yeah," Cal says. "You messed it up pretty good. I got most of the paint off, but there's some in the cracks. You can work on it with a toothbrush sometime."

The kid still looks wary. "I would say you can leave the door open in case you want to run," Cal says, "but it's too windy for that. Your call."

After a minute Trey makes up his mind. He moves

into the room, shuts the door behind him and thrusts the egg box at Cal. There's one left.

"Thanks," Cal says. "I guess. Stick it in the fridge."

Trey does. Then he sits down across the table from Cal, chair pushed well back and feet braced, just in case. He's wearing a dirty army-green parka, which is a relief; Cal has been wondering if the kid even had a winter coat.

"You want something to eat? Drink?"

Trey shakes his head.

"OK," Cal says. He pushes back his chair—Trey flinches—takes his plate to the sink, then goes into his room and comes back with a notebook and a pen.

"First off," he says, pulling his chair back up to the table, "most likely I won't find out anything. Or if I do, it'll be just what your mama already told you: your brother ran off. You OK with that?"

"He didn't."

"Maybe not. What I'm saying is, this might not go the way you got in mind, and you need to be ready for that. Are you?"

"Yeah."

Cal knows this is a lie, even if the kid doesn't. "You better be," he says. "The other thing is, you don't bullshit me. I ask you a question, you give me all the answer you've got. Even if you don't like it. Any bullshit, I'm out. We clear?"

Trey says, "Same for you. Anything you find out, you tell me."

"We got a deal," Cal says. He flips open his note-book. "So. What's your brother's full name?"

The kid is straight-backed, with his hands clamped on his thighs, like this is an oral exam and he needs to ace it. "Brendan John Reddy."

Cal writes that down. "Date of birth?"

"Twelfth of February."

"Where'd he live, up until he went missing?"

"At home. With us."

"Who's 'us'?"

"My mam. My sisters. My other brother."

"Names and ages?"

"My mam's Sheila Reddy, she's forty-four. Maeve's nine. Liam's four. Alanna's three."

"You said before you had three sisters," Cal says, writing. "Where's the other one?"

"Emer. She went up to Dublin, two years ago. She's twenty-one."

"Any chance Brendan's staying with her?"

Trey shakes his head hard.

"Why not?"

"They don't get on."

"How come?"

Shrug. "Brendan says she's thick."

"What's she do?"

"Works at Dunnes Stores. Stacking shelves."

"How 'bout Brendan? Was he working? In school? College?"

"Nah."

"Why not?"

Shrug.

"When'd he leave school?"

"Last year. He got his Leaving Cert, he didn't drop out."

"He have anything he wanted to do? He apply to any colleges, any jobs?"

"He wanted to do electrical engineering. Or chemistry. He didn't get the points."

"Why not? He dumb?"

"No!"

"Then why?"

"Hated school. The teachers."

The kid is shooting out answers like he's on the timed round of a quiz show. Cal can tell, watching him, that it feels good. This—the two of them facing each other across this table, the notebook and pen— is what Trey has been working towards, all this time.

"Gimme a little more about him," Cal says. "What's he like?"

Trey's eyebrows twitch together; clearly he has never tried to articulate this before. "He's a laugh," he says, in the end. "He talks a lot."

"You sure you're related?"

Trey gives Cal a blank stare. "Never mind," Cal says. "Just joshing you. Go on."

The kid makes a baffled what-do-you-want-from-me grimace, but Cal waits. "He can't sit still," Trey says, in the end. "Mam gives out about that. He got in hassle in school for it, and for messing."

When Cal keeps waiting: "He likes motorbikes.

And making stuff. Like when I was a kid, he made me little cars that actually went, and experiments out the back field to blow stuff up. And he's not thick. He has ideas. In school he made a load of money buying sweets in town and then selling them at lunch, till the teachers found out." He glances at Cal, checking whether that's enough.

Cal is thinking that it sounds like Brendan takes after his daddy a lot more than Trey does, and look what Daddy ended up doing. "Good," he says. "I like to get an idea who I'm looking for, see what direction it points me. Your brother have any medical conditions? Mental illnesses?"

"No!"

"It's not an insult, kid," Cal says. "I need to know."

The kid is still affronted. "He's grand."

"Never went to the doctor for anything?"

"He broke his arm one time. Came off a motorbike. But he went to the hospital for that, not the doctor."

"He ever seem depressed to you? Anxious?"

Clearly these aren't concepts to which Trey has given a lot of thought. "He was well pissed off when he didn't get into college," he offers, after considering this.

"Pissed off like what? Like staying in his room all day? Not eating? Not talking? What?"

Trey gives Cal a look like he's being a drama queen. "Nah. Like pissed off. Like he swore a lot, and he went out on the lash that night, and he was in a humor all week. Then he said fuck college anyway, he'd be grand."

"OK," Cal says. That doesn't sound like a tendency towards depression, but family aren't always the best observers. "Who'd he hang out with?"

"Eugene Moynihan. Fergal O'Connor. Paddy Fallon. Alan Geraghty. Some other lads as well, but mostly them."

Cal writes those down. "Which one was he closest to?"

"He doesn't have a best friend, like. Just whichever of them are about."

"He have a girlfriend?"

"Nah. Not the last while."

"Exes?"

"He went out with Caroline Horan for a couple of years, in school."

"Good relationship?"

Trey shrugs. This is an extravagant one that means **How the hell would I know?**

"When'd it end?"

"A while back. Before Christmas."

"Why?"

Another shrug. "She dumped him."

"Any beef there? She accuse him of anything? Hitting her, cheating on her?"

Shrug.

Cal underlines Caroline's name. "Where would I find Caroline? She work around here?"

"In town. Or she did when Bren was going out with her, anyway. Shop that sells shite to tourists. And sometimes she usedta give Noreen a hand—her mam and Noreen are cousins. I think she's in college now, but, so I dunno."

"He have any problems with anyone else?"

"Nah. Fought with the lads, sometimes. Nothing serious, but."

"Fought like what? Arguments? Yelling? Fists? Knives?"

Trey gives Cal the drama-queen look again. "Not **knives.** All the rest, yeah. Didn't mean anything."

"Just guys being guys," Cal says, nodding. This may well be true, but it needs checking. "What's he do for fun? Any hobbies?"

"Plays hurling. Goes out."

"He a drinker?"

"Sometimes. Not every night, like."

"Where? Seán Óg's?"

That gets an eye-roll. "Seán's is old fellas. Brendan goes into town. Or people's houses."

"What's he like drunk?"

"He's not a bad drunk or nothing. He goes messing, like him and his mates robbed a load of signboards from outside shops in town and put them in people's gardens. And one time Fergal's parents were away and he had a party, and he passed out drunk, so the rest of them put a sheep in his bathroom."

"Brendan ever get rowdy?" Cal asks. "Start fights?"

Trey makes a dismissive **pfft.** "Nah. He gets into fights the odd time, like once a bunch of lads from Boyle jumped on them in town. But he doesn't go looking."

"What about drugs? He ever do any of those?"

That gives Trey his first real pause. He eyes Cal warily. Cal looks back at him. He's got no duty to nudge and cajole, not here. If Trey decides he doesn't want to do this after all, that's fine by Cal.

"Sometimes," Trey says, finally.

"What kinds?"

"Hash. E. Bitta speed."

"Where's he get it?"

"There's a few lads around the townland that always have stuff. Everyone knows to go to them. Or he'd buy it in town, sometimes."

"He ever do any dealing?"

"Nah."

"Would you know?"

"He told me things. I wouldn't rat on him. He knew that."

There's a quick fierce flare of pride in Trey's eyes. Cal is getting the flavor of this. The kid was Brendan's pet brother, and everything about that was special.

"He ever have any problems with the police?"

The corner of Trey's mouth twists scornfully. "Mitching off school. This fat lump comes down from town and gives us shite."

"He's doing you guys a favor," Cal says. "He could

report it to child protective services, get you and your mama in big trouble. Instead, he takes the time to come out here and talk to you. Next time you see him, you thank him real nice. Brendan run into police any other ways?"

"He got caught speeding, coupla times. Racing, like, with his mates. Nearly lost his license."

"Anything else?"

Trey shakes his head.

"What about stuff he didn't get caught for?"

They look at each other. Cal says, "I told you. Any bullshit, we're done."

Trey says, "He robs off Noreen sometimes."

"And?"

"And off places in town. Nothing big. Only for the laugh."

"Anything else?"

"Nah. You gonna tell Noreen?"

"Pretty sure she already knows, kid," Cal says dryly. "But don't worry, I'm not gonna say anything. How'd Brendan get on with your daddy?"

Trey doesn't flinch, just one blink. "Bad."

"Like what?"

"They'd fight."

"Argue? Or it got physical?"

Trey's eyes snap furiously with the fact that this is none of Cal's damn business. Cal sits and watches, letting the silence stretch, while the kid's instincts drag him two ways.

"Yeah," Trey says, in the end. His face has tightened up.

"How often?"

"Few times."

"Over what?"

"Dad said Brendan was a waster, sponging. Bren said look who's talking. And sometimes . . ." Trey's chin jerks sideways, but he keeps going. He's sticking to his side of the deal. "To make Dad leave Mam or one of us alone, sometimes. If he was raging."

"So," Cal says, staying back from that, "it's not likely Brendan headed off to join your dad."

Trey makes a harsh, explosive noise that's something like a laugh. "No chance."

"You got a phone number for your dad, or an email address? Just in case."

"Nah."

" 'Bout for Brendan?"

"Know his phone number."

Cal flips to a fresh page in his notebook and passes it to Trey. He writes carefully, pressing the pen down hard. The wind is still going outside, rattling the door and pushing in at its edges to wrap cold around their ankles.

"He have a smartphone?" Cal asks.

"Yeah."

An hour with that number, and the techs at work would have known every single thing that was on Brendan's mind. Cal has none of their skills, none of their software and of course none of their rights.

Trey passes the notebook back. "You tried calling him?" Cal asks.

That gets him the moron look. "Course. Off the land line, every time my mam's not around."

"And?"

For the first time that day, that terrible, tense wretchedness rises up in Trey's face. He's been keeping it down hard. "Voicemail," he says.

"OK," Cal says gently. "Straight to voicemail? Or it rings out?"

"First day, it rang out. Now it's straight to voicemail."

That could, of course, mean Brendan is being held captive by bad guys who haven't provided a charger in his dungeon. Or it could mean he switched to a new phone when he got wherever he was headed. Or it could mean he hanged himself from a tree, somewhere up in the mountains, and his phone lasted a little longer than he did.

"OK," Cal says. "That's enough background stuff to keep me going, for now. Good job."

Trey lets out his breath.

"Nah," Cal says. "We're not done yet. I need to hear about the last time you saw Brendan."

After a second Trey takes another breath and braces himself again. It takes an effort this time. He looks drawn and shadowy-eyed all of a sudden, and too young for this, but Cal has talked to plenty of kids who were too young for this, and none of them were there by their own demand. He says, "Twenty-first of March, you said."

"Yeah."

"What day of the week was that?"

"Tuesday."

"So go back a few days before that. Anything out of the ordinary happen? Brendan have a fight with your mama? With one of his buddies? Guys in town?"

"My mam doesn't have fights. She's not like that."

"OK. Someone else?"

Trey shrugs. "Dunno. He didn't say he did."

"He get turned down for a job? Mention a girl he met? Stay out later'n usual? We're looking for anything out of his routine."

The kid thinks. "He was a bit off that week, maybe. Narky, like. The day he went, he was grand, but. Mam said, 'You're very cheerful,' and he said, 'No point sitting around sulking, sure, I haven't got time for that.' That's all."

"Huh," Cal says. An escape plan would cheer a guy up, all right. "So let's talk about the twenty-first. Start at the beginning. You got up."

"Didn't see Bren then. He was in bed. I went to school. Got home and he was watching the telly. I went in to him. After a while he went out."

"What time?"

"Five, maybe. 'Cause when Mam called us for tea he said nah, he was going out, and then he went."

"What kind of ride he have? Car, motorbike, bike?"

"Nothing. Mam's got a car, but he didn't take it. He doesn't have a motorbike. He was just walking."

"He tell you where he was going?"

"Nah. I thought he was meeting the lads. He was checking his watch like he had to be somewhere."

Or he could have had a bus to catch. The buses to Dublin and Sligo both pass on the main road, just a couple of miles away, and while they don't officially stop, Noreen has assured Cal that most of the drivers are good-natured about being waved down. Cal writes down **Bus timetables 4–8 p.m. Tues.**

"You guys talk about anything, while you watched TV?"

"My birthday. Bren said he'd get me a decent bike; I've only his old one and it's pure shite, the chain keeps jamming. And just the program on the telly. One of them singing shows, don't remember what one."

"How'd he seem? Good mood? Bad mood?"

"Fidgety, like. He was talking the whole time, slagging off the people singing. Sitting on different bits of the sofa. Poking me if I didn't answer him."

"That normal for him?"

Trey twitches one shoulder. "Sorta. He's always up and down like a fiddler's elbow, my mam usedta say. Only not like that."

"How was that day different?"

The kid pulls at a frayed place in the knee of his jeans, trawling through his mind for the right words. Cal swallows the urge to tell him to knock it off.

"Bren," Trey says in the end, "he's a messer, mostly. He'd always be making me laugh. Making everyone laugh, but . . . we had jokes, like. Just us. He liked making me laugh."

Cal gets a little bit of a glimpse of what Brendan leaving meant to Trey. The kid doesn't look like he's laughed since.

"But that day he wasn't looking for laughs," he says.

"Yeah. Not even once. He was the same kind of fidgety like during the exams." Trey shoots Cal a sudden sharp frown. "That doesn't mean he was planning on—"

"Focus," Cal says. "How was he dressed? Like he was heading into town? What?"

Trey thinks. "Just normal. Jeans and a hoodie. Not like for going out in town, like not a good shirt or nothing."

"He take a coat?"

"Bomber jacket, just. It wasn't raining."

"He say anything about when he was aiming to get back? 'Keep me some dinner,' 'Don't wait up,' anything like that?"

"Dunno." Trey's face is tightening again. "Can't remember. I tried."

Cal says, "And he didn't come back."

"Yeah." The kid's shoulders have hunched up inside his parka, like he's cold. "Not that night, or when I got back from school next day."

"He ever do that before?"

"Yeah. Stayed with one of his mates."

"So that's what you figured he was doing."

"At first. Yeah." Trey looks pinched and curled in on himself, the look street kids get, flooded with more of life than they can absorb. "I wasn't even worried."

"When'd you get worried?"

"Day after that. Just starting to. My mam rang him, only his phone rang out. Day after, she rang round asking people was he there. Only no one'd seen him. Not even the night he went out. They said, anyway."

"She didn't call the police?"

"I **said** to." The flash of pure fury in Trey's eyes takes Cal by surprise. "She said he just went off, same as my da. Cops won't do anything about that."

"OK," Cal says. He writes a **1** next to Sheila Reddy's name, and circles it.

"I did go looking for him," Trey says abruptly. "All along the roads, and up the mountain. For days, I went. In case he caught his foot in a hole and broke his leg, or something."

For a moment Cal sees it, the kid bent into the wind, tramping between great slopes of heather and moor grass, boulders patched with moss and lichen. He says, "Any reason why he'd be up the mountain?"

"He usedta go there sometimes. Just to be on his own."

Those aren't the Rockies out there, but Cal knows they're plenty big enough and bad enough to take a man if he makes a mistake with them. He says, "You go through his stuff?"

"Yeah."

"Find anything you didn't expect?"

Trey shakes his head.

"Anything missing?"

"Dunno. Wasn't looking for that."

The sharp downwards flick of the kid's eyes tells Cal what he was looking for. A note, with his name on it. **Here's where I'm going,** or **I'll be back,** or anything at all.

"Find any money?" he asks.

That makes Trey's eyes snap up again, hot with anger. "I wouldn't've taken it."

"I know," Cal says. "Find any?"

"Nah."

"You expect to? Brendan normally keep cash at home?"

"Yeah. Envelope stuck to the underneath of his jumper drawer. Sometimes he'd give me a fiver out of it, if he'd done a nixer. See? He knew I wouldn't rob it."

"And the envelope was empty."

"Yeah."

"When was the last time you saw cash in there?"

"Coupla days before he went. I came in, he was counting it on the bed. Few hundred, maybe."

And the day Brendan disappeared, so did his savings. Trey is no dummy. There's no way he's missed where that points.

Cal says, "And you think someone took him."

Trey bites down on his lip. He nods.

"OK," Cal says. "Is there someone you've got in mind, who might do something like that? Someone around here who's dangerous, who's maybe done sketchy stuff before?"

Trey stares at Cal like the question is beyond an answer. In the end he shrugs.

"I don't mean pissant crap like shoplifting or moonshining. Anyone who's ever kidnapped someone before? Hurt someone real bad?"

Another shrug, this one more exaggerated: **How would I know?**

"Anyone your mama tells you to stay away from?"

"Gurny Barry Moloney. He tries to get kids to come with him for sweets, and if you say no he cries."

"He ever try that on you?"

Trey blows air scornfully out of the corner of his mouth. "When I was a kid."

"What'd you do?"

"Legged it."

"How 'bout Brendan, he ever have trouble with this guy when he was little? Or any of your other brothers and sisters?"

"Nah. Gurny Barry's not . . ." Trey's lip curls in disgust. "He's pathetic. People throw things at him."

"Anyone else you've been warned about?"

"Nah."

Cal puts down his pen and leans back in his chair, rubbing mattress ache out of his neck. "You gotta spell it out for me, kid," he says. "How come you think your brother's been kidnapped? You're telling me no one had any beef with him, he wasn't mixed up in any bad stuff, just a regular guy. How come you're so sure he didn't just take off?"

Trey says, with absolute bedrock certainty, "He wouldn't do that."

Cal reached the point a long time ago where those words make him tired for all of humanity. All the innocents say that, and believe it to the bone, right up until the moment when they can't any more. **My husband would never do that to our children, my baby ain't no thief.** Cal feels like he ought to stand on a street corner handing out warnings, little pieces of paper that just say: **Anyone could do anything.**

"OK," he says. He closes his notebook and goes to slide it into his breast pocket, out of habit, before he realizes he doesn't have one. "Let's see where we get. How do you get from here to your place?"

That gives Trey's head a wary backwards tilt. "Up past Mart Lavin's about a mile, then there's a road goes off that way, to the mountain. We live a coupla miles up there. Why?"

"Your mama know you come here?"

Trey shakes his head, which comes as no surprise. "No one," he says.

Cal is less confident about that than Trey is, given Mart's view of his backyard, but he decides not to bring this up. "For now," he says, "let's keep it that way. So if I show up at your place and start visiting with your mama, you never saw me before. Can you do that?"

Trey looks less than delighted at the idea of Cal showing up at his place. "You want me to do this or not?" Cal asks.

"Yeah."

"Then do what I say. I know how to go about this. You don't."

Trey acknowledges this with a nod. He looks wrung out and loosened, like he just made it through having a tooth pulled with no anesthetic. He says, "Is this how you did it when you were a cop?"

"Near enough."

Trey watches him and turns things over, behind those gray eyes. "How come you became a cop?"

"Seemed like a good steady job. I needed one of those." Alyssa was on the way, and the fire department wasn't hiring.

"Was your dad a cop?"

"Nah," Cal says. "My daddy wasn't a steady man."

"What'd he do?"

"Little bit of this, little bit of that. Traveling around selling things, mostly. Vacuum cleaners, for a while. Another time it was toilet paper and cleaning supplies, to businesses. Like I said, he wasn't steady."

"But they let you be a cop anyway."

"Sure. They didn't care if my daddy was a billy goat, long as I could do the job right."

"Was it fun?"

"Sometimes," Cal says. His feelings for the job, which started out wholehearted and powerful, gradually got tangled enough that these days he prefers not to think about it. "Sounds like Brendan's good with electrical stuff. He ever do anything like that for people on the side, pick up a few bucks?"

Trey looks baffled. "Yeah. Sometimes. Fixing things, like."

"Could he do some rewiring in this place, if I needed it?"

Trey gives him a look that says Cal has lost his mind.

"This isn't like my badge days," Cal says, "when I could wade on in asking any questions I wanted. If I'm gonna go around bringing up your brother's name in conversation, I need a reason."

Trey considers this. "He fixed the wiring in our sitting room before. He's gone, but. People know that."

"Yeah, but I might not," Cal says. "I'm just a stranger that hasn't got the hang of who's who around here. If I hear a name mentioned as a guy who did some electrical work, how'm I supposed to know where he is or isn't?"

For the first time that day, a small smile lands on Trey's face. "You're gonna act thick," he says.

"You think I can pull that off?"

The grin widens. "No problem to you."

"Smartass kid," Cal says, but it pleases him to see the drawn look dissolve. "Now get outa my hair. Before your mama wonders where you've gotten to."

"She won't."

"Then get before I change my mind."

The kid bounces out of his chair with alacrity,

but he grins at Cal again as he does it, to show he's not worried. He takes for granted that Cal, his word once given, won't go back on it. Cal finds this both more touching and more intimidating than he would have expected.

"Can I come back tomorrow? See what you've found out?"

"Jeez, kid," Cal says. "Give me time. I don't want you expecting anything for at least a week or two. Maybe never."

"Yeah," Trey says. "Can I come anyway?"

"Yeah, you can. You got an appointment with a desk and a toothbrush."

Trey nods, a single definite jerk, making it clear he takes that seriously.

"Come in the afternoon," Cal says. "I got places to go in the morning."

The kid's ears prick up. "What're you gonna do?"

"Less you know, the better."

"I wanta do something."

He's all charged up and fizzing with energy, practically bouncing on his toes. Cal likes seeing him that way, but at the same time it makes him wince. He's already pretty sure what he's going to find. Brendan is textbook runaway, ticks just about every box: a bored, restless, underachieving kid with a shitty home life, no job or girlfriend or close friends to root him down, no career plan, in an area that offers him no prospects and no fun. On the other side of the scales, there's apparently nothing: no serious criminal activity, no serious criminal associates, no mental illness, nothing. Cal puts this at about five percent chance of an accident, five percent suicide, ninety percent up and gone. Or maybe eighty-nine percent up and gone, one percent something else.

"OK," he says. "You check if any of your brother's stuff is missing. You guys share a room?"

"Nah. He shares with Liam."

"Who else shares with who?"

"Me and Maeve. Alanna's in with my mam."

And Sheila hasn't moved her out. She's left Brendan's space waiting for him, even after six months. That sounds to Cal like she told Trey the truth: she thinks Brendan took off, and he'll be back. The question is whether that's just hope, or whether she's got reasons.

"Huh," Cal says. "Liam's four, right? So he's gonna notice if you go snooping. Wait till he's out playing or something. You don't get a good opportunity, leave it for another day."

Trey gives Cal a look that says **Duh.** He zips his parka. That sharp wind is still rattling around the door, looking for a way in and not giving up.

"Look for stuff like Brendan's phone charger," Cal says, "or his razor. Stuff that could fit in pockets, that he might want with him if he was planning on being gone a couple of days. If he's got a rucksack, or a backpack, check for that. And for missing clothes, if you know what he's got."

Trey has glanced up, instantly alert, from fighting

with his zipper. "You think? He went somewhere on purpose, and then they kept him?"

"I don't think anything," Cal says. "Not yet." All of a sudden he has that sensation he kept getting, back when Trey was an unknown quantity and Cal was deciding what to do about him: an intense awareness of the spread of the dark countryside all around his house; a sense of being surrounded by a vast invisible web, where one wrong touch could shake things so far distant he hasn't even spotted them.

He says, "You're sure about this, kid. Right? Because if you're not sure, this is when you need to tell me."

The kid throws him an eye-roll like Cal just told him to eat his broccoli. "Seeya tomorrow," he says, and he flips up his hood and steps out into the dark.

EIGHT

The mountainside is colder than the grassland below. The cold has a different quality from what Cal gets down at his place, too, finer and more challenging, coming straight for him on a honed wind. After decades of classifying weather in broad categories of nuisance value—wet, frozen, sweltering, OK—Cal enjoys noticing the subtle gradations here. He reckons at this point he could draw distinctions between five or six different types of rain.

As mountains go, these aren't much to write home about, a long sweep of hunches maybe a thousand feet high, but contrast gives them a force out of proportion to their size. Right up to their feet the fields are easy, gentle and green; the mountains rise brown and wild out of nowhere, commandeering the horizon.

The slope pulls in Cal's thighs. The road isn't much more than a track, twisting upwards between heather and rocky outcrops, weeds and wild grass leaning in from both sides. Above him, thick patches of spruce cling to the mountainside. Somewhere a bird sends up a high warning cry, and when Cal looks up he sees a raptor tilting down the wind, small against the thin blue sky.

Trey's directions turn out to be good: a couple of miles up the mountainside, Cal comes across a low, pebbledashed gray house, set back from the road in a poorly defined yard of balding grass. A beat-up silver Hyundai Accent with a 2002 license plate sags in one corner. Two little kids, presumably Liam and Alanna, are banging a piece of rusty metal with rocks.

Cal keeps going. A hundred yards farther up the road, he finds a boggy patch of ground and sinks one foot in it up to the ankle. Pulling it out again is harder than he expected; the bog hangs on to his boot startlingly tight, trying to keep it. Once he's free, he turns around and heads back to the house.

The kids are still squatting over their piece of metal. When Cal leans on the gate, they stop banging and watch him.

"Morning," Cal says to the bigger one, the boy. "Is your mama home?"

"Yeah," the boy says. He has overgrown dark hair, a worn-out blue sweatshirt and enough of a look of Trey that Cal knows he's in the right place.

"Can you ask her to come out here for a minute?"

Both kids stare. Cal recognizes that slight drawing back: the wariness of kids who already know that a stranger looking for your parents is likely some incarnation of the Man, and the Man is never there to make things better.

"I was out having a nice walk," Cal says, grimacing ruefully, "and look what I went and did to myself." He holds up his wet foot.

The little girl giggles. She has a sweet dirty face and brown hair pulled up in two uneven pigtails.

"Yeah yeah yeah," Cal says, mock-offended. "You go ahead and laugh at the dummy with the soggy boot. But I was wondering if your mama might be able to give me something to dry it off a little, so I don't have to squelch my way down this mountain?"

"Squelch," the little girl says. She giggles again.

"That's right," Cal says, grinning back at her and waggling his foot. "Squelch all the way home."

"We'll get Mammy," the boy says. He pulls on the girl's sleeve, hard enough that she overbalances and sits down on her behind in the dirt. "Come on." And he runs off round the back of the house, with the little girl trying to keep up and look back at Cal at the same time.

While they're gone, Cal looks the place over. It's run-down, with the window frames peeling and sagging, and moss growing between the roof tiles. Someone has made an effort here and there, though. There are flowerpots on each side of the door, with a multicolored crop only just dying off, and to one side of the yard is a play structure built of random pieces of wood and rope and piping. Cal would have expected a woman alone up here with a mess of kids to have a dog or two, but there's no sound of barking.

The kids come back circling a tall, scraggy woman in jeans and the kind of bafflingly ugly patterned sweater that only exists secondhand. She has rough red-brown hair pulled back in a sloppy bun, and a weather-beaten, high-boned face that must have been verging on beautiful, way back when. Cal knows she's a few years younger than him, but she doesn't look it. She has the same wary expression as the kids.

"Sorry to disturb you, ma'am," Cal says. "I was out walking, and I was foolish enough to step off the road. Found myself a nice big puddle."

He holds up his foot. The woman gazes at it like she has no idea what it is and doesn't much care.

"I live a few miles down thataway," Cal says, pointing, "and that's a long walk with a wet foot. I was wondering if you might be able to help me out."

The woman moves her gaze to his face, slowly. She has the look of a woman who's had too much land on top of her, not in one great big avalanche but trickling down little by little over a lot of years.

"You're the American," she says in the end. Her voice is rusty and unaccustomed, like she hasn't done much talking lately. "In O'Shea's."

"That's me," Cal says. "Cal Hooper. Pleased to meet you." He holds out his hand over the gate.

Most of the wariness fades. The woman comes forwards, wiping her hand on her jeans, and gives it briefly to Cal. "Sheila Reddy," she says.

"Hey," Cal says, with pleased recognition, "I've heard that name before. Now where . . ." He snaps his fingers. "That's it. Lena. Noreen's sister. She was telling me about her young days, and she mentioned you."

Sheila looks at him without curiosity, waiting for what he wants.

Cal grins. "Lena said the two of you used to run wild together. Get out your windows at night and hitch rides to discos."

That finds Sheila, enough to get a faint twitch of a smile. One of her top teeth is missing, near the front. "That was a long time ago," she says.

"Know what you mean," Cal says ruefully. "I remember when, if I went out, I was heading half a dozen different places and I wasn't coming home till daylight. Nowadays, three beers in Seán Óg's and I've had just about all the excitement I can handle for one week."

He gives her a sheepish smile. Cal has had plenty of practice being harmless. At his size, he has to put the work into that, specially with a lone woman. Sheila doesn't seem afraid, though, not now that she's placed him. She's not the timid kind. Her first wariness wasn't of him as a man, but of whatever authority he might be carrying with him.

"Back then," he says, "I'd have thought nothing of walking home wet. These days, though, my circulation isn't too good; by the time I make it all the way down the mountain, I won't be able to feel my toes.

Could I trouble you for a handful of paper towels to soak up a little of this, or an old cloth? Maybe even a dry pair of socks, if you've got some to spare?"

Sheila examines his foot again and finally nods. "I'll get something," she says, and she turns and goes back behind the house. The kids hang off the play structure and watch Cal. When he smiles at them, their expressions don't change.

Sheila comes back carrying a roll of paper towels and a pair of men's gray socks. "Now," she says, passing them over the gate.

"Miz Reddy," Cal says, "you just saved my day. Much obliged to you."

She doesn't smile. She watches, arms folded at her waist, as he makes himself comfortable on a boulder by the gatepost and takes off his boot. "Excuse my foot," he says, with an embarrassed grin. "It was clean this morning, even if it's not now." The kids, who have edged closer to watch, giggle.

Cal wads up paper towel and presses it inside his boot to soak up some of the water, taking his time. "It's beautiful country round here," he says, nodding at the mountain slope rising behind the house.

Sheila takes one glance over her shoulder and then looks away again. "Maybe," she says.

"Good place to raise a family. Clean air and plenty of space to run wild; there's not much else a kid needs."

She shrugs.

"I was raised a country boy," Cal explains, "but I was in the city a long time. This here looks like paradise to me."

Sheila says, "I'd be happy enough if I never saw it again."

"Oh?" Cal says, but she doesn't answer.

He tests the boot, which is about as dry as it's going to get. "I'm fond of hillwalking," he says. "The city turned me fat and lazy. Now that I'm here, I'm getting back into good habits. Although I better get back into the habit of looking where I put my feet."

That doesn't get a response, either. Sheila is harder work than he bargained for—Noreen and Mart and the guys in the pub have given him high expectations of the small talk around here—but at least now he knows where Trey got his conversational skills. And she doesn't seem to mind him talking away. She's watching him wrap his wet sock in more paper towel and tuck it away in his pocket, without interest, but without giving the impression that she has anything urgent to get back to.

"Ahh," Cal says, pulling on the dry sock, which is worn but whole. "Now that's an improvement. I'll give these a good wash and get them back to you."

"No need."

"I guess I wouldn't want my socks back once they'd been on some stranger's big ol' muddy feet, either," Cal says, lacing up his boot and grinning. "In that case, I'll bring you a new pair, soon as I get into town. In the meantime . . ." He produces two Kit Kat bars out of his jacket pocket. "I brought these to eat along my way, but now that I'm turning back early, doesn't seem like I'll need them. Would it be OK if I offered them to your young 'uns?"

Sheila comes up with a trace of a smile. "They'd like that, all right," she says. "They do love the sweet stuff."

"That's kids," Cal says. "My girl, when she was that size, she'da eaten candy all day long if we'da let her. I could tell if my wife had candy anywhere in the house, because my girl was like a bird dog, pointing right at it." He mimes. Sheila's smile grows, and softens. A freebie, even a little one, does that to poor people; it loosens them. Cal still recognizes that in himself, even though it's been twenty-five years since he was that kind of poor. It's the sweet warm wave of astonishment that, just for once and out of the blue, the world is feeling generous to you today.

"Hey," he calls, getting up and holding out the chocolate over the gate. "You guys like Kit Kats?"

The kids glance at their mama for permission. When she nods, they edge closer, shouldering each other, till they can grab the bars.

"Say thank you," Sheila says automatically. They don't, although the little girl gives Cal a big happy grin. The two of them retreat to the play structure fast, before someone can take the chocolate back.

"You just have these two?" Cal asks, propping himself more comfortably on the gate.

"Six. Those are my little ones."

"Whoa," Cal says. "That's a lot of hard work. Your big kids in school?"

Sheila looks around like one of them might materialize from somewhere, which Cal agrees is entirely possible. "Two," she says. "The others are grown."

"Wait a minute," Cal says, delighted to have made the connection. "Is Brendan Reddy your boy? The one who did the electrical work for that guy, what's his name, skinny old guy with a cap?"

Sheila spaces right back out, instantly and completely. Her eyes skid off Cal's face and she gazes up the road like she's watching some action unfold. "Don't know," she says. "He might've done."

"Well, there's a piece of luck," Cal says. " 'Cause, see, my house, O'Shea's place? I've been fixing it up myself. I'm doing OK with most stuff, the plumbing and the painting. But I don't wanna go messing around with any wires, not till someone's taken a look who knows what he's doing. Brendan knows his way around electrics, right?"

"Yeah," Sheila says. Her arms have come up to wrap tightly under her bosom. "He does, yeah. But he's not around."

"When'll he be back?"

Her shoulders twitch. "Don't know. He went off. Last spring."

"Oh," Cal says, with dawning understanding. "He moved out?"

She nods, still not looking at him.

"He go somewhere close by, where I could maybe give him a call?"

She shakes her head, a quick jerk. "He didn't say."

"Well, that's rough," Cal says peacefully. "My girl, she did that one time. When she was eighteen. Got a bee in her bonnet about how me and her mama didn't give her enough freedom, and off she went." Alyssa never did any such thing. She was always a good kid, stuck to the rules, hated making people unhappy. But Sheila's eyes have come back to him. "Her mama wanted to look for her, but I said no, let her win this one. If we go find her, she'll be even madder, and she'll just go farther next time. Let her go, and she'll come back when she's ready. You been looking for your boy?"

Sheila says, "Wouldn't know where."

"Well," Cal says, "he got a passport? Can't get too far without one of those."

"I never had him one. He could've got it himself, but. He's nineteen. Or you can get to England without."

"Any places he wanted to see? People he talked about visiting? Our girl always did say she liked the sound of New York, and sure enough, that's where she ran to."

She lifts one shoulder. "Plenty of places. Amsterdam. Sydney. Nowhere I can go look for him."

"When my girl went," Cal says reflectively, rear-ranging his forearms on the gate and watching the kids take apart their chocolate, "her mama kept thinking we should've seen it coming. All that talk about New York, she figured that was a hint we should've caught. She tore herself up pretty bad about it. Boys, though, they're different." Cal never did like to use a daughter in his work stories; he mostly preferred to stick with his imaginary son, Buddy. Sometimes, though, a girl makes for a better angle. "They keep quiet, don't they?"

"Brendan doesn't," Sheila says. "He's a great talker."

"Yeah? He dropped hints he was thinking about leaving?"

"Nothing about leaving. He said he was sick of it, only. Sick of having nothing to do. No money. There was a load of things he wanted, always, and he could never . . ." She throws Cal a glance that's a mix of shame and defiance and resentment. "It wears you out."

"That it does," Cal agrees. "Specially if you can't see your way out. That's hard on a young man."

"I knew he was fed up. Maybe I should have . . ." The wind is slapping straggles of hair across her face; she wipes them away, hard, with the back of a work-reddened hand.

"You can't blame yourself," Cal says gently. "That's what I told my wife. You're not a mind reader. All you can do is work with what you've got."

Sheila nods, unconvinced. Her eyes have slipped off him again.

"The other thing that hurt her," Cal says, "was the note our girl left. Telling us how mean we were, and how it was all our fault. Me, I figured she was just working up a good head of steam to get herself out the door, but her mama didn't see it that way. Your boy leave you a note?"

Sheila shakes her head again. "Nothing," she says. Her eyes are dry, but her voice has a raw, scraped sound.

"Well, he's young," Cal says. "Same as my girl was. That age, they don't realize what they're doing to us."

Sheila says, "Did your girl come back?"

"Sure did," Cal says, grinning. "Took her a couple of months, but once her point was made and she got tired of working in a diner and sharing a studio full of roaches, she came running. Safe and sound."

She smiles, just a twitch. "Thank God," she says.

"Oh, we did," Cal says. "God and the roaches." And then, more soberly: "The waiting was hard, though. We were worrying every minute, what if she's fallen in with some guy that doesn't treat her right, what if she's got nowhere to stay. And worse things." He blows out air, looking up at the mountain. "Tough times. Maybe it's different with a boy, though. You worry about him? Or you figure he can take care of himself?"

Sheila turns her face away from him, and he sees the long cord in her neck move as she swallows. "I worry, all right," she says.

"Any particular reason? Or just 'cause you're his mama, and that's your job?"

The wind whips strands of her hair against the sharp peak of her cheekbone. This time she doesn't push them away. She says, "There's always reasons to worry."

"I don't mean to pry," Cal says. "Pardon me if I've overstepped. I'm just saying, kids do the darnedest things. Most times, it all comes out in the wash. Not always, but mostly."

Sheila takes a quick breath and turns back to him. "He'll be grand," she says, with a crisp snap to her voice all of a sudden; she doesn't sound spacey any more. "Sure, I don't blame him. He's only doing what I should've done myself, when I was his age. Are you right, now, with them socks?"

"I'm a new man," Cal says. "Thanks to you."

"Right," Sheila says. Her body is half-turned towards the house. "Liam! Alanna! Get off that yoke and come in for your dinner!"

"Much obliged," Cal says, but she's already hurrying off across the grass. She barely turns to nod over her shoulder before she's gone behind the house, herding the kids in front of her with sharp flaps of her hands.

Cal walks back down the mountain. Apart from the patches of spruce, trees are few and far between; just the odd lonesome one, spiky and contorted, bare for winter and blown permanently sideways by the memory of hard prevailing winds. In the crook of a hill, someone's been dumping garbage: a rusty iron bedstead, complete with stained mattress, and a heap of big plastic bags ripped open and spilling. Once he passes the stone-wall scraps of an abandoned cottage. An old crow, perched amid the grass that's seeded in the cracks, opens its beak wide and tells him to keep moving.

He's come across plenty of people like Sheila, both in his childhood and on the job. Whether they started out that way or got brought to it somehow, their focus isn't much broader than a prey animal's. They're all used up by scrabbling to keep their footing; they don't have room to aim for anything bigger or farther than staying one jump ahead of bad things and snatching the occasional treat along the way. He gets another inkling of what a brother like Brendan must have meant to a kid like Trey, in that house.

Sheila told the kid the truth, or at least she told him the same thing she's telling herself: she believes Brendan got fed up and ran away, and he'll be back. That may well be true, but Sheila hasn't offered Cal anything to nudge him farther in that direction than he already was. Her belief is built purely out of hope, piled on top of nothing, solid as smoke.

Her worry, on the other hand, is dense and sharp-cornered as a lump of rock. Sheila's got reasons to worry about Brendan, even if she's not about to share them with Cal. One of Brendan's buddies might, though.

Cal thought he was done with this stuff for good, the day he turned in his badge. **Well, would you look at that,** he thinks, with a feeling he can't identify. **I guess I still got it.**

Donna would have rolled her eyes and said, **I knew it, the only surprise is that it took you this long.** She said Cal was addicted to fixing things, like a guy jabbing on and on at a slot machine, unable to leave it alone until the lights flashed and the prize came pouring out. Cal objected to that comparison, given the amount of hard work and skill he put into fixing things, but that just made Donna throw up her hands and make an explosive noise like a pissed-off cat.

Probably Donna was right, or a little bit right, anyway. The restless feeling is gone.

———

Mart is leaning on Cal's gate, staring out across the fields and smoking one of his hand-rolled cigarettes. When he hears the crunch of Cal's boots on the road, he whips round and greets him with a whoop and a fist pump. "Get up, ya boy ya!"

"Huh?" Cal says.

"I heard you were over at Lena's place the other day. How'd you get on? Did you get the ride?"

"Jesus, Mart."

"Did you?"

Cal shakes his head, grinning against his will.

Mart's screwed-up eyes are alight with mischief. "Don't be letting me down, bucko. Did you get a kiss and a cuddle, at least?"

"I got to cuddle a puppy," Cal says. "Does that count?"

"Ah, for Christ's sake," Mart says, disgusted. More philosophically, he adds, "Well, it's a step, anyhow. The women do love a man that likes puppies. You'll be in like Flynn before you know it. Are you taking her out?"

"Nope," Cal says. "Might take the puppy, though."

"If it's outa that beagle of hers, you might as well. That's a fine dog. Is that where you've been the day? Cuddling puppies?"

"Nah. Went for a walk up the mountain. Stood in a patch of bog, though, so I came home." Cal holds up his wet boot.

"Watch yourself around them bogs, now," Mart says, inspecting the boot. Today he's wearing a dirty orange baseball cap that says BOAT HAIR DON'T CARE. "You don't know their ways. Step in the wrong patch and you'll never step out again. They're fulla tourists; eat 'em like sweeties, so they do." He shoots Cal a wicked slantwise look.

"Gee," Cal says. "I didn't realize I was taking my life in my hands."

"And that's before you start on the mountainy men. They're all stone mad, up there; split your head open as soon as look at you."

"Tourist board wouldn't like you," Cal says.

"Tourist board hasn't been up them mountains. You stay down here, where we're civilized."

"I might do that," Cal says, reaching to open his gate. And, when Mart doesn't move: "I haven't been to town, man. Sorry 'bout that."

The mischief falls off Mart's face instantly and completely, leaving it grim. "I'm not here looking for biscuits," he says. He takes one more hard draw on his cigarette and throws it into a puddle. "Come on up to my back field. I've something to show you."

Mart's sheep are clumped together in the near field. They're edgy, jostling and picking up their feet nervously, not grazing. The far field is empty, or almost. In the middle of the green grass is a rough pale heap, not immediately identifiable.

"One of my best ewes," Mart says, swinging the gate open. His voice has a flat tone so far from its usual snappy lilt that Cal finds it a little bit unsettling. "Found her this morning."

Cal walks round the ewe the way he would walk a crime scene, keeping his distance and taking his time. Clusters of big black flies are busy among the white wool. When he moves closer he waves an arm to make them rise, looping and buzzing angrily, so he can get a clear view.

Something bad has got at the sheep. Its throat is a mess of clotted blood; so is the inside of its mouth, lolling too wide open. Its eyes are gone. A rectangular patch on its side, two hand-spans across, is flayed to the ribs. Under its tail is a great red hole.

"Well," Cal says. "This isn't good."

"Same as Bobby Feeney's," Mart says. His face is hard.

Cal is examining the grass, but it's too springy to hold prints. "I looked," Mart says. "In the muck out by the road, as well. There's nothing to see."

"Kojak pick up any trail?"

"He's a herd dog, not a tracking dog." Mart tilts his chin at the ewe. "He didn't like this at all, at all. He went pure mental. Didn't know whether to attack it or run for his life."

"Poor guy," Cal says. He squats to look more closely, still keeping some distance—the rich smell of rot is already starting to seep from the ewe. The edges of the wounds are clean and precise, like they were made by a sharp knife, but Cal knows from shooting the shit with the Homicide guys that dead skin can do strange things. "Bobby lost any more sheep?"

"He has not," Mart says. "He's been out on his land half the nights this last while, hoping to spot the little green men coming down for more, and he hasn't seen hide nor hair of anything worse than a badger. You tell me: what animal is cute enough to take just the one sheep from a farm, and then move on from a place where it knows there's food, as soon as the farmer's on guard?"

Cal was wondering the same thing. "Big cat might,

maybe," he says. "But you don't have those here, do you?"

"They're cute hoors, all right," Mart says. He narrows his eyes at the hills. "We haven't, not native, anyhow. But who knows what someone mighta wanted to get rid of. They're a great place for getting rid of things, them mountains."

Cal says, "A human would be smart enough to move on after one sheep."

Mart doesn't look away from the mountains. He says, "Someone that's gone in the head, is what you're talking about. Gone rotten in his mind."

"Anyone round here fit that description?"

"No one that I know of. But we mightn't know, sure."

"In a place this size?"

"You'd never know what maggot's ating someone's mind," Mart says. "The Mannions' lad—lovely young fella, never a bit of trouble to his mammy and daddy—a few year back, he threw a cat on a bonfire. Burned it up alive. No drink on him or nothing. He just fancied doing it."

Anyone could do anything; even, apparently, here. Cal says, "Where's the Mannion kid these days?"

"He went to New Zealand, after that. Hasn't been back."

"Huh," Cal says. "So you gonna call the police? Animal Control?"

Mart flicks him a glance exactly like Trey's moron look. "OK," Cal says. He's wondering what Mart wants from him here. Things have got plenty out of hand already; he doesn't plan on adding a dead sheep to his caseload. "Your sheep, your call."

"I want to know what done this," Mart says. "Your bitta woods there, that's thick enough to keep me hid. I'm asking you to let me spend the nights in there for a while."

"You think it'll come back?"

"Not to my sheep. But that bitta woods has a great view of P.J. Fallon's land, and he's got a fine flock. If this creature goes after them, it'll find me waiting."

"Well, be my guest," Cal says. He's not crazy about the idea of Mart out there on his own. Mart is a scrawny little old guy with rickety joints, and Cal knows, in a way that Mart might not, that a shotgun isn't a magic wand. "I might join you. Keep all the angles covered."

Mart shakes his head. "I'll do better on my own. One man can stay hid better than two."

"I've done my share of hunting. I know how to keep still."

"Ah, no." Mart's face crunches into a grin. "The size of you; sure, whatever's out there, it'd see you from space. You stay indoors and don't be freezing your bollocks off for something that's likely long gone anyway."

"Well," Cal says. "If you're sure about that." He needs to warn Trey not to make any more night-time visits, or he's liable to end up with an ass full of shotgun pellets. "You let me know if you change your mind."

The flies have resettled into tight, roiling clumps. Mart pokes the ewe with the toe of his boot and they rise again, briefly, before getting back to work. "I never heard a sound," he says. He kicks the ewe one more time, harder. Then he turns and stumps off, hands deep in his jacket pockets, towards his house.

———

The mailman has been by: Cal's firearm license is waiting for him on the floor by the door. When he applied for that license, he did it with a hankering for homemade rabbit stew rather than with any sense of real need. One of the things that had caught his attention, when he first started looking into Ireland, was the lack of dangers: no handguns, no snakes, no bears or coyotes, no black widows, not even a mosquito. Cal feels like he's spent most of his life dealing with feral creatures, one way or another, and he liked the thought of passing his retirement without having to take any of them into account. It seemed to him that Irish people were likely to be at ease with the world in ways they didn't even notice. Now that rifle feels like something it would be good to have in the house, the sooner the better.

He makes himself a ham sandwich for lunch. While he eats it, he manages to get the internet to show him bus timetables. On Tuesday evenings, a bus headed for Sligo goes by on the main road sometime around five, and one headed for Dublin goes past a little after seven. Both of these are possible, although neither one leaps out at Cal as the obvious answer. The main road is about a three-mile walk from the Reddy place, and Trey says Brendan left the house around five, just as Sheila was serving tea, which around here means dinner. Trey's sense of time has a haphazard quality that means his guess might well be off, and Cal doubts that Sheila serves meals on a strict schedule, but even four-fifteen would be cutting it close for the Sligo bus. On the other hand, five or even five-thirty would be too early to leave for the Dublin bus, specially if it meant skipping dinner unnecessarily. Overall, if Brendan was going any distance, Cal inclines towards him getting a ride from someone.

He calls Brendan's number, just for the hell of it. Like Trey said, it goes straight to voicemail: **Hi, this is Brendan, leave a message.** His voice is young, rough-edged, quick and casual, like he dashed this off in between two more important things. Cal takes a few shots at the voicemail password, in case Brendan left it on the default, but none of them get him anywhere.

He finishes his sandwich, washes up and heads for Daniel Boone's Guns & Ammunition. Daniel Boone's is concealed down multiple back roads, and Kevin—Daniel's real name—is a loose-limbed, scraggly-haired guy who looks like he would be more at home running a mildewy basement record store, but he knows his wares inside out and he has Cal's Henry .22 oiled, ready and waiting.

It's been a long time since Cal held one of these, and he'd forgotten the pure physical satisfaction of it. The warm solidity of the walnut stock is a sheer pleasure to his palm; the action is so smooth he could rack the lever back and forth all day. "Well," he says. "This was worth waiting for."

"Don't get a lot of demand for those," Kevin says, leaning his hip against the counter and eyeing the rifle sourly. "Or I wouldn't've had to order it in." Kevin took that personally. He clearly felt he had let himself down, and possibly let down his country while he was at it, by allowing some Yank to find him unprepared.

"My granddaddy had one," Cal says. "When I was a kid. Don't know what happened to it." He lifts the rifle to his shoulder and sights, enjoying the elegantly balanced weight of it. Cal could never muster up much fondness for his duty Glock, with its thuggish lines, the insolent swagger with which it wore the fact that it existed to be pointed at human beings. It carried nothing but aggression; it had no dignity. The Henry is, to him, what a gun should be.

"They haven't changed much," Kevin says. "You'll have your eye back in before you know it. Down to the range now, is it?"

"Nah," Cal says. He's a little nettled by the idea

that he looks like someone who needs a range to shoot. "Gonna go get myself some dinner."

"I do love a rabbit," Kevin says. "Specially now, with them good and fat for winter. Bring me one in and I'll give you a few bob off bullets."

Cal heads home planning on doing exactly that, to earn Kevin's forgiveness for the Henry. His plans change because Trey is sitting against his front door, knees up, eating a doughnut.

"Quit swiping shit from Noreen," Cal says.

The kid gets out of the way so Cal can unlock the door. He digs around in his coat pocket and hands Cal a paper bag containing another, slightly mashed doughnut.

"Thanks," Cal says.

"You got a gun," Trey points out, impressed.

"Yep," Cal says. "Your family doesn't have any?"

"Nah."

"How come? If I lived all the way up there, no one for miles around, I'd want some protection."

"My dad had one. He sold it before he left. You find out anything yet?"

"I told you. It's gonna take time." Cal heads inside and leans the rifle in a corner. He doesn't feel like showing Trey where he keeps his gun safe.

Trey follows him. "I know, yeah. What'd you find out today, but?"

"You keep bugging me about it, I'm gonna make you get lost and not come back for a week."

Trey stuffs the rest of his doughnut in his mouth and thinks this over while he chews. Apparently he concludes that Cal means it. "You said you'd teach me how to use that," he says, nodding at the gun.

"I said maybe."

"I'm old enough. My dad showed Bren when he was twelve."

Which isn't relevant, seeing as that gun was gone before Brendan was, but Cal files it away in his mind anyway. "You got a job to do," he reminds the kid. He opens his toolbox and tosses Trey the old tooth-brush. "Warm water and dish soap."

Trey catches the toothbrush, dumps his parka on a chair, gets himself a mug of soap and water, and tips the desk carefully onto its back so he can kneel beside it. Cal, spreading his drop sheet and levering the lid off his paint can, watches him sideways. The kid sets to work at a pace that he's not going to be able to keep up: proving himself all over again, after his outburst the other day. Cal pours paint into the roller tray and leaves him to it.

"I checked Bren's things," Trey says, without looking up.

"And?"

"His phone charger's there. And his razor and his shaving foam, and his deodorant. And his bag from school, that's the only one he's got."

"Clothes?"

"Nothing missing that I can tell. Only what he was wearing. He doesn't have a lot."

"He got anything he wouldn't leave behind? Anything that's precious to him?"

"His watch, that was my granddad's. My mam gave him that on his eighteenth. It's not there. He always wears it anyway, but."

"Huh," Cal says, dipping the roller. "Good job."

Trey says, louder, with a flash of triumph and fear, "See?"

"That doesn't mean much, kid," Cal says gently. "He mighta figured someone would notice if he snuck things out. He had cash; he could replace all that stuff."

Trey bites the inside of his cheek and bends his head back over the desk, but Cal can tell he's working towards saying something. He starts putting a second coat of paint on his wall, and waits.

It takes a while. In the meantime, Cal finds that he likes his work rhythm better with the kid there. On his own the last few days, he got ragged, speeding up and slowing down; not enough to make any difference to the job, just enough to get on his nerves. With the kid needing to be shown how to do it right, he stays nice and even. Gradually Trey's ferocious pace slows to something steadier.

Eventually he says, "You went to my house."

"Yeah," Cal says. "You might've actually been in school, for once."

"What'd my mam say?"

"What you thought she would."

"Doesn't mean she's right. My mam, she misses things. Sometimes."

"Well," Cal says, "don't we all. What'd she say to you?"

"She didn't tell me you were there. Alanna did. Said a beardy fella with a wet shoe gave them Kit Kats."

"Yep. I was out for a walk, had the misfortune to step in the bog right by your mama's place. What's the odds?"

Trey doesn't smile. After a second he says, "My mam's not mental."

"Never said she was."

"People say it."

"People say a heap besides their prayers."

Trey obviously has no idea what this means. "Do you think she's mental?"

Cal thinks this over, noticing along the way that he would strongly prefer not to lie to Trey if he can help it. "No," he says in the end, "I wouldn't have said mental. She seems to me more like a lady who could really use a few pieces of good luck."

He can tell by the twitch of Trey's eyebrows that he hasn't looked at things in this light before. After a minute he says, "So find Brendan."

Cal says, "Brendan's buddies, that you told me about. Which of 'em's the most reliable?"

Clearly Trey hasn't considered this. "Dunno.

Paddy's an awful blow, he'd say anything. And Alan, he's a spacer, wouldn't know his arse from his elbow. Fergal, maybe."

"Where's Fergal live?"

"Out the other side of the village, 'bout half a mile down the road. Sheep farm, white house. You gonna question him?"

"Which one's the smartest?"

Trey's lip curls. "Eugene Moynihan thinks he is. He's doing a course in Sligo Tech, business or something. Thinks he's only brilliant."

"Good for him," Cal says. "He move to Sligo for that, or is he still around?"

"He wouldn't want to be stuck in digs. Bet he goes in every day. He has a motorbike."

"Where's Eugene live?"

"In the village. That big yella house with the conservatory on the side."

"What're they like?"

Trey blows a scornful puff of air out of the side of his mouth. "Eugene's a wanker. Fergal's thick."

"Huh," Cal says. He figures this is as much detail as he can hope to get. "Sounds like Brendan doesn't have much of a gift for picking good buddies."

That gets him a glare. "Not a lot to choose from, round here. What's he supposed to do?"

"I'm not criticizing, kid," Cal says, lifting his hands. "He can run with whoever he wants."

"You gonna question them?"

"I'm gonna talk to them. Like I told you before. We talk to the missing person's associates."

Trey nods, satisfied with this. "What do I do?"

"You do nothing," Cal says. "You stay away from Eugene, stay away from Fergal, keep your head down." When Trey's mouth gets a mutinous set: "Kid."

Trey rolls his eyes and goes back to work. Cal decides against pushing it; the kid knows the deal, and he's no dummy. For now, anyway, the likelihood is that he'll do what he's told.

When the sky in the window starts to burn orange behind the tree line, Cal says, "What time do you reckon it is?"

Trey gives him a suspicious look. "Says on your phone."

"I know that. I'm asking for your best guess."

The suspicious look stays, but in the end Trey shrugs. "Seven, maybe."

Cal checks. It's eight minutes of. "Close enough," he says. If Trey figures Brendan left at five, he probably isn't too far off. "And late enough that you need to get home. I want you to keep away from here after dark, the next while."

"Why?"

"My neighbor Mart, something killed one of his sheep. He's not a happy guy."

Trey thinks this over. "One of Bobby Feeney's sheep got killed," he says.

"Yep. You know of anything around here that might go killing sheep?"

"Dog, maybe. That happened before. Senan Maguire shot it."

"Maybe," Cal says, thinking of the neat flayed patch on the ewe's ribs. "You ever see a dog running free, when you were hanging around here at night? Or any other animal big enough to do that?"

"It's dark," Trey points out. "You don't always know what you're seeing."

"So you've seen something."

The kid shrugs, one-shouldered, eyes on the neat back-and-forth of the toothbrush. "Seen people going into houses where they shouldn'ta been, coupla times."

"And?"

"And nothing. I went away."

"Good call," Cal says. "Now get. You can come back tomorrow. Afternoon."

Trey stands up, dusting his hands on his jeans, and nods at the desk. Cal goes over and examines it. "Looking good," he says. "Another hour or two's work and it'll be back on track."

"When I'm done," Trey says, shoving an arm into his parka, "you can teach me that." He jerks his chin at the gun and heads out the door before Cal can answer.

Cal goes to the door and watches the kid stride off, keeping to the hedge line. There are small flickers of movement among the long grass in his field, rabbits out for their evening meal, but the Henry and stew aren't on his mind any more. Once Trey turns up the road towards the mountains, Cal gives him a minute and then goes to the gate. He watches the kid's skinny back as he lopes up the road, hands in his pockets, between the blackberry brambles into the thickening dusk. Even after Trey is invisible Cal stays there, leaning his arms on the gate and listening.

NINE

Cal has always liked mornings. He draws a distinction between this and being a morning person, which he isn't: it takes time, daylight and coffee to connect up his brain cells. He appreciates mornings not for their effect on him, but for themselves. Even smack in the middle of a temperamental Chicago neighborhood, dawn sounds rose up with a startling delicacy, and the air had a lemony, clean-scoured tinge that made you breathe deeper and wider. Here, the first light spreads across the fields like something holy is happening, striking sparks off a million dewdrops and turning the spiderwebs on the hedge to rainbows; mist curls off the grass, and the first calls of birds and sheep seem to arc effortless miles. Whenever he can make himself, Cal gets up early and eats his breakfast sitting on his back step, enjoying the chill and the earthy tang of the air. The doughnut Trey brought him yesterday is still in pretty good shape.

The Wi-Fi is in an obliging mood, so Cal pulls up Facebook on his phone and pokes around for Eugene Moynihan and Fergal O'Connor. Eugene is dark and narrow, with a semi-arty shot of him in profile on a bridge somewhere that looks Eastern European.

Fergal has a big grin, a moon face with spit-shined red cheeks like a kid's, and a raised pint.

Brendan has a Facebook account, too, although his last post was a year ago, some like-and-share attempt to win tickets to a music festival. His photo has him on a motorbike, grinning over his shoulder. He's thin, brown-haired, with the kind of sensitive high-boned features that are good-looking in some moods and not in others, and that imply quick changes. Cal sees Sheila in him, in the cheekbones and around the mouth, but he can't find any look of Trey.

If Eugene is a student and Fergal is a farmer, then Cal has no doubts about which of them is more likely to be up early on a Saturday morning. He walks down through the village, where Noreen's and Seán Óg's and the decorous little ladieswear boutique are still shuttered and asleep, and the road is empty: only an old woman putting flowers in the Virgin Mary grotto at the crossroads turns to say good morning. Half a mile on are a set of broad fields full of fat, feisty sheep, and a sprawling white farmhouse. In the yard, a big young guy in a fleece and work pants is unloading sacks from a trailer and hauling them to an impressive corrugated-iron shed.

"Morning," Cal says, at the gate.

"Morning," says the young guy, hefting the next sack. He's a little out of breath. The exercise has given his face the same shine it has in the pub photo, and he has the same look of pleased expectation for Cal as he had for the camera, like Cal might be here to bring him a surprise snack.

"That's a fine bunch of sheep you've got out there," Cal says.

"They'll do," Fergal says, hoisting the sack more firmly onto his shoulder. He's chubby, with soft brown hair and womanish hips. He looks like most things might take him a while. "Oughta be more of them, but sure, we'll make the most of what we've got."

"Yeah? Why's that?"

That makes Fergal pause and give Cal a wide-eyed look, like he's startled anyone might not know this. "The drought last summer, sure. We'd to sell off some of the flock because we couldn't feed 'em."

"That's a bad blow," Cal says. "Plenty of rain this summer, though."

" 'Twas better, anyway," Fergal agrees. "Last year the drought went on right through breeding season. Hurt the lamb crop something fierce."

"I wasn't here for that," Cal says. He squints up at the sky, which is mottled in pearly whites and grays. "Hard to imagine this place getting more sunshine than it can handle. That's not what they sell on the tourist websites."

"I love the sunshine, so I do," Fergal confesses, with a bashful grin. "It was a mad feeling last year, hating the sight of it. I didn't know if I was coming or going."

Cal likes this kid, he likes this conversation, and

he would be perfectly content to continue it along these same lines. He feels a jab of aggravation at Trey and his dumbass brother.

"Cal Hooper," he says, holding out his hand. "I'm in the old O'Shea place, out the other side of the village."

Fergal clumps over to him, readjusting the sack so he can free up a hand and shake. "Fergal O'Connor," he says.

"Well, look at that," Cal says, pleased. "I heard you might be the man I need, and here you are. Can I give you a hand with that while we talk?"

While Fergal is working his way through this, Cal goes in the gate, closes it carefully behind him and pulls a sack off the trailer. He gets it up on his shoulder, appreciating the realization that four months ago he would probably have ripped half a dozen muscles trying. The sacks have a line drawing of a sheep and the words QUALITY RATION underneath. "These go in the shed?" he asks.

Fergal is looking perplexed, but he can't come up with anything reasonable to do about Cal, so he goes along with him. "They do, yeah," he says. "Sheep feed."

Cal follows Fergal into the shed. It's clean, high-roofed and airy, divided into long rows of metal-barred pens; bales of hay and sacks of feed are stacked along one wall. Up in the rafters a couple of fledgling swallows are swooping around their nest. "You got some lucky sheep," Cal says. "This is a nice place."

"We'll be needing it soon enough," Fergal says. "The aul' fellas are saying it'll be a bad winter." He keeps looking over his shoulder, but he can't work out what question to ask.

"The old guys mostly get it right?"

"They do, yeah. Mostly, anyway."

"Well then," Cal says, dumping his sack on top of a neat pile, "I sure hope you can help me. I'm aiming to get my house in shape before that winter hits us, and I'm looking to rewire my kitchen. Some guy in the pub, he mentioned that Brendan Reddy was the go-to guy for that stuff."

He glances over to see how Brendan's name strikes Fergal, but Fergal merely blinks at him, perplexed.

"I went looking for him," Cal says, "but Miz Sheila Reddy told me he's not around these days. She said you might be able to help me out."

Fergal's bafflement deepens. "Me?"

"That's what she said."

"Sure, I haven't a clue about electrics. Brendan does, all right. But he's not here."

Cal notes the **does.** "Well, shoot," he says. "Looks like I got it wrong. Don't I feel like the idiot." He grins ruefully at Fergal, who grins back, obviously familiar with that feeling. "Sorry to have disturbed your work. Least I can do is finish these up with you, to make up for it."

"Ah, no. You're grand, sure. Sorry I'm no good to you."

"Now I'm wondering if Miz Reddy was just trying

to get rid of me," Cal says, as they head back towards the trailer, "and you being Brendan's best buddy, you were the first person who popped into her mind." He hefts another sack onto his shoulder and makes way for Fergal to do the same. "See, I think I put my great big foot in my mouth there. I just waded right in, asking where I might find Brendan. I didn't know the story, then."

The speed with which Fergal's head turns towards him is what gives Cal his first inkling that Brendan Reddy may not just have run off to the bright lights. It comes to him with the clarity of a sound, a neat small chink like metal hitting stone.

Fergal says, "What story?"

Cal looks mildly into his round, startled blue eyes. "What'd his mam say?"

"Well, it's not so much what she said," Cal explains. "It's more what I gathered."

"What . . . ?"

Cal waits a little, but Fergal just stares. "Let's put it like this," Cal says in the end, picking the words carefully and letting the care show. "When people say Brendan's not around, they don't mean he packed his things and kissed his mama good-bye and found himself a nice little apartment in town, and he comes back every Sunday for a home-cooked dinner. Now do they?"

Fergal is looking wary. His features aren't constructed for this, and it gives him a comical frozen look, like a kid with a bug sitting on him. "I dunno," he says.

"Here's the thing," Cal says. "Brendan's family's pretty worried about him, son."

Fergal blinks at him. "Worried like what?" He hears himself, figures that was a stupid question, and goes redder.

"They're afraid he might've been taken."

That leaves Fergal utterly astounded. "Taken? Ah, God, no. **Taken?** By who?"

"Well, you tell me, son," Cal says, reasonably. "I'm a stranger around here."

"Dunno," Fergal says, eventually.

"You're not worried about him?"

"Brendan's not—sure, he . . . He's grand."

Cal looks surprised, which doesn't take much doing. "You're telling me you know this for a fact, son? You've seen him in the last six months? Talked to him?"

All this is considerably more than Fergal was prepared for, this morning. "Ah, no, I haven't— I haven't talked to him, or anything. I just think he's grand. Bren always is, sure."

"See," Cal says, shaking his head, "this is how I know I'm getting old. Young folks always think old folks worry too much, and old folks always think young folks don't worry enough. Your buddy's been missing for months, and all you think is, 'Gee, I guess he's OK.' To an old guy like me, that sounds downright crazy."

"I'd say he just got spooked, is all. Not **taken.** Sure, what would anyone take him for?"

"Spooked by what? Or by who?"

Fergal shifts the weight of the sack on his shoulder, looking increasingly uncomfortable. "I dunno. No one."

"You said he got spooked, son. Meaning someone musta spooked him. Who would that be?"

"I just meant . . . He's like that, sure. My mam says all the Reddys suffer terrible from their nerves. He'll be back once he's settled."

"Miz Reddy's wearing herself to a thread," Cal says, "worrying about him. How would your mama feel, if you were gone this long without a word?"

This gets to Fergal. He throws a hunted look towards the house. "Not great, I'd say."

"She'd be down on her knees day and night, sobbing her heart out and praying for her boy to come home. Not to mention," Cal says, pushing on the weak spot, "what would she say if she knew you were keeping another mama in that kind of pain, when you could ease her mind?"

Fergal glances wistfully at the shed. Clearly he'd like to go in there, either to sit down on a stack of feed sacks and think this over, or else to stay hidden until Cal gives up and goes away.

"If anyone can help her out, son, it's you. You're the one Brendan went to meet the evening he headed off. You give him a ride somewhere?"

"What? He did not!"

The astonishment on Fergal's face seems as genuine as any Cal has ever seen, but Cal looks skeptical anyway.

"He wasn't meeting me. The last time I saw him was two or three days before. He called in looking to borrow a few quid. I gave him a hundred. He said, 'Sound, I'll get it back to you,' and he went off."

"Huh," Cal says. If Brendan was planning on taking off, then every little bit would help, but Cal does wonder why the sudden rush. "He say what he needed it for?"

Fergal shakes his head, but there's a very slight shifty dip to it, and he blinks too fast. "And I didn't see him after that," he says. "I swear."

"I musta misheard that part," Cal says. "My point is, if you know where Brendan's fetched up, you need to say something to his mama. Right away."

"I haven't a notion where he is. Honest to God."

"Well, the part you don't know isn't gonna be much help to Miz Reddy, son," Cal points out. He doubts it will occur to Fergal to wonder why some stranger is getting so exercised about Sheila Reddy's feelings. "What's the part you do know? Brendan told you what he was planning, is that it?"

Fergal moves his feet in the dirt like a restless horse, trying to get back to work, but Cal stays put.

"I dunno," Fergal says, in the end. His face has smoothed out; he's retreated into vacant blankness. "I just think he'll come back in a while."

Cal knows that look. He's seen it on plenty of street corners and in plenty of interview rooms. It's the look you get, not from the kid who did it, but from his buddy, the one who can convince himself that he knows nothing because he wasn't there; the one who just got told about it, and is determined to prove himself worthy of that little bit of secondhand adventure by not being a snitch.

"Now, son," Cal says, lifting a tolerant eyebrow. "I look dumb to you?"

"What? . . . No. I didn't—"

"Well, that's good to hear. I'm a lotta things, but I'm not dumb, at least not so far as anyone's told me."

Fergal is still holding on to the vacant stare, but it has little twitches of worry going on around the edges. Cal says gently, "And I was a wild kid myself, once upon a time. Whatever Brendan's been up to, I probably did worse. But I never left my mama scared out of her wits for months on end. I don't blame you for not wanting to deal with Miz Reddy yourself, but she has a right to know what's going on. Any message you've got for her, I'm willing to pass it along. I don't need to tell her where it came from."

But he's run into a barrier in Fergal's mind, a mixture of confusion and loyalty that's set like concrete. "I dunno where Brendan went," Fergal says, more solidly this time. He's planning to keep on saying it, and nothing else. Like most people just quick enough to understand that they lag a little behind, he knows he can beat all the quicker ones with this.

Cal has ways of chipping away at this barrier, but he doesn't want to use them. He never liked rubbing dumb people's dumbness in their faces. It feels too much like playground picking on the weak kid, and besides, once you do that there's no going back. He's not looking to make an enemy in this place.

"Well," he says, with a sigh and a shake of his head, "that's your call. I hope you change your mind." He can't work out whether Fergal actually knows something that needs keeping quiet, or whether this is just reflex. He allows for the possibility that he's over-thinking things, out of professional deformation: back on the job that was always one of the main time-wasters, people keeping their mouths shut for no good reason, but Cal didn't expect to run into it here in the land of the gift of the gab. "When you do, you know where to find me."

Fergal mumbles something and heads off towards the shed as fast as he can go. Cal ambles along after him and asks a question about sheep breeds, which are what they talk about while they finish unloading the sacks. Fergal has relaxed a fair amount by the time they get done and Cal heads back towards the village, turning over Fergal and Brendan in his mind.

Being nineteen didn't sit right with Cal. He thought it did at the time, when he was running wild in Chicago, giddy on freedom, working as a bouncer at skeevy clubs and playing house with Donna in a fourth-floor walkup with no air-conditioning. It was only a few years later, when they found out Alyssa was on the way, that he realized running wild never had suited him. It had been a lot of fun, but deep down, so deep that he'd never spotted it there, Cal yearned after getting his feet on the ground and doing right by someone.

He feels that nineteen-year-olds, almost all of them, don't have their feet on the ground. They're turning loose from their families and they haven't found anything else to moor themselves to; they blow like tumbleweed. They're unknowns, to the people who used to know them inside out and to themselves.

The people who know a nineteen-year-old best are his buddies, and his girl if he has a good one. Fergal, who knows Brendan's mind a lot better than his baby brother or his mama or Officer Dennis, thinks Brendan is in the wind by his own choice, and that he's running not towards something but away from something, or someone.

This place has one thing in common with the tougher neighborhoods Cal used to work: in fine weather people spend much of their time outside, which is handy when you want to run into them by chance. In the driveway of the big yellow house with the conservatory, just on the edge of the village, a dark-haired young guy in skinny jeans is waxing a motorbike.

The bike is a weedy little Yamaha, but it's pretty near brand-new, and it wasn't cheap. Neither was the giant black SUV parked beside it, or the famous conservatory, come to that. The front garden has neat flower beds around a water feature shaped like a stone pagoda, with a lit-up crystal ball on top that keeps changing color. Cal knows from pub talk that Tommy Moynihan is some kind of big shot in the meat-processing plant a couple of townlands over. The Moynihans—like the O'Connors, although in a different way—are a whole lot better off than the Reddys.

"Nice bike," he says.

The guy glances up. "Thanks," he says, favoring Cal with a half smile. His features are finely modeled enough that plenty of people, himself included, probably consider him good-looking, but he's got a skimpy jaw and no chin.

"Gotta be tough to keep it looking good, on these roads."

This time Eugene doesn't bother to look up from his microfiber cloth. "It's not a problem. You just have to be willing to put the time into it."

This guy doesn't give Cal the same urge to hang around shooting the breeze as Fergal did. "Hey," he says, struck by a thought. "You Eugene Moynihan, by any chance?"

At that Eugene does take the trouble to look at him. "I am, yeah. Why?"

"Well, that's a piece of good luck," Cal says. "I was told you were the man I should talk to, and here you are. It was the bike that gave you away. I heard you had the prettiest bike in these parts."

"It's all right," Eugene says, shrugging and giving the glossy red paintwork an extra swipe. He has a light, pleasant voice with most of the local accent scrubbed off it. "I'm planning on trading up soon enough, but this'll do for now."

"I used to have a motorcycle," Cal says, leaning his arms on the big stone gatepost. "Back when I was about your age. Little bitty fourth-hand Honda, but man, did I love that thing. Just about every cent I made went straight into it."

Eugene isn't interested, and isn't going to bother pretending. He lifts his eyebrows at Cal. "You were looking for me?"

Cal, who is coming to agree with Trey's assessment of Eugene's personality, brings out his story about the rewiring and Brendan and Sheila Reddy giving him Eugene's name. By the end Eugene doesn't look wary, like Fergal did; he just looks mildly disdainful. "I don't do electrical work," he says.

"No?"

"No. I'm doing finance and investment. In college."

Cal is suitably impressed. "Well then," he says, "you're right not to waste your time on odd jobs. I ain't an educated man myself, but I know that much. If you done earned yourself an opportunity like that, why, you gotta make the most of it."

He can see the look, wry and guarded, that Donna used to give him when he did that, slouched into the thick backwoods drawl of his granddaddy's buddies. Rednecking up, she called it, and she hated it—she never said so, but Cal could tell. Donna was a Jersey girl from the hood, but she never leaned on her accent, or hid it either; people could take her or leave her. She thought Cal was lowering himself by playing to people's dumb preconceived ideas. Cal has his pride, but it doesn't run in that direction. Acting like a hick can be all kinds of useful. To Donna, that was beside the point.

Donna's opinions don't change the fact that Eugene's glance has just the right dismissive flick to it. "Yeah," he says. "I'm planning to."

"Looks like I got the wrong end of the stick," Cal says, taking off his baseball cap so he can scratch his head thoughtfully. "But Brendan Reddy does wiring, doesn't he? I got that part right?"

"He did, yeah. But I don't know where he is these days. Sorry."

This puzzles Cal. "You don't?"

"No. Why would I?"

"Well," Cal says, readjusting his cap, "nobody else seems to. It's a mystery, seems like. But folk keep on telling me you're the big genius around these parts. I reckoned if anybody would have an idea where Brendan went, it'd be you."

Eugene shrugs. "He didn't say."

"He got himself in hot water some way or other, didn't he?"

Another shrug, one-shouldered. Eugene concentrates on buffing his paintwork, squinting along it to make sure there's not a single streak.

"Oh," Cal says, grinning. He isn't going to bother trying the mama-guilt card, not with this kid. "Now I get it. A smart guy like you, it's easy for me to forget you're still a kid. You still think you can't tell tales or you'll get beat up in the playground."

Eugene looks up sharply at that. "I'm not a kid."

"Right. So what the heck did your little buddy do?" Cal is still grinning, propping himself more comfortably on the gatepost. "Lemme guess. He spray-painted bad words on a wall, got scared he'd catch a whipping from his mama?"

Eugene doesn't lower himself to answer that.

"Knocked up some girl, had to get out of town before her daddy found his shotgun?"

"No."

"Then what?"

Eugene sighs. "I don't actually know what Brendan got mixed up in," he says, tilting his head to examine the sheen from a fresh angle, "and I don't care. All I know is, he isn't as smart as he thinks, and that's a great way to end up in hassle. That's all."

"Huh," Cal says, his grin widening. He registers the **isn't**. "You're telling me this kid Brendan came up with some shenanigans fancy enough that you can't make head or tail of 'em, but he's the dumbass here?"

"No. I'm telling you I don't **want** to make head or tail of it."

"Uh-huh. Right."

"What do you care?"

If Cal had ever talked that way to a man old

enough to be his daddy, he wouldn't have been able to sit down for a week. "Well," he drawls, "I guess I'm just nosy-like. I'm from a little backwoods town where people like knowing each other's business." He scratches something off the back of his neck and examines it. "And back home there were plenty of people who talked like they knew it all, only when you got down to it, they didn't know shit from Shinola. Guess that's the same all over the world."

"Look," Eugene says, irritated. He sits back on his haunches, preparing himself to explain this in small words. "I know Brendan had some plan to make money, because he's always skint, and then all of a sudden he was going on about how this summer we could go to Ibiza. And I know it was dodgy, because a few days before he left we were hanging out here and a couple of Guards went past, and Brendan freaked **out.** I thought maybe he had some hash on him, so I was like, 'God, chill out, they didn't come all the way down here just for your spliff,' but he was all, 'You don't get it, man, this could be bad, like really bad,' and he took off like his arse was on fire. So I'm very happy not having a clue about the details, thanks very much. I'm not interested in spending days in some interrogation room answering pointless questions from some half-wit Guard. OK?"

"Right," Cal says. He finds himself despising Eugene a little bit. He understands that Eugene and Brendan were friends due to happenstance and habit rather than to choice. Cal has those childhood friends, some of whom grew up to do various things that landed them in prison, or to do nothing at all except sit on their porches drinking 40s and make kids they can't support. He still stays in touch with them, and when their needs get urgent he still lends them a few bucks he'll never see again. It seems to him that the least Eugene could do is care what kind of mess Brendan got himself into. "What were the Guards here about?"

"I haven't got a clue," Eugene says. He drapes his cloth neatly over his bumper, picks up a can of lube and starts carefully spraying his cables. "I doubt it was anything serious. I saw them leaving like twenty minutes later. But knowing Brendan, if the Guards weren't after him that time, that would just make him figure everything was grand and go right back to his big plan, instead of doing the smart thing and dropping it before they actually **did** come after him. That's what I mean about Brendan not being as smart as he thinks. He's **intelligent** enough, but he doesn't think things through. If he'd used his brain in school instead of mitching off to get stoned, he could have got into college. And if he'd used it to think through his brilliant idea, he wouldn't have ended up so terrified of the Guards that he's probably sleeping in a **doorway** somewhere."

Cal says, "He wouldn't get in touch with you, if it came down to that? Borrow a few bucks, sooner than sleep rough?"

"Oh," Eugene says, considering that for the first

time. "I mean, obviously I'd, if he really needed . . . But he wouldn't. Brendan's ridiculous about money. Like, you can't even offer to buy him a pint, or he gets the hump about charity and storms off home. It's like, fuck's sake, we're all just trying to have a good night out together here, what's your problem? You know?"

Cal figures Eugene's manner of offering might be the kind that would have sent him storming off home, too, at nineteen. He wholeheartedly agrees with Brendan's decision to go to Fergal, rather than Eugene, for extra cash. For him to do even that, the need must have been urgent. "Well, some folks are touchy that way," he says. "He didn't say nothing to you that day, about where he was headed?"

"What day?"

"The day he left. He was meeting you, wasn't he?"

Eugene stares at Cal like he shouldn't be allowed out alone. "Um, no? What with me being in Prague with the lads from college? It was Easter hols?"

"Right," Cal says. "Easter hols. Sounds like I can't count on Brendan coming home any time soon, huh?"

Eugene shrugs. "Who knows, with him. He could take a notion and be home tomorrow, or he might never come back at all."

"Huh," Cal says. "There anyone else that might be able to help me out?"

"I wouldn't know," Eugene says. He dabs away a trickle of excess lube and leans back to examine the bike. "Think I'll take this for a spin, get it properly dried out."

"Good idea," Cal says, straightening up off the gatepost. "If you hear from Brendan, tell him there's work waiting for him."

"No problem," Eugene says, picking up his helmet from the drive and flicking a speck of something off it. "Don't hold your breath."

"I'm an optimistic kind of guy," Cal says. "Nice talking to you."

He watches Eugene roar off up the road, weaving the Yamaha neatly around potholes. Only a little bit of the motorbike made it into Brendan's Facebook shot, but he's pretty sure it was this one. Eugene was at least generous enough to give his buddy a ride on his bike. Either he doesn't share his helmet, or Brendan was too much of a dumbass to wear it.

Cal heads back through the village, which has its Saturday up and running now. The aging blond woman who owns the boutique is decking out her window mannequin in an outfit running riot with ferocious tropical flowers, Noreen is polishing the brasswork on her door, and Barty the barman is giving the windows of Seán Óg's a wipe with news-paper. Cal nods to them all, and picks up his pace when he sees Noreen whip round with her polishing cloth raised and a gleam in her eye.

He walks the lanes for a while before he heads for home. In his mind, he's spreading out and arranging what he's got so far. If Eugene is right and Brendan is on the run from the police, then at the top of the list of potential reasons has to be drugs. Brendan had contacts, even if they were just low-level ones, and he wanted cash. Maybe he wanted to start selling, or actually had started selling, but he didn't have the constitution for it. The first time the police came sniffing around—or maybe the first time his suppliers got a little bit scary, and Cal knows suppliers can get plenty scary—he panicked and ran.

Officer O'Malley up in town didn't mention anything about a drugs op focused on the village, or about Brendan Reddy being in anyone's sights. But then, Officer O'Malley might not know.

Or Brendan's business plan might not have involved drugs at all. There are plenty of ways for a kid to pick up some cash on the wrong side of the law around here: running stolen cars across the border, helping out the guys who launder agricultural diesel. And those are only the ones that run close enough to the surface that even a stranger can see them. A kid like Brendan, with ideas and an entrepreneurial streak, could have come up with a lot more.

Another possibility, one that Eugene the boy genius hasn't thought of, is that Brendan's money-making scheme and his fear of the police were two separate things. Maybe he was planning on taking his odd-jobs business legit, or getting famous on YouTube. And meanwhile, unrelated, he was doing something bad.

And then there's the possibility that neither the

moneymaking scheme nor the bad thing was ever real. Brendan's mind could have been misfiring. Everything Cal has heard puts him on the unsteady side: one minute on top of the world and spinning big plans, the next minute panicked and running away from nothing, the next minute blowing it all off. Nineteen is the right age for a lot of things that can start misfiring inside someone's mind.

Among the cases Cal liked least were the ones where he was trying to pick up a trail that had never existed outside someone's mind. If a guy ran to Cleveland because his favorite cousin was there, or his old cellmate, or the girl who got away, the trail was solid; Cal could find it and follow it. If he ran to Cleveland because a voice from the TV told him an angel was waiting for him in a shopping mall there, then the trail was made of nothing but wisps and air. Cal needs to find out whether Brendan's mind was making things out of air.

He considers the possibility that Brendan is up in the mountains, living off the grid in some abandoned cottage, and coming down at night to slice sheep to rags. The image unsettles him a little bit more than it should. He sincerely hopes that he'll never have to pass it on to Trey.

In fact, when it comes to Trey, Cal isn't inclined to pass on any of the morning's events, at least not until he finds out why Brendan was running scared of the police. He promised to tell the kid anything he found out, but he feels it would be allowable to wait until he has something real, rather than a foggy cluster of hints and possibilities. There are things Brendan could have done that the kid would need to be told carefully.

It occurs to Cal that this is the first time he's made the decision to take on a case. On the job, he took cases because they got assigned to him. He never spent much time weighing up the intricacies of whether the people concerned and the wider society and the forces of good would be best served by him taking on the investigation; partly because he was going to do it anyway, but mainly because he believed that it was in fact the right thing to do in a general sense, if not necessarily in every particular instance. Most of the guys felt the same, at least the ones who cared one way or the other. There were exceptions—occasionally some short-eyes got himself beat up and the witnesses somehow never did get tracked down, or some pimp with a worse-than-average rep ended up shot and no one put too much effort into unraveling who had pulled the trigger—but on the whole, your name came up so you did your job. This is the first time Cal has been in a position to choose whether or not to take a case, and has made the choice to do it. He hopes, even more sincerely, that he's doing the right thing.

TEN

On his way home Cal stops by Mart's place, to check if Mart made it through his night watch. Mart answers the door with a paper towel tucked in the neck of his sweater and Kojak, snorting threateningly, at his knee. The house smells of old turf smoke, cooking meat and a baffling mix of spices.

"Just checking that the aliens didn't abduct you," Cal says.

Mart giggles. "Sure, what would they want with the likes of me? You're the one who should be watching yourself, great big fella like you. Plenty there to probe."

"I better make myself a tinfoil suit," Cal says, cupping his hand for Kojak to sniff.

"Ask Bobby Feeney for a lend of his. I'd say he has one hanging in his wardrobe, to wear when he's out hunting the little green men."

"You see anything last night?" Cal asks.

"Nothing that'd do what we saw. I protected your property from a big bruiser of a hedgehog, but that's as dangerous as it got." Mart grins at Cal. "Were you afraid I was lying out in them woods with bits cut off me?"

"Just wanted to know if I could cross those cookies off my shopping list," Cal says.

"Don't be holding your breath, boyo. Whatever done that, it'd better bring its friends and relations if it wants to take me on." Mart holds the door wider. "Come in, now, and have a bit of spaghetti and a cup of tea."

Cal was about to say no, but the spaghetti catches his curiosity. He had Mart down as a meat-and-potatoes guy. "You sure you've got some to spare?" he asks.

"Sure, I've enough there to feed half the townland. I do make a big pot of whatever I fancy, and then see how long it lasts me. Go on." He motions Cal in.

Mart's house isn't dirty, exactly, but it has an air of having been low priority for a long time. It has sludge-green walls and a lot of linoleum and Formica, and most surfaces have been worn down till they're speckled. In the kitchen, Kylie Minogue is singing the Locomotion from a big wooden transistor radio.

"Sit down there," Mart says, pointing at the table, where his meal is laid out on an old red-checked oilcloth. It looks like spaghetti Bolognese, barely started. Cal takes a seat, and Kojak flops down by the fireplace and stretches out with a pleasurable groan.

"Here I thought you'd have your place painted every color of the rainbow," Cal says. "After all the shit you gave me about plain white."

"I didn't paint this place at all," Mart informs

him, with the air of a man scoring a point. He pulls another plate and another mug out of a cupboard and starts scooping spaghetti out of a big pot on the cooker. "My mammy, God rest her, she did it up this way. When I do get around to painting it, you can bet your life it won't be any plain white."

"Yeah, but you won't get around to it," Cal tells him. He figures it's past his turn to yank Mart's chain a little bit. "You can tell yourself whatever you want, but if you haven't done it by now, it's because deep down, you like it this way."

"I do not. It's the color that'd come out of the arse of a sick sheep. I'm thinking bright blue in here, and yella out in the hall."

"Won't happen," Cal says. "Bet you ten bucks: this time next year, every wall you own is still gonna be sheep-shit green."

"I'm not putting any deadlines on myself," Mart says with dignity, setting a heaped plate in front of Cal. "Not to suit you or anyone else. Now: get your laughing-tackle round that."

The spaghetti needs plenty of chewing and the Bolognese sauce is heavily seasoned with mint, coriander and something that tastes like aniseed. It kind of works, as long as Cal takes it on its own terms.

"It's good," he says.

"I like it," Mart says, pouring Cal tea from a teapot shaped like a Dalek. "And I've only myself to please. There's great freedom in that. As long as the mammy was alive, nothing but good aul' meat and potatoes came in this house. She'd boil them till you couldn't tell one from the other if you'd your eyes closed, and no seasoning: she said the spices were half the reason foreign places had the divorce and the gays and all. The spices got in their blood and addled their brains." He pushes a carton of milk and a bag of sugar across the table to Cal. "Once she was gone, I went a bit experimental for myself. I went into Galway, to one of them fancy yuppie shops, and I bought every spice they had. The brother didn't like it, but sure, he'd burn water, so he had to lump it. Dig in there, before it goes cold on you."

He pulls up his chair and settles back to his food. Cal has apparently stumbled on the one circumstance where Mart doesn't believe in conversation: he eats with a hard worker's single-minded dedication, and Cal follows his lead. The kitchen is warm from the cooking; outside the window, the hills are soft with mist. Kylie has wrapped it up and another woman starts singing, pure and sweet, with practiced soulfulness: **no frontiers . . .** In his sleep Kojak makes little huffing noises and twitches his paws, chasing something.

"The rain'll hold off," Mart says eventually, pushing his plate away and squinting out the window, "but that cloud's going nowhere for a while yet. No matter: anything I don't see, I'll hear."

"You gonna be out there again tonight?"

"I will, later on," Mart says, "but I'm off duty this evening. I might see if P.J. fancies taking the odd shift, if you've no objection. I can't be missing my beauty sleep forever." In fact he looks surprisingly bright-eyed. The only sign that he spent the night sitting out under a tree is an extra hitch to his movements, like his joints are troubling him more than usual, but he says nothing about it.

"P.J.'s welcome to hang out in my woods," Cal says. He knows P.J. a little bit: a long-legged, hollow-cheeked guy who nods to Cal over walls without starting conversations, and who sometimes sings as he goes about his evening rounds, melancholy old ballads in a surprisingly poignant tenor. "How long are you gonna give this?"

"Wouldn't I love to know that myself," Mart says, topping up his tea. "Whatever this creature is, it's got to get hungry sooner or later. Or get bored, maybe."

"Lotta sheep around here," Cal says. "You got any particular reason to think it's gonna come after P.J.'s?"

"Well, sure," Mart says, glancing up from the sugar with his face crinkling into a grin, "I can't watch every sheep in Ardnakelty. P.J.'s are convenient."

"Right," Cal says. He has a strong impression that Mart is keeping something back.

"Besides," Mart points out, "don't we know the creature likes this area? And a lot of the other farms around here are cattle, and they mightn't be any good to it: it mightn't be big enough to take down a cow. If I was this yokeymajig, P.J.'s is where I'd be heading next." He taps his temple. "The aul' psychology," he explains.

"Never hurts," Cal says. "Has it been just those two sheep, yours and Bobby Feeney's? Or has this been going on awhile?"

"There was one other, beginning of the summer. Francie Gannon's, beside the village." Mart grins and points his mug at Cal. "Don't you be going all Columbo on me, now, asking questions. This is under control."

So the sheep-killing started not long after Brendan went missing. Cal thinks of that tumbledown cottage again, or a cave in the mountainside. There were wild men out his granddaddy's way, or at least rumors of them. Cal and his buddies never saw them, but they saw campfire sites and snare wires, coolers hidden in underbrush, animal skins pegged to branches to dry, deep in the woods where no one should have been spending any amount of time. One time Cal's buddy Billy almost fell into an expertly hidden pit trap. Whoever dug it, probably he started out as a restless teenager prowling the perimeter of his life for an escape route.

"Now," Mart says, scraping back his chair, "I know what you need, to finish off with." He bends over with a painful grunt, pokes around in a cupboard and comes up holding a packet of cookies. "There you go," he says, putting it triumphantly on the table. "Time you found out what all the fuss is about."

He's so delighted with his inspiration that it would be unmannerly for Cal to refuse. The cookie tastes exactly like it looks: sugar and foam rubber, in a variety of consistencies. "Well," Cal says. "We don't get these back home."

"Have another one there, go on."

"I'll leave 'em to you. Not really my style."

"You can't be coming over here insulting the Mikados," Mart says, miffed. "Every child in Ireland is weaned on these."

"No disrespect intended," Cal says, grinning. "I don't have much of a sweet tooth."

"D'you know what that is?" Mart demands, struck by a thought. "That's them American hormones. They're after wrecking your taste buds. The way, when a woman's pregnant, she'll eat fruitcake with sardines. Come back to me in a year and try those again, once we've got you recalibrated back to normal, and we'll see what you think of them then."

"Will do," Cal says, still grinning. "Cross my heart."

"Come here to me, Columbo, while I have you," Mart says, dipping a cookie into his mug. "Tell me you don't suspect that little scutter Eugene Moynihan of getting at my sheep."

"Huh?" Cal says.

Mart throws Cal one bright-eyed glance. "I heard you were having a great aul' chat with him this morning. Were you interrogating him? I'd say he'd crack in minutes, that fella. One stern look offa you and he'd be bawling for his mammy. Was he?"

"Not that I noticed," Cal says. "But I didn't give him anything to bawl about."

"Eugene didn't touch my ewe," Mart says. "Nor did Fergal O'Connor."

"Never thought they did," Cal says, truthfully.

"So what were you at with them?"

"All I want," Cal says, with mounting irritation, "is someone who'll help me rewire my kitchen so I can put in a washing machine and wash my damn underpants in my own home, instead of hauling them to town every week. Only I keep getting the runaround. One guy says I need this guy, so I go looking and nah, he's not around, I need this other guy. Track him down and he doesn't know a cable from his ass, I need this other guy. Track him down"—Mart has started giggling—"and he acts like I asked him to unclog my toilet with his bare hands. I'm trying to give work to local folk here, outa plain good manners, but I'm about ready to give up on that bullshit and hire a professional, just so I have that washer before I get too old to work it."

Mart is wheezing with laughter. "God almighty," he says, wiping his eyes, "cool your jets there, buckaroo, or you'll give yourself a heart attack. I'll find you someone local who'll put in a washing machine for you. Get you one at a good price too."

"Well," Cal says, settling himself down but still a little bit ruffled. "I'd appreciate that. Thanks."

"And sure, how would Eugene Moynihan be any use to you, anyway? He wouldn't lower himself to get his hands dirty wiring anything," Mart points out, with vast scorn. "Who was it told you he would?"

"Well," Cal says, scratching his beard thoughtfully, "I'm not rightly sure. It was some guy in the pub. He pointed me towards a coupla people who might be able to help me out, but I can't seem to remember his name—I'd had a few beers when I was talking to him, and I gotta admit, I haven't got everybody straight yet. Old guy, seems like. Short hair. Few inches taller'n you, maybe, but I could have that wrong. Got a cap."

"Spanner McHugh? Dessie Mullen?"

Cal shakes his head. "All I know is, he sounded like he knew what he was talking about."

"Not Dessie, so," Mart says with finality.

Cal grins. "Well, he didn't exactly turn out to be on the right track. Mighta been Dessie after all."

"I'll ask him. He can't be sending strangers on wild-goose chases like that. He'll give us a bad name." Mart finds his tobacco packet and tilts it at Cal.

"Appreciate the offer, but I better get moving," Cal says, pushing back his chair and picking up his plate. "Much obliged for the meal."

Mart cocks an eyebrow. "Where's the rush? Got a big date?"

"Date with YouTube," Cal says, putting his plate

in the sink. "Seeing as no one else around here is gonna help me rewire my kitchen."

"Don't be messing about with that YouTube; you'll have the place burned to the ground. I told you I'll get that washer sorted for you." Mart points his cigarette at Cal. "And come here to me: if you don't have a date, let you come down to Seán Óg's tonight."

"What's going on?" Cal asks. "It your birthday?"

Mart laughs. "Holy God, no. I gave up them yokes years ago. Just come on down, and you'll see what you'll see." He blows a thin stream of smoke between his teeth and gives Cal an extravagant wink.

Cal leaves him there, tilting his chair back and humming along to Dusty Springfield, and lets himself out. Kojak thumps his tail and rolls one eye at him as he passes. Cal walks home wondering what it was, somewhere around P.J. and his sheep and the killings, that Mart decided not to tell him.

In the end, Trey doesn't show up till late afternoon. "Hadta do the messages," he says by way of explanation, knocking mud off his sneakers against the doorstep.

"Well, that's good," Cal says. "You gotta help your mama out." After some bewilderment at the start, he worked out that around here "the messages" is the grocery shopping. One of the reasons he picked

Ireland was so he wouldn't have to learn a new language, but sometimes he feels like the joke is on him.

Trey is wired tight today; Cal can see it, in the jut of his chin and the shift of his feet on the step. He takes a quick glance behind him, like someone might be watching, before he comes inside and shuts the door.

"I was just tidying up this thicket of mine," Cal says, sweeping beard clippings off the table into the cardboard box he uses as a wastebasket. His beard was getting pretty unruly, and it occurred to him that if he's going to go round asking nosy questions, it wouldn't hurt to look respectable. "Whaddaya think?"

Trey shrugs. He fishes a packet out of his parka and hands it to Cal. Cal recognizes the wax-paper packaging: half a dozen sausages, out of Noreen's fridge. It hits him, all of a sudden, why Trey keeps bringing him things. This is payment.

"Kid," he says. "You don't have to bring me stuff."

Trey ignores this. "Fergal and Eugene," he says. "What'd they say?"

"Were you following me?" Cal demands.

"Nah."

"Then how'd you know I already talked to them?"

"Heard Eugene's mam saying to Noreen, when I was getting the messages."

"Jesus," Cal says, heading for the fridge to put the sausages away. "A guy can't pick his nose around here without the whole townland telling him to wash his hands." He wonders how much longer he can keep this thing under wraps, and what the townland will think when it comes out. He finds that he has no idea, either of the answer or even of what factors might influence it. "What'd Eugene's mama say?"

Trey follows him. "Just that you were asking for someone to do wiring. Face on her like a bulldog licking piss off a nettle. What'd they say?"

"How come? She doesn't like the look of me?"

" 'Cause Eugene's too good for that. And 'cause you thought he'd need the bitta extra cash."

"Well, I'm just a big dumb stranger that doesn't know his way around," Cal says. "What'd Noreen say to that?"

"Said there's no harm in honest work, and a job would do Eugene good. She doesn't like Mrs. Moynihan. What'd they **say**?"

The kid is standing in the middle of the kitchen floor, feet planted apart, blocking Cal's way. Cal can feel him practically vibrating with tension.

"They haven't heard from your brother since he went, neither one of them. They both think he's alive, though." Cal doesn't miss the slackening of relief in Trey's spine. Regardless of how sure the kid claims to be about Brendan's state of mind, he came in here scared that Brendan's buddies knew different. "And I've gotta tell you, kid, they don't think anyone took him. They think he went of his own accord."

"They coulda been lying."

"I was a cop for twenty-five years. I've been lied to by the best in the business. You think a big goof like Fergal O'Connor can bullshit me?"

Trey acknowledges that. "Fergal's thick, but. Just 'cause he thinks something, that doesn't mean he's right."

"I wouldn't pick him to build me a rocket ship, but he knows your brother. If he thinks Brendan went off . . ."

Trey says, looking Cal straight in the eyes, "Do you think he's alive?"

Cal knows better than to leave even the smallest pause there. Luckily he also knows what to say, having said it a few hundred times over the years. "I don't think anything, kid," he says. "Right now I'm just collecting information. I'll do my thinking later on, once I've got a lot more of that. All I can tell you is, I don't have one single piece of information that points to him being dead." All of which is true, and Sheila Reddy's face as she looked up at the mountains isn't information. The words still leave a bad taste in Cal's mouth. It comes to him, more powerfully than ever, that he has got himself into territory he doesn't understand.

Trey holds that straight stare for another moment, checking for cracks; then he nods, accepting that, and lets his breath out. He heads over to the desk and starts poking at it, seeing what's left to do.

Cal leans back against the kitchen counter and

watches him. "What kinda drugs do you get round here?" he asks.

Trey flashes him a fast, unexpected grin, over his shoulder. "You looking?"

"Funny guy," Cal says. "I'll pass, thanks. But say I was. What's on offer?"

"Lotta hash, lotta benzos," Trey says promptly. "E, off and on, like. Special K. Coke, sometimes. Acid, sometimes. Shrooms."

"Huh," Cal says. He wasn't expecting a full menu, although maybe he should have been. Lord knows back home the smallest towns, where the kids had nothing else to keep them occupied, were the ones where you could get your hands on any drug you'd heard of and a few you hadn't. "Crack?"

"Nah. Not that I ever heard."

"Meth?"

"Not a lot. Few times I heard someone had some."

"Heroin?"

"Nah. Anyone who gets on that, they leave. Go to Galway, or Athlone. Round here, you wouldn't know what'd be around when. Junkies haveta know they can get it anytime."

"The dealers around here," Cal says. "You know where they get their stuff? Is there some local guy in charge of distribution?"

"Nah. Buncha lads bring it down from Dublin."

"Did Brendan know these guys? The ones from Dublin?"

"Bren isn't a dealer," Trey says, instantly and hard.

"I never said he was," Cal says. "But you think bad people took him. I need to know what kind of bad people he could've run into around here."

Trey examines the desk, running a fingernail along cracks. "Them Dublin fellas are bad news, all right," he says in the end. "You'd hear them, sometimes: they come down in them big Hummers, race them across the fields at night, when there's a moon. Or in the daytime, even. They know the Guards won't come in time to catch 'em."

"I've heard 'em," Cal says. He's thinking about that huddle of guys in the back of the pub, every now and then, guys too young and dressed wrong for Seán Óg's and eyefucking him for just a second too long.

"Kilt a coupla sheep that way, one time. And they bet up a fella from up near Boyle because he didn't pay them. Bet him up bad, like. He lost an eye."

"I know the kind," Cal says. "They start out dangerous, and they get a whole lot worse if someone pisses them off."

Trey looks up at that. "Bren couldn't have pissed them off. He doesn't even know them."

"You sure about that, kid? Certain sure?"

"They wouldn't sell direct to the likes of him, that only does the odd bit here and there. Bren just bought from the local lads, when he wanted something. He wouldn't be around them fellas."

Cal asks, "Then who took him? These are the only bad guys anyone's mentioned around here. You tell me, kid: if not them, then who?"

"They could've got it wrong. Got him mixed up with someone else." Trey scrapes at paint residue with a thumbnail and watches Cal to check what he thinks of this theory.

"Maybe," Cal says. He can't imagine any likely way this could have played out, but if Trey needs it, he can keep it, at least for now. "That type mostly aren't geniuses, I'll give you that. If Brendan didn't hang with these guys, who does? Any of his buddies?"

Trey blows out a dismissive puff of air. "Nah. You saw Fergal, and Eugene. You think they're on the gear?"

"Nah," Cal says. "Never mind." He's thought of one person who knows plenty about the Dublin guys. Donie McGrath has been at the edge of that huddle in the pub, most times.

Trey glances sideways at him, with a glimmer of that grin creeping back. "You ever do any drugs? Before you were a cop, like?"

For a second Cal isn't sure what to say to this. When Alyssa asked him this same question, the thought of her on drugs kicked him in the stomach so hard that all he could do was tell her stories of things he'd seen and beg her never to go near anything stronger than weed. She hasn't, as far as he knows, but then she probably wouldn't have anyway. Here, the right answer could matter.

In the end he goes with the truth. "I tried a few things, back in my wild days. Didn't like any of 'em one little bit, so I quit trying."

"What'd you try?"

"Doesn't matter," Cal says. "I wouldn't've liked anything else any better." The fact is, everything he tried repelled him with an intensity that startled him and that he was unwilling to admit even to Donna, who back in those days accepted the odd drag or snort with cheerful ease. He hated the way every drug in its different way scooped the solidity right out of the world and left it quicksand-textured, cracked across and wavering at the edges. They did the same thing to people: people on drugs stopped being what you knew them to be. They looked you right in the face and saw things that had nothing to do with you. One of the happy side effects of having Alyssa and leaving his wild days behind was not having to hang out with people who were on drugs.

He asks casually, his eyes on the desk, "How 'bout you? You ever try any of that stuff?"

"Nah," Trey says flatly.

"You sure?"

"No way. Makes you stupid. Anyone could get you."

"True enough," Cal says. He's thrown by the strength of the relief. "I guess if you're not the trusting type, drugs probably aren't for you."

"I'm not."

"Yeah, I picked up on that. Me neither."

Trey looks at him. He seems thinner in the face

this week, and paler, like this is taking something out of him. He says, "Now what're you gonna do?"

Cal is still turning that over in his mind; not what to do, exactly, so much as how to go about it. What he does know right now is that the kid needs something good to happen today. He says, "I'm gonna teach you how to use that rifle."

The kid's mouth opens and he lights up like Cal just handed him that birthday bike. "Easy, tiger," Cal says. "You're not gonna just pick it up and be a sharpshooter. Mostly what you're gonna do today is learn how not to shoot your foot off, and miss a few beer cans. If we have time, maybe you can miss a few rabbits."

Trey tries to give him an eye-roll, but he can't wipe the grin off his face. Cal can't help grinning back.

"But," Trey says, his face suddenly falling. "That's not finished." He indicates the desk.

"So it'll get finished some other day," Cal says, straightening up off the counter. "Come on."

The gun safe looks out of place on Cal's bare bedroom floorboards. The only other things in the room are the mattress and sleeping bag, the suitcase where Cal keeps clean clothes and the garbage bag where he keeps dirty ones, and the four damp-mottled indigo walls; amid those, the tall dark metal box has an air of sleek, alien menace. "This is a gun safe," Cal says, giving the side of it a slap. "My gun stays in here until I'm planning on shooting it, because it's not a toy and this isn't a game; this thing was built for killing, and if I ever catch you disregarding that, you'll never lay a finger on it again. We clear?"

Trey nods, like he's scared to talk in case Cal changes his mind.

"This," Cal says, lifting it out, "is a Henry twenty-two lever-action rifle. One of the finest guns ever made."

"Ah, man," Trey says, on a reverent rush of breath. "My dad's gun wasn't like that."

"Probably not," Cal says. Next to the Henry, he finds most other guns seem either runty or bad-tempered. "They used this rifle in the Wild West, on the frontier. If you ever watch old cowboy movies, this is the gun those boys use."

Trey inhales the scent of gun oil and runs a finger down the rich walnut of the stock. "Beauty," he says.

"First thing, before you do anything else with it," Cal says, "you gotta check that it's unloaded. Magazine comes out like this, lever goes down like this, make sure there's no round in the chamber." He slides the magazine tube back into place and holds out the gun to Trey. "Now let's see you do it."

The kid's face when he takes the gun in his hands makes Cal glad he decided to do this. His private opinion about a lot of the baby thugs and delinquents he encountered on the job was that what they really yearned after, whether they knew it or not, was a rifle and a horse and a herd of cattle to drive through dangerous terrain. Given those, plenty of them—not all, but plenty—would have turned out fine. Failing that, they got as close as they could, with results ranging from bad to disastrous.

Trey checks the gun with the same neat-handed, intent care he puts into the desk. "Good," Cal says. "Now see this here? This is the hammer. You pull it back all the way, it's cocked, ready to fire. But you bring it back just a little bit, like this, so you hear it click? That means it's safe. You can pull the trigger all you want, nothing'll happen. To go from cocked to safe, you ease the trigger back, just a little bit, then click the hammer forwards. Like this."

Trey does it. His hands on the rifle look little and delicate, but Cal knows he has more than enough strength to handle it. "There you go," he says. "Now it's safe. But remember: safe or not, loaded or not, you don't ever point it at any creature unless you're prepared to kill it. You got that?"

"I got it," Trey says. Cal likes the way he says it, with a level unblinking gaze across the gun in his hands. The kid is feeling the weight of this, and he needs that.

"OK," he says. "Let's go give it a try."

He gets the plastic bag where he keeps empty beer cans and gives it to Trey to carry. He puts the rifle on his shoulder, and they go out into air that's soft and heavy with mist and rich with wet-earth smells. The first of the evening is just starting to seep in; off to the west, where the clouds thin here and there, their edges are gold.

"We need to pick ourselves a good spot," Cal says.

"Somewhere we're not gonna hit anything we don't intend to."

"Will we shoot them?" Trey asks, flicking his chin at the rooks, who are arguing over something in the grass.

"Nah."

"Why not?"

"I like having 'em around," Cal says. "They're smart. Besides, I don't know if they're good eating, and I don't kill creatures for kicks. We get something, we're gonna skin it, gut it, cook it and eat it. You OK with all that?"

Trey nods.

"Good," Cal says. "How 'bout we set up here?"

The low dry-stone wall of Cal's back field has clear views of open grass all around; no one can walk into their firing line unexpectedly. It's also on the side of the land overlooked by silent, incurious P.J., rather than the side overlooked by Mart, although right now even P.J. is nowhere to be seen. They balance beer cans on the rough stones, stacked there who knows how long ago by what ancestors of Mart's and P.J.'s and Trey's, and retreat across the field. Their feet swish in the damp grass.

Cal shows Trey how to pull out the magazine tube, drop the bullets into its slot and slide it back into place. They've picked a good day: the cloud keeps the low-angled light from dazzling them or throwing shadows, and the breeze is just an easy brush along one cheek. The beer cans are silhouetted sharply against the green fields, like tiny standing stones. The brown mountains rise behind them.

"OK," Cal says. "You can shoot standing, kneeling, or flat on your belly, but we're gonna start with kneeling. One leg under you, one knee up. Like this."

Trey imitates him carefully.

"The stock goes in the hollow of your shoulder, right here. Good and tight against you, so it won't kick too hard." The balance of the rifle is perfect; Cal feels like he could kneel there all day long without his muscles getting tired. "See that bead on the end of the barrel? That's the front sight. This half-moon here, that's your rear sight. You line up the two of 'em right on your target. I'm aiming for the third can from the left, so I've got those sights lined up on it. I'm gonna take a breath and then let it out again, nice and easy, and when all that breath is gone I'm gonna squeeze the trigger. Not hard; this isn't a gun you need to haul at. It'll work with you. You just breathe out through your mouth, and then out through the gun. Got it?"

Trey nods.

"Good," Cal says. "Now let's see if I still got it."

Somehow, after all these years, Cal's eye with a rifle is still there. He knocks the can clean off the wall with a triumphal ring of metal on metal that echoes across the fields, over the gun's sharp report.

"Ah **yeah**," Trey says, awed.

"Well, look at that," Cal says. He inhales the smell of gunpowder and finds himself smiling. "Your turn."

The kid holds the rifle well, settling it into his

shoulder like it belongs there. "Elbows in. Let your cheek fall against the stock, nice and easy," Cal says. "Take your time."

Trey squints down the barrel, carefully picking his can and lining up the sights. "It's gonna go bang," Cal says, "and it's gonna kick into your shoulder a little bit. Don't get startled."

Trey is too focused to bother with the eye-roll. Cal hears his long slow breath in and out. He doesn't wobble in anticipation of the kick, and he doesn't flinch when it comes. He misses, but not by too much.

"Not bad," Cal says. "All you need is some practice. Pick up your shell casing; you gotta leave a place the same way you found it."

They take turns till the magazine is empty. Cal bags himself five beer cans. The kid gets one, which lights him up so vividly that Cal grins and trudges across the field to retrieve the holed can for him. "Here," he says, passing it over. "You can hang on to that. Your first kill."

Trey grins back, but then he shakes his head. "My mam'd want to know where I got it."

"She go through your stuff?"

"Didn't useta. Only since Brendan went."

"She's worried, kid," Cal says. "She just wants to know that you're not thinking of going anywhere."

Trey shrugs, tossing the can into the plastic bag. The light has gone out of his face. "OK," Cal says. "Now that you've got the idea, let's get ourselves some dinner."

That pulls the kid back; his head snaps up again. "Where?"

"That piece of woodland over there," Cal says, nodding towards it. "Rabbits got a bunch of burrows at the edge of that. I see them up feeding most evenings, around this time. Come on."

They collect the beer cans and set themselves up far enough from the little wood not to spook the rabbits, but close enough that the kid stands a chance. Then they wait. The gold in the west has shifted to pink and the light is starting to fade, turning the fields gray-green and insubstantial. Off in Cal's garden, the rooks are having their bedtime powwow; distance gentles their racket to a comfortable babble, running under the high scattered chitchat of the smaller birds.

Trey has the rifle resting carefully on his knee, ready to raise. He says, "You said your granddaddy taught you to shoot."

"That's right."

"How come not your dad?"

"Like I told you. He wasn't around a lot."

"You said not steady."

"That's right."

Trey thinks this over. "How come your mam didn't teach you? Was she not steady either?"

"No," Cal says, "my mama was steady as they come. She worked two jobs to pay our way. Thing is, that meant she wasn't home enough to watch me.

So she sent me to stay with my granddaddy and my grandma, most of the time, till I got big enough to watch myself. And that's why he's the one that taught me to shoot."

Trey absorbs this, watching the edge of the wood. "What jobs?"

"Care assistant in an old folks' home. And wait-ressing in a diner, in her time off."

"My mam used to work in the petrol station up the main road," Trey says. "When Emer went off, but, there was no one to mind the little ones while we were in school. My granddads and grannies're all dead."

"Well," Cal says, "there you go. People do their best with what they've got."

"What about your brother and sisters? Did they go with you?"

"Well, they've got different mamas," Cal explains. "I'm not sure what-all they did."

"Your dad was a hoormaster," Trey says, light dawning.

It takes Cal a second to figure that one out; when he does, he lets out a crack of laughter that he has to stifle. "Yeah," he says, still laughing. "That about covers it."

"Shht," Trey says suddenly, nodding upwards at the wood. "Rabbit."

Sure enough, at the edge of the wood there's move-ment in the long grass. Half a dozen rabbits have come up for their evening feed. They're at their ease, trying out leaps and lollops just to stretch their legs, pausing now and again to nibble some delicacy.

Cal looks down at Trey, who is nestling the rifle into his shoulder, his whole body alert and eager. His buzzed hair looks like the baby fur on Lena's puppy. Cal feels an impulse to lay his hand on the top of the kid's head.

"OK," he says. "See if you can get us some dinner."

The bullet zips over the rabbits' heads, and they leap for the undergrowth and are gone. Trey looks up at Cal, dismayed.

" 'S OK," Cal says. "They'll be back. You got close enough that it'll take 'em a while, though, and it's time we were both heading home." The dusk is coming down thicker; soon enough, Mart or P.J. will be heading for the wood to keep watch.

"Aah! Five more minutes. I almost had that one."

The kid looks bereft. "So you'll get one next time," Cal says. "No rush; they're not going anywhere. Now lemme show you how to unload."

They unload the gun and start back across the field towards the house. Trey is whistling to himself, something Cal hasn't known him to do before, a jaunty little tune that sounds like something that might come out of the tin whistle in Seán Óg's; like it might be about setting out on a spring morning to see a pretty girl. The rooks are settling down and the first of the night creatures are out: a bat dips over the tree line, and something small scuttles in the long grass at their approach.

"Nice one," Trey says, glancing up sideways at Cal. "Thanks."

"My pleasure," Cal says. "You got a good eye. You'll learn fine."

Trey nods and, with nothing left to say, slopes off towards the cover of the hedge. Cal tries to watch after him, but long before he reaches the road he's invisible, vanished into the dusk.

Cal finds himself curious about what's going down at Seán Óg's tonight. He makes a grilled cheese sandwich for dinner and then takes a bath, to spruce himself up for whatever it might be. It's Saturday, so he phones Alyssa, but she doesn't pick up.

ELEVEN

When Cal sets out for the pub, the darkness has a sawtooth edge of cold. Smoke is rising from Dumbo Gannon's chimney, and as Cal passes his house he catches the scent of it, rich and earthy: the turf that people round here cut from peat bogs up in the mountains, dry out, and burn. The fields and hedges seem filled with sharp, restless movement; all the animals are feeling the countdown to winter.

The door of Seán Óg's opens on brightness and a warm fug, leaping with loud voices and music and curling with smoke. Mart, at his alcove table surrounded by his buddies, lets out a welcoming roar when he sees Cal step in. "The man himself! Come here to me now, Sunny Jim, and take a seat. I've something for you."

Mart's alcove is crowded: Senan is there, and Bobby, and a bunch of other guys whose names Cal isn't sure of. All of them have a high-colored, glittery-eyed look, like they're a lot drunker than Cal would expect at this hour. "Evening," he says, nodding to them.

Mart moves along the banquette to make room

for him. "Barty!" he calls up to the bar. "A pint of Smithwick's. You know this shower of reprobates, amn't I right?"

"We're mostly acquainted," Cal says, taking off his jacket and settling himself on the banquette. Mart has never invited him into his corner before, except when they need a fourth for cards. Tonight the musical corner has a fiddle and a guitar as well as a tin whistle, and they're singing some song that involves roaring out "No! Nay! Never!" and hitting the table. Deirdre is singing along, half a beat behind, almost smiling and more animated than Cal has ever seen her. "What's going on?"

"There's a gentleman here I'd like you to meet," Mart says, gesturing with a flourish to a slight, thin-faced guy tucked into a corner. "This is Mr. Malachy Dwyer. Malachy, this is my new neighbor, Mr. Calvin Hooper."

"Pleasure," Cal says, shaking hands across Mart and starting to get a clearer sense of what tonight is all about. Malachy has messy brown hair and a dreamy, sensitive look that doesn't match the wild renegade he was picturing. "I've heard plenty about you."

"Mal, meet Cal," says Bobby, getting the giggles. "Cal, meet Mal."

"The state of you," Senan says in disgust.

"I'm grand," Bobby says, miffed.

"Mr. Dwyer," Mart tells Cal, "is the finest distiller in three counties. A master craftsman, so he is." Malachy smiles modestly. "Every now and then, when Malachy has a particularly fine product on his hands, he's gracious enough to bring some of it in here to share with us. As a service to the community, you might say. I thought you deserved an opportunity to sample his wares."

"I'm honored," Cal says. "Although I feel like if I had any sense I'd be scared, too."

"Ah, no," Malachy says soothingly. "It's a lovely batch." He produces, from under the table, a shot glass and a two-liter Lucozade bottle half-full of clear liquid. He pours Cal a shot, careful not to spill a drop, and hands it over. "Now," he says.

The rest of the men watch, grinning in a way that Cal doesn't find reassuring. The liquor smells suspiciously innocuous. "For Jaysus' sake, don't be savoring the bloody bouquet," Mart orders him. "Knock that back."

Cal knocks it back. He's expecting it to go down like kerosene, but it tastes of almost nothing, and the burn doesn't have enough harshness even to make him grimace. "That's good stuff," he says.

"Didn't I tell you?" Mart says. "Smooth as cream. This fella's an artist."

Right then the poteen hits Cal; the banquette turns insubstantial beneath him and the room circles in slow jerks. "Whoo!" he says, shaking his head.

The alcove roars with laughter, which comes to Cal as a pulsing jumble of sound some distance away. "That's some serious firepower you got there," he says.

"Sure, that was only to give you the flavor of it," Malachy explains. "Wait till you get started."

"Last year," Senan tells Cal, jerking a thumb at Bobby, "this fella here, after a few goes of that stuff—"

"Ah, now," Bobby protests. People are grinning.

"—he got up out of that seat and started shouting at the lot of us to bring him to a priest. Wanted to make his confession. At two o'clock in the morning."

"What'd you done?" Cal asks Bobby.

He's not sure whether Bobby will hear him, since he's finding it hard to gauge exactly how far apart they are, but it works out fine. "Porn," Bobby says with a sigh, leaning his chin on his fist. The drink has given him an air of dreamy melancholy. "On the internet. Nothing shocking, like; just people having a bit of a rattle. It didn't even download right. But whatever was in that batch of Malachy's, it gave me palpitations, and I got it in my head I was having a heart attack. I thought I oughta confess my sins, in case I died, like."

Everyone is laughing. "That wasn't my stuff giving you them palpitations," Malachy tells him. "That was your guilty conscience coming out." Bobby tilts his head, acknowledging the possible justice of this.

"Did you take him to a priest?" Cal asks.

"We did not," says Senan. "We put him in the back room to sleep it off. Told him we'd say the rosary over him till he woke up."

"They didn't do it," Bobby says, aggrieved. "They

forgot I was there at all. I woke up the next morning and thought I was dead."

That gets another wave of laughter, and Cal is swept along, rocking helplessly with it. "He was still half cut," Senan says. "Rang me asking was he dead, and what should he do about it."

"At least," Bobby says with dignity, raising his voice to be heard, "I never broke my nose trying to jump a wall I hadn't leaped since I was eighteen—"

"Damn near made it," Mart says, lifting his pint and winking at the rest.

"—or took a dare and knocked on aul' Mrs. Scanlan's window buck naked and got cold water thrown on me."

A guy on the far edge of the group gets a collective whoop of approval and a couple of back-slaps, and shakes his head, grinning. Cal likes seeing them all this way, the wild boys shining through the solid farmers. For a moment he wonders which one of them was Brendan back in the day, the restless one on the hunt for hustles and escape routes, and how he ended up.

"Have another one there," Mart says, eyes alight with mischief, reaching for the bottle. "You've some catching up to do."

Cal is surface drunk but not deep-down drunk, and he reckons he ought to keep it that way. Booze has never bothered him the way drugs do—it doesn't hollow out reality, and people, in the same way—but the air of this room has a high giddy spin, like under the right circumstances things could get out of control with free-fall speed, and this situation has a flavor of initiation rite that could well turn out to be the right circumstances. "Sounds to me like I should take it slow," he says. "So I don't wind up buck naked outside Miz Scanlan's window."

"Nothing wrong with that," Mart assures him. "Sure, it could happen to a bishop."

"You boys were weaned on this stuff," Cal points out. "If I try to keep up with you, I'm gonna end up going blind."

"Not on mine, you won't," Malachy says, his professional pride touched.

"Ah, stop your fussing and foostering, man," Mart orders Cal. "You're not some tourist that comes in for a pint of Guinness with the quaint natives and then heads back to his hotel. You're a local man now; you'll do as we do. Don't be telling me you never done anything mad on the gargle before."

"Mostly just crashed parties," Cal says. "Made friends with some strangers, sang some songs. Stole the occasional street sign. Nothing fancy like you guys get up to."

"Well," Mart says, putting the glass back into Cal's hand, "we've no street signs and no strangers handy, and you're already at the only party around, so let's get you singing."

"Are you going to carry him home?" Barty demands, from behind the bar. "The size of him."

"Sure, isn't that my point exactly," Mart says. "It'll take more than the one to do the job on a fella his size. More than the two, but we'll start there and see where we get."

What makes up Cal's mind isn't the fact that quitting now would earn him an ineradicable reputation as a pussy and a tourist, or at least not primarily. What does it is the effortless rhythms of the talk snapping back and forth across the table. Cal has been missing the company of men he's known a long time. His four best buddies were among the reasons he left Chicago; the depth and detail with which they knew him had come to feel unsafe, something to be kept at as much distance as possible. By that point he couldn't be sure what there might be, inside him, that they would spot before he did. All the same, somewhere in the back of his head, his hunger for an evening in the bar with them has grown, so gradually that he's only just noticing its magnitude. He may not know these men, but they know each other, and there's comfort in being around that.

He resigns himself to the likelihood of waking up in a ditch with his pants missing and a goat tied to his leg. "Here's mud in your eye," he says, and throws back the shot, which is considerably larger than the first one. There's a burst of half-mocking cheers.

This one smooths everything over. The room starts moving again and the banquette turns even mistier, but this feels only natural and right. Cal is glad he did this. He almost laughs at how close he came to chickening out.

In the other corner, the song builds to a crescendo, ends on a whoop, and dissolves in a round of applause. "Isn't that great timing," Mart says. "What's your song, boyo?"

Cal's song, at parties that went this way, was always "Pancho and Lefty." He opens his mouth and starts to sing. Cal is no opera singer, but he can carry a tune, and he has a deep rambling voice that holds a room and suits a song about open spaces. The last of the applause trickles off, and people lean back in their seats to listen. The man with the guitar picks up the shape of the song and sends a loose, pensive river of notes drifting alongside it.

When Cal finishes there's a moment of silence, before the burst of clapping. Hands reach out to slap him on the back, and someone shouts to Barty to get him another pint. Cal grins, pleased and all of a sudden a little bit startled at himself. "Well done," Mart says in his ear. "That's a fine pair of lungs you've got on you."

"Thanks," Cal says, reaching for his beer. He finds himself a bit sheepish, not about the singing itself but at the unfeigned approval around the table and the depth of the pleasure he takes in it. "I enjoyed that."

"Sure, we all did. 'Tis great to have someone who can spice up the aul' singsong. We've all been listening to each other all our lives; we need the new blood."

The guy who showed up buck naked at Mrs. Scanlan's window starts singing, in a clear tenor: "Last night as I lay dreaming of pleasant days gone by . . ." The musicians take up the tune, and a few people hum along in a deep soft underscore. Mart tilts his head back to listen, his eyes half closed.

"When I was a young lad," he says, after a while, "you'd never have a night out without a bit of a sing-song. Do the young people still sing at all, except when they're trying to get themselves on the telly?"

"I wouldn't know," Cal says. He wonders if Alyssa and her friends sing at parties. You need someone with a guitar, mostly, to start things off. Ben is the type of guy who would consider learning an instrument to be frivolous. "Been a while since I was young."

"Come here to me, Sunny Jim," Mart says. "You're sure you want someone to rewire that kitchen, are you?"

"Huh?" Cal says, blinking at him.

"I'm not putting my reputation on the line," Mart explains, "getting one of these lads to take time out of his busy schedule, and then have you change your mind on us. Do you want the job done?"

"Sure," Cal says. "Course I do."

"Then it's as good as done," Mart says, clapping him on the shoulder and breaking into a grin. "Locky! Mr. Hooper needs his kitchen rewired, and he needs a dacent washer that won't cost the earth. Can you look after that for him?"

"I can, o' course," says a stocky guy with little eyes and a drinker's nose. Locky doesn't look all that reliable to Cal, but he doesn't feel he's in a position to express any doubts, even if he were sober enough to frame them delicately, which he isn't. "Give me a few days and I'll be down to you."

"Good man," Mart says happily, beckoning for the Lucozade bottle, which has worked its way around the pub and back again. "Now, mister: there'll be no more need for you to go chasing uppity young lads all over the townland, getting yourself all worked up and frustrated. Locky'll have you sorted inside the fortnight."

"Well, thank you," Cal says. "I appreciate that."

Mart fills Cal's shot glass and raises his own. "No bother. We have to look after each other around here. No one else is going to do it, amn't I right?"

They clink glasses and drink. Cal comes unmoored from the room again, but this time he's expecting it and finds himself able to enjoy the ride. The buck-naked window guy finishes his song and nods gravely at the round of applause, and the far corner strikes up something smart and snappy that starts "Whatever you say, say nothing."

"Now that I have you loosened up," Mart says, louder, pointing his glass at Cal. "How're you getting on with the lovely Lena?"

That gets a scattering of whoops and laughter from the other men. "She's a nice lady," Cal says.

"She is. And since I was good friends with her

daddy, God rest him, I think I should ask you: what's your intentions there?"

"Well," Cal says, taking it slowly and carefully, "I might intend to take one of her pups. But I haven't made my mind up yet."

Mart is shaking his head vigorously and waving a finger at Cal. "Ah no no no. That won't do at all. You can't be leading on a fine woman like Lena Dunne and then letting her down."

"I only met her twice," Cal points out.

"We've got the bloody village matchmaker here," someone says.

"Even if I was," Mart tells him, "there's nothing I could do for the likes of you. I like to see people settled and happy, is all. This fella needs a woman."

"No point in him courting Lena," a deep voice says from the corner of the alcove, "if he'll be heading back off to Yankeestania before the winter's out."

There's a splinter of a pause. Across the pub, the tin whistle lets out an ear-piercing trill.

"He's going nowhere," Mart says, a little bit louder, glancing around the table to make sure everyone hears him. "This man's a fine neighbor, and I'm planning to hang on to him." He adds, with a grin to Cal, "Sure, none of this shower would be arsed getting me them biscuits."

"If Lena won't have him," someone else says, "we'll sort him out with Belinda."

There's a burst of laughter. Cal can't get the flavor of it. There's mockery in it, but around here mockery is like rain: most of the time it's either present or incipient, and there are at least a dozen variants, ranging from nurturing to savage, and so subtly distinguished that it would take years to get the hang of them all.

"Who's Belinda?" he asks.

"A blow-in, like yourself," Senan says, grinning. "D'you fancy the redheads?"

"I wouldn't say the carpet matches the curtains there," someone else says.

"What would you know? You haven't been next nor near a woman since Elvis was number one."

"That's not what your sister says."

"Go on outa that. My sister'd roll the likes of you into a ball and use you to polish her floors."

"Belinda's an English one," Mart tells Cal, taking pity on him. "She has a wee cottage up by Knockfarraney, been there near twenty year. Mad as a brush, so she is. Covered in great big purple shawls and jewelry with Celtic yokes on. She came here because she thought she'd have the best chance at meeting the Little People round this way."

"Did she?" Cal asks. "Meet them?" The room is still realigning its angles every time he blinks, but less dramatically.

"She says she gets glimpses of them at the full moon," Mart says, grinning. "Out in the fields, like, or in the woods. She does paint pictures of them and sell them in the tourist shops in Galway."

"I seen her paintings," someone says. "They've

some fine sets of knockers on them, the Little People. I'll have to start spending more time in them fields at night myself."

"Off you go. You might be lucky and meet Belinda."

"Dancing round a fairy ring in the nip."

"Tell her you're the king of the fairies."

"Belinda's grand," Mart says. "She may be a Sassenach and she may be gone in the head, but there's no harm in her. She's not like your man Lord Muck."

They all laugh. The mockery is right up front this time, loud and ferocious, an aggression.

"Who's Lord Muck?" Cal asks.

"No need to worry your head about him," Senan says, reaching for his pint, still grinning. "He's gone."

"Another blow-in," Mart says. "Englishman. He was here for a bit of peace, so he could write a great novel. About a genius who rides the arse off a load of young ones because his wife doesn't appreciate his poems."

"I'd read that book," someone says.

"You never read a book in your life," someone else tells him.

"How would you know?"

"What've you read? Bitta Shakespeare, is it?"

"I'd read that one."

"If it was a picture book."

Mart ignores this. He says, "About eight year ago, it was, Lord Muck moved here."

"All ready to civilize us savages," Senan says.

"Ah, no," Mart says fairly. "He started out grand.

Lovely manners on him: always **Excuse me, Mr. Lavin,** and **Might I trouble you, Mr. Lavin.**" Senan snorts. "Don't be jeering, you. A few more manners would do you no harm."

"D'you want me to call you Mr. Lavin, is it?"

"Why not? Bring a bit of elegance to this aul' place. You can bow to me off your tractor, when you go past."

"I will in me arse."

"Where it all went off the rails," Mart tells Cal, settling to his story, "is when Lord Muck found out about the badger-baiting. D'you know what that is?"

"Not exactly," Cal says. The first violent flare of the poteen is dying down, but it still feels smarter to stick to short sentences.

"It's against the law," Mart says, "but the cattlemen don't like the badgers. They spread TB to the cattle, d'you see? The government does cull them, but some of the men, they prefer to take matters into their own hands. They'll send a coupla terriers into a sett to find the badger, and then the men'll dig it out. They might shoot it or they might let the dogs finish it, depending what kind of men they are."

"A few of the lads were making plans one night, in here," Senan says. "And didn't Lord Muck over-hear them."

"He didn't approve of that carry-on, at all," someone else says. "Outrageous, it was."

"Persecuting the helpless creatures."

"Disgraceful."

"Barbaric."

The men laugh again. This time there's a low rumble to it, a dark layer running underneath.

"The English are pure mad," Mart tells Cal. "They've more compassion for animals than they have for any human being. There's childer going hungry in that fella's own country, his army does bomb the living shite outa civilians all round the Middle East, and he wouldn't bat an eyelid, but the thought of that badger had him almost in tears. And him only on his second pint."

"Fuckin' sap," says Senan.

"I don't like the badger-baiting myself," Mart says. "I done it once, when I was a young lad, and I never done it again. But I don't have cattle. If a man's afraid the badgers'll ruin his livelihood, it's not my place to tell him to sit back and hope for the best. And if it's not my place, then it's not the place of some blow-in that was never on a farm in his life except to write a poem about it."

"A pity Lord Muck didn't see it that way," Senan says.

"He did not," Mart says. "Lord Muck showed up at that sett on the night, with a big torch in one hand and a video camera in the other."

"Screaming and yelling out of him," someone else says, "about how he was going to take his footage to the Gardaí and the television."

"He'd have the whole townland thrown in jail. Get the **bloody rotten operation** shut down."

"He never got that footage to the Gardaí and the

media," Malachy says, "the poor creature. Somehow or another, his video camera didn't survive the night."

"Ah, he smashed it himself," someone says. "Throwing himself about like a lunatic, he was."

"Trying to batter people away from the sett with that torch."

"Gave himself a bloody nose with it."

"Coupla black eyes, and all."

"One of the dogs went for him, and didn't the little fucker up and kick it in the ribs. Some animal-lover, hah?"

"He shot John Joe in the arm," Bobby says impressively.

"What are you on about?" Senan demands. "What the hell would he shoot John Joe with?"

"A gun. What the hell do people usually—"

"How would he hold a gun? He'd the torch in one hand, the video camera in the other—"

"How would I know how he held it?"

"—he wasn't a fuckin' octopus—"

"Maybe he'd the torch in his teeth."

"Then how did he shout at them?"

Bobby says stubbornly, "All I know is, John Joe showed me the bullet wound."

"Your man caught John Joe a clatter with his torch, is all he ever done. If John Joe showed you a bullet wound, he done it to himself; that fella wouldn't know one end of a rifle from . . ."

An impassioned all-parties argument gets under

way, and Cal is left looking at Mart, who is smiling back at him.

"Don't be listening to them eejits," Mart tells him, "about Belinda. She'd have your head melted. She'd want you out dancing round fairy rings at the full moon, and you haven't the build for it. You stick to Lena."

Cal's sense of distance is still screwy; Mart's face seems very close, and slightly watery around the edges. "So," Cal says, "Lord Muck doesn't live round here any more."

"I'd say he went back to England," Mart says, considering the possibilities. "He'd be happier there. I wonder if he ever got that novel written."

Cal says, "What you guys do to badgers is none of my business."

"I don't do anything to badgers," Mart reminds him. "Sure, I said that already. I don't believe in harming any creature unless there's a need."

Cal would like his head to be a lot clearer. He takes a swig of his beer, in the hope that it might dilute the poteen in his blood.

"D'you know what you did that was great," Mart says, aiming a knobbly finger at Cal, "when you first moved in? You asked for advice. Always asking me what was the best builders' providers, and what to do about the septic tank. I thought well of you for that. It takes a wise man to spot when he needs the bitta advice from someone that knows his way around. **This fella won't end up like Lord Muck,** I thought to myself; **this fella'll do grand.**" He peers reproachfully at Cal, through the haze of smoke that has thickened in the air. "And then you stopped altogether. What happened there, boyo? Did I lead you astray some way, and you never told me?"

"Not that I know of," Cal says. "Did you?"

"I did not. So why are you not asking my advice any more? Do you not think you need it, hah? You've got the measure of this place now, you're grand on your own?"

"OK," Cal says. "Gimme some advice."

"Now," Mart says approvingly. "That's better."

He settles himself deeper into the banquette and gazes up at the damp-stains on the ceiling. The music has slowed to something old and haunting, the tin whistle spinning a tune whose shapes are strange to Cal, the fiddle a long low drone underneath.

"After the brother died," Mart says, "I was at a bit of a loose end. All on my ownio in them dark winter evenings, no one to chat to. I wasn't myself, like; my mind wouldn't settle. 'Twasn't healthy. So I'll tell you what I did. I went into a bookshop in Galway, and I got them to order me a load of books on the aul' geology. I read them books from cover to cover. I can tell you everything there is to know about the geology round here."

He points at the little window, coated thickly with darkness. "D'you know those mountains out there," he says, "where you went for your wee bit of a saunter the other day? Those are red sandstone. Four hundred million years ago, those were laid down, when the land was right down by the equator. 'Twasn't green then; it was nothing but red desert, hardly a living thing on it. But it got the rain then, too, torrents of it. If you go up in those mountains and you dig about a bit, you'll find layers of pebbles and sand and muck, and that tells you there were flash floods out in that desert. A few million years after that, a coupla continents smashed into each other, and they crumpled up those mountains like bits of paper; that's why some of those rocks do be standing up vertical. A volcano shot rocks into the air and sent lava flowing down the mountainside."

He reaches for his pint, smiling at Cal. "When you went for your wee wander," he says, "that's what you were wandering over. It's a great comfort to me, knowing that. The things we do up those mountains, your walk and Malachy's still and all the rest of it, they don't make a blind bit of difference. No more than the midges."

He raises his pint to Cal and takes a long swallow. "That's what I did," he says, wiping foam off his lip, "when I caught my mind getting restless."

Cal says, "I don't know if geology's my style."

"Doesn't have to be the geology," Mart reassures him. "Whatever you fancy yourself. Astronomy, maybe—sure, haven't you the whole sky at your disposal, now you're away from the city lights? Get yourself an aul' telescope and a few charts, and away you go. Or a bitta Latin might suit you. You strike me as a man who never got all the education he could handle. We've a great tradition here of going out and getting our own education, if no one offers it to us on a plate. Seeing as you're here now, it's only right you should join in."

"Is this like buying Bobby a harmonica?" Cal asks. "Keep me busy, so I don't start doing crazy shit?"

"I'm looking out for you, is all," Mart says. The twist of mockery is, for once, gone from his voice; his eyes are steady on Cal's. "You're a dacent man, and I'd like to see you happy here. You deserve that."

He claps Cal on the shoulder, his face breaking into a grin. "And if you go alien-mad like Bobby, I'm the one that'll have to listen to you. Get yourself a telescope. And go on up there and get me a pint, in exchange for all that good advice."

By the time Cal returns, walking very carefully, with Mart's pint and his own, the conversation is clearly over: Mart is deep in an argument with a couple of the guys about the relative merits of two TV game shows Cal has never heard of, and breaks off only long enough to throw Cal a wink as he takes his glass.

The night goes on. The argument about TV shows gets heated enough that Cal keeps a hand on the table in case someone tries to turn it over, and then somehow dissipates in a burst of insults and laughter.

Deirdre sings "Crazy" in a mournful contralto, her head thrown back and her eyes closed. The Lucozade bottle empties, and Malachy produces another one from under the table. The musical corner takes off into a wild reel that has people stamping and slapping tables to the beat.

"D'you know what we thought when you first came?" Bobby shouts over the music, louder than necessary, to Cal. His hair is straggling out of its neat combover and he's having trouble focusing on Cal's face. "We thought you were one of them American preachers, and you'd be standing in the road shouting about Judgment Day."

"I didn't," Senan says. "I thought you were one of them hipster shites and you'd be asking Noreen for avocados."

"It was the beard that done it," Mart explains to Cal. "We don't see many like that around here. It needed accounting for."

"This fella thought you were on the run," someone else says, nudging his neighbor.

"Just lazy," Cal says. "I let the shaving slide for a while, and next thing you know, this happened."

"We'll give you a hand with that," the deep-voiced guy in the corner says.

"I've got used to it," Cal says. "I think I'll hang on to it a while longer."

"Lena's got a right to see what's under there, before she gets herself into anything."

"You'll be only gorgeous."

"Noreen's got razors."

"Barty! Give us the shop key there!"

They're all grinning at Cal, leaning forwards, glasses going down. The reel beats in the air like a pulse.

Cal has been sizing them up all evening, just in case. The deep-voiced guy in the corner is his top priority. He and Senan are going to be trouble, and probably Malachy; if Cal can take care of them, the rest are likely to back down. He readies himself, as best he can.

"Get outa that," Mart tells them, throwing an arm around Cal's shoulders. "I told ye all from the start, this fella was sound as a pound. And wasn't I right? If he wants a big Chewbacca head on him, he can have one."

For a moment the alcove is still, balanced on the edge and ready to tip either way. Then Senan roars with laughter and the rest join in, like they were just kidding all along. "The face on him," someone says, "thought he was about to be fuckin' sheared like a sheep," and someone else shouts, "Look at him there, ready to take on the lot of us! Get up, ya boy ya!"

They settle back into their seats, still laughing, with their eyes still on Cal, and someone shouts to Barty to bring this madman another pint. Cal stares right back at them and laughs as long and loud as the rest. He wonders which of these men is the most likely to spend his nights in a field with a sheep and a sharp knife.

Senan sings something in what must be Irish, long melancholy phrases with a quaver at the end, his head back and his eyes closed. The deep-voiced guy, whose name turns out to be Francie, slides over to introduce himself to Cal; this somehow spirals into a full account of how Francie's true love left him because he had to look after his mother through her twelve-year decline, a story heartrending enough that Cal is moved to buy Francie a pint and they both need another shot of poteen. At some point Deirdre is gone, and so is the buck-naked window guy. Someone sets off the rubber fish behind the bar when Barty isn't looking, and they all sing "I Will Survive" along with it, at the top of their lungs.

By the time people start to leave, Cal is drunk enough to accept a ride home from Mart, mainly out of a confused feeling that it would be uncivil to refuse, given that he owes Mart his beard. Mart sings all the way, in a cracked tenor with surprising volume, jaunty songs about girls who are all the prettiest in town, with some of the words missing. Cold air streams through the open windows, and the clouds are breaking up so that stars and darkness whisk dizzyingly across the windshield. At every pothole the car soars. Cal figures either they'll get home or they won't, and joins in on the choruses.

"Now," Mart says, pulling up with a jolt outside Cal's gate. "How's the aul' stomach holding up?"

"Pretty good," Cal says, fumbling for his seat-belt clip. His phone buzzes in his pocket. It takes him a moment to work out what on earth that might be. Then it comes to him that it must be Alyssa, WhatsApping him: **Sorry I missed you, catch you later!** He leaves the phone where it is.

"It is, of course. No better man." Mart's wispy gray hair is sticking straight out on one side of his head. He looks beatifically happy.

"Barty looked pretty glad to get rid of us," Cal says. The last time he looked at his watch, it was three in the morning.

"Barty," Mart says with magnificent scorn. "Sure, that pub's not even rightly his. He only got his hands on it because Seán Óg's son fancied himself sitting in an aul' office, the big jessie. He can put up with us having a wee carouse every now and again."

"Should I have given Malachy a coupla bucks?" Cal asks. "For the"—he can't come up with the right word—"the 'shine?"

"Sure, I looked after all that," Mart tells him. "You can sort me out some other time. You'll have plenty of oppornoon—opteroon—" He waves a hand at Cal and gives up.

"Whoops," Cal says, as he clambers out of the car. He regains his footing. "Thanks for the ride. And the invitation."

"That was some night, bucko," Mart says, leaning

over a little too far to talk through the passenger window. "You'll remember that one, hah?"

"Not sure I'll remember a damn thing," Cal says, which makes Mart laugh.

"Arrah, you'll be grand. Get a good sleep, that's all you need."

"I intend to," Cal says. "You too."

"I will," Mart says. His face crunches into a grin. "Here I was planning on taking over guard duty from P.J. halfway through the night, d'you remember? I shoulda known better. That was never on the cards. But I've been an optimist all my life." He waves to Cal and revs off up the road, taillights weaving.

Cal decides not to bother getting as far as the house just yet. Instead he lies down on his grass and looks up at the stars, which are thick and wild as dandelions right across the sky. He thinks about that telescope Mart suggested, and decides it wouldn't suit him. He feels no urge to understand the stars better; he's contented with them as they are. It's always been a trait of his, whether for better or for worse, to prefer setting his mind to things he can do something about.

After a while, he sobers up enough to feel the rocks poking at his back and the cold seeping into him. It also occurs to him, gradually, that it might not be smart to lie out here with something or someone on the loose that takes the throats out of sheep.

When he picks himself up his head spins, and he has to lean over with his hands on his thighs for a little bit till it stops. Then he trudges across the lawn, which feels very wide and bare, towards his house. There's no movement in the fields, and no sound in the hedges or the branches; the night has come to its deepest point, the deserted pre-dawn borderland. His clump of woods is a dense smudge against the stars, silent and still. Mart's house is dark.

TWELVE

Cal wakes up late: sun is pouring in at his bedroom window. His head is a little tender and feels like it's been stuffed with sticky carpet fluff, but apart from that he's in surprisingly OK shape. He runs his head under the cold tap, which clears it a little bit, and fixes himself some fried eggs and sausages, a couple of painkillers and a lot of coffee for lunch. Then he tosses his bag of dirty laundry into the trunk of his car and heads for town.

The day is deceptively bright, with a hard chill in the shadows and a little breeze that flirts its way close and then slices right in. The Pajero bumps rhythmically over the potholes at an easy lope. Alongside, the shadows of small clouds glide across the brown mountains.

Cal is clear that last night he got warned. The warning, however, was done with such subtlety that—whether by design or not—he's unsure what, exactly, he was being warned off. He has no idea whether Ardnakelty has worked out that he's looking into Brendan Reddy's disappearance and wants him to knock that shit off, or whether he's just been poking around too much for a stranger and needs instruction in local customs.

One interesting part is where and how the warning was delivered. Mart could have just given him a few quick pointers in private, over the gate some afternoon; instead, he saved it up for the poteen party. Either he wanted Cal to hear the message from a bunch of people at once, to drive it home, or he wanted to make sure everyone else knew Cal had been warned. Cal has come away with the strong impression that it was the second one, and that this was for his protection.

He's unsure what circumstances might make this necessary. Cal is accustomed to being in the dark at the start of an investigation, which means it's taken him a while to realize that this is an entirely different thing. He has no idea, not just what the people around him know and what they believe, but also what they might think of it, what they want, why they want it, or how they might go about achieving it. Their decades of familiarity, which seemed like a comfort at the beginning of last night, weave themselves into an impenetrable thicket; its layers obscure every action and every motivation till they're near indecipherable to an outsider. He understands that this effect is, at least in part, deliberate and practiced. The guys like him blindfolded. It's not personal; keeping him that way is, to them, an elementary and natural precaution.

Cal is aware that he seems like the kind of placid, amenable guy who would heed that warning. That appearance has come in handy plenty of times. He'd love to let it keep being useful here: let the townland relax into the belief that he's gone back to minding his own business and painting his house. The trouble is, he has no options that allow for that. Back on the job, he could have stayed accommodatingly away from Brendan's associates and focused on the behind-the-scenes stuff for a while: hooked up with the techie guys to dump Brendan's phone and track his locations and go through his emails, got the bank to check whether and where his bank card had been used, run all those associates through the system, talked to Narcotics about the Dublin drug boys. He could have bounced possibilities off his partner, O'Leary, a little cop-bellied cynic with a deceptive air of laziness and a keen sense of the ridiculous, and got O'Leary to do some legwork for him.

Here, all that artillery and all those allies have been stripped away. There is no behind the scenes to take cover in. He's in this empty-handed and alone, out in the wide open.

Cal's original plan for today was to track down Donie McGrath, but that's changed. For one thing, Donie is likely to be a huge pain in the ass to interview, and Cal's head can't take it. More importantly, he doesn't have a good enough handle on what's going on. Even if people were warning him away from Brendan, all they know so far is that he's trying to find out where a runaway kid ran to, in order to reassure his worried mama or just out of pure nosiness. But Cal knows they'll be keeping an eye on

him. If he talks to Donie, or anyone else who has
connections to the Dublin drug boys, they'll know
what he's thinking. Cal isn't inclined to take that
step until he's good and ready.

He does have one thing on his list that won't show
any more of his hand and that needs a weekend. In
town, he hands in his clothes to the laundromat and
heads for the gift shop.

Caroline Horan is still Facebook friends with
Brendan, which makes Cal figure the breakup wasn't
too shitty. Her profile shot shows her and two other
girls on a beach with their arms around each other,
laughing and windblown. Caroline has disorga-
nized brown curls and a round, freckled face with
an engaging smile. She also has "Studies at Athlone
Institute of Technology" on her profile, meaning
that if she's still working at the gift shop, she's likely
to be pulling weekend shifts.

Sure enough, when he pushes open the gift-shop
door with a tinkle of bells, there she is, reorganizing a
stand of nameplates with leprechauns on them. She's
shorter than Cal expected, with a neat, rounded figure. Her curls are smoothed into a ponytail and she's
wearing a little bit of makeup, just enough to look
groomed but still wholesome.

"Afternoon," Cal says, looking around, a little be-
wildered by the amount of stuff. The place is small
and chockablock with green things, things made of
wool, and things made of marble. Most of them have
either shamrocks or twirly Celtic symbols on them.

In the background some guy is singing a cheesy ballad that even Cal can tell has nothing in common with the music in Seán Óg's.

"Hiya," Caroline says, turning to smile. "Can I help you with anything?"

"Well, I'm looking to buy a present for my niece in Chicago," Cal says. "She's gonna be turning six. Maybe you could give me a few recommendations?"

"No problem," Caroline says cheerfully. She heads behind the counter, picking things off racks and shelves on her way: a gauzy green fairy doll, a shamrock T-shirt, a silver necklace in a little green box, a fuzzy black-faced toy sheep. "If she likes fairies, she'd love this. Or if she's more sporty, maybe a top and a baseball cap?"

Cal leans on the countertop, keeping a respectful distance, and nods along, taking stock of Caroline. She hasn't scraped off her accent for college, the way Eugene has; it's almost as strong as Trey's. Cal, who after nearly thirty years in Chicago still sounds like a North Carolina boy, approves of that. He likes her readiness of response and the efficiency of her movements, too. Brendan went for confident and competent. And if this girl wanted him, then he was no dummy, either.

"Or you can't go wrong with a claddagh necklace. It's the traditional Irish symbol for love, friendship and loyalty."

"This is pretty cute," Cal says, picking up the sheep. Alyssa used to love small soft creatures. Her

room had them on every surface, neat clusters ar-
ranged with care to look like they were having conversations or playing games. He would pick up a
couple of them and make them talk to each other,
while Alyssa giggled her head off. There was a raccoon who would sneak up on the others and tickle
them and then bounce away.

"They're as local as you can get," Caroline tells
him. "A lady in Carrickmore hand-felts them with
wool from her brother's sheep."

Cal glances up at her with his brows twitching
together. "I got a feeling you live round my way," he
says. "Did I see you helping Noreen out in Ardnakelty
store, one time?"

Caroline smiles. "You probably did, yeah. It's hard
to say no to Noreen."

"Tell me about it," Cal says, grinning and putting out a hand. "Cal Hooper. The American that's
bought the O'Shea place."

His name gets no reaction from Caroline, for
whatever that's worth. Her handshake is older than
she is, a professional's. "Caroline Horan."

"OK," Cal says, "lemme see if Noreen's taught me
anything. If you're Caroline, then you're the one that
broke her wrist falling off Noreen's ladder trying to
snitch some cake sprinkles. I get that right?"

Caroline laughs. "God, I was **six**. I'll never live
that down. And I didn't even get the sprinkles."

"Don't worry," Cal says, grinning back. "That's as

bad as it gets. Only other things I know are you used to date Brendan Reddy, the guy who's not available to do my wiring because he took off somewhere, and you're in college. What're you studying?"

Brendan's name does make Caroline blink. "Hotel management," she says, easily enough, turning away to get more sheep off the shelf. "You can go anywhere with that, you know?"

"Planning on traveling?"

She smiles over her shoulder. "Oh God, yeah. The more the better. And this way I can get paid for it."

Cal reckons Brendan's big mistake, or one of them anyway, was doing whatever he did to make Caroline dump him. This girl has the spark of a woman who's going places. She would have taken the pair of them as far as Brendan could dream of, and then some.

"Now," she says, lining up half a dozen more sheep in different colors on the counter. "Take your pick. I like the expression on this one."

"Looks kinda loco to me," Cal says, examining the sheep's white-rimmed stare. "Like it's waiting for the right moment to attack."

Caroline laughs. "It's just got personality."

"If I give my niece nightmares, my sister's gonna come over here and beat me up."

"How about this one?" She picks out a cream-colored one with a black head. "Look at the face on that. It wouldn't hurt a fly."

"That one's scared of the crazy one. Look." Cal

puts the timid sheep hiding behind the others, with the loco one staring them down. "It's shaking in its hooves."

Caroline is laughing again. "Then you oughta get it out of here. Give it a safe new home and it'll be grand."

"OK," Cal says. "I'll do that. My good deed for the day."

"You can tell your niece it's a rescue sheep," Caroline says. She starts putting the extra sheep back on their shelf.

"You know," Cal says, turning the green baseball cap in his hands, "I don't want to interfere, but I was talking with Brendan Reddy's mama the other day, and she's pretty worried about him. If you've heard from him, maybe you might take a minute to let her know he's OK."

Caroline glances back at him, but only for a second. She says, "I haven't heard from him."

"You don't need to tell me. Just tell his mama."

"I know. I haven't, though."

"Even if he mentioned somewhere he might be headed. She's not handling it too well. Anything would help."

Caroline shakes her head. "He never said anything about it to me," she says. "There's no reason he would, sure. We weren't really in touch, after we broke up."

The hurt in her voice hasn't healed over. Whatever went wrong between the two of them, she liked Brendan a lot.

"He took it hard?" Cal asks.

"Sort of. Yeah."

"You worried about him too?"

Caroline comes back to the counter. She runs a finger down the sheep's nose.

"I'd like to know," she says.

"You got any guesses?"

Caroline picks a curl of gray fuzz off the sheep's back. "The thing about Brendan," she says. "He gets ideas, and he gets carried away by them. He forgets to take other people into account."

"How's that?"

"Like," Caroline says, "OK, we both really like this singer Hozier, right? And he was playing in Dublin last December. So Brendan picked up any bits of work he could find, to get together the money for tickets and the bus and a B and B. For my Christmas present. Which would have been amazing, only he got them for the night before my last exam."

"Oh, man," Cal says, grimacing.

"Yeah. Not on purpose, like; he just forgot to check with me. Then when I said I couldn't go, he was genuinely shocked. And angry. Like, 'You only care about college, you think I'm not worth the hassle because I'm going nowhere . . .' Which I didn't think at all, but . . . yeah."

"But you're not gonna get that through to a guy who's feeling sensitive," Cal says.

"Yeah. That's why we broke up, basically."

Cal considers this. "So you think he went off

chasing a big idea," he says, "and he forgot his mama would worry?"

Caroline glances at him; then her eyes slide away again. "Maybe," she says.

Cal says, "Or . . . ?"

Caroline asks, "Will I gift-wrap this for you?"

"Well, that'd be great," Cal says. "I'm not much of a hand with wrapping stuff."

"No problem," Caroline says, deftly whipping out some green tissue paper from under the counter. "Sure, if she's six she won't care either way, but your sister might. Let's do it right."

Cal tries spinning the baseball cap on one finger, listens to the singer crooning about homesickness, and considers Caroline, who is layering sheets of tissue paper in various shades of green. With Eugene, he played dumb, because Eugene wants people to be dumb. It's clear to Cal that Caroline wants people to be smart, and to get things done.

"Miss Caroline," he says, "I'm gonna ask you a couple of things, because I figure you're my best chance at getting good answers."

Caroline stops wrapping and lifts her head to look at him. She says, "About what?"

"Brendan Reddy."

Caroline says, "Why?"

She and Cal look at each other. Cal knows he's been lucky to get this far without anyone asking him that question.

"You could say I'm just nosy," he says, "or restless, or both. I can promise you this much: I'm not aiming to do him any kind of harm. Just find out where he's gone, is all."

Caroline nods, like she believes him. She says, "I've got nothing to say to you."

Cal says, "You want to know where he went. You gonna go asking around yourself?"

Caroline shakes her head. The sharp jerk makes Cal understand that she's afraid.

He says, "Then I'm the best hope you've got."

"And if you find out, you'll tell me."

"I can't promise you that," Cal says. A minute ago he might have, but that shake of her head has turned him wary. She doesn't seem like the type who scares easy. "But if I find him, I'll tell him he should give you a call. That's better'n nothing."

After a moment she says, without any expression, "OK. Fire away."

"How was Brendan, in his mind?"

"What way?"

"Was he depressed?"

"I don't think so," Caroline says. The answer comes promptly enough to tell Cal that she's thought about this before. "He wasn't happy, but that's a different thing. He didn't seem dragged down by it, you know? More just . . . frustrated. Annoyed. He's basically an optimist. He always reckoned something would turn up, in the end."

"I apologize for putting this harshly," Cal says, "but do you think there's any chance he might have taken his own life?"

"I don't," Caroline says. This comes out instantly, too. "I know you can't say someone's not the type for suicide, and people might be a lot worse off than they let on, but . . . the way Brendan thinks: always 'Sure, I'll find a way, it'll be grand in the end one way or another . . .' That doesn't seem like it goes with suicide."

"I wouldn't have thought so," Cal says. He tends to agree with Caroline, although he also shares her reservations. "He ever seem out of touch with reality? Saying stuff that didn't make sense?"

"You mean like schizophrenia, or bipolar disorder."

"Or anything else along those lines."

Caroline thinks for a moment, her hands lying still on the tissue paper. Then she shakes her head. "No," she says, with certainty. "He gets unrealistic, sometimes, like with the tickets and my exam—'It'll be grand, just do all your studying beforehand and we'll catch the early bus home the next day . . .' But that's different from being out of touch with reality."

"That it is," Cal says. **He's, he gets.** Caroline, just like Fergal and Eugene, thinks Brendan is alive. Cal doesn't set too much store by that. To them, the idea of someone their age dying is impossible. He hopes it can stay that way a while longer. "That unrealistic attitude make him any enemies?"

Caroline's eyes widen, just a flicker, but her voice

stays even. "Not like you're talking about. People got annoyed with him, sometimes. But . . . sure, we've all known each other all our lives. Everyone knows what he's like. It was never a big deal."

"I know how that goes," Cal says. "Is he reliable? Say he tells you he's gonna do something for you, or get you something. Would you expect that he'd get it done, or that he'd forget the whole thing?"

"He'd follow through," Caroline says immediately. "It's a matter of pride for him, like. His dad was an awful man for making promises and forgetting them. Brendan hated it. He didn't want to be like that."

"Well, there you go. People can forgive a man for being a little bit unrealistic, as long as he's reliable." Cal puts the baseball cap back on the counter and pats it into shape. "I'm guessing that means he wouldn't have up and left if he thought you were pregnant."

He's betting on Caroline having more sense than to get huffy about that. Sure enough, she says matter-of-factly, "No way. He'd've done everything he could to be the perfect daddy. Anyway, there's no reason he'd think that. I'd no scare or anything."

"You said money was tight for Brendan, and he worried that you thought he was going nowhere. He have any plans to try and fix that?"

Caroline blows out air through a small wry smile. "I bet he did, yeah. He said—when we were breaking up, like—he said he'd show me he was going places."

"He mention how?"

She shakes her head.

Cal says, "Maybe by getting involved in something he shouldn't've?"

"Like what?"

Caroline's voice has sharpened. "Well, like something against the law," Cal says mildly. "Stealing, maybe, or running drugs."

"He never did anything like that. Not when we were going out."

"How'd he get the money for the band tickets?"

"One of our friends' uncle does furniture removals, so Brendan got a few days with him. And he gave grinds." At Cal's uncomprehending look, she says, "Tutored people from our school in chemistry, and engineering—they're his best subjects. Stuff like that."

Back on the job, Cal could have verified all this. Now all he's got is his gut, which is telling him that Caroline wants to think well of Brendan, but also that she's no fool. "Smart thinking," he says. "Not gonna make a guy rich, though."

"No, but you see what I mean. He didn't do anything dodgy."

"You're not telling me he never would, though," Cal points out.

Caroline goes back to her tissue paper, folding it around the sheep with deft quick fingers. Cal waits.

"There were rumors going round," Caroline says in

the end, "after Brendan went." Her hands are moving faster, and her voice has tightened. She doesn't enjoy talking about this. "People were saying he'd raped me, and he went on the run because I was going to the Guards."

"And that wasn't true?"

"No, it wasn't. Brendan never laid a finger on me that I didn't want. I squashed that one quick, once I heard about it. But there were plenty of others I couldn't do anything about. That he ran because he beat up his mam. Or because he got caught peeping in women's windows. Probably worse ones that no one told me."

She pulls a piece of tape off the dispenser with a snap. "That's what Ardnakelty was like to Brendan, all his life. Because he came from that family, people always believed the worst about him, whether there was any reason to or not. Even my parents— and they're not like that—they were horrified when I started going out with him, only they said I had sense, so if I saw something in him then it was probably there. But they didn't like it. Even when they saw he was good to me, they didn't like it." She glances up at Cal. The fast jerk of her head has anger in it. "So I'm just saying, don't be believing everything people tell you about Brendan. Most of it's a load of shite."

"Then you tell me," Cal says. "Would he do anything criminal, or not?"

"I'll tell you what Brendan's like," Caroline says. Her hands have stopped moving; she's forgotten all about the toy sheep. "He has a rake of little brothers and sisters, right? Most people, when they start going out with someone, they ignore everyone else. But Brendan: even when we first started going out, when we were pure mad about each other, he'd be saying, 'I can't meet up tonight, I've to go watch Trey's football match,' or 'Maeve's after having a row with her best friend, I'll hang around home and cheer her up.' Their parents weren't doing any of that, so Brendan did it. Not like it was a pain in the arse. Like he wanted to."

"He sounds like a good man," Cal says. "But good men break the law, sometimes. You haven't told me whether he would or not."

Caroline goes back to folding the edges of the paper. In the end she says, "I hope not."

Her face has tightened up. Cal waits.

She starts to say something, and then stops. Instead she says, "I'd just like to know he's OK."

Cal says gently, "I haven't heard anything to say he's not."

"Right." Caroline takes a quick breath. She's not looking at Cal any more. "Yeah. I'd say he's grand."

"Tell you what," Cal says. "I'll say to Miz Reddy, if she does hear from Brendan, she should let you know."

"Thanks," Caroline says politely, unrolling green

ribbon from a spool. The conversation is over. "That'd be great."

She wraps up the sheep nice and pretty, and twirls the green ribbon in ringlets. When Cal thanks her for all her help, he leaves a second in case she might say something else, but she just gives him a bright impersonal smile and wishes his niece a happy birthday.

———

The outdoors, away from the clutter and the syrupy ballads, feels spacious and loose, peaceful. In the main square, families in their good clothes and old women in head scarves are coming out of the church; behind its spire, the wind chivvies scraps of cloud across the blue sky.

Cal was hoping Brendan might have talked to Caroline about his big moneymaking plan. Boys run their mouths, when they're trying to impress girls. Caroline isn't the type to be impressed by criminal activity, but Brendan could have been too young, too hasty and too desperate to notice that. Cal believes Caroline, though. Whatever was in the works, Brendan kept it to himself.

Cal hasn't come away empty-handed, though. Suicide is off the table, or as good as. Not because Caroline thinks Brendan wasn't the type, but because Caroline—and Cal considers her to be the best witness he's talked to so far—Caroline says Brendan set a lot of store by keeping his promises. Brendan said he'd get Trey a bike for his birthday, and Brendan said he'd pay back Fergal's hundred bucks—money he wouldn't have needed if all he was aiming to do was go up the mountain and hang himself. If Brendan was planning on going anywhere, he was also planning on coming back.

And Caroline thinks there was nothing going wrong in Brendan's mind. Cal is glad of this. If Brendan got spooked, if he ran, if he's hiding out in the mountains, then he had a reason that existed outside his mind. That means it must have left solid tracks, somewhere along the way.

It might be that Caroline does have a guess at what Brendan was doing and it's not something she wants to discuss, at least not with a stranger and an ex-cop. On the other hand, it might be that Cal isn't the only person who's had a warning.

Cal doesn't hold out much hope of finding the police station open on a Sunday, but Garda O'Malley is sitting at his desk, reading his paper and eating a big piece of chocolate cake with his fingers. "Ah, God, it's Officer Hooper," he says, beaming and trying to work out whether to stand up. "I won't shake your hand, look—" He holds up his sticky fingers. "My little fella's after turning eight, and the size of the cake my missus made, we'll be ating it for his ninth as well."

"No problem," Cal says, grinning. "Looks like good cake."

"Ah, it's gorgeous. She does watch all them bake-off shows. If I'da known you were coming, I'da brought you a slice."

"Catch you next year," Cal says. "I just dropped in to let you know I got that rifle in the end. Thank you kindly for your help."

"No problem at all," O'Malley says, relaxing back into his seat and sucking frosting off his thumb. "Have you taken it out yet?"

"Just shooting at tin cans, getting my eye back in. It's a good gun. I got rabbits on my land, so I'm gonna try and bag me a few of those."

"Cunning little bastards," O'Malley says, with the melancholy of experience. "Good luck."

"Well," Cal says, "the only other thing I got to hand is a tree full of rooks messing up my lawn. Maybe you can tell me: they good eating?"

O'Malley looks startled, but he considers the question out of politeness. "I've never et rook my-self," he says. "But my daddy told us his mammy used to make rook stew when he was a little fella, if they'd nothing else. With potatoes, like, and the bit of onion. I'd say you'd get a recipe on the internet; sure, they've everything on there."

"Worth a try," Cal says. He has no intention of

shooting any of his rooks. He has a feeling the survivors would make bad enemies.

"I wouldn't say it'd be nice," O'Malley says, thinking it over further. "Awful strong-tasting, I'd say."

"I'll save you a helping," Cal says, grinning.

"Ah, no, you're grand," O'Malley says, slightly apprehensive. "Sure, I'll still be working my way through this cake."

Cal laughs, gives the counter a slap and is turning for the door when a thought strikes him. "Almost forgot," he says. "Some guy was telling me a couple of officers got called out to Ardnakelty, back in March. Would that have been you?"

O'Malley thinks that over. " 'Twasn't, no. The only times I've been out that way this year, I was up the mountain, trying to get those Reddy childer to get an education. Ardnakelty doesn't have much call for our services."

"Well, that's what I thought," Cal says, frowning a little. "You got any idea what that thing in March was about?"

"Can't have been anything serious," O'Malley assures him. "Sure, if it was, I'd have heard about it."

"I'd love to know, all the same," Cal says, his frown deepening. "I can't rest easy unless I know what I'm living with. Side effect of the job—I mean, hey, who am I telling, right?"

O'Malley doesn't look like this angle has ever occurred to him before, but he nods along vigorously all the same. "Tell you what I'll do," he says, an idea striking him. "You hang on here a minute, and I'll look it up in the system."

"Well, that's kind of you," Cal says, surprised and pleased. "I'd appreciate that. I'll bring you some rook stew for sure."

O'Malley laughs, extracts himself from his chair with a few loud creaking noises, and heads back to the office. Cal waits and looks out the window at the sky, where the clouds are thickening, getting darker and more ominous. He can't imagine ever getting accustomed to the effortless hairpin turns of the weather around here. He's used to a hot sunny day being a hot sunny day, a cold rainy day being a cold rainy day, and so on. Here, some days the weather seems like it's just fucking with people on principle.

"Now," O'Malley says, coming back out, happy with his results. "Like I told you: nothing serious at all, at all. March the sixteenth, a farmer reported signs of intruders on his land and a possible theft of farm equipment, but when the boys got out there, he told them 'twas all a mistake." He resettles himself in his chair and pops a chunk of cake into his mouth. "I'd say he found out 'twas the local young scally-wags messing, like. They do get bored; sometimes the bold ones'll hide something just for the crack, to see the farmer go mental looking for it. Or maybe it was robbed, but the farmer found out who done it and got the stuff back, so he left it at that. They're like that, around here. They'd rather keep us out of it, unless they've no choice at all."

"Well, either way," Cal says, "that sets my mind at ease. I don't have any farm equipment to get stolen. I got an old wheelbarrow that came with the place, but if anyone wants it that bad, they're welcome to it."

"They're more likely to put it on top of your roof," O'Malley says tolerantly.

"It'd probably improve the look of the place," Cal says. "There's designer guys who charge yuppies thousands of bucks for ideas like that. Who was the farmer?"

"Fella called Patrick Fallon. I don't know the man. That means he's not a regular, anyway; there's no local feud going on, nor nothing like that."

Patrick Fallon is presumably P.J. "Huh," Cal says. "That's my neighbor. I haven't heard him mention any trouble since I got here. I guess it must've been a once-off thing."

"Lads messing," O'Malley says, with comfortable finality, breaking off another big hunk of cake.

———

Looking at that cake has made Cal hungry. He finds a café and gets himself a slice of apple pie and more coffee, to pass the time till his laundry is ready. While he finishes the coffee, he gets his notebook out of his jacket pocket and turns to a fresh page.

He tosses around the possibility that Brendan was setting himself up as a source of stolen farm equipment, boosted P.J.'s stuff, got spooked and gave it back when he found out the cops had been called in, and skipped town to avoid the fallout or was run out, like the cat-killing Mannion kid. It doesn't sit quite right—anyone with half a brain would have expected police, and Brendan is or was no dummy— but maybe he didn't think the theft would be noticed so soon. Caroline said he didn't take people's reactions into account.

He writes: **Farm equipment 3/16. What was stolen? Was it recovered?**

The other thing hanging around the edges of his mind is the thought of those dead sheep. Mart isn't sitting up in those woods on the off chance. He has some reason for thinking P.J.'s sheep are next.

Cal draws himself a quick sketch of Ardnakelty townland, with help from internet maps. He marks in Mart's land, P.J.'s and Bobby Feeney's; he doesn't know where Francie Gannon's is exactly, but "beside the village" gives him a rough idea. Then he marks in all the other sheep farms he knows about.

Geographically, those four have nothing to single them out from the rest. They're not the nearest ones to the mountains or a wood where some creature might stay hidden, not all close together, not the nearest to the main road for a quick getaway. There's no reason, at least none that Cal can see, why they would be an obvious set of targets for either man or beast.

He writes: **Francie/Bobby/Mart/P.J. Links? Related? Beef w Brendan? W anyone?**

He can think of one person who had beef with Mart, anyway, not long before Mart's sheep got killed. He writes: **W Donie McG?**

The last of the coffee has got cold. Cal buys his groceries, including Mart's cookies and a three-pack of socks, picks up his laundry, and heads out of town.

The road up into the mountains feels different in a car, rockier and less welcoming, like it's biding its time to puncture Cal's tire or send him sideslipping into a patch of bog. He parks outside the Reddys' gate. There's no shoulder, but he's not too worried that another car will need to get by.

This time the Reddys' yard is empty. The breeze nips at his neck, and the ropes hanging from the climbing structure sway restlessly. The front windows of the house are blank and dark, but as Cal crosses the yard, he feels watched. He slows down, letting them get a good look.

It takes Sheila a long time to come to the door. She holds it a foot open and looks at Cal through the gap. He can't tell whether she recognizes him. From somewhere inside the house comes faint, bright cartoon laughter.

"Afternoon, Miz Reddy," he says, staying well

back. "Cal Hooper, who you helped out with dry socks a couple of days back, remember?"

She keeps looking at him. This time the wariness doesn't dissolve.

"I brought you these," he says, holding out the socks. "With my thanks."

That brings a spark of life into Sheila's eyes. "I don't need them. I'm not so poor that I can't afford to give away a pair of old socks."

Cal, taken aback, ducks his head and shifts his feet on the step. "Miz Reddy," he says, "I didn't intend to give any offense. You saved me a long wet walk home, and I was raised not to be ungrateful. My gramma would sit up in her grave to yell at me if I didn't bring you these."

After a moment the resentment fades and she looks away. "You're grand," she says. "Just . . ."

Cal waits, still abashed.

"I've the children. I can't be letting strange men call round."

When Cal lifts his head, startled and affronted, she says almost angrily, "It's nothing to do with you. People are fierce talkers, round here. I can't give them an excuse to say worse about me than they already do."

"Well," Cal says, still being a little miffed, "I apologize. I don't mean to cause you any trouble. I'll get out of your hair."

He holds out the socks again, but Sheila doesn't

take them. For a moment he thinks she's going to say something more, but then she nods and starts to close the door.

Cal says, "You hear anything from your boy Brendan?"

The flash of fear in Sheila's eyes tells him what he was looking to know. Sheila's been warned, too.

"Brendan's grand," she says.

"If you do," Cal says, "you might let Caroline Horan know," but before he's finished the sentence, Sheila has shut the door in his face.

———

On his way home Cal drops off the cookies at Mart's place, as a thank-you for last night and an indication that he spent today behaving himself. Mart is sitting on his front step, watching the world go by and brushing Kojak.

"How's the head?" he inquires, shoving Kojak's nose away from the cookies. He looks perky as ever, although he could do with a shave.

"Not as bad as I expected," Cal says. "How 'bout you?"

Mart throws him a wink and a finger-point. "Ah, you see, now, that's why we love Malachy. His stuff's pure as holy water. It's the impurities that'll destroy you."

"Here I thought it was the alcohol," Cal says, rubbing behind Kojak's ears.

"Not at all. I could drink a bottle of Malachy's finest, get up in the morning and do a day's work. But I've a cousin over the other side of the mountains, I wouldn't touch his stuff with a ten-foot pole. The hangover'd last till Christmas. He does always be inviting me to call in for a wee drop, and I've to find a new excuse every time. It's a social minefield, so 'tis."

"P.J. see anything last night?" Cal asks.

"Not a sausage," Mart says. He pulls a fluff of fur out of the bristles and tosses it onto the grass.

Cal says, "That guy Donie McGrath isn't too fond of you right now."

Mart stares at him for a second and then bursts into high-pitched giggles. "Holy God," he says, "you'll be the death of me. Are you talking about that wee kerfuffle in the pub? If Donie McGrath went around killing sheep on every man who put him back in his box, he'd never get a night's sleep. He hasn't got the work ethic for it."

"P.J. put him back in his box lately?" Cal inquires. "Or Bobby Feeney?"

"If it's not one thing with you, Sunny Jim, it's another," Mart says, shaking his head. "Never mind that telescope; what you need is a game of Cluedo. I'll buy you one myself, and you can bring it down to Seán Óg's for us all to play." He gets rid of the last of his giggles and snaps his fingers for Kojak to come back to the brush. "Will you be in tonight, for a straightener?"

"Nah," Cal says. "I gotta recover." He doesn't feel

any desire to go to Seán Óg's, tonight or in general. He always liked the glint and speed of the men there, of their talk and their shifting expressions, but now, when he thinks back, all that looks different: light flashing on a river, with who knows what underneath.

"A fine strong fella like you," Mart says, more in sorrow than in scorn. "What's the younger generation coming to, at all?" Cal laughs and heads back to his car, with the pebbles of Mart's driveway crunching under his feet.

———

When he gets home, he takes out his notebook and settles himself in the armchair to read through everything he's got. He needs to order his thoughts. He's never much liked this phase of an investigation, when things are messy and layered, forking off in multiple directions, and too many of them didn't actually happen. He hangs in there for the part when, if he's lucky, he gets to strip away the misty theories and take hold of the solid things hidden among them.

This time the process has a personal quality that he's not accustomed to. The fear in Sheila's eyes, and Caroline's, told him that last night's warning wasn't a general caution against being a busybody. It was about Brendan.

Cal would love to know what or who, exactly, he's

supposed to be scared of. Brendan appears to have been frightened of the Guards, and Sheila might well be wary of them either on his behalf or by reflex. But Cal has a hard time finding a reason why Caroline, or Mart, or he himself should be terrified of Garda Dennis, unless the whole townland is up to its neck in some vast criminal enterprise that could be blown sky-high if he goes asking too many questions, which seems unlikely.

The obvious alternative, in that they seem to be the only threat anyone can point to, is the drug boys from Dublin. Cal assumes that, like drug gangs everywhere else, they wouldn't think twice about getting rid of anyone who caused them inconvenience. If Brendan became inconvenient one way or another, and they disappeared him, they wouldn't be best pleased about some nosy Yank poking around. The question is how they would know.

Cal feels it's getting close to time for him to talk to Donie McGrath. Now, at any rate, he has an unimpeachable reason for doing that. Mart knows Cal was feeling protective after the pub argument. It would be only natural for him to go rattle Donie's cage a little bit about that sheep. That wouldn't violate last night's warning; not unless Mart thinks the sheep have something to do with Brendan. Cal is interested to see what happens after he talks to Donie.

He sits with his notebook for a while, looking at the map and considering where Ardnakelty, rightly or wrongly, thinks Brendan has gone, and why.

Outside the window, the clouds are still holding their rain, but the green of the fields is dimming as the light starts to fade. Evening has its own smell here, dense and cool, with a heady tinge of plants and flowers that play no part in the daytime. Cal gets up to turn on the light and put his shopping away.

He was planning to send the woolly sheep to Alyssa, but now he's not sure whether that would be a dumb idea. She might think he's treating her like a little kid, and take offense. In the end he unwraps the sheep from its green tissue paper and stands it on his living-room mantelpiece, where it leans wearily to one side and gives him a sad reproachful stare.

THIRTEEN

First thing next morning, Cal texts Lena. **Hi, Cal Hooper here. Wondering if I might be able to come see how that pup's doing sometime today. No problem if that's not convenient. Thanks.**
The clouds opened up during the night. Even in his sleep, Cal heard the heavy unceasing drum of rain on his roof; it drilled its way through his dreams, which seemed important at the time, although he can't now remember them. He eats breakfast watching it streak past the window, dense enough to blur the fields beyond.

He's doing the dishes when Lena texts him back. **I'm in all morning till half twelve. Pup is twice the size.**

Given the weather, Cal takes the car. The windshield mottles with big splatters too fast for the wipers to keep up, and his tires send fans of muddy water spraying from potholes. The smell of the fields comes through the cracked car window, fresh with wet grass and fertile with cow dung. The mountains are invisible; beyond the fields there's only gray, cloud blending into mist. The herd animals stand still, huddled together, with their heads down.

"You found the place again," Lena says, when she opens the door. "Fair play to you."

"I'm getting the hang of the area," Cal says. He stoops to pat Nellie, who, delighted to see him, is wagging her whole hind end. "Little by little."

He expects Lena to put on a jacket and come out, but instead she holds the door open for him. He scrapes his boots on the mat and follows her down the hall.

Lena's kitchen is big and warm, made up of things that have seen plenty of use but are solid enough that they've held up: gray stone floor tiles worn smooth in spots, wooden cabinets painted a chipped butter-yellow, a long farmhouse table that could be decades old or centuries. The lights are on against the dark day. The room is clean but not neat: there's a tumble of books and newspapers spread across the table, and piles of ironing waiting to be put away on two of the chairs. The place makes it clear that whoever lives there has only themselves to please.

Mewling and rustling noises come from a big cardboard box tucked in a corner. "There they are," Lena says.

"They moved indoors in the end, huh?" Cal says. The mama dog lifts her head and lets out a low rumble, deep in her chest. He turns away and fusses over Nellie, who's brought him a chewed sneaker.

"That bit of frost the other night did it," Lena says. She kneels down and cups the mama dog's jaw to calm her. "Midnight, she came scratching at the door with a pup in her mouth, wanting to bring them all into the warm. They'll have to go out again once they start running about—I'm not cleaning the floor after them. But they'll do grand here for another few days."

Cal ambles across and squats beside Lena. The mama dog doesn't object, although she keeps one wary eye on him. The cardboard box is lined with thick layers of soft towels and newspaper. The pups are clambering over each other, making sounds like a flock of seabirds. Even in these few days, they've grown.

"There's your fella," Lena says. Cal has already spotted the ragged black flag. She reaches into the box, scoops out the pup and passes it to him.

"Hey, little guy," Cal says, holding up the pup, which squirms and paddles its paws furiously. He can feel the change in it, both its weight and its muscle. "He's gotten strong."

"He has. He's still the smallest, but it's not getting in his way. That big black-and-tan bruiser there barges right over the rest, but your fella's having none of it: gives as good as he gets."

"Attaboy," Cal says gently to the pup. It can hold up its head without wobbling now. One of its eyes is beginning to open, showing a droplet of hazy gray-blue.

"Will you have a cup of tea?" Lena asks. "You look like you could be there a while."

"Sure," Cal says. "Thanks." She gets up and goes to the counter.

The pup has started to struggle. Cal settles himself on the floor and brings it in to his chest. It relaxes against his warmth and his heartbeat, turning soft and heavy, nuzzling a little. He runs one of its ears between his fingers. At the counter, Lena moves about, filling the electric kettle and taking mugs out of a cabinet. The room smells of toast, ironing and wet dog.

Cal figures Noreen is bound to have every kind of cardboard box in the land. He could get one the right size and line it with old shirts, so his smell would be a comfort to the pup. He could put it right beside his mattress, where he could keep one hand on the pup during the night, just till it settles in and gets used to doing without its mama. The thought hits him powerfully. Even in imagination, it changes his sense of his house.

"I was expecting I'd be mobbed with children looking to pet them," Lena says, over the building hiss of the kettle. "I remember doing that when we were little, the whole lot of us running down to anyone that had puppies or kittens. But there's only been a few."

"The rest of them too deep in their screens?"

Lena shakes her head. "There's no rest of them. Like we were talking about before. It's not just this generation that headed for the towns. Ever since they started being allowed to do good jobs, the girls go. The lads stay if there's land being left to them, but most people round here don't leave land to girls. So they head off."

"You can't blame them for that," Cal says, thinking of Caroline. The pup is starting to teethe. He shoves at Cal's finger with both tiny forepaws, finally manages to get a corner of it into his mouth, and does his best to gum it to death.

"I don't. I'd've done the same if I hadn't fallen in love with Sean. But it means the lads have no one to marry. And now we've no children coming to see these, and a load of aul' bachelors up on the farms."

"That's tough on the area," Cal says.

The kettle bubbles and clicks off, and Lena pours the tea. "More ways than one," she says. "Men with no children get to feeling unsafe, when they get older. The world's changing and they've no young people to show them it's grand, so they feel like they're being attacked. Like they need to be ready for a fight the whole time."

"Having kids can do the same thing," Cal says. "Make you feel like you need to fight things."

Lena glances over at him, as she drops tea bags into the trash can, but she doesn't ask. "That's different. If you've kids, you're always looking out into the world to see if anything needs fighting, because that's where they're headed; you're not barricading yourself indoors and listening for the Indians to attack. It's not good for a place, having too many aul' bachelors out on their land with no one to talk to, feeling like they need to defend their territory, even though they're not sure from what. D'you take milk?"

"Nope. Just the way it comes."

She takes milk from the fridge for herself. Cal likes the way she moves around the kitchen, efficient but not rushed, at ease with the place. He considers what it would be like to live your life in a place where your personal decisions, whether to get married or to have kids or to move away, alter the entire townland. Outside the windows, the rain is still coming down thick as ever.

"So what'll happen when all the bachelors die off?" he asks. "Who'll take over the farms?"

"Nephews or cousins, some of them. God knows about the rest."

She brings the mugs of tea over to Cal on the floor and sits down, with her back against the wall and her knees up. One of the pups is scrabbling at the edge of the box. She scoops it into her lap. "I like them this age," she says. "I can come and have a cuddle whenever I fancy one, and then put them back when I've had enough. Another week or two and they won't stay put for it; they'll be getting under my feet instead."

"I like 'em this way," Cal says, "but I like 'em a little bit bigger, too. When they get to playing with you."

"They're always needing something then. Even if it's just an eye out so you don't step on them." She holds her tea out to the side, away from her pup, which is trying to clamber up her knees. "Once they're out of the basket, I can't wait for them to get big enough to have a bit of sense. That's why I got a half-grown dog and not a pup. And now look at me."

"You find homes for the rest?"

"Two. Noreen'll take the others, if no one else does. She says she won't, but she will."

"Your sister's a good woman," Cal says.

"She is. She drives me mental sometimes, but the world wouldn't get far without the likes of her." She smiles. "I do make fun of her sometimes because her youngest, Cliona, she's exactly the same as her mam, but the truth is I'm glad of it. Without someone to take over Ardnakelty when Noreen gets old, the place'd fall apart."

"Cliona the one that's around ten or eleven?" Cal asks. "Red hair?"

"That's the one."

"She was helping out one time I went into the store. She told me I was buying the wrong dish soap, it'd dry out my hands and wouldn't get my dishes shiny, and she went up that ladder to fetch me the one she recommends. Then she asked me why I moved here and why I'm not married."

Lena laughs. "There you go. We're in safe hands."

Cal shifts so he can hold the pup one-handed and drink his tea, which is strong and good. He says, "I've been asking around about Brendan Reddy."

"I know, yeah," Lena says. Her puppy, exhausted by its efforts, has collapsed on her lap. She tickles the tiny pads of one paw. "Why?"

"I met your old friend Sheila. She's pretty cut up about her boy going off."

Lena shoots him an amused look. "Knight in shining armor?"

"Just saw a question that needed answering," Cal says. "My neighbor Mart, he thinks I'm bored, looking for something to occupy my mind. He might be right."

Lena blows on her tea and regards him across the mug, still with that wry quirk to one corner of her mouth. "How're you getting on with it?"

"Not too good," Cal says. "I've heard plenty about Brendan, but no one wants to talk about where he might have gone, or why."

"Maybe they don't know."

"I've talked to his mama, his two best buddies, and his girlfriend. Not one of them had anything to say. If they don't know, who would?"

"Maybe no one knows."

"Well," Cal says, "I did wonder about that. But then Mart warned me to back off, the other night. He thinks I'm gonna get myself in trouble. That sounds to me like someone knows something, or thinks they do."

Lena is still watching him sideways on, as she drinks her tea away from the pup. "Are you one of those people that can't rest easy? If they don't have any trouble in their lives, they go looking for some."

"Not me," Cal says. "What I went looking for

was peace and quiet. I'm taking what came my way. Same as you are."

"These pups are hassle. They're not trouble."

"Well," Cal says, "no one's explained to me how Brendan Reddy might be trouble, either. Who's Mart scared of?"

Lena says, "I didn't think Mart Lavin was ever afraid of anyone."

"Maybe not. But he thinks I should be."

"Then maybe you should."

"I'm contrary by nature," Cal explains. "The more people try to shoo me away from something, the more I dig my heels in. I always was that way, even as a little guy." His puppy has eased its gnawing on his finger; when he looks down he sees that it's fallen asleep, sprawled gracelessly against his chest, in the cup of his palm. "I figure," he says, "if anyone in this townland's gonna give me a straight answer about Brendan Reddy, it'll be you."

Lena leans back against the wall and examines him, drinking her tea and stroking her pup with her free hand. In the end she says, "I don't know what happened to Brendan Reddy."

"But you could take a guess."

"I could, yeah. But I won't."

"You don't strike me as the kind that scares easy," Cal says. "Any more than Mart does."

"I'm not scared."

"Then what?"

"I don't get involved in things." She grins suddenly. "That does people's heads in. There's always someone trying to get me to join the Countrywomen's Association, or the Tidy Towns. Probably if we'd had kids I'da done it: the PTA and sports clubs, and all the rest. But we never did, so I don't have to. Sure, Noreen's involved enough for the two of us."

"That she is," Cal says. "Some people are built that way, and some aren't."

"Tell that to Noreen. She's been that way since the day she was born; it drives her mental that I'm not the same. That's one reason why her and the rest are always trying to matchmake me. They think if I get myself a nice fella who's up to his neck in the townland's business, he'll pull me in as well." Lena gives Cal another grin, frank and mischievous, unembarrassed. "Which kind are you?"

"I enjoy being the kind that doesn't get involved," Cal says. "That suits me down to the ground."

Lena's eyebrows lift a little, but all she says is, "You can do that; no one'll give you hassle. People around here respect a man who keeps to himself. It's just a woman that makes them nervous as cats."

"Well, I'm not asking you to get involved," Cal says. "I'm just asking for your thoughts."

"And I'm not planning on sharing them. You're well able to get your own." She glances up at the clock ticking on the wall. "I've to head in to work. Tell me now, do you want this pup, or did you just want an excuse to ask me about Brendan?"

"Little bit of both."

Lena eases her own pup back into the basket and holds out her hands for Cal's. She says, "So you'll take this fella."

Cal puts the pup gently into her hands, trying not to wake it, and gives it a last stroke along the white blaze on its nose. The pup, still mostly asleep, lifts its face and licks his finger.

He says, "Gimme another week or two. Just to be sure."

Lena looks at him for a moment, unsmiling. Then she says, "Fair enough." She turns away from him and tucks the pup carefully in among the rest.

———

Trey shows up late in the afternoon. The rain has finally worn itself out, so Cal is sitting on his back step, having a beer and watching the rooks. Their day seems to be winding down. Two of them are playing tug-of-war with a twig; another two are taking turns preening each other, lazily, exchanging remarks about what they find. Another one is off under the dripping hedge, burying something and throwing sneaky glances over his shoulder.

The sound of feet in wet grass makes Cal turn. Trey comes tramping around from the front of the house and dumps a packet of little white-frosted cupcakes onto the step. "You need to quit doing that," Cal says. "Noreen's gonna call the cops on you."

"Those aren't from Noreen's," Trey says. He looks tense and skinny again. To Cal, squinting up at him from the step, he also looks a shade taller, like he might be starting his teenage growth spurt. "I knocked."

"Didn't hear you," Cal says. "I was thinking."

"I called round earlier. And yesterday. You weren't in."

"Nope."

"What were you doing? You find out anything?"

Cal finishes the last of his beer and gets up. "First things first," he says, brushing off his rear end, which is damp from the step. "I'm gonna get my gun and we can have another try at those rabbits."

Trey follows him indoors, close on his heels. "I wanta know."

"And I'm gonna tell you. But if we want a chance at the rabbits, we need to get ourselves set up before they come out for their dinner."

After a moment Trey accepts this with a nod. Cal gets his gun out of the safe and fills up his pockets with the other things they might need—bullets, his hunting knife, a bottle of water, a plastic bag—and they head for their spot facing the edge of the wood. The sky is one motionless spread of sulky gray cloud, with streaks of pale-rinsed yellow under the western edge. The grass is heavy with rain, and the earth gives underfoot.

"We're gonna get wet," Cal says. "And muddy."

Trey shrugs.

"OK," Cal says, settling himself on one knee in the

grass. "You remember everything I showed you the other day?"

Trey gives him the moron look and holds out his hands for the gun.

"OK," Cal says, handing it over. "Let's see."

Trey checks the gun, clicks the safety on and loads it, slowly but neatly and methodically, making no mistakes. Then he looks up at Cal.

"Good," Cal says.

Trey keeps looking at him, unblinking. "Rabbits aren't out yet."

"All right," Cal says. He sits himself down in the wet grass, takes the gun from Trey and rests it across his knees. He didn't want to tell Trey that Brendan had some plan till he knew what it was, but nobody appears to have any intention of sharing that information with him, and he needs to get it somehow. "Here's your update. I've talked to a bunch of people. What I'm getting is that Brendan had got pretty frustrated with being poor, so he came up with some plan that he reckoned would fix that. That fits with what you told me about him promising you a bike for your birthday. When's your birthday?"

"Third of May." The kid's eyes are fixed on Cal like he's a preacher about to hand down the Word. It makes Cal edgy. He turns his voice a few notches more casual.

"So he figured the cash would be coming in pretty soon. You got any idea what his plan might've been?"

"He gave grinds sometimes. Coulda been more of those. Exams were coming up."

"I doubt it. He also talked about taking a vacation in Ibiza, and about showing people he was going places. Tutoring a few kids wasn't gonna cover all that. He was thinking bigger."

Trey lifts his shoulders, baffled.

"No ideas?"

The kid shakes his head.

"The other thing I heard," Cal says, "is that your brother was nervous about police, the week before he went missing."

"Bren's not dodgy," Trey says instantly and fiercely, glaring. "Just 'cause he's a Reddy, everyone thinks—"

"I'm not saying he's dodgy, kid," Cal says. "I'm just telling you what I've heard, from people who care about him. Can you think of any reason why he mighta been scared of police?"

"Maybe he had a bitta hash on him. Or a few yokes."

"He was scareder than that. This wasn't some piss-ant little thing he was dealing with. Like I said, your brother was thinking big. And if his big plan was on the up-and-up, then how come no one can tell me what it was?"

"He mighta wanted to surprise people," Trey says, after a moment. "Like, ye all thought I was a waster, fuck you."

"You ever think he was a waster?"

"No!"

"Then why would he need to surprise you?"

Trey shrugs. "Just felt like it, maybe."

"Lemme ask you something," Cal says. "When Brendan was planning out what he wanted to do in college, he tell you about it?"

"Yeah."

"When he was thinking about doing tutoring?"

"Yeah."

"He tell you his plan to get Caroline tickets to some singer for Christmas?"

"Yeah. Hozier. They broke up first, but, so he sold the tickets to Eugene. Why?"

Cal says, "So Brendan told you his plans, when there was no particular reason he shouldn't."

"Yeah. He did."

"Which means, whatever his big idea was, there was a reason why you shouldn't know about it."

Trey is silent. Cal is quiet too, leaving him to turn that over and fit it into his mind. At the edge of the woods, the branches hang heavy with leftover rain. Above them, swallows arc tiny and black against the cloud, sending down their high twittering.

After a few moments Trey says suddenly and savagely, "I wouldn'ta ratted him out."

"I know that," Cal says. "I bet he did too."

"Then why would he not—"

"He wanted to keep you safe, kid," Cal says gently. "Whatever he was getting into, he knew it could bring trouble. Bad trouble."

Trey goes silent again. He picks threads out of a hole in the knee of his jeans.

"I think we can make a fair guess," Cal says, "that when Brendan left your house that day, acting like he had somewhere important to be, it was connected to his plan some way or other. I'm not taking it as definite, but I'm gonna go ahead and work on that assumption. Either he was skipping town because he got spooked, or else he was going to do something that would move that plan forwards."

The kid is still messing with his jeans, but his head has tilted towards Cal. He's listening.

"He promised you the bike that same afternoon, and a couple days earlier he borrowed a few bucks from Fergal and said he'd pay him back. So it doesn't seem likely he intended to leave for good. He might have been planning on lying low just for a few days, till whatever spooked him had died down, but in that case I'd expect him to take his phone charger, deodorant, coupla changes of clothes. Seeing as all he took with him was his cash, it seems more likely he was headed to buy something, or to give someone money."

Trey says, low and tight, "And they kidnapped him."

"Could be," Cal said. "We're not far enough on to settle on that yet. Something could've gone wrong, maybe, and he had to run. Where would he meet someone? He have anywhere special he liked to go?"

Trey's eyebrows twitch together. "Like a pub?"

"Nah. Somewhere private. You said when he

needed a little privacy, he went up the mountains. Anywhere in particular that you know of?"

"Yeah. One time he said he was going for a walk and I followed him, 'cause I was bored. Only when I found him, he was just sitting there. He gave me a clatter and told me to fuck off 'cause he wanted some privacy. Like that?"

"Sounds about right," Cal says. "Where was he?"

Trey jerks his chin at the mountains. "Aul' cottage. Empty, like."

"How long ago was that?"

"Few years back. But he went there again after. 'Cause I followed him a couple more times, when I was bored again."

For a minute Cal sees the kid trudging up those bare windy hillsides, trailing after the one person in his life worth following. "You look there since he left?"

Trey says, "Looked everywhere."

"Any sign of him?"

"Nah. Bits of aul' rubbish, just." The kid's eyes skid away. The memory is a hard one. He went there hoping he would find either Brendan or something he'd left, a message, and afraid he would find something bad.

Cal says, "Any reason why you didn't tell me about this place?"

Trey gives him the moron stare. "Why would I? It's not where he went."

"Right," Cal says. "I'd like to take a look at it for myself. Could you tell me how to get there?"

"Up past our place maybe a mile. Then off the road, up the mountain a bit. Through some trees."

"Uh-huh. You gonna send out a search party when I'm not back in a few days?"

"I know the way. I could bring you there." The kid is up off his knee, halfway to a runner's stance, like one word from Cal and he'll shoot right off.

"I'd rather the two of us didn't get spotted wandering around together," Cal says. "Specially not round there."

Trey's face is lit up fiercely. "I'll go on my own. No one'll spot me. Lend me your phone, I'll take photos, bring them back to you."

"No," Cal says, more sharply than he intends. "You stay away from that cottage. You hear me?"

"Why?"

"In case, is why. Did you hear me?"

"I'm not gonna get kidnapped. I'm not thick."

"Good for you. You stay away from it anyway."

"I wanta **do** something."

"That's what you got me into this for. To do things. So let me do them."

The kid is opening his mouth to argue. Cal says, "You wanna do something useful, get us dinner." He puts the rifle into Trey's hands and nods towards the edge of the wood. The rabbits have come out to feed.

After a second of indecision, Trey drops the argument. He eases himself slowly into position, settles the rifle against his shoulder and squints down the sight. "Take your time," Cal says. "We're in no hurry."

They wait and watch. The rabbits are feeling frisky; a few half-grown ones chase each other through the grass, springing high, in the long slants of gold light slipping under the cloud. P.J. is singing to his sheep as he looks them over: scraps of some plaintive old ballad, too fragmented to catch, drift across the fields.

"That big guy there," Cal says softly. One rabbit is turned broadside on to them, working away at a clump of white-flowered weed. Trey shifts the rifle a fraction, lining up his sights. Cal hears the long whisper of his breath, and then the gun's roar.

The rabbits whirl and streak for cover, and a high screaming starts. It sounds like a child being tortured.

Trey swings round to Cal, his mouth opening and nothing coming out.

"You got it," Cal says, standing up and taking the gun from Trey. "We'll have to finish it off."

He pulls his hunting knife out of his pocket on his way across the field. Trey half-runs to keep up. His eyes are flaring with pure wild panic at the runaway momentum of what he's set in motion. He says, "We could try to fix him."

"It's in bad shape, kid," Cal says gently. "We need to stop it suffering. I'll do it."

"No," Trey says. He's white. "I shot him."

One of the rabbit's forelegs has been taken half off and is bleeding in fast bright-red spurts. It lies on its side, jerking, with its back arched; its eyes are white-ringed and its mouth is open, lips pulled back, showing strong teeth and a bloody foam. Its screaming fills up the air.

"You sure?" Cal says.

"Yeah," Trey says tightly, and holds out his hand for the knife.

"Back of the neck," Cal says. "Right here. You need to cut through the spine."

Trey positions the knife. His mouth is set like he's stopping himself from throwing up. He takes a breath and lets it out long, like he's about to fire the rifle. It eases the shake in his hand. He comes down hard on the knife, with his weight behind it, and the screaming stops. The rabbit's head lolls.

"OK," Cal says. He digs in his pocket for the plastic bag, so he can get the rabbit out of the kid's sight. "It's done now. You did good." He picks up the rabbit by the ears and maneuvers it into the bag.

Trey wipes the hunting knife on the grass and gives it back to Cal. He's still breathing hard, but the panic has gone out of his eyes, and his face is starting to get its color back. It was the suffering he couldn't take.

"Gimme your hands," Cal says, finding his water bottle.

Trey looks down at his hands. They're crisscrossed with fine lines of blood droplets, from the arterial spray.

"Come here," Cal says. He pours water over Trey's

hands, while Trey rubs at the blood, till it's run off into the grass. "That'll do for now. You can scrub up good and hard once we're done with the messy part."

Trey dries off his hands on his jeans. He turns his face up to Cal, still a little stunned, like he needs to be told what to do next.

"Here you go," Cal says, holding out the plastic bag. "It's your kill."

Trey looks down at the bag, and it sinks in. "Hah!" he says, a sound halfway between a burst of breath and a triumphant crack of laughter. "I did it!"

"You did, all right," Cal says, grinning down at him. He feels an impulse to clap the kid on the shoulder. "Come on," he says instead, turning towards the house. Its wall is lit to pale gold by the setting sun, so that it stands square-set and radiant against the gray sky. "Let's take it home."

———

They dress the rabbit on Cal's kitchen counter. He shows Trey how to take off the feet, make a slit across the rabbit's back and hook his fingers under the skin to pull it off, twisting the head away with it; then how to cut open the belly, free the organs and coax them out. He's pleased to find the skill coming back to him so smoothly, after all these years. His mind hardly remembers what to do, but his hands still know.

Trey watches intently and follows Cal's instructions,

with the same methodical neatness that he brought to the desk and to the gun, as Cal shows him how to pinch out the urine sac cleanly and how to check the liver for disease spots. Together they strip off silverskin and sinew and the mangled front leg, then cut away the three good legs, the belly and the loin. "There's your eating meat," Cal says. "Next time I'll make stock from the rest, but today we're gonna put a little bit of this back where we got it." It's what he and his granddaddy did with his first squirrel, way back when: gave the parts they didn't need back to the wild. It seems like the right thing to do with a first kill.

They take the offal down to the back of the garden and leave it on the stump, for the rooks or the foxes or whoever gets to it first. Cal whistles up to the rooks, but they're settling into their tree and ignore him, except for a halfhearted rude remark or two.

"Well, we did offer," he says. "You hungry? Or that take the edge off your appetite?"

"Starving," Trey says promptly.

"Good," Cal says, glancing up at the sky. The strip of pale yellow has dimmed into a clear green. "I was planning on stew, but that takes a while. We'll just fry it up." He wants Trey home before it gets too late. "You like garlic?"

"I guess."

It occurs to Cal, looking at his blank face, that he may not know. "Let's find out," he says. "You cook?"

Trey shrugs. "Sometimes. Sorta."

"OK," Cal says. "You're gonna cook today."

They scrub up, and Cal puts on some Waylon Jennings to help them work. Trey grins up at him.

"What?"

"Aul'-fella music."

"OK, DJ Cool. What do you listen to?"

"Nothing you've heard of."

"Smartass," Cal says, getting ingredients out of the little kitchen cupboard with the busted hinge. "Lemme guess. Opera."

Trey snorts.

"One Direction."

That gets him an outraged stare that makes him grin. "Well, thank the Lord for small mercies. Quit complaining and listen. Maybe it'll teach you to appreciate good music." Trey rolls his eyes. Cal turns up the volume another notch.

He shows Trey how to shake the chunks of meat in a plastic bag of flour, salt and pepper, and then fry them up in oil, with strips of bell pepper and onion and some garlic Cal picked up in town. "If I had tomatoes and mushrooms," he says, "we could throw those in too, but Noreen's tomatoes weren't looking too perky this week. This'll do fine. We'll have it with rice." He microwaves packet rice while Trey, frowning with concentration, turns the meat frying in the pan. The kitchen is warm, condensation veiling the window, and starting to smell good. For a minute Cal thinks of the dusk thickening outside that window, and about the fear in Sheila's eyes and Caroline's, but he puts them out of his mind.

Cal is waiting for Trey to bring up Brendan again, or the cottage, but he doesn't. For a while Cal is wary of this; he's inclined to take it as a sign that the kid is making plans he's not sharing. Then he happens to glance over, checking how the rabbit is doing. The kid is poking at the frying pan and nodding his head along to "I Ain't Living Long Like This," his lips pursed in a goofy half whistle, his cheeks rosy from the heat of the stove. He looks several years younger than he is, and completely at ease. It comes to Cal that, for once, the kid's mind isn't taken up by worrying about Brendan. He's rewarded himself for the rabbit by allowing himself to put that away, just for a little while.

Trey looks askance at his plate when they sit down at the table, but after one bite his doubts disappear. He shovels in the food like he hasn't eaten in weeks. His face is practically touching the plate.

"Turns out you like garlic, huh?" Cal asks, grinning.

The kid nods, over another big forkful.

"This dinner's down to you," Cal says. "Start to finish. No farmer, no butcher, no factory, no Noreen: just you. How's that feel?"

Trey is smiling a particular small, private smile that Cal has come to realize means he's specially happy. "Not bad," he says.

"If I had my way," Cal says, "I'd do this for every

piece of meat I ever ate. It's harder and messier than buying a hamburger, but that seems fitting. Eating a creature shouldn't be a light thing."

Trey nods. They eat without talking for a while. Outside the window, twilight is setting in and the cloud has started to break up, leaving patches of sky a luminous lavender-blue, edged by the lacy black silhouette of the tree line. Somewhere far away, a fox barks sharply.

"You could live up the mountains," Trey says. He has clearly been thinking this over. "If you got good at it. Never come down again."

"You can't shoot jeans," Cal points out. "Or sneakers. Unless you want to sew your clothes out of hides, you'd have to come down sometimes."

"Once a year. Stock up."

"You could, I guess," Cal says. "I'd get lonesome, though. I like having someone to talk to, now and again."

The kid, scraping his plate, throws him a glance that says they differ widely on this. "Nah," he says.

Cal gets up to fix Trey a second helping. From the stove he says, "You wanna bring one of your friends with us, next time we go hunting?"

The last thing he wants is more random kids hanging around his house, but he feels pretty safe; he just wants to confirm a suspicion he has. Sure enough, Trey stares at him like he just suggested inviting a buffalo to dinner, and shakes his head.

"Your call," Cal says. "You got friends, though, right?"

"Huh?"

"Friends. Buddies. **Compañeros.** People you hang out with."

"I did have. I'll get back with them sometime."

Cal puts Trey's plate in front of him and goes back to his own dinner. "What happened?"

"They're not allowed hang around with me any more. They don't care, but; they would anyway. I just . . ." He twitches one shoulder, sawing at a chunk of rabbit. "Not now."

An edge of tension has slid back into his body. Cal says, "How come they're not allowed to hang out with you?"

"We did some stuff together," Trey explains through a mouthful, "like we robbed a coupla bottles of cider and got drunk. Stuff like that. There was the four of us in it—the cider wasn't my idea, even. But their parents reckoned it was all my fault 'cause I'm the bad one."

"You don't seem like a bad kid to me," Cal says, even though Trey doesn't seem particularly upset about it. "Who says you are?"

Trey shrugs. "Everyone."

"Like who?"

"Noreen. Teachers."

"What'd you do that's so bad?"

Trey twists one corner of his mouth, implying a surfeit of examples. Cal says, "Pick one."

"Teacher was giving me hassle today. For not paying attention. I told her I don't give a shite."

"Well, that's not **bad**," Cal says. "It's unmannerly, and you shouldn'ta done it. But it's not a question of morals."

The kid is giving him that look again. "That's not manners. Manners is like chew with your mouth closed."

"Nah. That's just etiquette."

"What's the difference?"

"Etiquette is the stuff you gotta do just 'cause that's how everyone does it. Like holding your fork in your left hand, or saying 'Bless you' if someone sneezes. Manners is treating people with respect."

"I don't always," Trey says.

"Well, there you go," Cal says. "Maybe it's your manners that need work. You could do with keeping your mouth shut when you chew, too."

Trey ignores that. "Then what's a question of morals, so?"

Cal finds himself uncomfortable with this conversation. It brings back things that put a bad taste in his mouth. Over the last few years it's been brought home to him that the boundaries between morals, manners and etiquette, which have always seemed crystal-clear to him, may not look the same to everyone else. He hears talk about the immorality of young people nowadays, but it seems to him that Alyssa and Ben and their friends spend plenty of their time concentrating on right and wrong. The thing is that many of their most passionate moral stances, as far as Cal can see, have to do with what words you should and shouldn't use for people, based on what problems they have, what race they are, or who they like to sleep with. While Cal agrees that you should call people whatever they prefer to be called, he considers this to be a question of basic manners, not of morals. This outraged Ben enough that he stormed out of Cal and Donna's house in the middle of Thanksgiving dessert, with Alyssa in tears running after him, and it took him an hour to cool down enough to come back in.

In Cal's view, morals involve something more than terminology. Ben damn near lost his mind over the importance of using the proper terms for people in wheelchairs, and he clearly felt pretty proud of himself for doing that, but he didn't mention ever doing anything useful for one single person in one single wheelchair, and Cal would bet a year's pension that the little twerp would have brought it up if he had. And on top of that, the right terms change every few years, so that someone who thinks like Ben has to be always listening for other people to tell him what's moral and immoral now. It seems to Cal that this isn't how a man, or a woman either, goes about having a sense of right and wrong.

He tried putting it down to him getting middle-aged and grumpy about young people these days, but then the department went the same way. They brought in a mandatory sensitivity training session— which was fine by Cal, given the way some of the guys treated, for example, witnesses from bad hoods and rape victims, except the session turned out to be all about what words they were and weren't allowed to use; nothing about what they were doing, underneath all the words, and how they could do it better. Everyone was always talking about talking, and the most moral person was the one who yelled at the most other people for doing the talking all wrong.

He's afraid to answer Trey, in case he leads him wrong and gets him into all kinds of trouble, but no one else is going to do it. "Morals," he says in the end, "is the stuff that doesn't change. The stuff you do no matter what other people do. Like, if someone's an asshole to you, you might not be mannerly to him; you might tell him to go fuck himself, or even punch him in the face. But if you see him trapped in a burning car, you're still gonna open the door and pull him out. However much of an asshole he is. That's your morals."

Trey chews and considers this. "What if he was a psycho killer?"

"Then maybe I wouldn't help him up if he fell down and broke his leg. Still wouldn't leave him in that car, though."

Trey thinks that over some more. "I might," he says. "Depending."

"Well," Cal says, "I got my code."

"You don't ever break it?"

"If you don't have your code," Cal says, "you've got nothing to hold you down. You just drift any way things blow you."

"What's your code?"

"Kid," Cal says, with a sudden surge of weariness, "you don't want to listen to me about this stuff."

"How come?"

"You don't want to listen to anyone about this stuff. You gotta come up with your own code."

"But what's yours?"

"I just try to do right by people," Cal says. "Is all."

Trey is silent, but Cal can feel more questions shaping themselves in his mind. He says, "Eat your dinner."

Trey shrugs and does as he's told. When he finishes his second helping, he sets down his fork and knife, leans back in his chair with his hands on his belly and gives a satisfied sigh. "Stuffed," he says.

Cal hates to bring the kid's mind back to Brendan, but if he doesn't provide a plan for the next step, Trey is liable to come up with one of his own. After he clears the table, he finds a pen and a fresh page in his notebook, and puts them in front of Trey. "Draw me a map," he says. "How to get to the cottage where Brendan hung out."

The kid genuinely tries, but Cal can tell within a minute that it's hopeless. All the landmarks are shit like BIG GORSE BUSH and WALL THAT BENDS LEFT. "Forget it," he says in the end. "You're gonna have to take me there."

"Now?" The kid is half off his seat.

"No, not now. We'll go tomorrow. Up to here"— Cal taps the map at a bend in the mountain road—"I can follow what you're driving at. I'll meet you here. Three-thirty."

"Earlier. Morning time."

"Nope," Cal says. "You got school. Which means right now you need to go home and get your home-work done." He stands up and takes the notebook away, ignoring the look that says Trey will do no such thing. "Take one of those cupcakes with you, for your dessert."

On his way out the door Trey turns, unexpect-edly, to give Cal a great big grin over his shoulder, through the half of the cupcake that's already stuffed in his mouth. Cal grins back. He wants to tell the kid to be careful out there, but he knows it wouldn't do any good.

FOURTEEN

During the night, something happens. It reaches Cal through his sleep, a snag somewhere in the night's established rhythms, a disturbance. As he comes awake he hears, away across the fields, a hard savage howl of pain or rage or both.

He goes to the window, cracks it open and looks out. The cloud has cleared some, but the moon is slim and he can see very little except different densities and textures of darkness. The night is cold and windless. The howl has stopped, but there's still movement, far off and ragged, ruffling the edge of his hearing.

He waits. After a minute or two, the sounds grow and sharpen, and his eyes pick out a shape among the grass in his back field. It's loping towards the road at a good pace but with an odd ungainly gait, like it's injured. It could be a big animal, or a hunched-over human being.

When it moves out of his sight line, Cal pulls on his jeans, loads his rifle and goes to his back door. He switches lights on as he goes. Mart has a shotgun, presumably P.J. does too, and the other thing might have or be anything. Cal isn't aiming to take anyone by surprise.

He sweeps the fields with his flashlight, but it's not strong enough to make much of a dent in this dark. The hunched shape is nowhere to be seen.

"I'm armed!" he shouts. His voice spreads out a long way. "Come out with your hands where I can see 'em."

For a moment there's sharp silence. Then a cheery voice yells back, from somewhere off on P.J.'s land, "Don't shoot! I surrender!"

A narrow beam of light flicks on and bobs across the fields, getting closer. Cal stays where he is, keeping the rifle pointed down, until a figure stumps into the pale spill of light from the windows and lifts an arm in a wave. It's Mart.

Cal goes to meet him in the back field, making a few more sweeps with his flashlight on the way. "Holy God, Sunny Jim, put that away," Mart says, nodding at Cal's rifle. His face is alive with excitement and his eyes glitter like he's drunk, although Cal can tell he's stone-cold sober. He's holding his flashlight in one hand and a hurling stick in the other. "D'you know what you sounded like there? You sounded like something off that **Cops** show. You'd make a great aul' Garda, so you would. Are you going to tell me to get down on the ground?"

"What's going on?" Cal says. He clicks the safety

on, but keeps his finger ready. Whatever that creature was, it went somewhere.

"I was right about that yoke coming after P.J.'s sheep
next, is what's going on. And there was you doubting
me. You'll know better next time, won't you?"

"What was it?"

"Ah," Mart says ruefully, "that's the only hitch. I
didn't get a good look. I was otherwise occupied, you
might say."

"Did you get it?" Cal asks, thinking of the creature's lopsided run.

"I hit it a coupla good skelps, all right," Mart says
with glee, slapping his hurling stick against his leg.
"There I was, sitting up in your bitta woods, thinking I was outa luck again. I'll be honest with you, I
was almost nodding off there. Only then I heard a
bit of a kerfuffle down among P.J.'s sheep. I couldn't
see a feckin' thing in this dark, but I snuck down
there nice and quiet, and sure enough, there was a
sheep down, and something on it. So busy it didn't
even hear me coming. I caught it a great aul' clatter,
and it let a howl out of it like a banshee. Did you
hear that?"

"That's what woke me up," Cal says.

"I was aiming to knock it out, but I must not have
got it right. I took it by surprise, though, anyhow. I
got in another skelp before it worked out what was
happening." He hefts the stick, savoring the weight
of it in his hand. "I was afraid I mighta lost the

knack with the hurl, after all these years, but it's like riding a bike: it never leaves you. If I'da been able to see that creature, I'd say I'da took the head clean off it. Sent it flying halfway to your door."

"It do anything to you?"

"Didn't even try," Mart says, with contempt. "Maiming sheep is all it's fit for; the minute it was up against something that'd fight back, it turned tail and ran. I went after it, but I have to face facts, I'm no T. J. Hooker. All I did was banjax my back."

"Shoulda thrown the stick at it," Cal says.

"Last I saw, it was heading your way." Mart looks up at Cal, his face creased into a guileless squint. "You didn't happen to get a good look at it, did you?"

"It didn't come close enough," Cal says. Something about Mart's look bothers him. "It was pretty big, is all I saw. Coulda been a dog, maybe."

"D'you know what it looked like to me?" Mart says, pointing his stick at Cal. "If I didn't know better, I'da thought it was a cat. Not a little pussycat, like. One of them mountain lions."

The way it moved didn't look like a cat to Cal. He says, "Main thing I noticed was it looked like it was limping. You musta got it pretty good."

"I'll get it better if it comes back," Mart says grimly. "It won't, but. It's had its fill."

"How come you decided on that?" Cal asks, nodding at the hurling stick. "Me, I'da brought my gun."

Mart giggles at him. "Barty's right about you

Yanks. Ye'd bring your guns to mass, so ye would. What would I want a gun for, at all? I'm out here trying to save P.J.'s sheep, not shoot the poor feckers because I can't see a yard in this dark. This yoke here did the job grand." He examines the hurling stick with satisfaction. There's a wide dark smear near the tip that could be mud, or blood. Mart spits on it and wipes it on his pants.

"Guess it did," Cal says. "How's the sheep?"

"Dead. The throat's taken out of it." Mart arches his back experimentally. "I'd better go give P.J. the news, before this stiffens up on me. You go back to your bed, now. The excitement's over for tonight."

"Glad all that waiting paid off," Cal says. "Give P.J. my condolences on his sheep."

Mart tips his cap and heads off, and Cal turns back towards his house. Inside the garden gate, he switches off his flashlight and moves into the thick dark under the rooks' oak tree.

The night is so still that the patches of stars and cloud don't even shift in the sky, and the cold has an edge that cuts through the sweatshirt Cal has taken to wearing in bed. After a few minutes, a light goes on in P.J.'s house. A minute after that, two flashlight beams bob and crisscross their way across the fields, stop and focus in on something on the ground. Cal hears or imagines he hears, very faintly, the low, anger-filled rhythms of their discussion, and the restless jostling of the unsettled sheep. Then the two beams work their way back to P.J.'s place, more slowly. Mart and P.J. are dragging the dead sheep, a leg each.

Cal stays where he is and watches the land. A few late moths whirl in the light from his windows. Nothing much else is moving, only the usual small things in the hedges and the occasional call from a nightjar or a hunting owl, but he waits and watches anyway, just in case. Whatever Mart met, it might have taken cover when Cal came out, and it might be patient.

The unease that started with Mart's innocent in-quiring look has grown and worked its way to the surface. Mart knew that, out of all the sheep in Ardnakelty, this creature would go after P.J.'s.

The more Cal thinks about it, the less he likes that hurling stick. Only a fool would risk getting up close and personal with something that rips the soft parts out of sheep, when he has a perfectly good shotgun that would let him keep a safe distance. Mart is no fool. The only reason he would have left his gun at home was if he was expecting to meet something he wouldn't shoot. Mart was sitting up in that wood waiting for a human being.

Cal finds himself afraid. He feels the fear first, and understands it only gradually. It has to do with the kid, and the way people around here treat him and his family like shit, and the way his brother leaving threw him into a savage, desperate tailspin. It has to do with the matter-of-fact, unflinching neatness—which seemed like a good quality at the time—with which he killed and butchered that rabbit. He couldn't handle causing suffering, but then the sheep didn't suffer, or only for a second or two.

Cal thinks, **That's a good kid. He wouldn't do that.** But he knows that no one has ever made it clear to Trey what, exactly, good and bad mean, or the importance of finding the line between them and staying on the right side.

After a while, a lone flashlight beam makes its way up the fields from P.J.'s place to Mart's. A while after that P.J.'s lights go out, and finally Mart's do too. The countryside is dark.

Cal heads for home. On his way up the garden he shines his flashlight over at the stump. Something has taken away the remains of the rabbit, clean as a whistle, not a scrap left behind.

———

When Cal gets to the meeting point, at three-twenty and by a long rambling route, Trey isn't there. The mountainside is so deserted that he feels like an intruder. Along the way grazing sheep turned their heads to stare at him, and he passed fragments of lichen-mottled field walls; but up here the only signs of human existence are the dirt track he's been following, with weeds growing tall along the middle, and the occasional dark scar in the heather where someone was cutting turf sometime.

Last night's unease builds higher. The only way
the kid would miss this is if he was hurt too badly
to come.

Cal turns in a circle, scanning the mountain. The
wind combs the heather and gorse with a low cease-
less rustle. Its smell has a sweetness almost too cold
to catch. The sky is a fine-grained gray, and from
somewhere in its heights a bird sends down a pure
wild whistling.

When he turns back, the kid has materialized on
the road above him, like he was there all along.

"You're late," Cal says.

"Doing my homework," Trey says, with the edge
of a sassy grin.

"Sure you were," Cal says. He can't see any bruises
or gashes. "You get home OK last night?"

Trey gives him a suspicious look, like this is a
weird question. "Yeah."

"I heard noises, later on. Like an animal got
hurt, maybe."

The kid shrugs, implying that this is both possible
and not his problem, and turns to head up the road.
Cal watches him walk. His long, springy lope is the
same as ever; he's not favoring anything, or holding
himself like anything hurts.

Some of the worry goes out of Cal, but a residue
stays. He's more or less satisfied that the kid isn't the
one hurting sheep, but this no longer seems like the
central point, or at least not the only one. It's been

brought home to him that he's not clear, or anything like clear, on what Trey is and isn't capable of.

Beyond the bend Trey strikes off the path, upwards into the heather. "Mind yourself," he says over his shoulder. "Boggy bits."

Cal watches where Trey puts his feet and tries to match him, feeling the ground sink under him here and there. The kid knows this terrain better, and suits it better, than Cal does. "Shit," he says, as the bog sucks at his boot.

"You haveta go faster," Trey says, over his shoulder. "Don't give it a chance to get holda you."

"This is as fast as I go. Not all of us are built like jackrabbits."

"Moose, more like."

"You remember what I told you about manners?" Cal demands. Trey snorts and keeps moving.

They pass between gorse bushes, around old turf-cutting scars, under a sheer cliffside where tufts of grass sprout in the cracks between boulders. Cal keeps an eye out for watchers, but nothing moves on the mountainside, except heather stirring in the wind. This isn't a place anyone would stumble across by accident. Whatever Brendan was doing up here, he wanted to do it undisturbed.

Trey takes them up a slope steep enough to use up Cal's breath, and plunges into a thick plantation of spruces. The trees are tall and neatly spaced, and the ground is padded with years' worth of needles. The wind doesn't reach them here, but it rakes the tree-tops with an unceasing restless mutter. Cal doesn't like the stark contrasts in this terrain. They have the same feel as the weather, of an unpredictability deliberately calculated to keep you one step behind.

"There," Trey says, pointing, as they step out of the trees.

Brendan's hideout is below them, sheltered from the worst of the winds in a slight dip, with its back up against the mountainside. It isn't what Cal expected. He was picturing one of those clusters of raggedy stone-wall scraps with maybe a piece of roof here and there, left to nature's slow devices for generations. This is a squat white cottage no older than his own, and in much the same shape as his own was when he arrived. Its door and window frames even have most of their red paint left.

Cal finds this more unsettling than his original image. A derelict two-hundred-year-old house fits into the ways of nature: things have their time and then fall apart. For a relatively new and usable house to be abandoned seems to imply some unnatural event, sharp-edged and final as a guillotine. The place has a look he doesn't like.

"Wait," he says, putting out a hand to block Trey as he starts towards it.

"Why?"

"Just give it a minute. Let's be sure no one else had the same idea as your brother."

"That's why Bren came here. 'Cause no one else ever—"

"Just wait," Cal says. He moves back, nice and easy, to stand among the spruce trees. Trey rolls his eyes impatiently, but he follows.

Nothing comes from the cottage, neither movement nor sound. The weeds growing high against its walls have been trampled away on the path to the front door. Its windows are mostly broken out and plenty of its roof slates are missing, but someone has been trying to remedy this, not long ago: a tarp has been tacked down over one patch of roof, and there's plywood in the windows.

"You said you've been in there since Brendan went," Cal says. "Right?"

"Yeah. Coupla days after."

That means they're unlikely to walk in on his dead body. A pair of swifts skim in and out under the eaves, unhurried, practicing their acrobatics in the cool air. "Looks OK," Cal says, at last. "Let's go take a look."

Down in the dip, sound is condensed in a way that comes as startling after the open space above. Their steps are sharp and loud on the grit of the path. The swifts set up an angry chittering and dive for cover.

The door has a big splintered dent near the bottom, where someone has kicked it in with a nice combination of precision and dedication. Not too long ago: the broken wood is only starting to discolor. A steel hasp, its padlock still attached, hangs loose from its staple; there are holes in the door where it was wrenched free. Cal pulls his jacket sleeve down over his hand before he pushes the door open.

"Was it like this last time you were here?"

"Like what?"

"Kicked in. Lock broken out."

"Yeah. Just walked in." Trey is right at Cal's heel, like a barely trained hunting dog pulsing with impatience.

Inside, nothing is moving. There's a little fall of weak light somewhere in the back room, but apart from that, the plywood makes the house too dark to see. Cal finds his pocket flashlight and sweeps it around.

The front half of the house is one mid-sized room, with no one in it. The next thing Cal notices is that it's clean. The first time he walked into his own place, it was layered up with cobwebs, dust, mold, dead bugs, dead mice, forms of gunge he couldn't even identify. This has bare floorboards with only a thin coating of dust. The wallpaper, columns of fancy pink and gold flowers, is damp-stained, but any peeling pieces have been ripped away.

In one corner is a propane camping stove, brand-new, with a few spare tanks beside it. Under one boarded-up window is a cooler, also brand-new. Along the back wall are a shitty white MDF side-board, not new, a broom and dustpan, a mop and bucket, and a row of big plastic water bottles. There are scuff marks on the floorboards where things have been dragged in and maybe out.

Nothing moves as they step inside. "Wait there," Cal says. He goes swiftly through to the back. Here, in what used to be a kitchen and a bedroom, no one has bothered cleaning. The floors are scattered with fallen plaster and random pieces of dilapidated furniture, and dusty cobwebs hang heavy as lace curtains from the ceiling. The back windows are unboarded, yellow-flowered weeds swaying behind them, but the mountainside presses close enough to block much of the light.

"See?" Trey says, at his shoulder. "No one."

"So we wasted two minutes," Cal says. "Better'n walking into trouble." He heads back into the front room, squats down by the cooler with the kid hanging over his shoulder, and opens it through his sleeve. It's empty. He examines the camping stove, which is set up ready to go but looks like it's never been used. He rocks each of the spare propane tanks on its base: one full, two empty. He moves to the sideboard, pries the doors open by their corners and points his flashlight in there.

Inside the cabinet are three packs of rubber gloves, three bottles of household cleaners, a pile of dirty scrubbing sponges and cleaning cloths, a few Tupperware containers, a big pack of coffee filters, a coiled-up rubber hose, two sets of lab goggles, a pack of lab safety masks, and a stray battery that's rolled into a corner.

Cal's heart zigzags. For a second he can't move. He wanted something that would burn off all the hazy possibilities and show him the solid thing in their midst. Now that he's got it, he finds he doesn't want it one bit.

He had Brendan wrong. He was picturing a wild kid galloping after the first and easiest idea that sprang up in his head, all hopped up on resentment and the prospect of showing everyone they'd underestimated him. But Brendan went about this methodically, systematically, taking his time and setting all his pieces in place. A half-cocked kid in a huff can get himself into plenty of shit. A kid with method is less likely to get himself into shit, but if he does, the shit is a whole lot deeper.

He can feel Trey crouched beside him watching every flicker of his face, catching the instant of stillness. "Huh," he says easily, straightening up. "Here, hold this for me." He hands over the flashlight.

"What for?" Trey asks. He's coiled tight, barely containing his electricity.

Cal finds his phone and switches on the camera. "When you're investigating, you document. You never know."

Trey doesn't move. His eyes are still on Cal's face.

"Start right there," Cal says, nodding to the front door. "Then sweep it round the room, nice and slow."

After a moment, Trey does as he's told without comment. He moves the flashlight evenly while Cal videos the room, then holds it steady for photos of the cooler, the sideboard, the stove, the propane tanks, the water bottles. Then Cal takes videos

of the back rooms, without the flashlight. The unboarded back windows were a good call. If you're
going to do what Brendan Reddy was going to do in
here, you want plenty of ventilation.

The place smells of nothing but damp, rain and
spruce. Brendan never got started. He had most
everything in place, maybe everything, and then
something went wrong.

When they finish up the photos, Cal takes the
flashlight back and walks the front room, keeping
the beam on the floor. "What you looking for?" Trey
asks, hovering.

"Anything I can find," Cal says. "Nothing there,
though." He's looking for bloodstains. He can't see
any, but that doesn't mean they're not there—the
floor's been cleaned not too long ago, although there's
no way to know whether it was before Brendan
went or after. Luminol would still show blood, but
he hasn't got Luminol. "Take a good look round.
Anything different from when you were here last?"

Trey scans every room, taking his time. Finally he
shakes his head.

"OK," Cal says. He puts his phone away. "Let's go
take a look around outside."

Trey nods, hands Cal the flashlight and heads for
the door. Cal has no idea what he's making of all
this. He can't tell whether this is just because the
kid is the way he is, or whether Trey is deliberately
keeping his thoughts to himself.

They walk the overgrown area that used to be the

yard, but there's no convenient stash and no sign of digging. All they find is a midden from the house's inhabited days: a little heap of broken crockery and glass bottles, half buried under years' worth of silted-up dirt and weeds.

Trey finds a stick and beats down nettles. "Knock it off," Cal says.

"How come?"

"I'd rather not tell the world that someone's been here."

Trey glances at him, but says nothing. He throws the stick onto the midden.

Up here has a silence that separates it from the lowlands. Down below, there's always a lavish mix of birds fussing and flirting, sheep and cattle conversing, farmers shouting, but up here the air is empty; nothing but the wind and one small cold call like pebbles being tapped together, over and over again.

They work their way up the sides of the dip, poking into clumps of long grass, going systematically back and forth to make sure they miss nothing. They find a rusted garden hoe with half a handle, and a snarl of barbed wire, also rusty. When they reach the top they crunch through the spruce grove, kicking at piles of fallen needles and squinting up into the branches for caches. A couple of old nests make them look twice.

Cal knew from the start it was hopeless. There's too much space up here for one man and a kid ever to cover. What he needs is a CSI team swarming all over the house, and a K-9 unit combing the mountainside. He feels like the world's biggest fool, out here in a foreign country playing cop with no badge and no gun, and a thirteen-year-old kid and Officer Dennis for backup. He tries to imagine what Donna would say, but the truth is, Donna wouldn't say anything at all; she would give him a stare where sheer incredulity beat out a number of other things for top spot, and then throw up her hands and walk away. Even Donna's extravagant supply of words and noises didn't contain anything to cover this.

"Well," he says, in the end. "I guess we've seen about all there is to see around here." It's time to go. The light is starting to shift, the spruce shadows stretching down the side of the dip towards the house.

Trey looks up at him sharply, inquiring. Cal ignores that and heads deeper into the trees. He's glad to get away from this place.

After a minute or two, he realizes he's walking fast enough that the kid is trotting to keep up. "So," he says, slowing down. "What do you make of that?"

Trey shrugs. He jumps to snap a branch off one of the spruces.

Cal feels a powerful need to have some idea of what's going on in the kid's head. "You know Brendan," he says. "I don't. That house give you any idea what he might've been planning?"

Trey whips the branch against a trunk as they pass. The hiss and smack are compressed by the trees all around. Nothing flaps or scuttles in response.

"When I went there," he says, "after Bren went. I thought maybe he was living there. 'Cause I saw how he'd fixed it up, the roof and all, and the cooker and the cooler. Those didn't use to be there before. I thought maybe he'd got sick of us and moved in there. I waited all night for him to come back. I was gonna ask could I come too." He whips the branch against another trunk, harder this time, but the sound still flattens to insignificance. "I only copped on in the morning: I was fucking thick. There's no mattress or sleeping bag or nothing. He wasn't living there."

This is the longest speech Cal has ever heard the kid make. He's not surprised Trey didn't mention the cottage earlier, not after that long night and that stinging slap of disappointment. "Doesn't look like it," he says.

After a shorter silence, Trey says, glancing up at him sideways, "All that stuff in the sideboard."

Cal waits.

"Cleaning gear. Brendan coulda been meaning to do up the rest of the place. Rent it out, on the QT, like. To hikers, backpackers. Only the people who own the house found out, and they got pissed off. And that's who Bren was going to meet. To sort it. Give them cash."

"Could be," Cal says, ducking under a branch. He can feel the kid watching him.

"And that's who took him."

"You know who owns the place? Who lived there last?"

Trey shakes his head. "But some of them up the mountains, they're rough."

"Well," Cal says. "Looks like I might need to have a look at property registers."

"You're gonna find him," Trey says. "Right?"

Cal says, "I'm aiming to." He doesn't want to find Brendan Reddy any more.

Trey starts to say something else, then checks himself and goes back to whacking tree trunks with his branch. They make their way through the spruces and back down the mountainside in silence.

When they get back onto the path, at the bend where they met up, Cal slows. "Where's Donie McGrath live?" he asks.

Trey is kicking a rock down the path in front of him, but he looks up at that. "What for?"

"I want to talk to him. Where's he live?"

"Just this side of the village. That gray house that's in bits. With the dark blue door."

Cal knows it. People in the village take pride in their homes, keeping their windows clean, their brasses polished and their trim painted. A run-down house means an empty house. Donie's is the exception.

"By himself?"

"Himself and his mam. His dad died. His sisters married away, and I think his brother emigrated." The rock has gone off the path. The kid nudges it out of a clump of heather with his toe. "Donie and his brother, they usedta pick on Bren, back in school. In the end they bet him up bad enough that my mam went in, and Donie's mam hadta as well. She was like, 'My boys would never, they're lovely lads, we're a **decent** family'—even though everyone knew the dad was a drunk and a waster. Thought she was great just 'cause she's from town and her brother's a priest. School didn't give a shite either way, 'cause it was only us." He glances up at Cal. "Now, but, Bren could beat the shite outa that little scut any day. Donie didn't take him."

"I never said he did," Cal says. "I just want to talk to him."

"How come?"

"Because. And I want you to stay away from him. Far away."

"Donie's only an arsewipe," Trey says, with complete scorn.

"OK. Stay away from him anyway."

Trey kicks his rock, hard, into the heather. He gets in front of Cal and stops, blocking the path. His feet are set apart and his chin is out.

"I'm not a fucking **baby.**"

"I know that."

"'Stay away from this, stay away from him, do nothing, you don't need to know—'"

"You wanted me to do this 'cause I know how to do it right. If you can't stay outa my way while I—"

"I wanta talk to Donie. He'll say nothing to a blow-in."

"And you think he'll talk to some kid?"

"He will, yeah. Why not? He thinks the same as you: I'm a baby. He can say anything to me; there's nothing I can do about it."

Cal says, "What I'm telling you is, I find out you've been anywhere near Donie, I'm done here. No second chances. Clear?"

Trey stares at him. For a second Cal thinks the kid is going to flip his shit, the way he did when he smashed up the desk. He gets ready to dodge.

Instead, the kid's face shuts like a door. "Yeah," he says. "Clear."

"Better be," Cal says. "I'll talk to him tomorrow. Come round the day after, I'll update you." He wants to tell the kid not to get seen on the way, but the sleazy ring of it stops him.

Trey doesn't argue any more, or ask any more questions. He just nods and lopes off, into the heather and gone behind the shoulder of the mountain.

Cal understands that the kid knows. He knows something happened inside that house; something solidified and came into sharp focus, and the stakes shot up. He knows that was the moment when this situation went bad.

Cal wants to call the kid back and take him hunting again, or feed him dinner, or teach him how to build something. None of those will fix this. He turns and starts to walk home, by the same meandering route he took to get here. Below him the fields are yellowing with autumn. The shadow of the mountainside is spilling onto the path, with a chill inside when he crosses it. He wonders if, a week or two from now, the kid will hate his guts.

At least now he knows what farm equipment got stolen back in March. Brendan went out with a hose and a propane tank one night, or a couple of nights, and siphoned off a little bit of P.J.'s anhydrous ammonia. Only he got busted: maybe he got sloppy and left a piece of duct tape stuck to the tank where he'd attached his hosepipe, maybe P.J. spotted the brass fitting turning green. Either way, P.J. called the cops. Cal would love to know what Brendan said to him to make him call them off.

He could probably have those CSIs and that K-9, if he went to the police—not cheery Garda Dennis, but the big boys, the detectives up in Dublin. They would take him seriously, specially once they saw those photos. Brendan wasn't setting up some pissant shake-n-bake op in that cottage. He was going for the real thing, the pure high-yield technique, and he had the chemistry knowledge to make it work. It seems like a fair assumption that he also had the connections in place to sell the meth once he made it. The detectives wouldn't fuck around.

Cal would be lighting the fuse on something

whose blast would reverberate through Ardnakelty in ways he can't predict.

No matter what he does or doesn't do, he can't see a way that this might turn out well. That's what that shift in the air meant, the one he and Trey both felt as they squatted by the sideboard, the cold implacable shift that's familiar to him from a hundred cases: this isn't going to have a happy ending.

FIFTEEN

The loss of one of their number hasn't scared the rabbits off. In the morning an easy dozen of them are bounding around Cal's back field like they own it, breakfasting off his dew-wet clover. He watches them from his bedroom window, feeling the cold creep in at him through the glass. Whatever people do, right up to killing, nature absorbs it, closes over the fissure and goes on about its own doings. He can't tell whether this is a comforting thing or a melancholy one. The rooks' oak tree is every shade of gold, leaves twisting down to add to a pool lying like a reflection beneath it.

It's a Wednesday, but Cal feels safe in assuming Donie McGrath won't be spending his day in gainful employment. He also assumes Donie isn't an early riser, so he takes his time over his morning. He fixes himself a big breakfast, bacon, sausages, eggs and black pudding—he hasn't worked out whether he likes black pudding, exactly, but he feels he should occasionally eat it out of respect for local custom. This could take a while, so he might as well be prepared for a long wait and no lunch.

A little after eleven he heads down to the village. Donie's house is on the fringe of the main street, maybe a hundred yards from the shop and the pub. It's a narrow, ungainly two-story house, its windows crowded, at the end of a mismatched row facing right onto the sidewalk. The gray pebbledash is flaking off in patches and there's a sturdy crop of weeds growing out of the chimney.

Opposite Donie's place is a pink house with boarded-up windows and a low stone wall outside. Cal settles his ass on the wall, turns up the collar of his fleece against the lush wet wind, and waits.

For a while nothing happens. The sagging lace curtains in Donie's front window don't move. There are little china ornaments on the windowsill.

A skinny old guy Cal has seen in the pub a few times shuffles past, giving him a nod and a sharp look. Cal nods back, and the guy heads on to the shop. Two minutes after he leaves, Noreen pops out with a watering can and tiptoes to aim it at her hanging basket of petunias. When she cranes her head over her shoulder to peer at Cal, he gives her a wave and a great big grin.

By evening, all of Ardnakelty will know he was looking for Donie. Cal has had enough of being discreet. He figures it's time to kick a few bushes and see what scuttles out.

He waits some more. Various old people go past, and a couple of mothers with babies and little kids, and a fat ginger cat that gives Cal an insolent stare before sitting down on the sidewalk and washing its nether parts to show him what it thinks of him. Something moves behind Donie's mama's lace curtains, and the folds waver, but they don't move aside and the door doesn't open.

A beat-up yellow Fiat 600 bumps down the street and pulls up in front of Noreen's, and a woman who has to be Belinda gets out. She has a lot of dyed-red hair going in a lot of directions, and a purple cape which she swirls around herself before she goes into the shop. When she comes back out, she slows down as she drives past Cal, flutters her fingers and gives him a huge glowing smile. He nods briefly and pulls out his phone like it's ringing, before she can decide to stop and introduce herself. It looks like Noreen has changed her mind about setting him up with Lena.

The movement behind the lace curtains becomes more frequent and more agitated. Not long after two o'clock, Donie cracks. He throws open his front door and heads across the street towards Cal.

Donie is wearing the same shiny white tracksuit that he wore to Seán Óg's. He's aiming for a threatening swagger, but this is hampered by the fact that he's limping a little bit. He also has a swollen black-and-blue lump, with a gash down the middle, over one eyebrow.

Cal has no doubt that Donie McGrath could have earned himself a few whacks in plenty of ways, but he didn't. Mart, the big expert on Ardnakelty and everyone in it, got this one wrong. Cal wishes he could see Mart's face when he finds out, on the slim chance that he hasn't already.

"What the fuck do you want, man?" Donie demands, stopping in the middle of the road, a safe distance from Cal.

"What you got?" Cal asks.

Donie evaluates him. "Fuck off," he says.

"Now, Donie," Cal says. "That's impolite. I'm not bothering anybody. I'm just sitting here enjoying the view."

"You're bothering my mam. She's afraid to go to the shops. You fuckin' sitting there staring out of you, like a pervert."

"I promise you, Donie," Cal says, "I got no interest in your mama. I'm sure she's a lovely lady, but you're the one I've been waiting for. You sit down here and have a little talk with me, and then I'll be on my way."

Donie looks at Cal. He has a fat flat face and small pale eyes that don't show expressions well. "Got nothing to say to you."

"Well, I can sit here till kingdom come," Cal says amiably. "I got nowhere else to be. How 'bout you? Day off work?"

"Yeah."

"Yeah? What do you do for a living?"

"Bit of this, bit of that."

"That doesn't sound like enough to keep a man

occupied," Cal says. "You ever consider going into farming? Plenty of that to go round hereabouts."

Donie snorts.

"What, you don't like sheep?"

Donie shrugs.

"Seems to me you got some kinda grudge against them," Cal says. "One of 'em turn you down?"

Donie eyes him, but Cal is a lot bigger than he is. He spits on the street.

"How'd you get that?" Cal nods at Donie's eyebrow. "Fight."

"But I oughta see the other guy, right?"

"Yeah. Right."

"I gotta tell you, Donie," Cal says, "he looked OK to me. In fact, he looked happy as a clam. That's pretty sad, considering he's half your weight and twice your age."

Donie stares at Cal. Then he grins. His teeth are too small. "I could take you."

"Well, I bet you fight dirty," Cal says. "But then, so do I. Lucky for both of us, I'm in a talking mood, not a fighting mood."

He can see Donie's mind operating on two tracks at once. A small, slow surface part of it is taking in the conversation, more or less. The majority of it, running underneath and a lot more expertly, is assessing what he can get out of this situation and what, if anything, might be a threat. Although it's muted now that he's sober, he still has that bad, unpredictable hum that first made Cal pick him out: the look like there are none of the usual processes between his ideas and his actions, and the ideas aren't ones that would occur to most people's minds. Cal is willing to bet that, while the general concept of the sheep may not have been Donie's idea, the specifics were.

"Give us a cigarette," Donie says.

"I don't smoke," Cal says. He pats the wall next to him. "Take a load off."

"Am I under arrest?" Donie demands.

Cal says, "Are you **what** now?"

" 'Cause if I am, I'm saying nothing without a solicitor. And if I'm not, I'm going inside, and you can't stop me. Either way, fuck off from outside my house."

Cal says, "You think I'm a cop?"

Donie snickers, enjoying the look on his face. "Ah, man. Everyone knows you're Drugs. Sent over from America to give our lot a hand."

By now Cal should be used to the unfettered panache of the townland's rumor mill, but it still has the power to catch him by surprise. This is not a story that he wants taking hold.

"Son," he says, grinning. "You're overrating yourself. No police force in the whole of America gives a shit about you and your pissant drug ops."

Donie gives him a disbelieving stare. "Then what're you doing here?"

"Here like Ardnakelty, or here like outside your house?"

"Both."

"I'm in Ardnakelty because the scenery's so pretty, son," Cal says. "And I'm outside your house because I live in this neighborhood, and I'm curious about a coupla things that've been going on around here."

He smiles at Donie and lets him decide. With the beard and the hair and all, he looks a lot more like a biker or a survivalist loon than like a cop. Donie eyes Cal and considers which of the possibilities he likes least.

"If I was you," Cal advises him, "I'd just sit down, answer a few easy questions without making a big fuss about it, and then go on about my day."

"I know nothing about drugs," Donie says.

This is exactly the kind of fucky conversation, with exactly the kind of pointless shitweasel, that Cal has been congratulating himself on never having to put up with again. "You already admitted you do, you fucking moron," he says. "That's OK, though, because I don't give a shit about your pissant drug ops either. I'm just a good Southern boy who was raised to be neighborly, and there's been some things happening to my neighbors that I'd like to understand better."

Donie should go indoors right about now, but he doesn't. This could just be because he's dumb or bored, or because he's still looking for some way he can benefit. Or it could be because he feels the need to find out what exactly Cal knows.

"I need a smoke," he says. "Give us a tenner."

"Left my wallet at home," Cal says. Even if he was inclined to give Donie money, that would only land him with weeks' worth of made-up bullshit, punctuated by demands for more cash. "Have a seat."

Donie evaluates him for another minute, mouth open in a small feral grin. Then he sits himself down on the wall, out of Cal's reach. He smells like some meal, cabbage and deep-fried stuff, cooked a few days back.

Cal says, "You've been killing my neighbors' sheep."

"Prove it." Donie pulls a pack of cigarettes out of his tracksuit pocket and lights one, not bothering to blow the smoke away from Cal.

"You got some unusual tendencies, son," Cal says, "but seeing as I'm not a shrink, I don't give a shit about that, either. My only question is, when you go slicing the private parts out of sheep, is that for your own personal enjoyment, or you got a bigger agenda going on?"

"Don't worry about it, man. There won't be any more sheep killed."

"Well, that's nice to know," Cal says. "But my question still stands."

Donie shrugs and smokes. Noreen is watering her petunias again. He hunches his back to her, like she might not recognize him.

"I got sort of the same question," Cal says, "when it comes to Brendan Reddy."

Donie's head comes around sharply and he stares at Cal. Cal looks pleasantly back. Even Donie's stringy little bangs, which look like Donie saves time and motion by keeping them permanently matted in place with months' worth of grease, are getting on his last nerve.

"What question?" Donie demands.

"Well," Cal says, "I don't much care what happened to him. But I'd sure like to know whether it was just some little personal affair, or whether it was part of what you might call a grander scheme of things."

"'Grander scheme,'" Donie says, and snorts.

"I think that's the phrase I'm looking for," Cal says, considering. "If you got a more fitting one, I'm all ears."

"Why do you care what happened to Brendan?"

"Any intelligent man likes to know what he's dealing with," Cal says. "I'm sure you feel the same way. You get edgy when you don't know what you're dealing with, don't you, Donie?"

Donie says, "You in business?"

"My business is beside the point, son," Cal says. "The point is that I like staying out of other people's business. I like it a lot. But in order to do that, I need to know where other people's business lies."

"Do a bitta fishing for yourself," Donie says, and blows smoke at Cal. "Get a few chickens. That'll keep you out of other people's business."

"Everyone in this townland appears to think I need a hobby," Cal says.

"You do. So did Bren Reddy."

"Well, I do love me some fishing," Cal says. "But what I want you to take in here, son, is that I'd very much appreciate some clarity on the situation."

"Yeah? How much?"

"Depends on what kind of clarity I get."

Donie shakes his head, grinning.

"OK, Donie," Cal says. "Lemme do some of the work for you. Brendan Reddy fucked up." He has no intention of letting on that he knows about the meth lab. He doesn't want that house burned down; he might have a use for it at some point. "Your buddies from Dublin got rid of him, one way or another. My neighbors found out. And you've been given the job of warning them to keep their mouths shut."

Donie stares at Cal. He sniggers.

"How'm I doing?"

"You want a lot of shit for free, man."

"I'm asking nicely," Cal says. "So far. That oughta count for something, even these days."

Donie stands up and picks his tracksuit pants out of his ass. "Get fucked," he says. He throws his cigarette into the road, swagger-limps back to his house and slams the door behind him.

Cal waits a few seconds, waves good-bye to the lace curtains and heads for home. There's no point in sticking around. The only things that will move Donie are gain and pain. Anything fancier will have no more effect on him than it would on a wolverine.

He didn't expect to get much out of Donie, anyway.

His main goals were to find out whether Donie is connected to whatever happened to Brendan, which he is, and to kick those bushes. Which, for better or for worse, he certainly has done.

All the same, the conversation has left him stirred up and restless. Putting away guys like Donie used to be one of Cal's favorite parts of the job. These guys aren't hankering for a rifle and a horse and a herd of cattle; you could give them all those things, and within a week they would get themselves shot for cheating at cards, or stealing horses, or raping someone's wife. The only useful thing you can do with them is lock them up where they can't harm anyone except each other. With that option off the table, Cal gets the same feeling he got in the pub when Donie was squaring up to Mart, that sense of not being quite able to get his feet on the ground. He ought to do something about Donie, but the context prevents him from understanding what that might be.

———

In the end Cal takes Donie's advice and goes fishing. His restlessness makes the house feel cramped and nagging, full of shit he needs to do and can't settle to. On a more practical level, he doesn't want to be home if Trey gets impatient and comes looking for news.

Cal is no longer particularly interested in finding out where Brendan went. While the cop part of him jerks a knee at the thought of abandoning a case that still has plenty of candy in it, the overriding priority here is the fact that, at least for the foreseeable future, Trey needs to stop looking.

The river is sluggish today, moving in muscular, viscous-looking twists. Leaves fall onto its surface, drift for a second, and are pulled under without a swirl or a trace. Cal thinks about telling the kid that Brendan fetched up in there, some accidental way. He could come up with a convincing story, maybe involving Brendan scouting locations for a business running fishing trips for tourists on heritage pilgrimages, or nature retreats for suits in search of their inner wild men, either of which is the kind of thing that the dumbass kid should have fucking gone for to begin with.

He might pull it off. Trey trusts him, as much as he trusts anyone. And although the kid would fight the suggestion that Brendan is dead, he'd welcome the thought that Brendan didn't deliberately go off and leave him without a word. He would also welcome the opportunity to think of Brendan as a fine upstanding entrepreneur in the making. He might even welcome it enough not to wonder why Brendan would have taken his savings with him to check out suitable locations for actuaries to build tree forts, or why the actuaries would need lab masks.

Cal can't tell whether he ought to do it. This seems like the kind of thing he should know instantly, on instinct, but he has no idea whether it would be right or wrong. This unsettles him right down to the bottom of his guts. It implies that somewhere along the way he got out of practice doing the right thing, to the point where he doesn't even know it when he sees it.

That feeling is one of the things that drove Cal out of his job. He associates it, even though he knows the reality is nowhere near that simple, with a scrawny black kid called Jeremiah Payton, who, a few months before Cal retired, robbed a convenience store with a knife and jumped bail. Cal and O'Leary tracked him down at his girlfriend's house, at which point Jeremiah leaped out of a window and took off.

Cal was older than O'Leary, and heavier. He was three paces behind him rounding the corner. He heard O'Leary yell, "Let me see your hands!" and then he saw Jeremiah turning towards them with one hand rising and one dropping, and then O'Leary's gun went off and Jeremiah landed face-down on the sidewalk.

Cal was already on the radio calling for the ambulance as they ran towards him, but when they got there, Jeremiah shouted into the sidewalk in a voice that was pure terror, "Don't shoot me."

Cal got his hands behind his back and cuffed them there. Someone had started screaming. "You hit?" Cal asked Jeremiah.

He shook his head. Cal turned him over and checked him anyway: no blood.

"I miss him?" O'Leary said. He was cabbage-green and pouring sweat like he was melting. He still had his Glock in his hands.

"Yeah," Cal said. To Jeremiah he said, "You got anything on you?"

Jeremiah just stared up at him. It took Cal a minute to understand that he couldn't talk because he thought he was going to die.

O'Leary said, "He was going for his pocket. You saw him go for his pocket."

"I saw his hand drop," Cal said.

"For his fucking pocket. Pants pocket. I swear to God—" O'Leary bent over, panting, and burrowed in Jeremiah's pocket. He came out with a switchblade.

"I thought it was a gun," O'Leary said. "Well, shitfuck," and he sat down on the curb like his legs had given way.

Cal wanted to sit down next to him, but the woman was screaming louder and people had started to gather. "It's gonna be OK," he said, pointlessly, and he left O'Leary there and headed off to cancel the ambulance and secure the scene.

Cal was feeling a little tender right then, what with Donna having just walked out on him. He had spent most of the past year fumbling in the dark trying to disentangle complications, and complications behind complications; he didn't seem to know how to stop. He was sure, absolutely, that O'Leary had believed Jeremiah was going for a gun in his pocket, which for a lot of guys would have been enough. But for Cal, that fact seemed to be overlaid and underlaid by so many layers that he couldn't tell whether or not it was important. What was important was that he and O'Leary were supposed to be out there keeping people safe. They had always considered themselves to be good cops, cops who tried to do right by everyone they came across. They had worked hard to be that, even when plenty of people hated their guts on sight, even when some of the other guys were getting meaner by the day and some had been rattlesnake-mean from the start. They had done their damn sensitivity training. And yet, somehow, they had ended up almost killing an eighteen-year-old kid. Cal knew it was unspeakably wrong that Jeremiah had come within a few inches of dying on that sidewalk, and that he had looked at the two of them and expected to die; but no matter how much time he spent fumbling at it, he couldn't put his finger on a point where he could have made things go right. He could have stayed outside Jeremiah's window to stop him taking off, but that doesn't seem like it would have fixed very much of anything.

He told Internal Affairs that Jeremiah was going for his pocket. Cal had a good record and fewer complaints against his name than most cops; IA believed him. It might be true—Cal thinks it is, he thinks that probably is what he saw. That doesn't alter the fact that he didn't say that to IA because he thought it was the right thing to do. He did it because he knew everyone around him believed it was, and he himself had no idea. He was so deafened by the locust buzz of all the anger and the wrongness and the complications surrounding him, he couldn't hear the steady pulse of his code any more, so that he found himself having to turn to other people's—a thing that in itself was a fundamental and unpardonable breach of his own.

When he put in his papers, and the sarge asked him why, he didn't mention Jeremiah. The sarge would have thought he had gone out of his ever-loving mind, losing his nerve over an incident where no one got hurt worse than a couple of scraped knees. Cal wouldn't have known how to explain that it wasn't that he couldn't handle the job any more. It was that one or the other of them, him or the job, couldn't be trusted.

The river, out of its endless supply of contrariness, has decided to be charming today. The perch are little, but inside half an hour Cal has enough of them to make up a good dinner. He keeps fishing anyway, even when the cold sets up an ache in his joints, making him feel old. He only packs up his gear when the light coming through the branches starts to tarnish and contract, turning the water green-black and sullen. He doesn't feel like walking home in the dark today.

As he comes up his lane he sees Mart leaning back against his gate, looking out across the road and the wild-grown hedge and the fields scattered with hay bales, to the gold in the sky. A thin curl of smoke trickles from his mouth and meanders off up the road. Beside him, Kojak nips through his fur after a flea.

As Cal gets closer, Mart turns his head and drops his cigarette under his boot. "Here comes the big bold hunter," he says, grinning. "Any joy?"

"Got a mess of perch," Cal says, holding up his kill bag. "You want some?"

Mart waves the perch away. "I don't eat fish. They depress me. I had fish every Friday of my life, till the mammy died. I've et enough fish for one lifetime."

"I oughta be that way about grits," Cal says. "But I'm not. I'd eat grits any day and twice on Sundays, if I could get them."

"What the feck is grits, anyhow?" Mart demands. "All the cowboys in the fillums do eat it, but they never have the courtesy to tell you what it is. Is it semolina, or what is it at all?"

"They're made of cornmeal," Cal says. "You boil 'em up and serve 'em with whatever you like best. I favor shrimp and grits, myself. If I could get my hands on some, I'd invite you over to try them."

"Noreen'd order that in for you. If you bat the big aul' baby blues at her."

"Maybe," Cal says. He remembers Belinda waving to him out her car window. He doesn't think Noreen is in the mood to special-order anything for him right now.

"Are you getting homesick on me, bucko?" Mart inquires, eyeing him sharply. "I've twenty quid on you, down at Seán Óg's, to stick it out here at least a year. Don't let me down."

"I got no plans to go anywhere," Cal says. "Who'd you bet against?"

"Don't be minding that. They're a crowd of aul' fools, down there; wouldn't know a good bet if it walked up and bit them."

"Maybe I oughta stick a few bucks on myself," Cal says. "What are my odds like?"

"Never you mind. If you win it for me, I'll give you a bit offa the top."

"You're looking good," Cal says. It's true. Mart doesn't have the raw materials to look fresh-faced, exactly, but both his perkiness and his movements have lost the effortful quality of the last few days. He appears to have no intention of explaining his presence at Cal's gate. "You get your beauty sleep last night?"

"Oh, begod, I did. Slept round the clock. Whatever that yoke was, it won't be bothering anyone's sheep again." Mart pokes Cal's kill bag with his crook.

"You did well there. What'll you do with the ones you don't eat?"

"I was thinking about that myself," Cal says. "That little freezer compartment won't hold 'em. If I knew where to find Malachy, I might give him a few, in exchange for the other night."

Mart considers this and nods. "Might not be a bad idea. Malachy lives up the mountains, but. You won't find his place. Give 'em to me; I'll see he gets them."

Mart and Kojak walk up to the house with Cal to get a bag for the fish, but they don't come in. Mart leans a shoulder in the door frame, a ragged and bumpy outline against the sunset. Kojak slumps at his feet.

"The mansion's looking well," Mart says, inspecting Cal's living room.

"It's slow work," Cal says. "I got a lot left to do before winter hits."

"I see you've got yourself an apprentice," Mart says, bending to pick brush out of Kojak's fur. "That oughta speed things up a bit."

"How's that?"

"Trey Reddy's been helping you out."

Cal has been waiting for this for weeks, but the timing is interesting. "Yep," he says, finding a big Ziploc bag in his cupboard. "Kid came round looking for work, I figured I could use a hand."

"Didn't I warn you about them Reddys?" Mart demands reproachfully. "Buncha gurriers. They'd rob the nose off your face, and sell it back to you the next day."

"You did," Cal says. "Kid didn't give a last name; took me a while to make the connection. And I'm not missing anything that I know of."

"Better keep an eye on them tools. They'd sell for a few bob."

Cal goes to the mini-fridge for his ice tray. "He seems like a pretty good kid to me. These gonna be enough to keep the fish cold till you can get them to Malachy?"

Mart says, "He?"

"Trey."

"Trey Reddy's a girl, bucko. Did you not spot that?"

Cal straightens up fast, ice tray in his hand, and stares.

Mart starts to laugh.

"Are you shitting me?"

Mart shakes his head. He can't talk. He's laughing so hard that he doubles over, banging his crook on the ground.

"Trey's a fucking **boy's name.**"

Cal's outrage sends Mart into a fresh gale of giggles. "Short for Theresa," he manages to explain, through them. "The face on you."

"How the hell was I supposed to know that?"

"Holy God," Mart says, straightening up and wiping his eyes with a knuckle, still giggling. Apparently this is the funniest thing that's happened to him in weeks. "That explains it. Here was me wondering what the bloody hell you were at, letting a young girl hang around you, and all the time you hadn't a notion she was a girl at all. Doesn't that beat Banagher?"

"The kid looks like a **boy.** The clothes. The fucking haircut."

"I'd say she might be a lesbian," Mart says, considering this possibility. "She picked the right time to be one, anyway, if she is. She can get married and all, these days."

"Yeah," Cal says. "Good for her."

"I voted for that," Mart informs him. "The priest in town was bulling at mass, swearing he'd excommunicate anyone that voted yes, but I didn't pay him any heed. I wanted to see what would happen."

"Right," Cal says, easing his voice. "What did happen?" Now that the initial shock is past, he doesn't feel like letting Mart know just how pissed off he is with Trey. In fact, he's not sure why he's so pissed off, given that Trey never claimed to be a boy, but he is.

"Not a lot," Mart admits, with some regret. "Not around here, anyway. Maybe up in Dublin the gays are all marrying the bejaysus out of each other, but I haven't heard of any in these parts."

"Well look at that," Cal says. He's only half-hearing Mart. "You went and pissed off the priest for nothing."

"Fuck him. He's only an aul' blow; too used to getting his own way. I never liked him, big Jabba the Hutt head on him. It's healthier for men to live with men, anyway. They don't be wrecking each other's heads. They might as well get married while they're at it, have a day out."

"Can't hurt," Cal says. He bangs the ice tray on the counter and throws cubes into the Ziploc.

Mart watches him. "If Trey Reddy's not robbing you," he says, "then what does she want out of you? Them Reddys, they're always looking for something."

"Learn a little carpentry," Cal says. "He didn't ask for pay—she. I was thinking about throwing her a few bucks, but I'm not sure if she'd take it right. What do you think?"

"A Reddy'll always take money," Mart says. "Mind yourself, but. You don't want her thinking you're a soft touch. Are you going to let her keep coming round, now you know she's a young one?"

There is no way on God's green earth that Cal would have let a little girl hang around his yard, never mind come inside his house. "Haven't had time to think about that," he says.

"Why would you want her about the place? Don't be telling me you need the help with that bloody desk."

"She's handy enough. And I've been enjoying the company."

"Sure, what kind of company is that child, at all? You'd get more chat out of that aul' chair. Do you ever get two words out of her?"

"Kid's not much of a talker, all right," Cal says. "She lets me know she's hungry, now and again."

"Send her packing," Mart says. There's a finality to his voice that makes Cal look at him. "Give her the few bob, tell her you won't be needing her no more."

Cal opens his kill bag and scoops up a couple of perch. "I might do that," he says. "How many would Malachy eat? He got a family?"

Mart hits the door with his crook, making a raw whack that echoes startlingly loudly in the half-bare room. "Listen to me, man. I'm looking out for you. If this place finds out Theresa Reddy's hanging round here, people'll talk. I'll tell them you're a sound man, and I'll tell them you thought she was a young fella, but there's only so far they'll listen to me. I don't want to see you bet up, or burned out of it."

Cal says, "You told me I didn't need to worry my head about crime round here."

"You don't. Not unless you go asking for it."

"You afraid you're gonna lose your twenty bucks?" Cal asks, but Mart doesn't smile.

"What about the child? D'you want the townland talking about her the way they'll be talking if they find out?"

This had not occurred to Cal. "She's a kid learning to be handy," he says, keeping his voice even. "Is all. If a few dumb fucks would rather she was out on the streets making trouble—"

"She'll be on the streets all right, if you don't get sense. They'll have her hunted out of here by Christmas. Where d'you think she'll go?"

"For fixing a desk and frying a rabbit? What the hell—"

"You'll give me blood pressure, so you will," Mart says. "Honest to God. Or palpitations. Would ye Yanks not learn to listen once in a while, so everyone around ye can have some fuckin' peace of mind?"

"Here you go," Cal says, handing over the Ziploc. "My compliments to Malachy."

Mart takes the bag, but he doesn't move to leave. "The other reason I voted for the marriage yoke," he says. "My brother was gay. Not Seamus, that lived here with me; the other fella. Eamonn. It was against the law, back when we were young. He went off to America because of it, in the end. I asked him would he not join the priesthood instead. Sure, they could do what they liked, and no one would say boo to them; I'd say half of them were riding the arse off each other. But Eamonn was having none of it. He hated all them bastards. So off he went. That was thirty year ago. Never heard another word out of him."

"You try Facebook?" Cal asks. He's not sure where this is going.

"I did. There's a few Eamonn Lavins on there. One's got no photo or nothing, so I sent him a message, just in case. He never got back to me, either way." Kojak is sniffing at the bag. Mart palms his nose away. "I thought maybe once we got the gay marriage, he'd come home, if he's alive. But he never did."

"He might yet," Cal says. "You never know."

"He won't," Mart says. "I had it wrong. 'Twasn't the laws that were the problem." He looks out over the fields, at the pink sky. "It's a hard aul' place, this. The finest place in the world, and wild horses wouldn't drag me out of it. But it's not gentle. And if Theresa Reddy doesn't know that by now, she'll learn soon enough."

SIXTEEN

What with one thing and another, Cal has been neglecting some stuff: the rooks, for example, and his daily walks around the countryside, and that desk. When he sees the morning—pristine in the sharp autumn sunlight, cold enough to chill his palate with each breath—he figures this is as good a time as any to get back to them. They'll keep him outdoors, which is where he wants to be when Trey comes around. And he needs to herd his mind off its dusty old detective trail, back to the pretty, scenic one he was thoroughly enjoying until the kid showed up smack in the middle of it.

He starts by walking his legs sore. After that he moves on to the rooks, who have been surveilling him for long enough that they ought to be comfortable with him by now. Alyssa used to have some book about kids who had done surprising things, among them a little girl who had made friends with a crow. There were photos of the presents the crow would bring her: candy wrappers, car keys, broken earrings and Lego figurines. Alyssa spent months trying to strike up a relationship with their neighborhood pigeons, who as far as Cal could tell were too dumb even to identify her as a living creature rather than a weird-shaped food dispenser. He would really like to send her a photo of some rooks bringing him presents.

He lays out a handful of strawberries on the stump, and then a trail of them leading from the stump to the back step, where he sits down to wait. The rooks tumble down from their tree, bicker over the stumpful, get halfway along the trail, then give Cal a collective eye-roll and head back to their business.

Cal tries to find his patience, but it appears to have gone missing somewhere along the way, and the step is cold. After nowhere near enough time, he decides the rooks can fuck themselves, and goes inside to fetch the desk and his tools. By the time he comes back outdoors, every strawberry is gone, and the rooks are back in their tree laughing their asses off at him.

The desk still has tricky deposits of white paint in crevices, and Trey cracked another shelf when she went at it. Disentangling the broken shelf from all the rest looks like a pain in the rear end, so Cal goes at the paint with a toothbrush and a cup of soapy water, a job that starts to irritate him almost immediately. Despite not having touched a drop of booze yesterday, he has the same feeling he associates with hangovers, a heavy, prickly disinclination towards everything around him. He wants today over and done with.

He gives up on the paint, wrangles the shelf loose and starts tracing its outline on a fresh piece of wood.

He's finishing up when he hears the swish of feet through the grass.

The kid looks the same as always, all ratty parka and unyielding stare. Cal can't see a girl there. For all he knows, she has bosoms of some degree, but he never had any occasion to examine that area in detail before and there's no way in hell he's going to do it now. It occurs to him that one reason he's pissed off with Trey is because he would have liked at least one person around this damn place to be exactly what they seem.

"I went to school," she informs him.

"Congratulations," Cal says. "I'm impressed."

The kid doesn't smile. "You talk to Donie?"

"Come here," Cal says. "Let's get this fixed up. You wanna do the sawing?"

Trey stands still for another moment, looking at him. Then she nods and comes tramping across the grass.

She knows Cal has something to tell her that she doesn't want to hear. She would never have asked for the mercy of a few extra minutes without it, but she's taking them when he puts them in her hand. The stoicism of her, complete and unthinking as an animal's, makes Cal feel blinded.

He wants to change his mind. But, shitty though his plan is, every other one he can think of is even worse. It feels like a vast, implacable failing in his character that he can't come up with just one good solution to offer this scrawny, dauntless kid.

He hands her the saw and moves so she can take over at the table. "You had a snack after school?"

"Nah," Trey says, squinting along the saw line.

Cal goes inside and comes out with a peanut butter sandwich, an apple and a glass of milk. "Say thank you," he says automatically.

"Yeah. Thanks." The kid drops cross-legged on the grass and aims herself at the sandwich like she hasn't eaten all day.

Cal goes back to his paint streaks. He doesn't want to say what he's about to say. He would like to leave this afternoon undisturbed, let it unroll itself in its own slow time across the newly plowed fields, to the rhythms of their work and the west wind and the low autumn sun, right up until the moment when he has to wreck everything.

But, Mart's theory notwithstanding, there are a couple of reasons Cal can think of why a girl might not want to look like a girl. If someone has been doing bad things to Trey, his plan will need to change.

"I got a bone to pick with you," he says.

Trey chews and gives him a blank look. Cal can't tell whether this relates to the subject at hand, or whether she just hasn't heard the expression before.

He says, "You never told me you're a girl."

The kid lowers her sandwich and watches him, with fast things zipping behind her eyes. She's trying to read in his face what this means. For the first time in a long time, she looks ready to run.

She says, "Never said I was a boy."

"You knew I thought you were, though."

"Never thought about it."

Her muscles are still primed for flight. Cal says, "Are you scared I'm gonna hurt you?"

"Are you pissed off?"

"I'm not mad," Cal says. "I'm just not crazy about surprises. Did someone do something bad to you 'cause you're a girl?"

Her eyebrows twitch together. "Like what?"

"Like anything. Anything that might make you feel better going around like a boy."

He's alert for the slightest flinch of tension or withdrawal, but the kid just shakes her head. "Nah. My dad, he went easier on us girls."

She has no idea what he's aiming at. Cal feels a flood of relief, chased by something thornier and harder to identify. The kid doesn't need his rescuing; there's no reason to change his plan. "Well then," he says. "Quit looking at me like I'm gonna throw this toothbrush at you."

"How'd you know? Did someone say it to you?"

Cal says, "What's with the hair?"

Trey swipes a hand over her head and checks it, like she's expecting a leaf or something. "Huh?"

"The buzz cut. Makes you look like a boy."

"I had lice. My mam hadta shave it."

"Great. You still got 'em?"

"Nah. Last year."

"Then how come it's still short?"

"Less hassle."

Cal is still trying to overlay a girl on top of the boy he's accustomed to. "What was it like before?"

Trey holds up a hand somewhere around her collarbone. Cal can't picture it. "When I was in school, kids would've given a girl shit for having her hair like that. No one does?"

The kid does a combination shrug, mouth-twist and eye-roll, which Cal takes to mean that this is the least of her problems. "They mostly leave me alone. 'Cause I bet up Brian Carney."

"How come?"

Trey shrugs again. This one means it's not worth going into. After a moment she says, with a quick glance at Cal under her eyebrows, "Do you care?"

"That you beat up Brian Whatsisname? Depends on why. Sometimes you got no choice but to set someone straight."

"That I'm a girl."

"At your age a kid's a kid," Cal says. "Doesn't make much difference what kind." He would love this to be true.

Trey nods and goes back to her food. Cal can't tell whether the subject is closed in her mind. After a little bit she says, "You got any kids?"

"One."

"Boy or girl?"

"Girl. She's grown."

"Where's her mam? Were you not married?"

"We were. Not any more."

Trey absorbs this, chewing. "How come? You a hoormaster like your dad?"

"Nope."

"Didja beat her?"

"No. Never laid a finger on her."

"Then how come?"

"Kid," Cal says, "I have no idea."

Trey's eyebrows twitch together skeptically, but she says nothing. She bites a chunk off the apple, puts it inside her last piece of sandwich and tries out the combination, with mixed results, going by the look on her face. It makes Cal's bones feel weak, how little she sometimes is.

She says, "Does your girl know you're here?"

"Sure. I talk to her every week."

"Is the desk gonna be for her?"

"Nah," Cal says. "She's got her own place, her own furniture. That's staying right here."

Trey nods. She finishes the apple and tosses the core, with a hard whip of her wrist, down the garden towards the rooks. Then she wipes her hands on her jeans and goes back to sawing.

The sounds of their work fall into a balance that could sustain itself forever. The swifts streak and crisscross in the cool blue sky, and the weaning lambs call to each other in wavery trebles. Off on Dumbo Gannon's land a red tractor lumbers patiently back and forth, small as a beetle with distance, leaving a broad band of dark upturned earth behind it.

Cal gives them as long as he can afford. Trey saws out the shelf, measures and checks, chisels and planes, squints and measures again. Cal scrubs cracks, wipes them down, scrapes a little with a blade when he needs to. Trey, finally satisfied, moves on to sanding.

The light is starting to condense, lying golden as honey across the fields. Cal needs to get this done.

"I talked to Donie," he says, hearing the words start something splitting like wood.

Trey's shoulders set. She puts down the shelf and the sandpaper, carefully, and turns to look at him. "Yeah," she says.

Cal can see the white around her eyes, and the flare of her nostrils when she breathes. He knows her heart is going like a runaway horse.

"It's not bad news, kid. OK?"

A hard breath comes out of her. She swipes the back of her wrist across her mouth. "OK," she says.

She's the same bad white as she was when she winged the rabbit. "You wanna sit down for this, get comfortable?" Cal asks. "It's a long story."

"Nah."

"Suit yourself," Cal says. He brushes paint dust off the desk and leans his forearms on the top of it, keeping his movements slow and easy, the way he would around a spooked animal; the way he did the first couple of times the kid came around, just a few weeks ago. "To start with: you wanted to know why I was aiming to talk to Donie. My thinking went like this. Brendan was planning to use that cottage to generate a good income. He had something shady in mind, or he'd've told you about it. Which means he would've needed to talk to people who have shady connections. The only people like that round here are the boys who come down from Dublin selling drugs. And I'd seen Donie hanging out with them in the pub."

Trey nods, one tight jerk. She's following him. She's still white, but the wildness has gone out of her eyes.

"So I went to call on Donie. I knew, like you said, he wouldn't be too eager to tell the story to a stranger—specially since, if you heard I was a cop, he had to have heard the same thing. But we came to an understanding in the end."

"Didja beat him up?"

"Nah. No need. You only have to meet Donie once to know he's not a big player. He's just some two-bit hanger-on, kissing the real guys' asses and scared shitless of them the whole time. So all I had to do was make it sound like I knew a lot more than I did, and then tell Donie if he didn't fill in the gaps for me, I was gonna make sure his city friends heard he'd been talking to a cop."

Trey clearly approves of this. "And he talked?"

"Sang like a little birdie," Cal says. "Donie isn't exactly a mastermind, so he mighta had some details wrong, but I think he got all the bones of the matter in place. Here's what he says, anyway. You know all that crap up in Brendan's hideout?"

Trey nods sharply.

"Sometimes people get hold of stuff they shouldn't have. Then they sell it on."

"Brendan's not a thief."

"Shut up and listen, kid. I'm not saying he is. What I'm saying is, sometimes it might take these people a while to find buyers. While they're looking, they need somewhere to store the stuff. Somewhere secure and out of the way, so no one's gonna stumble on it by mistake, and the cops won't find it unless they know exactly where to look. If these guys find the right place, run by someone reliable who's gonna keep their stuff safe, they'll pay decent rent."

"Like a warehouse."

"Yeah. Exactly like. And a place like here, not too far from the border, this is prime territory. Brendan saw a gap in the market, and he realized his hide-out was the perfect place to fill it. All he needed to do was fix it up some, and get in touch with people who'd use it."

Trey evaluates this. Apparently she can fit this level of shadiness into her idea of Brendan. She nods.

"So Brendan started fixing the place up. Maybe he even got a couple of local guys using it, here and there, but they'd be too small-time to be much use to him. He needed to land some bigger fish."

"The lads from Dublin," Trey says.

"This part's where Donie got a little hazy on the details," Cal says. "No one's gonna tell a dumbass like him more than they need to; he just got given the general gist of what went down. Best he can tell, Brendan waited till the Dublin boys were in town and asked them to put him in touch with people who might want his services. They were interested, but there was a little bit of disagreement among them about Brendan's operation. Some of them thought he'd be an asset, but some of them thought he'd be more of a liability. From what I can gather, they're planning on running something of their own up those mountains, and they didn't want Brendan and his clients drawing police attention in that direction."

"Guys like that," Trey says. She doesn't finish.

"Yeah," Cal says. "You don't want to piss them off. Brendan probably shoulda taken that possibility into account, but from what I've been told, he had a tendency to get carried away and forget to factor in other people's reactions. That sound right to you?"

Trey nods. Cal spent half the night smoothing the edges on this story and looking it over from different angles, making sure it holds together and incorporates all the pieces Trey has possession of. There are little holes here and there, but nothing that would make it fall apart under pressure. It has enough truth in it to act as glue. There's even a chance, and what a trip that would be, that with a few minor substitutions this hinky story is accidentally true.

"So," he says, "Brendan set up a meeting with them, thinking he was gonna pay them for a bunch of phone numbers and everyone would go away happy. By the time the meeting came around, though, the ones that thought he was a liability had shouted down the rest. They told him to get out of town and stay gone."

"Just told him to leave," Trey says. Her breath is coming fast and shallow. "They didn't take him? For definite?"

"Nah. What would they want him for? All they wanted from him was to get out of their hair, and he did that himself, right quick. He had more sense than to hang around till he got told again."

"So that's why he went. Not 'cause he wanted to."

"That's right," Cal says. "He didn't have a choice."

A hard breath comes out of Trey and her eyes skid away, one place and then another. The thought of Brendan walking out without a word, because he wanted to, has been eating her raw and bloody for months. Now that it's gone, she can't take in the clear space where it used to be.

Cal lets her be. After a minute she asks, "Where'd he go?"

"Donie's not sure. He thinks Scotland, for whatever that's worth. He says the boys didn't take any cash off Brendan, so he shoulda had enough to get him somewhere and get him set up. And if he's got sense, he won't be back for a while."

Trey says, coming down heavy on the words, "But he's alive."

"Far as anyone knows. No guarantees—he coulda fallen off the boat on the way over, or got hit by a car, same as anyone could. But there's no reason to think he's anything but."

"Then why didn't he ring? Even once, let us know he was OK?"

The question forces its way out against her will. This is the other half of what's been gnawing her to the bones. She wanted Brendan kidnapped because that would have been fixable.

"These are pretty scary guys, kid," Cal says gently. "My guess is, Brendan knows you well enough to figure that if you got any smell of what went down, you might go trying to fix things so he could come home. And that would've just made the situation worse. For him and you both. He liked to protect you, right?"

"Yeah. He did."

"That's what he was doing. If you want to do the same for him, the best thing you can do is trust him and stick to what he wanted you to do. Pull in your horns, keep your mouth shut and go about your business till he figures it's safe to come home."

Trey looks at him for another long minute. Then she says, "Thanks." She turns back to the table and starts sanding again, very carefully and very neatly.

Cal goes back to his toothbrush and his soapy water, even though the desk is already as clean as he can get it. Trey doesn't say another word, so neither does he. Their side of the mountains has darkened, its great shadow bleeding across the fields towards them, by the time the kid brings the shelf over to him.

Every edge is smooth as paper. Cal passes Trey the hammer and she fits the shelf carefully into place, a tap on one side and then a tap on the other. She stands back and looks up at Cal.

"Good job," he says. "You've done fine work on this, kid. Now you better get home."

Trey nods, dusting her hands on her jeans.

"So," Cal says. "You got your answer, near as I can come to it. Glad I could help out." He holds out his hand.

The kid looks at it, and then up at Cal's face, baffled.

"Case closed, kid," Cal says. "I hope your brother comes home when things settle down. See you round Noreen's sometime, if she doesn't ban you."

Trey says, "I'll come back anyway. Finish that." She jerks her chin at the desk.

"Nope," Cal says. "Nothing personal. You're handy and you're fine company, but I came here to get away from company."

The kid is staring at him with her face wiped blank by shock. Cal realizes, with a grief so deep and exhausting that he wants to sink to his knees and put his forehead down on the cool grass, how badly she wants to keep coming round.

He has experience in what happens if you try to make Trey Reddy give up on something she's set her heart on. His only course is to make her want to never come back.

If she doesn't realize what people will say, he can't bring himself to put that into her mind. Instead he says, "You wanted me to find out what happened to your brother, kid. I did that. What else do you want from me?"

Trey keeps staring. She looks like she might say something, but nothing comes out.

Cal lets a wry grin slide onto his face. "Huh," he says. "I did get warned about the Reddys and cash. Is that what you want? Pay for the work you've done? 'Cause I can probably spare fifty, sixty bucks, but if you're thinking about taking what you're owed when I'm not looking—"

For a second he thinks she's going to go for the desk again, or maybe for him. He's fine with either one. She can take the desk to splinters if that's what she needs. He even moves back to give her a clear shot. Instead she spits, swift and vicious as a rattlesnake striking, at his feet. It lands on his boot with a splat. Then she whips around and strides off, fast and hard, towards the road.

Cal waits a minute and goes to the gate. Trey is already far away, moving fast through the blotches of light and shadow that pattern the road, with her head down and her hands jammed deep in her pockets. He watches till she reaches the upwards slant in the road and is received into the bright muddle of sun and hedge-branches at the top, and a long time after. Nothing follows her.

He carries his tools inside, and his table, and

finally the desk. He puts the desk in the spare bedroom, where it won't be always catching his eye. He would have liked to finish that desk together with Trey, before he had to send her away.

Probably he should make the rest of yesterday's perch into dinner, but instead he gets himself a beer and takes it out to the back step. In the east the sky is deepening towards lavender; beneath it the red tractor stands still, abandoned in mid-furrow. The plowing has added a new layer to the air's smell, something richer and darker, thick with hidden things.

See? he tells Donna, in his head. **I can walk away from a case, if it's the right thing to do.** Donna, refusing to be obliging even in his imagination, rolls her eyes and makes a ferocious noise at the heavens.

Cal told Trey the truth: he does not, in fact, know why he and Donna split up. As far as he can tell, what happened was that in Alyssa's junior year of college she got mugged and beat up pretty bad, and two years later Donna walked out, and apparently there was some mysterious connection that Cal is too dumb to understand.

At the time, there was no indication that the first of these events would lead to the second. He and Donna flew out to Seattle so fast that they got there while Alyssa was still in recovery from surgery for a smashed shoulder bone. Once Cal was sure she was going to be OK, he left Donna to sit with her and headed down to the precinct. He knew exactly what priority would be assigned to a random mugging, but the mugging of a cop's daughter was a different matter, and the daughter of a cop who was all up in the precinct's grille was another thing again. Over the next couple of weeks Cal harried that precinct, politely and relentlessly, till they pulled CCTV footage from every camera in a block radius. That got them a couple of grainy shots of the mugger, which Cal and the precinct guys worked—some days Cal put in twenty hours—till they dragged up a runty, redheaded junkie called Lyle, who still had Alyssa's credit card in his jacket pocket.

When Cal told Alyssa, she was still too shaken up even to show relief; she just looked at him and then turned her head away. Cal understood: he had hoped she would be pleased, but he had seen enough victims to understand that trauma shapes feelings into forms you would never expect.

Over the next while, he and Donna were mostly taken up by worrying about Alyssa. She wouldn't let them stay with her, after the first couple of weeks, and she wouldn't come home, so they had to do their worrying long-distance. The attack had cracked her mind all over, like a dropped mirror where the pieces are still in place but the whole doesn't function right any more. Cal never did figure out whether it was the physical harm or the things Lyle had threatened to do to her—Alyssa had tried to talk him down, connect with him like one human being to another, and Lyle hadn't taken well to that. Either way, she would barely get out of bed, let alone go to class and hang out with her friends and whatever else she should have been doing.

Gradually, though, her mind healed over. She started going to classes again. One night she laughed on the phone. A few weeks later, when Cal phoned to tell her that Lyle was pleading guilty, she was at a bar with Ben. Cal knew the cracks were still there and still fragile, but he also knew how strong the drive towards life is in healthy young creatures. He put his trust in that, as far as he was capable of doing.

When Donna started giving him shit, at first Cal put that down to the same thing: delayed trauma, coming out now that she had room for it. The shit in question was initially a generalized buckshot spatter of anger, but gradually, as Donna talked her thoughts into clarity, it focused in on their time in Seattle: specifically, the fact that Cal had spent most of that time tracking down Lyle. Donna felt, apparently, that he should have spent it in Alyssa's apartment, with her and her roommates and Donna and Ben and whatever other friends had shown up to offer moral support and gossip and crap with chia seeds in it.

"What was I gonna do there?"

"Talk to her. Hug her. Just fucking **sit** there. Anything would've been better than nothing."

"I did something. I went out and got the guy. Without me, they would have—"

"She didn't need you out somewhere being a cop. She needed you right in that room being her father."

"She didn't want me there," Cal said, baffled. "She had you."

"Did you ask her?" Donna snapped, hands and eyebrows flying up. "Did you ever **ask**?"

Cal hadn't. It had seemed obvious to him that at a time like that, a kid needed her mama with her, and that Donna would do the talking and hugging part a lot better than he would. He had gone out and brought Alyssa the best he had to offer, which was Lyle's louse-ridden scalp. That didn't seem like nothing to him. Without his work, Lyle would still have been on the streets; every time she went out her door, Alyssa would have been watching for him on every corner. Now, at least for the next seven to ten years, she could go out without being afraid.

Either way, this did not, at first, seem like marriage-ending material. But over the next months it led them, via a series of leaps and skids that Cal barely managed to follow even at the time, into much darker and muddier places. They argued for hours on end, late into the night, far past the point where Cal became too punch-drunk and exhausted to understand what they were arguing about. In the end Donna got mad enough that she left, which stunned Cal to the bones. He had got plenty mad at Donna, in the course of their time together, but never mad enough that it occurred to him to walk out.

The only thing he took away from those arguments with any clarity was that Donna believed he would be a better husband, and a better father, if he wasn't a cop. Cal thought that was a load of hooey, but he found himself willing to run with it anyway. He had his twenty-five, Alyssa was out of college, and the job was no longer what it had been, or maybe what Cal had believed it was. He couldn't tell what it was, any more, but he was becoming clearer and clearer that he didn't like it.

He didn't tell Donna what he had decided until he had turned in his paperwork, got it all approved and got in writing the date when he would hand in his badge. He wanted to present her with something solid, so she would know he wasn't bullshitting. Maybe he left it too long, because when he told Donna, she said she had something to tell him, too, which turned out to be that she was seeing some guy called Elliott from her book club.

Cal didn't reveal that part to his buddies. They would have said that Donna had been banging Elliott all along and that was why she left to begin with, and Cal knows she wasn't. He would like to believe she was, for his own peace of mind, but he knows Donna better than that. She has her code too. Probably the thought of hooking up with Elliott never so much as crossed her mind while she and Cal were together, or she would never have laid a finger on him even after they split. He just told the guys that she had said it was too late, which she had, and the guys bought Cal more beer and they all agreed on the incomprehensibility of women.

But this, which should have provided some comfort, just made him feel worse. He feels like a fraud, because the other thing he took away from all those fights with Donna was that somehow, without ever intending to, he had let her and Alyssa down. All Cal ever wanted to be was a steady man who took care of his family and did right by the people around him. For more than twenty years, he went about his business believing he was that man. Only somewhere along the way, he fucked up. He lost hold of his code, and the worst part is that he can't understand what he did. Everything he's been since that moment has been worth nothing, and he doesn't even know what the moment was.

Cal finishes his beer and heads up the fading road. Mart and Kojak come to their door in a cloud of onions and paprika. "Well, would you look at that," Mart says happily. "It's Sunny Jim. How's she cutting?"

"I told Trey Reddy to get lost," Cal says. "She won't be coming round any more."

"Good man yourself," Mart says. "I knew my money was safe on you. You'll be glad you did it in the end." He waves Cal towards the kitchen. "Sit you down there now, and I'll get another plate. I'm after making a chicken and bacon paella that's only feckin' beautiful, if I do say so myself."

"I ate," Cal says. "Thanks." He gives Kojak's ears a rub and goes home, through the cold darkening air and the smell of smoke coming from somewhere.

SEVENTEEN

When Cal walks into Noreen's the next day, he's expecting a frosty stare if he's lucky, but she greets him with a block of cheddar, a long account of how Bobby came in asking for it and she told him that when his manners were as good as Cal Hooper's he'd get the same service Cal gets and the big eejit left practically in tears, and a reminder that in a couple of weeks Lena's pups will be old enough to leave their mammy. Cal has been in Ardnakelty long enough to interpret the nuances of this exchange. Not only does Noreen know that he's seen the light, and approve wholeheartedly, she's going to make sure the rest of the townland knows it too. Cal wonders whether Mart went as far as breaking the terms of his feud with Noreen to make this happen.

By way of confirmation, he tests out Seán Óg's that evening. He walks in the door and is hit by a burst of whoops and ironic cheering from Mart's corner. "Jaysus," Senan says, "the dead arose. We thought Malachy had kilt you."

"We reckoned you must have an awful delicate constitution altogether," says the buck-naked window guy, "to be put off the drink for life by a few sips of poteen."

"Who's **we,** kemosabe?" Mart demands. "I told ye he'd be back. He didn't fancy looking at your ugly mugs for a few days, is all. I don't blame him." He moves over to make room for Cal on the banquette, and signals to Barty to bring him a pint.

"Come here," Bobby says to Senan. "Ask him. He'd know."

"Why would he know?"

"It's probably some American yoke. The young people do all be talking American these days."

"Go on and educate me, then," Senan says to Cal. "What's a yeet?"

"A what?" Cal says.

"A yeet. I'm sitting on the sofa tonight after my tea, doing a bit of digesting, and my youngest lad comes running in, launches himself onto my feckin' belly like he's been shot from a cannon, yells 'Yeet!' out of him right in my face, and legs it out again. I asked one of my other fellas what he was on about, but he only laughed his arse off and told me I'm getting old. Then he asked me for twenty quid to go into town."

"Did you give it to him?" Cal asks.

"I did not. I told him to fuck off and get a job. What the hell is a yeet?"

"You never saw a yeet?" Cal says. He finds himself fed up to the back teeth with being tossed around by these guys like a beach ball. "They're pet animals. Like hamsters, only bigger and uglier. Great big fat faces and little piggy eyes."

"I haven't got a fat fuckin' face. You're telling me my young lad's after calling me a hamster?"

"Well," Cal says, "that word's used for something else, too, but I hope your boy wouldn't know about that. How old is he?"

"Ten."

"He got the internet?"

Senan is swelling up and turning red. "If that little fecker's been looking at porn, he can say good-bye to his drum kit, and his Xbox, and his—everything. What's a yeet? Did he call his own father a prick?"

"He's only winding you up, ye eejit," the buck-naked window guy tells him. "He's no more notion of yeets than you have."

Senan glares at Cal. "Never heard of 'em," Cal says. "But you're cute when you're angry."

Everyone roars with laughter, and Senan shakes his head and tells Cal where he can shove his hamsters. The guys order another round, and Mart insists on teaching Cal the rules of Fifty-Five, on the grounds that if he's planning on sticking around these parts he might as well make himself useful. Nobody says a word about Trey, or Brendan, or Donie, or dead sheep.

Nobody Cal meets, in fact, mentions any of those. Cal tries to take this as an indication that the whole thing is well and truly over—surely if the kid did anything dumb, he would hear about it, one way or another. He's not entirely sure that's the case.

Trey herself has dematerialized. Cal is prepared for anything from slashed tires to a brick through his window—he's moved his mattress into a corner out of range, and he keeps a lookout for missiles on his way in and out of the house. Nothing happens. When he sits on his step in the evenings, nothing rustles in the hedges but birds and small animals. When he works on his house or cooks his dinner, the back of his neck stays quiet. If he didn't know better, he could easily find himself believing that he imagined the whole thing.

He goes flat out on the house: gets the name of the local chimney sweep from Noreen, finishes painting the walls in the front room and moves on to stripping the wallpaper in the little second bedroom. Mart's buddy Locky comes round to do the rewiring and provide a washing machine, at a price that Cal knows better than to inquire into. Locky shows an inclination to chat, so Cal takes the opportunity to go into town and buy himself some new kitchen cupboards and an actual fridge-freezer. With them installed and a fire in the fireplace, the front room changes. It loses its remote, dismantled air and comes together into something whose bareness has a spare, solid warmth. He WhatsApps Alyssa a photo. **Oh wow,** she texts back, **it looks great!**

Getting there, Cal texts. **You should come see**

it. Alyssa comes back with, **Yes! As soon as work settles down** and an eye-roll emoji. Even though this is much what Cal expected, it leaves him sore and low, with the urge to call Donna and piss her off.

Instead he goes out to his woods and spends a couple of hours collecting dead branches to stack for firewood. The cold has settled in, and a fine net curtain of rain hangs in the air. Whenever Cal leaves the house, even just to take out the trash, he doesn't feel a drop hit him, but he gets back inside damp through. Somehow it seeps inside the house, too: no matter how long he keeps the fire burning and the oil heater on, his sleeping bag and his duvet always feel almost imperceptibly damp. He buys another heater for his bedroom, which helps some but not a whole lot.

He tries to take advantage of the fact that he can play his music as loud as he wants again, but it doesn't go to plan. He starts out well, cooking dinner to a good rousing dose of Steve Earle complete with full air drums, just like no one ever came peeping in the windows to see him make a fool of himself. Somehow or other, though, by the end of the evening he finds himself sitting on his back step with a beer, looking up into the darkening haze of the sky and feeling the mist of rain thicken on his skin and his hair, while Jim Reeves fills the air with an old tearjerker about a guy trudging through a blizzard who almost makes it home.

One of the few things that give Cal real pleasure

in these days is the discovery that he still has his eye
for a rifle. The weather lends itself more to fishing,
but he doesn't have the patience just now. He would
love to spend more time out with the Henry, drizzle
or no drizzle, but there's a limit to how much rabbit
he can eat. He stashes a couple in his new freezer and
takes two to Daniel Boone, who rewards him with
a discount on bullets and a tour of his favorite guns,
and a pair to Noreen, to make it clear that he sees and
appreciates her support. He knows he ought to take
one to Mart, but he can't bring himself to do it.

He could take one to Lena, except he's avoiding
her with such dedication that he feels like a damn
fool, skulking outside the shop trying to make sure
she's not in there before he can work up the cour-
age to go in himself. He would love to do all his
shopping in town for a few weeks, but he can't risk
offending Noreen at this delicate moment. This also
means he can't hurry in and out; he has to listen to
all the news about Angela Maguire's heart trouble,
complete with an explanation of how Noreen and
Angela are half cousins via a great-grandmother who
may or may not have poisoned her first husband, and
discuss what the new water park up beyond town
might mean for Ardnakelty. Normally he would be
happy to spend half his day on this, but if Lena sees
him she'll want to talk about the pup, and Cal isn't
going to take the pup.

For the first time since he arrived, Ireland feels

tiny and cramped to him. What he needs is thousands of miles of open highway where he can floor it all day and all night long, watching the sun and the moon pass over nothing but ochre desert and tangled brush. If he tried that around here, he would get about fifty yards before running into an unjustifiable road twist, a flock of sheep, a pothole the size of his bathtub or a tractor going the other way. He goes walking instead, but the fields are so sodden they squelch like bog under his feet, and the road verges are churned to extravagant pits and ridges of mud that stop him from ever finding a rhythm to his stride. Mostly these inconveniences wouldn't bother him, but right now they feel personally targeted: pebbles in his shoes, small but carefully chosen for their sharp corners.

Cal refuses to let his unsettled feeling faze him too badly. It's natural enough, after the disturbance Trey brought. If he lets it be and does plenty of hard work, the feeling will pass. This is what he did at times when, for example, his marriage or his job pinched him around the edges, and it worked: sooner or later, things shifted themselves around enough that he felt at ease amid them again. He reckons by the time he has the house ready for winter, he should have worn the restlessness down.

In the event, he doesn't get the chance. Less than two weeks after he sends Trey packing, he's sitting in his nice spiffed-up front room, in front of a wood fire. It's a high-tempered, unruly night, windy enough to make Cal wonder if his roof is as sound as he thought. He's reading the skinny local paper, and listening for the sound of smashing roof slates, when there's a knock at the door.

The knock has an odd quality, rough and sloppy, more like an animal's pawing. If it hadn't come in the lull between two gusts, Cal might have put it down to the wind hurling a branch up against the door. It's ten at night, past farmers' bedtime unless something is badly wrong.

Cal puts his paper down and stands for a moment in the middle of his front room, wondering whether to get his rifle. The knock doesn't come again. He crosses to the door and cracks it open.

Trey is standing on his doorstep, shaking from head to toe like a whipped dog. One of her eyes is purple and swollen shut. Blood is streaked across her face and pouring down her chin. She's holding up one hand, curled into a claw.

"Aw, shit," Cal says. "Aw, shit, kid."

Her knees are buckling. He wants to pick her up and carry her inside, but he's terrified to touch her in case he hurts her worse. "Get in here," he says.

She stumbles inside and stands there, wobbling and panting. She looks like she doesn't know where she is.

Cal can't see anyone coming after her, but he locks the door all the same. "Here," he says. "Come on.

Over here." He guides her to the armchair with his fingertips on her shoulders. When she drops into it she lets out a sharp hiss of pain.

"Wait," Cal says. "Wait there. Hold on." He gets his sleeping bag and duvet from his bedroom and tucks them around the kid, as gently as he can. Her good hand fastens on the duvet so hard the knuckles whiten.

"There you go," Cal says. "It's gonna be OK." He finds a clean towel and squats by the armchair to stem the blood dripping off her chin. Trey flinches away, but when he tries again she doesn't have the focus to stop him. He blots till he can see where the blood is coming from. Her bottom lip is split open.

"Who did this to you?"

The kid's mouth opens wide, like she's going to howl like a broken animal. Nothing comes out but more blood.

"It's OK," Cal says. He gets the towel to her mouth again and presses. "Never mind. You don't have to say anything. You just sit still awhile."

Trey stares past him and shakes. She breathes in shallow huffs, like it hurts. Cal can't tell if she knows what's going on, or if she took a blow to the head and wandered here in a daze. He can't tell how bad that hand is, or if any teeth are gone, or what other damage might be hidden under her hoodie. The blood from her mouth is everywhere.

"Kid," he says gently. "I don't need you to say

anything. I just need to know what hurts worst. Can you show me?"

For a moment he thinks she can't hear him. Then she lifts her curled hand and motions at her mouth and at her side.

"OK," Cal says. She knows what he's saying, at least. "Good job. We're gonna get you to a doctor."

The kid's good eye flares wide with panic and she starts struggling to get her feet under her. "No," she says, in a harsh growl blurred by the swollen lip. "No doctor."

Cal puts up his hands, trying to block her into the armchair. "Kid. You need X-rays. That lip, you could need stitches—"

"**No.** Get **away,** get—" She smashes his hands away and manages to stand up, rocking.

"Listen to me. If your hand's broken—"

"I don't care. Fuck off, get—"

She's ready to fight her way to the door and stumble back into the night. "OK," Cal says, stepping back and raising his hands. "OK. OK. No doctor. Just sit down."

He has no idea what to do if she won't, but after a minute, when the words get through, the fight goes out of her and she collapses back into the chair.

"There you go," Cal says. "That's better." He puts the towel back to her mouth. "You feel like you're gonna throw up?"

Trey shakes her head. The pain makes her suck in a breath. "Nah."

"Don't swallow the blood, or you will. Just spit it right into here. You dizzy? Seeing double?"

"Nah."

"Did you black out?"

"Nah."

"Well, that's all good," Cal says. "Doesn't sound like you have a concussion." Blood is creeping up through the towel in a rapidly widening patch of red. He switches to a clean part and tries to make himself press harder. He notices, off in a distant corner of his brain, the awareness that at some point, once he has this situation under control, he's going to kill someone.

"Listen," he says, when the red stain slows. "I'm gonna go outside just for one minute. I'll be right outside the door. You just sit tight. OK?"

Trey stiffens again. "No doctor."

"I'm not gonna call a doctor. I swear." He detaches her good hand carefully from the duvet, closes her fingers on the towel and arranges it against her lip. "You keep that there. Press as hard as you can stand. I'll be right back."

The kid still trusts him, or else she just has no choice. Cal doesn't know which possibility kills him worse. She sits there, holding the towel and staring at nothing, while he goes out and closes the front door gently behind him.

He keeps his back against the door, wipes his bloody hands on his pants and tries to scan the garden. The night is huge and wild with wind and stars.

Leaves scud and soar, and shadows roil on the grass. Anything could be out there.

Lena takes her time answering her phone, and her "Hello?," when it finally comes, has a definite coolness to it. She hasn't missed the slight to her pup, and she doesn't appreciate it.

Cal says, "I need your help. Someone's beat up Trey Reddy pretty bad. I need you to come over to my place and give me a hand."

A big part of him expects Lena to stick by her principle of not getting involved in other people's business, which would be the smartest response by far. Instead she says, after a silence, "What d'you want me for?"

"Look her over, see how bad she is and whether she's got any other injuries. I can't do that."

"I'm no doctor."

"You've seen to plenty of hurt animals. That's more'n I've done. Just find out if she's got anything that needs medical attention."

"It mightn't show. She could have internal bleeding. You need to get her to a doctor."

"She doesn't want one. I just need to know whether I should drag her kicking and screaming, or whether she's gonna survive without. And if I do have to drag her, then I'm gonna need you to hold her down while I drive."

There's another, longer silence, in which Cal can do nothing but wait. Then Lena says, "Right. I'll be down to you in ten minutes." She hangs up before he can say anything more.

Trey jumps violently at the sound of Cal coming back in. "Just me," he says. "I got a friend of mine coming over who's good at caring for hurt animals. I figure a hurt kid can't be too different."

"Who?"

"Lena. Noreen's sister. You don't need to worry about her. Out of everyone around here, she's the best person I know for keeping her mouth shut."

"What'll she do?"

"Just take a look at you. Clean up your face— she'll do it gentler than I can. Maybe stick on one of those fancy Band-Aids that look like stitches."

Trey clearly wants to argue, but she's got nothing left in her to do it with. The warmth from the coverings and the fire has eased her shaking, leaving her limp and slumped. She looks like she barely has the strength to keep holding the towel to her mouth.

Cal pulls over one of the kitchen chairs, so he can sit by her and catch it if she drops it. Her eye has got worse, plum-black and swollen so big that the skin is tight and shiny.

"Let's see how that cut's doing," he says. Trey doesn't react. Cal reaches out one finger and moves her hand away from her mouth. The bleeding has slackened, just slow bright drops welling up. Her teeth are all still there. "Better," he says. "How's it feel?"

Trey moves one shoulder. She hasn't looked straight at him once. When she tries, her eye skids away like his hurt her.

She needs to rinse out that cut with salt water, and someone needs to take a close look and see if it needs stitches. Cal has done first aid on babies, junkies and everyone in between, but he can't do it here. He can't take the risk that he'll put a finger wrong and break the kid. Just being this near to her makes his whole body sing with nerves.

"Kid," he says. "Listen to me. I can't make sure this situation goes nice and smooth unless I know what it is I'm dealing with. I'm not gonna say a word to anyone without your leave, but I need to know who did this to you."

Trey's head moves against the back of the chair. She says, "My mam."

The fury hits Cal so intensely that for a second he can't see. When it clears a little, he says, "How come?"

"They told her to. Said do it or we will."

"Who told her to?"

"Dunno. I was out. Got home and she said to come out back 'cause she hadta talk to me."

"Uh-huh," Cal says. He makes sure he has his cop face and his cop voice in place, peaceful and interested. "What'd she use?"

"Belt. And hit me. Kicked me a coupla times."

"Well, that's not good," Cal says. He wants Lena

to get here so badly that he can hardly sit still. "You got any idea why?"

Trey makes a ragged twitch that Cal recognizes as a shrug.

"You been stealing from anyone who might take offense?"

"Nah."

"You've been asking questions about Brendan," Cal says. "Haven't you?"

Trey nods. She doesn't have the wherewithal to lie.

"Dammit, kid," Cal begins, and then bites it back. "OK. Who've you been asking?"

"Went to see Donie."

"When?"

It takes her a while to figure that out. "Day before yesterday."

"He give you anything?"

"He just told me to fuck off. Laughed at me." Her words are sloppy and widely spaced, but she's making sense. Her mind is OK, depending on your definition of OK. "He said watch yourself or you'll end up like Bren."

"Well, Donie can say anything he likes," Cal says. "Doesn't make it so." The talking has opened up her lip again; a thin trickle of blood is making its way down her chin. "Hush, now. I'll take care of that part. All you gotta do is stay still."

Wind slams against the windows and sings furiously in the chimney, setting the fire fluttering and sending curls of rich-smelling smoke into the room. Firewood cracks and pops. Cal checks Trey's lip every now and then. When the bleeding stops again, he stands up.

The movement sends a jolt of panic through Trey. "What're you doing?"

"Getting you some ice to put on that eye, and that lip. That's all. Bring down the swelling, and ease the pain a little bit."

He's at the sink, popping ice cubes into a fresh towel, when he sees the sweep of Lena's headlights across the window. "Here's Miss Lena," he says, putting down the ice tray with a surge of relief. "I'm gonna go warn her not to pester you with questions. You just sit tight and keep this on your face."

Lena is getting out of her car by the time Cal comes outside. She slams the door and strides up the drive, hands shoved in the pockets of a man's green wax jacket. The wind whips pieces of her hair free from its ponytail and the starlight turns it a luminous, eerie white. As she reaches Cal, she raises her eyebrows for an explanation.

"Kid showed up at my door in bad shape," Cal says. "If you ask her for details she'll freak out, so don't ask. She's got a black eye, a split lip, something's wrong with her hand, and she says her side hurts pretty bad."

Lena's eyebrows flick higher. "Noreen told me a date with you would be different from the local lads," she says. "She's always right, that one," and she walks past him into the house.

The sight of her hits Trey with another jolt of panic. She drops the towel, ice cubes scattering, and looks like she's about to scrabble up from the chair again. "Hush," Cal says. "Miss Lena's here to take a look at you, remember? It's her or a doctor, so don't give her any hassle. OK?"

Trey sinks back into the chair. Cal can't tell whether that's because she's OK with Lena or because her strength has given out. "There you go," he says. "That's better." He goes to the cupboard and finds his first-aid kit.

"First thing is to get you cleaned up," Lena says matter-of-factly, pulling off her jacket and throwing it over the back of a chair, "so I can see what's what. Have you another cloth, Cal?"

"Under the sink," Cal says. "I'll be right outside." He puts the first-aid kit in Lena's hands and walks out the back door.

He sits down on the step, leans his elbows on his knees and breathes hard into his fingers for a while. He feels some kind of light-headed, or maybe sick, he can't tell which. He needs to do something, but he can't tell what that is either. "Fuck," he says quietly, into his fingers. "Fuck."

The wind shoves at him, trying to get around him and in the door. The treetops toss furiously and the garden has a deserted, tight-battened feel, like no creature that's not desperate or crazy would be out in this. No sound comes from inside the house, or nothing Cal can hear through the wind.

After a while his head starts to come back together again, at least enough to fumble for something like a plan. He has better sense than to go near Sheila Reddy, but nothing on earth is going to keep him away from Donie.

He can't do anything until he learns what Trey needs, though, and figures out how to get it for her. He considers slipping the kid a big dose of Benadryl and hauling her into the car when she gets drowsy. Even leaving aside the problematic aspects of showing up at a hospital with a drugged beat-up teenage girl, he's uneasy about a course of action that, among its many other less predictable consequences, would likely land the kid in foster care. Maybe she'd be better off there; he can't tell. Back when it was his job, he would have handed her over without a second thought and let the system do its thing.

Lena comes outside drying her hands on her jeans, closes the door behind her and sits down on the step next to Cal.

"She gonna make a run for it while you're out here?" Cal asks.

"I doubt it. She's exhausted. No reason why she would, anyway. I told her she doesn't need a doctor."

"Does she?"

Lena shrugs. "There's no emergency, as far as I can tell. Her stomach's not sore or swollen, and she's got no bruises there—she says she curled up in a ball—so no reason to think she's bleeding internally. I'd say she's got a cracked rib, but there's nothing a doctor could do about that. The hand seems like it's bruised, not broken, but she'll have to wait and see how it goes over the next couple of days. There's plenty more cuts and bruises on her back and her legs, but they're not serious."

"Right," Cal says. The image of Trey curled up feels like it's branding him. "Yeah. Well. There you go. You think the lip needs stitches?"

"It could do with them, all right, so it doesn't leave too bad of a scar. I told her that and she said no stitches, she doesn't give a shite about scars. So I had her rinse it out with salt water, and I put on one of your Steri-Strips. Gave her one of your Nurofen for the pain. Better than nothing."

"Thanks," Cal says. "I appreciate this."

Lena nods. "She oughta get seen, just in case. But she'll live without."

"Then she'll have to live without. She'd just do herself more damage, fighting all the way."

"If she gets worse during the night, she'll need to go. Like it or not."

"Yeah."

Lena pulls her hands up into her sweater sleeves to keep them warm. She says, "Are you going to keep her here for the night?"

Even if Sheila notices Trey is gone before morning, she's hardly likely to call the cops. "Yeah," Cal says. "Could I ask you to sit with her?" It comes out abrupt, but he can't wait to get moving. "I got somewhere I need to be. If she gets worse, call me and I'll come back."

"She was asking for you."

"Tell her I'll be back in the morning. And tell her don't worry, I'm not going for a doctor."

"She hardly knows me. It's you she wants."

Cal says, "I'm not gonna spend the night alone with a little girl."

Lena tilts her head back against the door frame to inspect him up and down. She doesn't look particularly impressed with what she sees. "Fair enough," she says. "I'll stay if you do."

It's a challenge, and it leaves Cal stymied. "What am I gonna do for her here?" he says.

"Same as I am. Give her more Nurofen, or a clean towel if her lip opens up. It's not like she needs brain surgery. What are you going to do for her anywhere else?"

"I told you," Cal says. He wishes he had called someone else, anyone else—not that there is anyone, unless he felt like getting on Facebook and messaging Caroline. "I got somewhere to be."

"Not somewhere smart."

"Maybe not. But still."

"If you leave," Lena informs him, "I'm leaving as well. This is your mess, not mine. I'm not sitting here all night waiting for your problems to come find me."

She doesn't look one bit nervous to Cal, but neither does she look like she plans on backing down. "These problems aren't gonna come looking for anyone," he says. "Not tonight, anyway."

"Imagine how you'll feel if you abandon a poor widow woman and an injured child to get bet up by hooligans."

"I've got a gun I can leave you."

"Congratulations. So do plenty of other people round here."

More than anything else, she looks amused at Cal's predicament. He runs his hands over his face. "Look," he says. "I know it's a lot to ask. You could take her to your place, if—"

"You think she'll go?"

Cal rubs his face harder. "My mind's not working too good right now," he says. "Are you serious about leaving if I do?"

"I am, yeah. I don't mind giving you a hand where you actually need it, but I'm not going to be left handling the real business while you chase off on some nonsense you've got into your head." She grins at him. "I told you I was a cold bitch."

Cal believes her. "OK," he says, like he has a choice. "You win." There's no way in the world he can leave Trey in this house alone tonight. "I've only got one bed, and the kid's getting that, but you can have the armchair."

"Well, would you look at that," Lena says, standing up. "Chivalry isn't dead." She holds the door open and ushers him inside with a sweep of her arm, in exchange.

With the shock and the pain ebbing, fatigue has hit Trey like a kick from a horse. Her head has fallen back in the armchair, the hand holding the ice pack has dropped into her lap, and her good eyelid is drooping. "Come on," Cal says. "Let's get you to bed before you fall asleep right there."

The kid catches her breath and rubs at her good eye. There are gouges on her hand where the belt buckle caught her. " 'M I staying here?"

"Yep, for tonight. You're gonna have my bed. Me and Miss Lena, we'll be right out here." Trey's lip, all tidied up and held together by the Steri-Strip, has a reassuringly professional look. Lena did a good job. "Now come on. I'm not gonna carry you; I'd throw my back out."

"You could do with the exercise," Trey tells him. Her lopsided shadow of a grin pretty near takes Cal to pieces.

"Ungrateful little so-and-so," he says. "Watch your manners or I'll make you sleep in the bathtub. Now move it."

Her sore places are stiffening. He has to half scoop her out of the armchair, set her on her feet and steer her into the bedroom. The movement makes her grimace, but she doesn't complain. Lena picks up the duvet and the sleeping bag and follows them.

"Here you go," Cal says, switching the light on. "The lap of luxury. I'm gonna let Miss Lena get you settled. You need anything in the night, or anything bothers you, you just call us."

Trey crumples onto the mattress in an ungainly pile of elbows and feet. Lena tosses the bedclothes beside her and moves to undo Trey's shoelaces. To Cal the scene looks lawless and incomprehensible, stained mattress on scuffed floorboards, harsh glare from the bare bulb, tangle of cheap bedclothes, the woman kneeling at the feet of the bruised and bloody child. He feels like he should at least be able to offer the kid something gentle, a feather bed with a ruffle, a soft-shaded bedside lamp and a picture of kittens on the wall.

He switches on the oil heater. "Well," he says. He thinks, fleetingly and ridiculously, of putting the toy sheep on Trey's pillow. "Good night. Sleep tight." She watches him over Lena's shoulder, with her one open eye beyond any expression, as he shuts the door.

The bloodied dish towels are scattered around the armchair. Cal collects them and throws them in his new washing machine. He doesn't turn it on, in case its whirring disturbs the kid. He switches on the electric kettle and sets out two mugs—what he needs is a shot of whiskey, but he might yet have to drive tonight, and he's learned enough to know that around here tea is an appropriate response to any situation at any time of day or night. Blood has dried in the lines of his knuckles; he washes his hands at the kitchen sink.

Lena comes out of the bedroom and closes the door quietly behind her. "How's she doing?" Cal asks.

"Asleep before I got the duvet on her."

"Well, that's good," Cal says. "You want some tea?"

"Go on."

Lena settles herself in the armchair, testing it out, and kicks off her shoes. The kettle boils, and Cal pours and brings a mug over to her. "I don't have milk. This OK?"

"You savage." She takes the mug and blows on it. She looks at ease in the armchair, as if it were her own. It's an ample, lopsided creation in a peculiar purplish green that might have been fashionable for a minute a long time ago, or might just have started out a different shade; it's surprisingly comfortable, but Cal never envisioned inviting anyone to sleep in it. He has that sense of being weightless again, off his feet and borne along with nothing to grab hold of.

The fire has burned low; he puts more wood on it. "She say anything to you that I oughta know?" he asks.

"She said nothing about anything, except what I told you. But I didn't ask."

"Thanks."

"No point. You're the one she trusts." Lena sips her tea. "She's been coming here a lot."

"Yeah," Cal says, taking his mug to the table. He can't imagine that Lena is aiming to lecture him on the unseemliness of letting Trey Reddy hang around, and sure enough, she only nods. "Are you gonna get any hassle for helping me out?"

She shrugs. "I doubt it. You might, but, depending what you do next. Are you going to bring her home in the morning?"

"You know anywhere else she can go?"

He feels Lena take in the implication. She considers and shakes her head.

"Aunt? Uncle? Grandparents?"

"Most of her relations are emigrated or dead or useless, depending on which side you mean. Sheila's got cousins over the other side of town, but they wouldn't want to get mixed up in this."

"I can see their point," Cal says.

"Sheila does the best she can," Lena says. "You and I might not think it's great, but we haven't spent twenty-five years on the wrong side of Johnny Reddy and Ardnakelty. Sheila's had all the fancy notions worn right out of her. All she wants is to keep the children she's got left alive and out of jail."

Cal has no idea what to say to this. He can't tell whether he's angry at Lena, or whether his anger at Sheila and whoever got to her is so high that it's spilling over onto her.

Lena says, "She's got used to doing whatever needs to be done. Right or wrong. She hasn't had much choice."

"Maybe," Cal says. He doesn't find that reassuring. If Sheila felt her best or only option tonight was to beat the living shit out of Trey, she might feel that way again sometime. "I might see if I can get a few things done before I send the kid back there."

Lena glances up from her tea. "Like what?"

"The stuff I shoulda been doing tonight."

"**Man** business," Lena says, mock-awed. "Too serious for a lady's delicate ears."

"Just business."

The firewood pops and shoots a spray of sparks upwards. Lena stretches out a toe to nudge the screen more snugly into place.

"I can't stop you doing something stupid," she says. "But I'm hoping if you have to leave it till morning, you might think better of it."

It takes Cal a minute or two to figure out why this comment startles him so much. He was assuming that the reason Lena made him stick around—apart from not wanting his business dumped in her lap, which is fair enough—was because the kid wanted him there. Instead, she sounds like her aim was to prevent Cal from getting his ass kicked, or something similar. Cal finds this unexpectedly moving. Mart has put considerable effort into the same goal, but it's different coming from a woman. It's been a while since a woman gave that much of a damn about Cal either way.

"Well, I appreciate that," he says. "I'll keep it in mind."

Lena makes a wry **pfft** noise, which leaves Cal

slightly chagrined even though he agrees that it's warranted. "I'm going asleep," she says, leaning to put her mug on the table. "Will we turn out the light?"

Cal switches it off, leaving only the firelight. He goes into the spare bedroom and brings out his heavy winter duvet—he hasn't got around to buying a cover for it, but it is at least clean. "I apologize for this," he says. "I'd like to be a better host, but this is all I've got."

"I've slept in worse," Lena says, taking out her pony-tail and snapping the hair band around her wrist. "I wish I'd brought my toothbrush, is all." She curls side-ways in the chair and tucks the duvet around herself.

"Sorry," Cal says, getting both his coats from their hook. "Can't help you there."

"I'll go down to Mart Lavin and ask if he has a spare, will I?"

Cal is so off-kilter that he spins around horrified. When he sees her grin, he's startled into a crack of laughter loud enough that he claps a hand over his mouth, glancing at the bedroom door.

"You'd make Ardnakelty's day," he says.

"I would, all right. It'd almost be worth it, only Noreen'd pat herself on the back so hard she'd do herself an injury."

"So would Mart."

"Jesus. Is he on this too?"

"Oh yeah. He's already decided that Malachy Dwyer's gonna cater the bachelor party."

"Ah well, feck the toothbrush, so," Lena says. "We can't let those two think they're right every time. 'Twouldn't be good for them."

Cal arranges himself in front of the fireplace and wraps both coats around him. By firelight the room is all warm gold flickers and pulses of shadow. It makes the situation bloom with a seductive, ephemeral intimacy, like they're the last people left awake at a house party, caught up in a conversation that won't count tomorrow morning.

"I don't know that we've got much choice," he says. "Unless you leave before dawn, someone's gonna see your car."

Lena thinks that over. "Mightn't be a bad idea," she says. "Give people something to talk about, keep their minds away from the other thing." She nods at the bedroom door.

"Are you gonna get hassle, though?"

"What, for being a loose woman, like?" She grins again. "Nah. The aul' ones'll talk, but I don't mind them. It's not the eighties; it's not like they can throw me in a Magdalen laundry. They'll get over it."

"How 'bout me? Is Noreen gonna show up with a shotgun if I don't marry you after this?"

"God, no. She'll blame me for letting you slip through my fingers. You're grand. The lads in Seán Óg's might even buy you a pint, to congratulate you."

"Win-win," Cal says. He stretches out on his back, with his hands behind his head, and wishes he'd thought to bring his extra clothes out of his bedroom. He's not planning to sleep if he can help it, in case of the various situations that might arise, but after a night on this floor he's going to be walking like Mart.

"Tell me something," Lena says. The firelight moves across her eyes. "Why aren't you going to take that pup?"

"Because," Cal says, "I'd want to guarantee that I'd take care of it right, and no harm would come to it. And it doesn't seem like I can do that."

Lena's eyebrows go up. "Huh," she says. "Here I thought you just didn't want anything tying you down."

"Nope," Cal says. He watches the fire. "Seems like I'm always looking for something to hold me down. It just never works out that way."

Lena nods. Wind, wearying to halfhearted gusts, ruffles the fire. It's burning low again, the heart of it darkening to a deep orange glow.

From the bedroom comes a thrashing of bed-clothes and a hoarse, inarticulate cry. By the time Cal's mind works out that a homicidal intruder is unlikely, he's at the bedroom door.

He stops and looks over at Lena. "You're up already," she says. "I'll go next time." Then she turns her shoulder to him, settling herself more comfortably in the chair, and pulls the duvet up to her chin.

Cal stands there, at the door. Another strangled cry comes from the bedroom. Lena doesn't move.

After a moment he opens the bedroom door. Trey

is up on her elbow, head turning wildly, whimpering through gritted teeth.

"Hey," Cal says. "It's OK."

The kid jumps and whips round to stare at him. It takes her a few seconds to see him.

"You had a bad dream, is all. It's gone now."

Trey lets out a long shaky breath and lies back, wincing as her rib catches. "Yeah," she says. "Just dreaming."

"That's right," Cal says. "Anything hurt? You need more painkillers?"

"Nah."

"OK. Sleep tight."

When he turns to go, she moves in the bed and makes a small rough sound. He turns back and sees her good eye looking at him, shining in the light coming through the door.

"What?"

The kid doesn't answer.

"You want me to stick around awhile?"

She nods.

"OK," Cal says. "I can do that." He eases himself down onto the floor and settles his back against the wall.

Trey rustles herself around so she can keep that eye on him. "What're you gonna do?" she asks, after a minute.

"Hush," Cal says. "We'll figure it out in the morning."

He can see her searching for the next question. To quiet her, he starts to sing, so low it's half a hum, hoping Lena won't hear through the wind. The song that comes out is "Big Rock Candy Mountain," same as he used to sing for Alyssa when she was little and couldn't sleep. Gradually Trey relaxes. Her breathing slows and deepens, and the shine of that eye fades among the shadows.

Cal keeps on singing. He used to fix up the words a little bit for Alyssa, change the cigarette trees to candy-cane trees and the lake of whiskey to one of soda. There doesn't seem to be much point in doing that for Trey, but he does it anyway.

EIGHTEEN

The wind blows itself out, and dawn comes to the window cold and still in a clear gold-green. Cal has been dozing off and on, in between watching the fire die down and checking on Trey by the light of his phone. As far as he can tell, she never budged once all night, even when he got close enough to make sure she was still breathing.

In the first light Lena takes shape, curled up in the armchair with her face buried in her elbow, her hair a pale scribble. Outside, the small birds are starting to toss out scraps of morning conversation, and the rooks are bitching at them to shut up. Cal is sore at every point where his bones pressed into the floor, and a lot of points in between.

He gets up, as quietly as he can, and heads to the sink to fill the kettle. He's light-headed with tiredness, but not in a fuzzy way; the chill and the dawn give everything a spellbound, airy lucidity. In his garden the rabbits are chasing each other in circles through the dew-wet grass.

Lena stirs in the armchair and sits up, arching her back and scrunching up her face. She looks baffled. "Morning," Cal says.

"Ah, Jaysus," Lena says, shielding her eyes. "If

you're planning on having guests on the regular, you need curtains."

"I'd need a lot more'n that," Cal says, keeping his voice down. "How you feeling?"

"Too old for this carry-on, is how I'm feeling. How about you?"

"Like I got hit by a truck. Remember back when we'd crash on people's floors just for kicks?"

"I do, yeah, but I was an awful eejit back then. I'd rather be old and have sense." She stretches, hugely and with appreciation. "Is Trey still asleep?"

"Yeah. I figure the longer she sleeps, the better. Can I make you some breakfast?" Cal finds himself hoping she says yes. Lena may not be the most accommodating person in the world, but she alters the balance of the house in a way he likes. "I got toast with bacon and eggs, or toast without bacon and eggs."

Lena grins. "Ah, no. I'd better head. I've to get ready for work, and I've to feed the dogs first, let them out. Nellie'll be going mental. She loses the head if I'm out past bedtime; by now she's probably et half the furniture." She unfurls herself from the chair and starts folding the duvet. "Will I call by here on my way in to work? Bring Trey home?"

"I'm not sure," Cal says. He thinks about what kind of scary it would take, to make a mother do that to her kid. For a second, before he can turn his mind away, he wonders what it would have taken to make him or Donna do that to Alyssa. "I'd rather get things cleared up a little bit first."

Lena tosses the folded duvet over the back of the armchair. "Here was me hoping by morning you'd have got sense," she says.

"I'm not gonna do anything stupid."

Lena's glance says this is a matter of opinion, but she doesn't comment. She pulls her hair band off her wrist and twists her hair back into its ponytail. "So I'm not bringing her home."

"Maybe later. OK if I see how the day goes, give you a call in a while?"

"Away you go. Have fun."

"If I needed you to stay here one more night," Cal says, "would you consider it? I'd run into town and buy an air mattress, so you wouldn't be back on that chair."

Lena startles him by bursting out laughing. "You," she says, shaking her head, "you're some tulip, d'you know that? And your timing is shite. Come back to me later, once the aches and pains wear off, and we'll see." She pulls on her shoes and her jacket and heads for the door.

Cal waits till he hears her car drive away. Then he takes a walk around his garden. He can't find any sign of intruders, but then he wouldn't either way. The evidence of the night's wind is everywhere. Leaves are scattered lavishly across the grass and banked high against walls and hedges, and the trees have a raw, defiant bareness. Under his windows, the earth has been scoured smooth.

He goes back indoors and starts cooking breakfast. The smell of frying bacon brings Trey out of the bedroom, barefoot and crumpled. Her fat lip has gone down some, but the eye is even more spectacular in daylight, and there's an ugly bruise on her cheekbone that Cal didn't notice before. Her hoodie and her jeans are crusted with patches and smears of dried blood. Cal looks at her and has no idea what to do about her. The thought of sending her out of this house makes him want to barricade everything and spend his time with his gun pointing out a window, in case someone comes for her.

"How you doing?" he asks.

"Shite. Hurts everywhere."

"Well, I took that for granted," Cal says. The fact that she's walking and talking fills him up with a relief that makes it hard to breathe. "I meant apart from that. You sleep OK?"

"Yeah."

"You hungry?"

The kid looks like she wants to say no, but the smell is too much for her. "Yeah. Starving."

"Breakfast'll be ready in a minute. Sit down there."

Trey sits, yawning and flinching as the yawn stretches her lip. She watches Cal while he turns the bacon and butters the toast. The way she's sitting, with her shoulders high and too much weight on her feet, reminds him of the way she used to stand when she first started coming around: ready to run.

"You want another painkiller?" he asks.

"Nah."

"Nah? Anything hurt worse than last night?"

"Nah. I'm grand."

With her face messed up, Cal finds it even harder than usual to tell what's going on in her head. "Here you go," he says, bringing the plates to the table. "Cut it up small, and don't let it touch that lip. The salt'll sting."

Trey ignores that and attacks the food, still keeping a wary eye on Cal. Her hand is better; she holds the fork clumsily, trying not to bend her fingers, but she's using it.

"Miss Lena just left a few minutes back," Cal says. "She's got work. She might be back later, depending."

Trey says brusquely, "Sorry I came here. I wasn't thinking straight."

"No," Cal says. "Don't be sorry. You did right."

"Nah. You told me not to be coming around any more."

All of Cal's relationships, which seemed perfectly straightforward and harmonious last night, appear to have got themselves out of joint while he wasn't looking. Never mind Brendan Reddy: the real mystery to which Cal would love an answer is how, while doing everything right as far as he can tell, he somehow manages to fuck everything up.

"Well," he says. "This was an emergency. That's different. You called it right."

"I'll go after this."

"No hurry. Before you go anywhere, we need to decide what you want me to do."

Trey looks blank.

"About last night. You want me to call the police? Or CPS—child protective services, whatever you call it?"

"No!"

"CPS isn't the boogeyman, kid. They'll find you somewhere safe to stay for a while. Maybe get your mama some help."

"She doesn't need help."

The kid is glaring, holding her knife like she's all ready to stab Cal with it. "Kid," he says gently. "What she did to you wasn't OK."

"She never done that before. She only done it this time 'cause they made her."

"So what if they make her again?"

"They won't."

" 'Cause what? You learned your lesson, now you're gonna behave yourself?"

"None a your business," Trey says, with a defiant glance.

"I'm asking you, kid. I need to figure out what to do here."

"You don't need to do anything. If you call child services, I'll tell 'em you done this."

She means it, too. "OK," Cal says. Seeing this

amount of fight out of her makes his spine go weak with relief. He got up this morning afraid to see her in case he found her smashed inside, a girl-husk that stared right through him, that had to be steered stumbling from place to place and sat with a bite in her mouth till she was reminded to chew and swallow. "No child services."

Trey eyeballs him for another minute. Apparently she believes him, because she goes back to her food. She says, "I know that was all bullshit, what you told me. About Bren going to Scotland. So's I'd fuck off and leave you alone."

Cal gives up. Whatever he was trying to do there, it hasn't worked. "Yeah," he says. "Donie gave me sweet fuck-all. Only I was bullshitting you about the leave-me-alone part, too. Truth is, I got no problem with you coming around. I enjoy your company."

Trey looks up at that. She says, "I don't want your fucking money."

"I know that, kid. I never thought you did."

She goes still, rearranging her mind around that. The loosening in her face hooks Cal right under the breastbone. "So how come you said all that shite?" she demands.

"For Christ's sake, kid. You think no one noticed what the two of us were up to? I got warned to back off. This right here"—he points his fork at Trey's face—"this is exactly what I was trying to avoid."

Trey gives an impatient hitch of her shoulders. "It's no big deal. I'll be grand."

"This time, you will. Because they got your mama to do it, and she only went as far as she thought would satisfy them. Next time, they'll go after you themselves. Or after your mama. Or your little brother and sisters. Or me. These are serious guys, doing serious business. They don't fuck around. They didn't kill you because they don't want the attention a dead kid would get, but they will if they have to."

The kid blinks fast at that. She goes back to shoveling food into her face, head down.

"Jesus Christ, kid," Cal says, suddenly right on the edge of blowing up. "What the fuck is it gonna take to make you knock it off?"

Trey says, "When I know. For definite. Not some bullshit that someone made up to get rid of me."

"Yeah? That's all you want? Just to know for certain?"

"Yeah."

"Yeah, it doesn't work like that. If you find out for certain that Brendan skipped town, you're gonna want to find out why, and then you're gonna want to track him down. If you find out for certain that someone ran him off, you're gonna want to get back at them. There's always gonna be just one more thing left to do. You gotta know when to stop."

"I do know. When—"

"**No.** When to stop is now, kid. Look at you. If they have to come after you again, what are they gonna do? When to stop is now."

Trey's face turns up to him like she's drowning. She

says, "I wanta stop now. I'm tired to fuckin' death of this. At the start, when I first came here, it was like you said: I'da kept going forever. Now I just want it gone. I wanta never think about him again. I wanta go back to doing my own things that I usedta do before. But whatever happened to Brendan, he deserves for someone to know. Just one person, even, to know."

Cal wasn't sure, until this moment, whether she understood the size of the chance that Brendan is dead. They sit there, listening to it settle into the crevices of the room.

"Then I'll stop," Trey says. "When I know."

"Well," Cal says, "there you go. You were asking about having a code. There's the beginning of it." He looks at that beat-up, half-comprehending face and feels his throat thicken for all the things the kid is just starting on, all the rivers she'll have to struggle across that she hasn't even glimpsed on the horizon. "Finish your breakfast," he says. "Before it gets cold."

Trey doesn't budge. "So are you gonna help me? Or not?"

"Truthfully," Cal says, "I don't know yet. First I need to track down the people who came calling on your mama yesterday, and have a talk with them. Once I've done that, I should either know what happened to your brother, or at least know whether we can keep looking without getting ourselves killed."

"What if we can't?"

"I don't know. We're not there yet."

Trey doesn't look like that satisfies her, but she goes back to scraping up egg yolk with her toast. "Tell me something," Cal says. "You think it was Donie who got your mama to do this?"

Trey snorts. "Nah. She'd tell him to fuck himself."

"Yeah, me neither. But these guys came calling two days after you talked to Donie. That's not a coincidence."

"You said if I talked to Donie, you were outa this."

"Yeah, well," Cal says. "Things change. How'd you get hold of him?"

"His mam goes to half-nine mass in town every day," Trey explains, with her mouth full. "She gets a lift with Holy Mike. I waited in the hedge by Mike's lane till I saw his car go off, and then I went across Francie Gannon's fields to Donie's back door."

"You see anyone on your way in or out?"

"Nah. Someone could've seen me, but. From a window. Nothing I could do about that, only go fast."

"Listen," Cal says. He gets up and takes the plates over to the sink. "I gotta go out for a little while. Not long. You gonna be OK here by yourself?"

"Yeah. Course."

The kid doesn't sound entirely happy about the idea. "No one knows you're here," Cal says, "so you don't need to worry. But I'm gonna lock the doors just in case. If anyone comes calling while I'm gone, don't answer, don't look out the window. Just sit tight till they go away. You got it?"

"You going to talk to Donie again?"

"Yeah. You gonna get bored? You want a book or something?"

Trey shakes her head.

"You could take a bath if you want. Wash last night off you."

The kid nods. Cal figures she won't do it. She doesn't look like she could manage anything that complicated. Just getting up for breakfast has tired her out; all of a sudden her face has a kind of exhaustion that's unnatural on a kid, a slack droop to her one good eyelid and deep grooves from nose to mouth. She looks, for the first time, a little bit like her mama.

"You just rest," he says. "Eat whatever you want out of the kitchen. I'll be back soon."

———

Cal heads for Donie's by the same route Trey took, down the back roads and across Francie Gannon's fields. The wind has ripped branches off trees and thrown them, scraggly and splintered, into the roads; the long gold autumn light laid over them gives them the look of a deliberate, sinister harvest. Cal heaves the bigger ones into ditches on his way. He knows he must be tired, but he can't feel it. The walk and the crisp air are shaking the aches out of his muscles, and he still has that light-headed clarity buoying him on. The only thing in his mind is Donie.

The farmers must have finished their morning rounds and gone in for breakfast; Cal encounters no one except a bunch of Francie's sheep, who freeze in mid-chew to fix him with indecipherable stares as he passes, and keep gazing after him for a disconcertingly long time. He still gets over Donie's back wall quicker than anyone could reasonably expect of a guy his age and size, just in case the neighbors look out a window or Francie decides to investigate what's paralyzed his sheep.

Donie's garden is a decrepit patch of overgrown grass, with wind-scattered plastic patio furniture that looks like it came from a supermarket giveaway. Through the window, the kitchen looks empty. Cal jimmies the back door with a loyalty card from his favorite Chicago deli, pushes it open nice and slowly, and steps inside.

Nothing moves. The kitchen is old, beat-up and ferociously clean, with an exhausted shine coming off the oilcloth and the linoleum. A slow drip falls from the tap.

Cal moves quietly through the kitchen and down the hall. The house is dim and smells powerfully of flowery cleaner and damp. It has too much furniture, most of it dumpy varnished pine turning a tawdry orange with age, and too much wallpaper with too much pattern. On the living-room mantelpiece, a dull red light flickers in the chest of a fey-looking Jesus who points at it with one finger and simpers reproachfully at Cal.

Cal keeps to one side of the staircase and puts his weight down gradually, but the steps still creak under him. He stops and listens for movement. The only sound is a faint, dedicated snoring coming from one of the bedrooms.

Donie's room has nothing in common with the rest of the house, except the pine furniture. Most of the surfaces are occupied by dirty clothes and video-game cases. One wall is taken up by a TV the size of a picture window; another one has a high-end sound system whose speakers bulge in every corner like roided-up biceps. The air is practically solid with the interleaved smells of sweat, cigarette smoke, beer farts and crusted sheets. At the heart of this accretion is Donie, spread-eagled facedown on the bed, wearing an undershirt and Minion-patterned briefs.

Cal crosses the room in three strides, gets a knee on the small of Donie's back, grabs his fat neck and shoves his face into the pillow. He keeps him there till Donie's bucking gets an extra edge of desperation, and then hauls his head up for one long gasp. Then he does it again, and then again.

Donie comes up the third time squealing for breath. Cal puts more weight on his spine, lets go of his neck and twists one arm high behind his back. Donie has the consistency of a wetsuit full of pudding.

"You dumb shit," he says into Donie's ear. "You fucked up."

Donie wheezes and writhes, and finally manages

to ratchet his head around and get a look at Cal.
The first thing across his face is relief. This isn't what
Cal is aiming for. Fear is one of the few things that
will spin Donie's hamster wheel. If he's more scared
of someone else than he is of Cal, that's a problem.
Luckily, Cal is in the right mood for fixing it.

"Brendan Reddy," he says. "Start talking."

"Don't know what you're—"

Cal pulls open the drawer of the bedside table, shoves
Donie's fingers in and slams it shut. When Donie
howls, Cal plunges his face into the pillow again.

He waits till he's sure Donie's done howling before
he eases his grip so the little shit can turn his head.
"You know what I want for Christmas?" he says, into
Donie's face. Donie pants and whines. "I want you
mopes to quit being **so fucking predictable.** I'm fed
up to the back teeth of 'Uhhh, dunno what you're
talking about, never heard of the guy.' You know
exactly what I'm talking about. I know you know.
You know I know you know. But still, Donie, **still**
you gotta come out with that shit. Sometimes I feel
like, I hear that shit **one more time,** I'm not gonna
be able to control myself."

He lets go of Donie, gets off the bed and upends a
chair to dump a bunch of nasty tracksuits onto the
floor. "Sorry to lay my personal troubles on you," he
says pleasantly, pulling the chair over to the bedside.
"But every now and again it seems like things build
up just a little bit higher than I can be expected to
put up with."

Donie heaves himself up to a sitting position, holding his fingers and blowing through his teeth. A glob of pale hairy belly pops out between his undershirt and his briefs. The eyebrow gash from his encounter with Mart's hurling stick is only half healed. Donie is having a tough couple of weeks, beating-wise.

"Looking good, son," Cal says.

"My fucking **hand,**" Donie says, outraged.

"Shake it off. You've got some talking to do."

"You fucking **broke** it."

"Ouch," Cal says, leaning in to inspect Donie's fingers, which are purple and swelling, scored with deep red grooves. The middle one is bent at an interesting angle. "I bet if someone stamped on that, it'd hurt like all hell."

"What the fuck do you **want,** man?"

"Jesus Christ, son, you miss the day they taught English in school? Brendan Reddy."

Donie considers going back into know-nothing mode, assesses Cal and thinks better of it. He doesn't look scared, exactly, but he looks a little more alive than usual, which for his kind is the same thing. "Who even are you, man? You in business? Or a cop? What?"

"Like we said before: I'm just a guy who needs a hobby. I'm not gonna pass this conversation on to anyone, if that's what you're worried about. Unless you piss me off."

Donie runs his tongue around the inside of his lip, where the pillow mashed it into his teeth, and examines Cal with those flat pale eyes. "You want me to convince you some more?" Cal asks. "We got at least an hour. I can be real convincing in an hour."

"Why d'you wanta know about Brendan?"

"Lemme get you started," Cal says. "Brendan was setting up as a meth cook for your buddies from Dublin. Take it from there."

"Little prick thought he was outa **Breaking Bad**," Donie says. "'All ye have is the shake-n-bake shite, I can make ye the pure stuff . . .' Fuckin' tosser." Cal watches his eyes in case he has a weapon stashed somewhere, but his focus is on his fingers. He examines them at various angles, experiments with flexing them and grimaces.

"You weren't a fan, huh?"

"I told them all along. Useless little prick, thinks he's the dog's bollox. He'll let you down."

"They shoulda listened to you," Cal agrees. "Woulda made all our lives a lot simpler."

Donie goes for the littered bedside table. Cal shoves him backwards onto the bed. "Nope," he says.

"I need a smoke, man."

"You can wait. I don't wanna breathe that shit; this room stinks bad enough already. You do anything useful for these Dublin boys, or they just keep you around for decoration?"

Donie picks himself up, carefully keeping his sore hand uninvolved. "They need me. You can't run the game without local lads."

"And I'm sure they appreciate you the way you deserve. You have anything to do with Brendan?"

"Hadta help the little prick clear out the aul' house where he was setting up. Get him what he needed." Donie bares his too-small teeth like he wants to bite. "Sending me out with a shopping list, like a fuckin' servant."

"Like what?"

"Sudafed. Batteries. Propane tanks. Generator. Yes sir, no sir, three bags full sir."

"Anhydrous?"

"Nah. Little prick said he'd do that himself, I'd only fuck it up." Donie sniggers. "He was the one that fucked it up."

"How?"

Donie shrugs. "How would I know? Took too much, maybe. Anyhow P.J. Fallon spotted it and called the Guards. Little prick musta talked him into sending them home again, but—"

"How'd he do that?"

"P.J.'s soft in the head. Anything'd do it." Donie puts on an unpleasant whine: "'My poor aul' mammy, if I get sent down she'll be all alone . . .' Only the little prick musta let slip to P.J. where he'd put the anhydrous."

"Which was where? His lab?"

"'Lab,'" Donie says, and sniggers. "Aul' tip of a house up the mountains. Little prick swore no one else knew about it. P.J. and a few of his mates went in and cleared it out. Not just the anhydrous. Generator, batteries, anything worth anything. Five, six hundred quid's worth, easy."

Cal doesn't need to ask who P.J.'s mates included. Mart, that know-it-all fuck: he really did know it all, or most of it anyway. All the time Cal was babbling on about big cats, and all the time he was wandering around asking innocent questions about wiring, Mart knew exactly who each of them was looking for, and why.

"The Dublin guys find out?" he asks.

Donie grins. "Ah, yeah."

"How?"

"I dunno, man. Maybe they had a lookout on the place, check for themselves was it really as safe as the little prick said." Donie's grin widens. He seems surprisingly at ease with this conversation, now that he's got accustomed to the idea of it. Cal has met people like Donie before: people who barely registered even pain or fear, let alone anything else, like their emotions never grew in right. None of them improved anyone's life in any way. "Little prick was shitting himself. I'd say he'd been hoping to keep it on the QT that he'd been snared. Try and get hold of the cash to replace all the gear before they found out."

"What'd they do?"

"Had me set up a meeting. Them and him."

"Where?"

"That aul' house."

"To do what?"

"Give him a few slaps, probably. For being a thick cunt and drawing attention. Only the little prick didn't show. He done a runner."

Donie's eye is wandering to the pack of cigarettes on the bedside table again. Cal snaps his fingers in his face. "Focus, Donie. That all they woulda done to him? A few slaps?"

"Long as he paid it back, yeah. They wanted him to do the work for them."

"He know that?"

Donie shrugs. "Fuckin' eejit didn't know his arse from his elbow. He was in over his head, know what I mean? You wanta work with these lads, you haveta be smart. Not fuckin' chemistry shite. Street smart."

"Were you at the meeting?"

"Nah. Other stuff to do."

Meaning he wasn't invited, and meaning he doesn't know whether or not the Dublin boys were telling him the truth about Brendan not showing up. Brendan was an optimistic guy; he could have gone bouncing out the door figuring he was about to put everything happily back on track, and only found out different when it was too late. Cal says, "Did the Dublin boys ask you where he could've gone?"

"How would I know? I wasn't his fuckin' babysitter."

"They go after him? Catch him?"

Donie shakes his head. "I'm not thick, man. I didn't ask."

"Come on, Donie. How pissed off were they?"

"What d'you fuckin' think?"

"Right. You figure they'd just let Brendan ride off into the sunset?"

"Don't wanta know. All I know is they told me to put the frighteners on those aul' fellas. Make sure they knew to keep their mouths shut, stay out of our business from now on."

"The sheep," Cal says.

Donie grins again, an involuntary grin like a spasm.

"Well, that musta been rewarding," Cal says. "Finally, something that made the most of your God-given talents."

"Just getting the job done, man."

Cal looks at Donie, sitting on the edge of his bed with his pudgy bare knees wide apart, poking at his broken finger, sneaking the odd speculative glance at Cal. Donie is keeping something back.

He didn't like Brendan one bit, which is understandable. Donie had been doing the donkey work for this gang for God knows how long, and all of a sudden Brendan came riding in, just an uppity kid talking big, and Donie was stuck being his errand boy. He wanted the little smartass gone, and Cal gets the distinct feeling that he took steps to make that happen. Maybe he told Brendan that that meeting would involve a lot more than a few slaps, scared the shit out of him, nudged him into skipping town. Or maybe he just accompanied Brendan along the way, and picked a lonely stretch of mountainside.

Cal considers getting the full story out of Donie, who is now removing fluff from his belly button. He decides against it, on the grounds that right at this moment he doesn't actually give a shit what happened to Brendan Reddy. He needs as much of this story as it takes to find out who made Sheila beat Trey, and why. The rest of it can wait.

"And once you got the job done," he says, "everything went back to normal."

"Yeah. Until you came sticking your nose in. I want a fucking smoke, man."

"Speaking of people sticking their noses in," Cal says. "Trey Reddy."

Donie's lip lifts. "What about her?"

"She came to see you the other day, asking about Brendan. And then someone beat her up pretty bad."

That makes Donie snigger. "No harm done there. The bitch was ugly to begin with."

Cal punches him in the stomach so fast Donie never sees it coming. He doubles up and collapses sideways onto the bed, wheezing and then retching.

Cal waits. He doesn't want to have to hit Donie again; every time he touches the guy, he's not sure he'll be able to stop. "Start over," he says, when Donie eventually drags himself back up to sitting, wiping a trickle of spit off his chin. "Get it right this time. Trey Reddy."

"Never touched her."

"I know you didn't, moron. You told someone she'd been here. Your Dublin buddies?"

"Nah, man. Never said a word to anyone."

Cal pulls back his fist again. Donie scoots his ass

backwards on the bed, yelping as he forgets and puts weight on his hand. "Nah nah nah, hang on. I said fucking **nothing.** Truth, man. Why would I? I don't give a shite about her. I told her to fuck off, forgot the whole thing. End of. Swear to God."

Cal recognizes the specific sense of injury that pours from a chronic liar who, for once, is being accused of something he genuinely didn't do. "OK," he says. "Anyone see her here?"

"I dunno, man. I wasn't looking."

"The Dublin boys got anyone else working for them round here?"

"Not in Ardnakelty. Couple up in town, one over in Lisnacarragh, one in Knockfarraney."

Except Donie might not know, specially not if the Dublin boys suspect him of causing trouble around Brendan. If they have someone keeping an eye on him, he definitely wouldn't know. Cal wishes he had waited till nighttime and found a way to catch Donie outside, instead of going off half-cocked, but it's too late now.

There are two phones on Donie's bedside table, in among the ashtrays and the weed baggie and the souring mugs and the snack wrappers: a great big shiny dickswing of an iPhone, and a shitty little My First Dumbphone. Cal picks up the burner and goes into the contacts list, which has half a dozen names. He holds up the screen to Donie. "Who's the boss?"

Donie eyes him. Cal says, "Or I can just phone all of them, and tell them where I got their numbers."

"Austin's the boss. Of the lads who come down here, anyway."

Cal copies Austin's number, and the rest, into his own phone, keeping one eye on Donie in case he decides to get smart. "Yeah? Austin due in town any time soon?"

"There's not, like, a schedule, man. They ring me when they need me."

"What's Austin like?"

"You don't wanta fuck with him," Donie says. "I'm telling you now."

"I don't want to fuck with anyone, son," Cal says, tossing the phone back onto the bedside table, where it lands in an ashtray with a dispirited puff of gray powder. "But sometimes life just turns out that way." He gets up and dusts the residue of Donie's chair off his pants. He feels like he needs a decontamination shower. "You can go back to sleep now."

"I'm gonna kill you," Donie informs him.

The flat eyes say he'll do it, if he doesn't fuck it up. "No you're not, you moron," Cal says. "You do that, you'll have a dozen detectives crawling all over this townland, interviewing the shit out of everyone about every piece of mopery that goes on in these parts. What do you think your Dublin buddies'll do to you if you bring that shitstorm down on their heads?"

Donie may be dumb as a bag of hair in most ways, but he has an expert's grasp of the intricate ways of trouble. He gives Cal a stare of pure vicious hatred, the kind that only comes from someone who's no threat.

"See you round," Cal says. He heads for the door, kicking a ketchup-crusted plate out of his way. "And clean this place up, for Christ's sake. You make your mama live with this? Change your fucking sheets."

On his way out Cal has himself a nice long wander around the lane behind Francie Gannon's fields, taking a deep interest in the verges and checking to see if anyone is watching Donie's place. He has a story about his lost sunglasses ready to go if anyone comes along asking, but the only person he sees is Francie Gannon, who waves cheerfully to him and calls something unintelligible, on his way somewhere with a bucket that looks heavy. Cal waves back and keeps looking, not urgently enough to make Francie come help him out.

When he reaches the conclusion that the place is clear, right now anyway, he walks home in a state of mounting irritation, more with himself than with anyone else. He reckoned all along, after all, that there was more going on underneath Mart's quirky-yokel shtick; he just never put things together, which for someone in his line of work is an unpardonable level of dumb. Cal supposes he should be grateful for Mart's protective herding, even if Mart was mainly

motivated by the desire to prevent Cal from bringing down more trouble on the townland, but he's not
fond of being made to feel like a fool.

The morning has turned lavishly beautiful. The
autumn sun gives the greens of the fields an impossible, mythic radiance and transforms the back roads
into light-muddled paths where a goblin with a rid-
dle, or a pretty maiden with a basket, could be waiting around every gorse-and-bramble bend. Cal is in
no mood to appreciate any of it. He feels like this
specific beauty is central to the illusion that lulled
him into stupidity, turned him into the peasant gazing slack-jawed at his handful of gold coins till they
melt into dead leaves in front of his eyes. If all this
had happened in some depressing suburban clot of
tract homes and ruler-measured lawns, he would
have kept his wits about him.

He needs to talk to Austin. Austin sounds like
a fun guy. If he's the boss man, though, even just
regionally, there's better than a fifty-fifty shot that
he's the calculating subspecies of psycho, rather than
the rabid kind. In this situation, unlike many, Cal
considers that a plus. If he can convince Austin that
Trey is no threat, then Austin is likely to abandon
his silencing campaign as an unnecessary risk, rather
than keeping it up just for entertainment. There's
even an outside chance Cal can persuade him to give
Trey some level of answer in exchange for guaran-
teed peace and quiet. In order to gauge Austin well

enough to wrangle him, though, Cal needs to do this face-to-face. He's going to have to phone Austin and set up a meeting, pick his strategy on the fly depending on what he finds, and hope his meeting goes better than Brendan's did.

The house and the garden look the same as they did when he left, and the rooks are happily doing their thing, making conversation and combing the grass for bugs, undisturbed. Cal unlocks the front door as quietly as he can, figuring the kid will likely be asleep again, and peeks into the bedroom. The bed is empty.

Cal spins round, his head blooming with fully fledged abduction scenarios. When he sees the bathroom door shut, he switches to picturing the kid collapsed on the floor, bleeding into her guts. He can't believe he didn't haul her to a hospital last night.

"Kid," he says, outside the bathroom, as calmly as he can. "You OK?"

After a bad second, Trey pulls the door open. "You were fuckin' ages," she snaps.

She's electric with nerves. So is Cal. "I was talking to Donie. Did you want me to do that or not?"

"What'd he say?"

The flare of terror in her eyes disintegrates Cal's irritation. "OK," he says. "Donie says your brother did get mixed up with the drug boys from Dublin. Not selling, you were right about that, but he was gonna be making meth for them. Only he fucked up, lost a bunch of their supplies. He was planning to meet up with them and make it right, and that's the last Donie heard of him."

He's not sure if some or all of this is going to be more than Trey can take, but he's done hiding stuff to protect her: look how well that worked out last time. The kid has a right, paid for and branded onto her, to true answers.

She absorbs it with an intentness that stills her jittering. "That what Donie actually said? No bullshit this time?"

"No bullshit. And I'm pretty sure he wasn't bullshitting me, either. Not sure he told me every single thing, but I reckon what he did tell me was true."

"Didja hurt him?"

"Yeah. Not too badly."

"You shoulda battered the fucker," Trey says. "Shoulda danced on his fucking head."

"I know," Cal says gently. "I would've loved to. But I'm after answers, not trouble."

"You haveta talk to them, the lads from Dublin. Didja talk to them?"

"Kid," Cal says. "Slow down. I'm gonna. But I need to work out the best way to go about it, so neither of us winds up with a bullet in our heads."

Trey thinks that over, biting off skin from around her thumbnail, wincing when she catches her lip. In the end she says, "Didja see Mart Lavin?"

"No. Why?"

"He came looking for you."

"Huh," Cal says, mentally kicking himself. Of

course Mart would have clocked Lena's car and headed straight down here, truffle-hunting for gossip, the second he got a chance. "He see you?"

"Nah. I saw him coming, hid in the jacks. He went all round the house, when you didn't answer the door. I heard him. Checking in the windows. Saw his shadow."

The kid is starting to twitch with adrenaline again at the memory. "Well," Cal says peacefully, "good thing my bathroom's got that sheet over the window." He takes off his coat and hangs it on its hook behind the door, moving nice and slowly. "You know why I put that up to begin with? 'Cause of you. Before we ever met. I knew someone was watching me, so I nailed that sheet up there to give me a little bit of privacy where it counts. And now it's coming in useful to you. Funny how things turn out, huh?"

Trey gives a one-shouldered shrug, but her jittering has slowed down. "I know what Mart wanted, anyway," Cal says, "and it's got nothing to do with you. He saw Miss Lena's car here, and he wants to know if me and her are hooking up."

The look on Trey's face makes him grin. "Are you?"

"Nope. There's more'n enough going on without adding that in on top. You want anything? A snack, maybe?"

"I wanta see this." The kid points at her face. "You got a mirror?"

Cal says, "It looks a lot worse'n it is, right now. The swelling'll go down in a day or two."

"I know. I wanta see it."

Cal finds his beard-trimming mirror in a cupboard and hands it to her. Trey sits at the table with it and spends a long time there, turning her head this way and that.

"We can still see if a doctor can fix up that lip," Cal says. "So it won't leave a scar. We'll tell them you fell off your bike."

"Nah. I don't give a shite about scars."

"I know. You might someday, though."

The kid makes Cal happy by giving him a full-bore moron stare. "I'd rather look like 'don't fuck with me' than look pretty."

"I think you got that covered," Cal says. "You need to get out in the village. Before those bruises go down."

Trey's head comes up sharply from the mirror. "I'm not going down there."

"Yeah you are. Whoever told your mama to do this, we need them to know that she did it, and did it right. That's why she went for your face: so they'd know. You need to get seen by someone who'll pass it on."

"Like who?"

"Well, if I knew that," Cal says. "Just go into Noreen's. Buy bread or something. Give her a good look at your face, walk like you hurt all over. She'll make sure word gets around."

"I've got no money."

"I'll give you some. You can bring the bread back here to me."

"I do hurt all over. I can't walk that far."

The kid's shoulders have a mutinous set. Everything in her is dug in against the thought of waving her family's dirty laundry in Noreen's face. "Kid," Cal says. "You want them coming back to make sure?"

After a second Trey pushes the mirror away. "Right," she says. "OK. Just, can I go tomorrow?"

The downswirl of fatigue dragging at her voice makes Cal feel like a heel. Just because the kid's still got fight in her, he fooled himself into believing she was more whole than she could possibly be right now. "Yeah," he says. "Sure. Tomorrow'll work fine. Today you just rest up."

Trey says, "Can I stay here?"

"Sure," Cal says. He's been turning over ways to suggest the same thing himself. Donie would have to be a dumbass of epic proportions to go whining to Austin about their conversation, but Cal learned a long time ago never to underestimate the spectacular natural wonder that is people's stupidity. And on the off chance that Austin does have someone watching Donie, and they spotted Cal, they know every word of that conversation by now. He thinks of the Austin variants he's known, and of the things they'll do to Trey if they feel the need to come back. Until he has the situation under some kind of control, the kid is staying put.

Trey yawns, suddenly and hugely, not bothering to cover her mouth. " 'M wrecked," she says, puzzled.

"That's 'cause you're hurt," Cal explains. "Your body's using a ton of energy on healing. Just gimme two minutes, and we'll get you back to bed."

He fetches his hammer and tacks, a chair and a drop sheet, and takes them over to the bedroom window. Trey follows him and collapses on the bed like someone cut her strings.

"I got beat up one time when I was about your age," Cal says. He climbs on the chair and starts tacking up the sheet over the window.

"Was it your mam that done it?"

"Nope," Cal says. "My mama had the softest heart in town. She couldn't swat a mosquito."

"Your dad?"

"Nah. He didn't have a mean bone in his body either. My dad, when he showed up, he'd bring me little toy cars and candy, flowers for my mama, show me card tricks, stick around a couple of weeks and then take off again. No, this was a couple of guys from school. I don't even remember what it was about. They got me pretty good, though. Two cracked ribs, and my face looked like a rotten pumpkin."

"Worse'n mine?"

"About the same. More bruises, less blood. What I remember most, though, is how tired I was afterwards. For most of a week, all's I could do was lie on the couch and watch TV, and eat whatever my gramma brought me. Getting hurt tires you right out."

Trey works this over in her head. "Didja get them back?" she asks. "The lads that bet you up?"

"Yep," Cal says. "It took a while, 'cause I had to wait till I grew as big as them, but I got there in the end." He steps off the chair and gives the drop sheet a tug. It stays in place. "There," he says. "Now you won't have to worry about hiding in the bathroom if anyone comes round. You just get all the rest you need."

The kid lets out another yawn, knuckling her good eye, and starts winding herself up in the bedclothes. "Sleep tight," Cal says, and closes the door behind him.

She sleeps for four hours. Cal strips wallpaper in the second bedroom, at a slow, steady rhythm, so as not to make any sudden noises. Dust motes whirl and flare in the sunlight slanting through the windowpane. Out among the harvested fields, sheep call back and forth, and a flock of tardy geese sets up a faraway clamor. No one comes looking for anyone.

NINETEEN

Hunger finally rouses Trey, and Cal makes them both peanut butter sandwiches and then locks Trey in again so he can head into town. Even if Donie called Austin straightaway, this is hardly going to be high enough on Austin's priority list to make him leap into action, but Cal still wants to be back home by dark. As he backs out of his driveway, the house, low and stolid amid his overgrown fields and the brown smudge of mountains on the horizon, looks very far away from anything else.

On the drive, he phones Lena. "Hey," he says. "How're the dogs doing?"

"Grand. Nellie destroyed one of my shoes to punish me, but it was an old one." In the background, men's voices are calling back and forth. She's at work. "How's Trey?"

"OK. Still kinda shaky, but better. How 'bout you? Did the aches and pains wear off yet?"

"You mean," Lena says, "have I blocked it out enough that I'd be on for doing it all over again."

"Well," Cal says, "that too. The kid wants to stay one more night at my place. Would you help me out again? If I get that mattress?"

After a moment Lena makes a sound that could

be laughter or exasperation, or both. "You should've just taken the pup," she says. "It would've been less hassle."

"It's just one more night." Cal is pretty sure this is true. This isn't something he can let lie for any length of time. "You could bring Nellie, if you want. Keep the rest of your shoes out of danger." He doesn't mention the part where a beagle's alert ears might come in handy, but he's pretty sure Lena catches it anyway.

The men's voices get smaller; Lena is moving away from them. She says, "One more night. If you get that air mattress."

"Heading there now," Cal says. "Thank you. If ever you need a favor, you know where to come."

"Next time one of the pups gets the runs all over the floor, I'm ringing you."

"I'll be there. Can I invite you to join us for dinner?"

"No, I'll make my own and call over to you after. Around eight, say. Can the two of ye protect yourselves till then?"

"We'll do our best," Cal says. "While I'm pushing my luck, could you do me one more favor? Can you call Sheila Reddy and tell her Trey's OK?"

There's a silence.

"She oughta know," Cal says. He's not feeling particularly warm towards Sheila, but it wouldn't be right to leave her wondering if Trey is helpless or dying somewhere on the mountainside. "Just tell her the kid's safe, is all."

"Ah, yeah, right. And when she asks where Trey

is, I just say I've no clue, is it? Or I say, 'Ha ha, not telling,' and hang up on her?"

"Just tell her, I don't know, tell her the kid doesn't want to talk to her right now, but she'll be home tomorrow. Something like that." Into another silence that has a distinct air of raised eyebrows, he says: "I'd do it myself, except Sheila might get upset if she finds out the kid's staying at my house. I don't want her calling the police on me. Or banging on my door."

"But it's grand if she does that on me, yeah?"

"She won't call the cops on you. If she comes to your place, you can show her you don't have the kid. And if she comes after eight, you won't be there anyway."

After a minute Lena says, "I'd be happier if I could figure out how I ended up in the middle of this."

"Yeah," Cal says. "Me too. The kid's got a gift."

"I've to go," Lena says. "See you later." And she hangs up. Cal thinks of the array of sound effects Donna would have come up with to convey the iceberg-tip of her feelings about this situation. He actually thinks about phoning her and telling her the whole story, just for the pleasure of hearing them one more time, but he doubts she would appreciate this the way he intends it.

Town has a weekday briskness, old women steaming along with wheeled shopping bags, young ones juggling strollers and shopping and phones, old guys having stick-waving conversations on corners. Cal has some trouble tracking down an inflatable mattress, but eventually the guy in the hardware store disappears into his back room for a long time and comes back with two of them, both coated in dust and sticky cobwebs. Cal takes them both. Even if he welcomed the prospect of a night in his armchair, a lone mattress might give Lena the impression that he has expectations.

In a shop hung with an impressive variety of resigned polyester-based clothing that explains Sheila's sweater, he finds a wire bin of polyester-based bedding, an extra duvet and a couple of pillows, as well as a set of pajamas, a blue hoodie and a pair of jeans that look to be around Trey's size. He loads up his supermarket cart with steak, potatoes, vegetables, milk, eggs, the most nourishing stuff he can find. While he's at it, he picks up a packet of Mart's cookies. He needs an excuse to go over and let Mart rib him about Lena, before Mart gets impatient enough to try calling round again.

Evening works its way in earlier, these days. By the time Cal leaves town, the light is lowering, throwing great swathes of shadow across the fields. He heads for home faster than he should, on these roads.

He's still figuring out how to approach Austin. Back on the job, he would have been going in equipped with an elaborate range of sticks and carrots in every shape, size and specification. He watches the slim low moon hanging in a lavender sky and the fields deepening with dusk as they flow past his

windows, and feels the wide immensity of his empty-
handedness all over again.

Austin isn't going to talk to an ex-cop, he's not
going to take kindly to a business rival, and he's not
going to give a random civilian the time of day. Cal
figures his best bet is to go in as a guy who used
to be in the life, retired before his luck could run
out, and moved far from home so he wouldn't get
sucked back in or tracked down: tough enough to
keep Trey in check and to merit some respect, not
active enough to be a threat.

He realizes that he's thinking like a detective again,
but not the kind of detective he ever was. This is undercover thinking. Cal never liked undercover work,
or the guys who did it. They moved in an atmosphere
of funhouse-mirror fluidity, and had a nimble, fly-
weight ease with it, that made him edgy down to
his bones. He's starting to feel that they would fit in
around these parts a lot better than he does.

By the time he parks in his driveway, his house
is two lighted rectangles and a roofline against indigo sky and first stars. Cal gets out of his truck
and goes around to the back to get out the air mattresses. When he registers the rush of feet in long
grass, he has just time to spin round and see the dark
shapes in near-darkness charging towards him, just
time to grab at the spot where his Glock should be,
before something rough and dusty comes down over
his head and he's yanked backwards off his feet and
slammed down flat.

The fall winds him. He heaves for breath, use-
lessly, like a fish mouthing at air. Then something
hard smashes down on his collarbone. He hears the
dull clunk of it striking bone and feels himself splinter. He heaves for breath again, pain shears through
his collarbone and this time he manages a lungful of
dust and grit, mixed with barely enough air.

He twists sideways, wheezing, his mouth clogged
with rough fabric, and flails out blind. He grabs an
ankle and yanks with all his might, and feels the
thud in the ground as the man goes down. A kick
in the back makes him let go. The hard thing cracks
into his kneecap, the pain whips his breath away
again, and a small clear part of his mind realizes that
there's more than one of them and that he is fucked.

A man's voice says, into his face, "You mind your
own business. D'you hear me?"

Cal punches out, connects and hears the man
grunt. Before he can get his knees under him, the
hard thing slams into his nose and it explodes, pain
blooming dazzlingly bright all through his head. He
breathes blood, gags on it, retches it up in great helpless hacks. Then the air splits open with a great roar
and Cal thinks they've hit him again, thinks this is
it, and then everything stops.

In the silence a hard clear voice, some way away,
shouts out, "Don't fuckin' move!"

It takes Cal a moment to make sense of the sound,
through the insistent singing fog of blood and
stars, and another to identify it as Trey's voice. In

the third moment, he realizes that Trey just shot off the Henry.

Trey shouts, "Where's Brendan?"

Nothing moves. Cal scrabbles at the cloth covering his head, but his fingers are useless with shaking. A man's voice shouts, very nearby, "Put that down, you little scut!"

The Henry roars again. There's a raw yell of pain from behind Cal's head, then a rising gibber of voices.

"What the hell—"

"Jesus Christ—"

"I told ye **don't move**!"

"I'm fuckin' shot, she fuckin' shot me—"

"**Where's my brother** or I'll kill the fuckin' lot of ye!"

Somehow Cal manages to get a grip on the bag and pull it off his head. The world tilts and seethes and he can see only one thing clearly: a lighthouse beam of gold spreading across the grass, and at its apex, silhouetted in the bright rectangle of the doorway, Trey aiming the rifle. Trey has come out of that house like a flamethrower, fueled to the brim with a lifetime's worth of rage, all ready to burn everything for miles to the ground.

"Kid!" Cal yells, and hears it echo out over the shocked dark fields. "Stop! It's me!" He claws himself to his feet, swaying and lumbering, one leg dragging, snuffling and spitting blood. "Don't shoot me!"

"Get outa my fuckin' way!" Trey shouts back. Her accent has turned rougher and wilder, straight down from the mountains on a saw-toothed wind, but her voice is clear and intent.

Behind Cal someone pants through gritted teeth, "My fuckin' arm," and someone else snaps, low, "Shut up." Then there's utter stillness, as far as he can hear through the pounding and bubbling in his head. The men watching Trey's every move know better, now, than to take her lightly.

Cal spreads his arms wide and lurches in front of them. "Kid," he shouts. "No." He knows there are words he's used to talk guns out of people's hands before, promises, soothing things. They're all gone.

"Get outa my way or I'll shoot you too!"

All around Cal things are rocking and rippling, but her silhouette in the doorway is steady as a monument; the heavy rifle at her shoulder doesn't even shake. If these men refuse her, or if they lie to her, or maybe even if they tell her the truth, she'll blow them all to kingdom come.

"Kid," he shouts. His voice comes out frayed by dust and blood. "Kid. Send them away."

"Where's Brendan?"

"Please, kid," Cal shouts. His voice cracks open. "Please. Just send them away. I'm begging you."

There are three breaths' worth of pure, cold nighttime silence. Then the Henry goes off again. The rooks explode from their tree in a vast black firework of wings and panic. Cal's head goes back and he roars like an animal up at the night sky.

When he gasps for air, paralyzed between lunging

for the rifle and lurching around to see the damage, he hears Trey's voice shout, "Now get ta fuck!"

"We're going!" a man shouts back, behind him.

It takes another second for Cal's jolted brain to catch up. Trey aimed high, into the treetops.

"Get ta fuck offa this land!"

"I'm bleeding, God almighty, look—"

"Come on, come on, come on—"

Rough panting, jumbled voices that Cal can't make into sense, feet hurrying through grass. When he turns to get a look at the men, his knee gives out and he collapses, gradually and ungracefully, into a sitting position. The men are already vanishing into the dark, three swift black shapes huddled together with their heads ducked down low.

Cal sits where he is and presses his coat sleeve to his streaming nose. Trey stays in the doorway, with the rifle to her shoulder. The rooks whirl, screaming abuse, and then gradually calm down and settle back into their tree to bitch in comfort.

When the muffled voices have faded up the lane, Trey lowers the gun and comes loping down the beam of light to Cal. He takes his sleeve off his nose long enough to say, "The safety. Put the safety on."

"I did," Trey says. She hunkers down to peer at him in the darkness. "How bad are you?"

"I'll live," Cal says. He starts trying to reorganize his limbs into some arrangement that will let him stand up. "We need to get inside. Before they come back."

"They won't come back," Trey says with satisfaction. "I got one fella goodo."

"OK," Cal says. He can't articulate the fact that, if they do come back, they'll come with guns of their own. He manages to get to his feet and stands there, wobbling gently and trying to work out whether his knee will carry him.

"Here," Trey says. She loops her free arm across his back, taking his weight on one skinny shoulder. "Come on."

"No," Cal says. He's thinking of her injuries, which at the moment he can't picture exactly but which he recalls as horrifying. Trey ignores him and starts towards the house, and Cal finds himself moving with her. They shamble across the grass, weaving in and out of the light, propping each other up like a pair of drunks. Both of them are panting. Cal can feel every inch of the darkness spread out around them, and every inch of their bodies that would make a perfect target. He tries to limp faster.

By the time he slams the door behind them and double-locks it, every muscle in his body is juddering. The sudden brightness smashes him right in the eyes. "Get me a towel," he says, dropping into a chair at the table. "And that mirror."

Trey leaves the Henry on the counter and brings him both, and then a bowl of water and his first-aid kit, and stands there hovering while he presses the towel to his nose. "How bad are you?" she asks again.

The tautness in her voice reaches Cal. He takes a

long breath and tries to steady himself. " 'Bout the same as you were the other night," he says, through the towel. "Pretty banged up, but I've taken worse."

The kid hovers for another minute, watching him and fingering her lip. Then she heads abruptly to the freezer and starts rummaging. While Cal waits for the bleeding to stop, he pulls up his pants leg and checks out his knee. It's purple and inflating, with a darker purple line scored right across it, but after some experimenting he's pretty sure it's not broken. His collarbone is at least cracked: it shoots out pain whenever he moves his shoulder. When he probes very carefully along it, though, the line is straight. It shouldn't need setting, which is good. Cal would much prefer not to explain any of this to a doctor.

Trey dumps two plastic bags of ice cubes on the table in front of him. "What else?" she asks.

"I'm gonna need a sling," Cal says. "That sheet over the bathroom window, that's long enough that we can cut off a strip at the bottom. Scissors in that drawer there."

Trey goes into the bathroom and comes back with a length of cloth, which she fashions into a dirty but serviceable sling. Once they have Cal's coat eased off him and the sling fixed on, she pulls herself up to sit on the countertop, where she can keep an eye out the kitchen window.

Cal's nose has stopped bleeding. He tests it, trying not to let the kid see him flinching at each touch. It's swollen to twice its size, but the line of it feels much the same as it ever did. His shaking has ebbed enough that he can clean up his face, give or take, with a corner of the towel dipped in the bowl of water. In the mirror, he looks just about how he expected: his nose is the shape of a tomato and he has two black eyes coming, although his are nowhere near as impressive as the kid's.

Trey is watching him. "Look at us," Cal says. His voice sounds just as muffled and blurred as it did through the towel. "Pair of beat-up stray mutts."

Trey nods. Cal can't tell how much this has shaken her. Her face still has the hard, intent focus that he heard in her voice across the yard and the gun. It seems wrong on a child. Cal feels like he ought to do something about it, but right this moment he can't work out what.

He leans back in the chair, settles one ice pack on his knee and the other one on his nose, and concentrates on slowing his body and his mind so they can work right. He goes back over previous beatings he's taken, in order to put this one into perspective. There were kids in school, a few times. There was the idiot who came after him with a piece of pipe outside a party Cal and Donna were at in their wild days, because he thought Cal had looked funny at his girlfriend—Cal still has a dent in his thigh where the end of that pipe dug in. That guy was aiming to kill him, and so was the guy jacked up on something or other who charged out of a back alley when Cal was on patrol and wouldn't quit till Cal broke his arm. And yet, somehow, here Cal still is, sitting halfway across the world in a back corner of Ireland, with yet another bloody nose. He finds this strangely comforting.

"We had a beat-up stray mutt one time," Trey says, from the counter. "Me and Brendan and my dad, we were going to the village, and we found him on the road. All scraped up and bleeding, and a bad leg. My dad said he was dying. He was gonna drown him so he wouldn't suffer. But Brendan, yeah? He wanted to fix the dog up, and in the end my dad said he could try. We had that dog six more years. He always had a limp, but he was grand. He usedta sleep on Bren's bed. He died of being old, in the end."

Cal has never heard her talk this much, especially for no apparent purpose. At first he thinks it's tension coming out as babble, but then he looks at her looking at him, and realizes what she's doing. She's using what she's learned from him: talking about whatever comes into her head, in order to soothe him down.

"How old were you?" he asks.

"Five. Bren said I could name him. I said Patch, 'cause he had like a black eye patch. Now I'd think of something better, but I was only little."

"You ever find out where he came from?"

"Nah. Not from round here, or we'da known about him. Someone dumped him out of a car on the main road, probably, and he crawled from there. He wasn't one of them fancy dogs. Just an aul' black-and-white mutt."

"Best kind," Cal says. "Your brother did good." He tests out his knee, which is working OK, now that the initial shock has worn off it. "Tell you something, I'm feeling better'n I expected to right now."

This is pretty much true. He's throbbing in various places and feels mildly nauseated from swallowing blood, but overall, he could have ended up a lot worse off. He would have done, if Trey and the Henry hadn't interrupted.

"Thanks, kid," he says. "For saving my ass."

Trey nods. She reaches for Cal's bread and sticks a couple of slices in the toaster. "You figure they woulda kilt you?"

"Who knows," Cal says. "I'm fine with not finding out." He doesn't want to take anything away from the kid, but he doubts he would have wound up dead, unless someone screwed up. He knows the difference; this beating wasn't intended to kill. Just like he said to Donie, the Dublin boys don't want the attention that a dead Yank would draw. What they wanted was to get their message across.

Now that Trey's gone and shot one of them, that might change. It depends on how level-headed this Austin guy is, how persuasive Cal can be, and how strong a hold Austin has on his crew. Cal is in no frame of mind to make that phone call tonight, but it needs to happen tomorrow morning, as soon as Austin can reasonably be expected to be awake.

Trey is alternating between watching the window, watching her toast and watching Cal. "You got that gun loaded up pretty quick," Cal says.

"I had it ready. Ever since you left."

"How'd you get it out of the safe?"

"Saw the combination when you opened it that time."

Cal feels he ought to lecture her about not touching guns unless she has both permission and a license, but in the circumstances that would seem unappreciative. "Right," he says. "How'd you know you wouldn't hit me?"

The kid looks like the question is so dumb it barely deserves an answer. "You were on the ground. I aimed higher up."

"Right," Cal says again. The thought of her getting one of those men in the head gives him an extra fillip of nausea. "Well then."

Trey's toast pops. She leans over to get the cheddar out of the fridge and a knife from its drawer. "You want some?"

"Not right now. Thanks."

Trey packs slices of cheese between the toast, not bothering with a plate, and pulls off a chunk so she can bypass her split lip. She says, "How come you didn't let me make them talk?"

Cal takes the ice pack off his nose. "Kid. You had

a **gun** on them. You'd already **shot** one of them. What did you think they'd say? 'Uh, yeah, it's our doing that your brother's gone, sorry 'bout that'? Nah. They woulda sworn blind they had no idea what happened to him, whether they did or not. And then you woulda had to pick between shooting them all dead and letting them go home. No matter what, you wouldn't have got your answer. I figured it was a lot smarter to skip straight to sending them home."

The kid thinks that over, eating hunks of sandwich carefully and swinging one foot. The taut focus has faded out of her. Her eye is blooming in lurid new shades, but she seems revived and energized, back in her body and her mind. Tonight did her good.

She says, "I wanted to shoot them."

"I know. But you didn't. That's a good thing."

Trey looks about half convinced. "I got the one fella, anyway."

"Yeah. I think you got him in the arm. He was moving fine, when they left. He'll be OK."

"He won't go to the cops."

"Nah," Cal says. "The hospital might call them, if he has to go there. But he'll say he had an accident cleaning his gun, something like that. They won't believe him, but there won't be a lot they can do about it."

Trey nods. She says, "They sound like Dubs to you?"

"Dunno. I wasn't paying much attention to that."

"Sounded local to me."

"Probably," Cal says. Austin wouldn't have had the

time, or likely the inclination, to send guys down from Dublin. This would have been a job for a few local foot soldiers. "You recognize any of 'em?"

Trey shakes her head.

"You see what they hit me with?"

"Looked like hurls. Couldn't see for sure, but." She glances up from her sandwich. "We haveta be getting close, right? Or they wouldn't bother coming after us."

"Maybe," Cal says. "Maybe not. Could be they're just fed up of the hassle. Or pissed off with me for beating up Donie."

"But maybe."

"Yeah," Cal says, only partly because she needs that, to make all this worth it. "We could be."

After a moment Trey says, "Are you raging?"

"I don't have time for that right now. I need to get things straightened out."

Trey thinks that over and rips off another piece of her sandwich. Cal can feel her wanting to say something, but he can't help her with that. He rummages through the first-aid kit till he finds his ibuprofen, and swallows a hefty dose dry.

Trey says, "It's my fault they done that to you."

"Kid," Cal says. "I'm not blaming you."

"I know. It is, but."

"You didn't beat me up."

"It was me that got you into this."

Cal looks at her and finds himself floored by both the vast importance and the vast impossibility of saying the right thing, at a moment when he can barely piece together a thought. He wishes Lena were there, until he realizes that she would be no help at all. He wishes Donna were there.

"All's you can do is your best," he says. "Sometimes it doesn't work out the way you intend it to. You just gotta keep doing it anyway."

Trey starts to ask something, but then her head snaps around. "Hey," she says sharply, in the same instant that headlights sweep across the kitchen window.

Cal pulls himself to standing, bracing himself on the table. His knee still hurts, but he's steadier on his feet. "Go in the bedroom," he says. "Anything happens, get out the window and run like hell."

"I'm not going to—"

"Yeah you are. Go."

After a moment she goes, slamming her feet down hard to make her views clear. Cal picks up the Henry and goes to the door. When the car's lights go off and he hears the engine cut out, he throws the door wide and stands in the doorway, leaving himself clear in the light. He wants whoever it is to see the rifle. He couldn't aim it even if he wanted to, but he's hoping the sight of it will be enough.

It's Lena, getting out of her car with Nellie bounding ahead of her, and lifting a hand to Cal in the door-beam of light down the grass. What with one thing and another, their plans slipped Cal's mind. He recognizes her just in time to avoid making a fool of himself by shouting the Lord only knows what.

Instead he remembers, after a moment, to raise a hand in return.

As she gets close, Lena's eyebrows shoot up. "What the holy Jaysus," she says.

Cal had forgotten what he looks like. "I got beat up," he says. It occurs to him that he's holding a rifle. He steps back inside and lays it down on the counter.

"I got that part, yeah," Lena says, following him. "Didja shoot anyone with that yoke?"

"No casualties," Cal says. "Far as I know."

Lena takes his chin in her hand and turns his face from side to side. Her hand is warm, rough-skinned and matter-of-fact, like she's examining a hurt animal. "Are you going to the doctor?"

"Nope," Cal says. "No real harm done. It'll heal."

"I've heard that somewhere before," Lena says, giving his face one more look and releasing it. "The pair of ye are a match made in heaven, d'you know that?"

Trey has emerged from the bedroom and squatted down to make friends with Nellie, who is joyously wriggling and licking. "How's the war wounds?" Lena asks her.

"Grand," Trey says. "What's her name?"

"That's Nellie. If you give her a bitta food, you'll have a friend for life." Trey heads for the fridge and starts rummaging.

"You oughta go home," Cal says. "They might come back."

Lena starts unloading the various pockets of her big wax jacket. "You never know your luck. If they do, I might do a better job of dealing with them than ye two have." The jacket contains an impressive quantity of stuff: a small carton of milk, a hairbrush, a paperback book, two cans of dog food, a clip-on book light, and a toothbrush, which she waves at Cal. "Now. I came prepared this time."

Cal feels that Lena isn't taking in the full weight of the situation, but if his face and Trey's haven't brought it home to her, he can't come up with anything that would. "I bought a couple of air mattresses," he says. "They're in the car. I'd appreciate it if you'd keep an eye out while I go fetch them."

One of Lena's eyebrows arches upwards. "You want me to cover you, is it? With that yoke?" She nods at the rifle.

"You know how to use it?"

"For Jaysus' sake, man," Lena says, amused, "I'm not going to crouch under the window playing snipers while you go twenty meters to your car. You're going nowhere, anyway: with that arm, you can't carry anything. I'll go. Where's your keys?"

Cal doesn't like that idea one bit, but he can't get round the fact that she has a point. He works his good arm around to fish his keys out of his pants pocket. "Lock it up once you're done," he says, although he's not sure what this will achieve.

"And you can't cover me, either," Lena points out, catching the keys. "That yoke needs two good arms."

"I'll do it," Trey says, from where she's sitting on the floor feeding ham slices to Nellie.

"No you won't," Cal says. He finds himself getting irritated with Lena. He was starting to feel that he had a grip on the situation, until she showed up, and now the whole thing seems to have slipped out of his hands and got itself stranded somewhere between dangerous and ridiculous. "You'll quit distracting that dog, is what you'll do, so it can go along with Miss Lena. Put that ham away."

"Now there's a stroke of genius," Lena says approvingly. "Nothing like a beagle to fight off a gang of desperate criminals. She hasn't had her supper; I'd say she could eat at least three of 'em, depending how much meat they have on them. Were they big ones?"

"If you're getting those mattresses," Cal says, "now would be a good time. There's some groceries in there, while you're at it."

"Sure, anyone'd be a narky fucker, after the day you've had," Lena tells him consolingly, and she heads out to the car. Cal follows her to the door to watch after her, regardless of what she thinks about that and of whether he could actually be any help if she needed it. Trey, after a brief pause to assess matters, goes right back to feeding Nellie.

By the time they—Lena and Trey, mainly—have unloaded the groceries, fed the dog, inflated the mattresses, set out one on each side of the fireplace and made up the beds, Trey is yawning and Cal is fighting it. All his good intentions with steak and green beans have gone out the window. Trey's cheese sandwich will have to get her through the night.

"Bedtime," he tells her. He throws her the clothes he got in town. "Here. Pajamas, and stuff for tomorrow."

Trey holds up the clothes like they have cooties, her chin goes out and she starts to say something that Cal knows is going to be about charity. "Don't give me any shit," he says. "Your clothes stink of blood. By tomorrow they're gonna be attracting flies. Throw 'em out here once you've changed, and I'll wash 'em."

After a moment Trey rolls her eyes to heaven, heads into the bedroom and bangs the door behind her. "You've got yourself a teenager," Lena says, amused.

"She's had a long couple of days," Cal says. "She's not at her best."

"Neither are you. You look about ready for bed yourself."

"I could sleep," Cal says. "If it's not too early for you."

"I'll read for a while." Lena finds her book and her clip light amid the stuff on the table, kicks off her shoes and makes herself comfortable on one of the mattresses—she has, sensibly, come wearing a soft-looking gray sweatshirt and sweatpants, meaning she has no need to change. Nellie is checking out the new space, snuffling into corners and under the sofa; Lena snaps her fingers, and Nellie lollops over and curls up at her feet. Lena props herself up on her pillow and gets to reading. Cal isn't in the mood for sleepover chitchat either, but he's irritated that she made the point before he did.

Trey opens the bedroom door, wearing the pajamas, and skids her dirty sweatshirt and jeans across the floor. Cal realizes that the pajamas are boy-type stuff with some kind of race car on the front. He still has trouble thinking of Trey as an actual girl.

"You want me to sit with you awhile?" he asks.

For a second she looks like she might, but then she shrugs. "Nah. I'm grand. Night." As she heads back into the bedroom she throws him a lopsided grin over her shoulder. "Call me if you need your arse saving," she tells him.

"Smartass," Cal says to the closing door. "Get outa here."

"Looks like she oughta be the one telling you a bedtime story, tonight," Lena says, glancing up over her book.

"This isn't a joke," Cal says. Lena's comfy sweat suit is annoying him all over again. He has no intention of asking for her help getting changed, which means he's going to have to sleep in his blood-covered clothes.

"Seems to me you're the one that hasn't been taking it seriously enough," Lena points out. "Are you done doing stupid things yet?"

"I'd love to be," Cal says. He's been trying to work out the least painful way to bend over for Trey's clothes. He gives up on the whole damn thing and heads for his mattress. "I just can't see any way around them." Lena flicks one eyebrow and goes back to her book.

Cal is almost dizzy with fatigue. He turns his back to Lena and keeps his eyes open by poking his sore knee till Lena's light clicks off, leaving the house dark, and till he hears her breathing slow down. Then, as quietly as he can, he disentangles himself from the bedding, gets up and inches the armchair over to the window. Nellie opens one eye at him, but he whispers, "Good dog," and she thumps her tail once and goes back to sleep. He lays the Henry along the windowsill and sits in front of it, looking out at the night.

There's a three-quarter moon, a rustler's moon, high over the tree line. Under its light the fields are blurred and unearthly, like a mist you could lose yourself in, an endless sweep of it crisscrossed by the sharp black tangles of hedges and walls. Only small things move, flickers among the grass and across the stars, intent on their own business.

Cal thinks of the boys who have left their lives out there on that land: the three drunk boys whose car soared off the road and spun among the stars up beyond Gorteen, the boy across the river with the noose in his hands; maybe, or probably, Brendan Reddy. He wonders, without necessarily believing in ghosts, whether their ghosts wander. It comes to him that even if they do, even if he were to take up his coat now and go walking the back roads and the mountainsides, he wouldn't meet them. Their lives and their deaths grew out of a land that Cal isn't made from and hasn't sown or harvested, and they've soaked back into that land. He could walk right through those ghosts and never feel their urgent prickle. He wonders if Trey ever meets them, on her long walks homewards under the dimming sky.

"Go get some sleep," Lena's voice says quietly, from her corner. "I'll watch."

"I'm fine here," Cal says. "Can't get comfortable on that thing. Thanks, though."

"You need sleep, after the day that's in it." He hears a ruffle of movement and a grumble from Nellie, and Lena's shape rises up off the mattress and pads across the floor to him. "Now," she says, laying a hand on his good shoulder. "Go on."

Cal stays put. They look out the window, side by side. "It's beautiful," he says.

"It's small," Lena says. "Awful small."

Cal wonders if things would have been any different for all those dead boys if they had had, stretching out beyond their doorsteps, one of those days-long empty highways he was dreaming of a few days back: something else to sing in their ears at night, instead of the drink and the noose. Probably not, for most of them. He's known plenty of boys who had the highway handy and still picked a needle or a bullet. But he wonders about Brendan Reddy.

"That's what I came looking for," he says. "A small place. A small town in a small country. It seemed like that would be easier to make sense of. Guess I might've had that wrong."

Lena lets out a small, wry puff of breath. Her hand

is still on his shoulder. Cal wonders what would happen if he were to lay his hand over hers, stand up out of the chair and take her in his arms. Not that he could do it even if he was sure he wanted to, given his various injuries, but still: he wonders whether she would lie down with him, and whether, if she did, he would wake up in the morning knowing, for better or for worse, that he was here for good.

"Go to bed," Lena says. She gives his shoulder a gentle shove out of the chair.

This time Cal moves with it. "Wake me up if anything happens," he says. "Even if it seems like nothing."

"I will, yeah. And just so you know, of course I can use a rifle. So you're in safe hands."

"That's good," Cal says. He drags his aching self over to the mattress and is asleep before he can pull up the duvet.

A few times during the night he half-wakes, from a burst of pain as he turns or a jerk of adrenaline out of nowhere. Every time, Lena is sitting still in the armchair, her hands resting on the Henry laid across her lap, her profile upturned as she watches the sky.

TWENTY

Cal sleeps late, and would sleep later except that Lena wakes him. His first movement rips a growl of pain out of him, but gradually his muscles loosen enough that he can sit up, wincing in half a dozen different ways. "Jesus," he says, slowly getting a handle on things.

"Breakfast," Lena says. "I figured you wouldn't smell it, with that nose."

"You were snoring," Trey informs him, from the table.

"Anything happen?" Cal asks. He hurts in all the places he expected and then some, but at least his voice sounds a little bit clearer. "Anyone come?"

"Not a peep," Lena says. "I saw nothing, heard nothing, Nellie didn't even twitch, I didn't have to shoot a single bandit. Come have your breakfast. And you snore too," she adds, to Trey, who gives her a skeptical stare.

The table is loaded with what looks like every piece of crockery Cal owns, all of it full of food and drink: bacon, eggs, a tower of toast. Trey is already stuffing her face. It's been so long since anyone made Cal breakfast that he finds this more touching than Lena probably intended it to be. "I only did it 'cause

I didn't know if you'd make a decent job of it," she says, laughing at the look on his face. "For all I know, you can't cook for shite."

"He can cook rabbit," Trey tells her, through a mouthful. "And fish. 'S only gorgeous."

"I don't eat rabbit for breakfast," Lena informs her. The two of them appear to have established some kind of understanding while Cal was asleep. "Or fish either. And I don't know your standards. I'd rather trust my own."

"I'll prove it to you sometime," Cal says, "if you'd like. As a thank-you. When things settle down a little bit."

"You do that," says Lena, who clearly doesn't care for the odds of things settling down in her lifetime, or at any rate in Cal's. "Eat this meanwhile, before it goes cold on you."

The breakfast is good. Cal finds himself craving rich salty things, and Lena has a lavish hand with them; she's fried every piece of bacon he had, and the toast is buttered till it drips. It's raining, not heavily but steadily, in long meandering sheets; out in the fields, the cows have banked themselves together under a flat gray sky and are keeping their heads to the grass. The day has a strange, unshakable wartime calm, as if the house is besieged so thoroughly that there's no point thinking about it until they see what happens next.

"Did you talk to her mama?" Cal asks, when Trey is in the bathroom.

"I did," Lena says, giving him a dry glance. "She's relieved enough that she didn't ask too many questions. All the same, but, Trey needs to go home soon enough. Sheila's got plenty on her plate without worrying about this one as well."

"She can't leave here till I get things under control," Cal says. "She's gone and pissed off some bad people."

"And when are you planning on getting things under control?" Lena inquires politely. "Just outa curiosity, like."

"I'm working on it. I'm aiming for sometime today." One good phone conversation should get Austin to rein in his boys till they can meet up and arrange matters to everyone's satisfaction. Cal tries to think how much cash he has in the bank, just in case.

"That'll be lovely," Lena says. "Let me know if you need a lift to the hospital."

"Could I ask you to stick around awhile?" Cal asks, ignoring that. "I need to go out for a little bit, and I don't want to leave the kid alone."

Lena gives him a long unimpressed look. "I've to go see to the other dogs," she says. "Then I can come back for a bit. I've to be in work at one, though."

"That'll give me plenty of time," Cal says. "Thanks. I appreciate it." He feels like this is the main thing he's said to her during their acquaintance.

Lena leaves Nellie behind to hang out with Trey, who is smitten with that dog to the point of sprawling on the floor with her, ignoring everything else.

The kid seems fully recovered, mentally if not physically—although Cal isn't about to trust this—and she doesn't appear to find anything remarkable about the current arrangement. As far as she's concerned, apparently, the three of them could keep on going like this for the rest of their lives.

Cal, with large amounts of caution, time and swearing, manages to change into clean clothes. When he comes out of his bedroom, Trey is using the leftover bacon to try and teach Nellie to roll over. Cal wouldn't bet money on the outcome either way: Nellie doesn't strike him as the smartest dog around, but Trey has plenty of persistence, and Nellie is happy to humor her as long as the attention and the bacon hold out.

"Your nose looks better," Trey says.

"Feels better, too," Cal says. "Sort of."

Trey moves the bacon in a circle, which just makes Nellie bounce and snap at it. She says, "Are you gonna give up on looking for Bren?"

Cal doesn't want to let her know that, after last night, walking away isn't an option any more. Austin and his boys aren't going to walk away from the fact that she shot one of them. "Nope," he says. "I don't take well to people trying to push me around."

He expects the kid to come at him with a volley of questions about his investigative plans, but that seems to be all she needs from him. She nods and goes back to waving the bacon at Nellie.

"I reckon you'd have better luck trying to train

one of the rabbits outa the freezer," Cal says. Her matter-of-fact trust moves him so much that he has to swallow. This morning he feels like he's made of marshmallow. "Leave that poor dumb dog alone and come do the dishes. I can't manage it with this arm."

————

When Lena gets back, it's almost eleven. Mart mostly takes a break around that time, for a cup of tea. Cal finds the cookies he bought yesterday and heads for the door, before Mart can take a notion to come calling. Mart had to hear those rifle shots, but with any luck he couldn't tell where they came from. Cal wants to make it clear that they had nothing to do with him.

"Take a bath," he tells Trey, on his way out. "I left you a towel in the bathroom. The red one."

Trey looks up from Nellie. "Where you going?" she asks sharply.

"Got stuff to do," Cal says. Lena, who has joined Trey on the floor to watch her patchy progress, doesn't react. "I'll be back in half an hour or thereabouts. You better be washed by then."

"Or what?" Trey inquires with interest.

"Or else," Cal says. Trey, unimpressed, rolls her eyes and goes back to the dog.

Cal's knee has settled down enough that he can walk that far, although he has a limp that feels set to last him a while. As soon as he's far enough up the road to be out of sight of his windows, he shelters against a hedge from the worst of the rain, changes his phone settings to hide his number, and calls Austin, who he feels can reasonably be expected to be awake at this hour. The call rings out to a snooty voicemail woman who sounds disappointed in Cal. He hangs up without leaving a message.

Mart's house, hunkered down among the fields, looks gray and deserted through its veil of rain, but Mart and Kojak answer the door. "Hey," Cal says, holding out the cookies. "Went to town yesterday."

"Well, holy God," Mart says, looking him up and down. "Look what the cat dragged in. What've you been doing with yourself at all, Sunny Jim? Have you been fighting banditos?"

"Fell off my roof," Cal says ruefully. Kojak is sniffing at him cautiously, tail down; the clean clothes haven't stripped away the reek of blood and adrenaline. "Climbed up there to check the slates, after that wind we got, but I'm not as limber as I used to be. Lost my footing and went flat on my face."

"G'wan outa that. You fell offa Lena Dunne," Mart tells him, cackling. "Was it worth it?"

"Aw, man, gimme a break," Cal says, rubbing the back of his neck and grinning sheepishly. "Me and Lena, we're buddies. Nothing going on there."

"Well, whatever nothing is, it's been going on two nights running. D'you think I've lost the use of my eyes, young fella? Or the use of my wits?"

"We were talking. Is all. It got late. I've got one

of those, what do you call them, for guests, the air mattresses—"

Mart is giggling so hard he has to hold himself up on the door frame. "Talking, is it? I did a bit of talking to women myself, back in the day. I'll tell you this much, I never made them sleep on an air mattress all on their ownio." He heads into the kitchen, waving Cal after him with the cookie packet. "Come in outa that and have a cup of tea, and you can give me all the details."

"She makes a mean bacon-and-egg breakfast. That's all the details I got."

"Doesn't sound like ye did that much talking," Mart says, switching on the kettle and rooting around for mugs and the Dalek teapot. Kojak flops down on his rug in front of the fireplace, keeping one wary eye on Cal. "Was it her brothers done that on you?"

"Uh-oh," Cal says. "She's got brothers?"

"Oh, begod, she does. Three big apes that'd rip your head off as soon as look at you."

"Well, shit," Cal says, "I might have to skip town after all. Sorry 'bout your twenty bucks."

Mart snickers and relents. "Don't worry your head about those lads. They know better than to get between Lena and anything she wants." He throws a generous handful of tea bags into the Dalek. "Tell me this and tell me no more: is she a wild one?"

"You'd have to ask her," Cal says primly.

"Come here," Mart says, his tangle of eyebrows

shooting up as a new idea strikes him, "is that what happened to you? Did Lena give you a few skelps? I'd say she'd have a fine aul' right hook on her. Does she have one of them fetishes?"

"No! Jesus, Mart. I just fell off the roof."

"Give us a proper look," Mart says. He leans in and peers at Cal's nose from various angles. "I'd say that's broken."

"Yeah, me too. It's straight, though, or as straight as it ever was. It'll heal."

"It'd better. You don't wanta lose your good looks, specially not now. What's the story on the arm? Didja break that too?"

"Nah. I think I cracked my collarbone. Gave my knee a pretty good whack, too."

"Sure, it could've been worse," Mart says philosophically. "I know a fella up near Ballymote that fell off his roof, the exact same as yourself, and didn't he break his neck. He's in a wheelchair to this day. His missus has to wipe his arse for him. You were lucky. Didja go to the doctor?"

"Nah," Cal says. "Nothing they could do except tell me to take it easy for a while, and I can do that myself for free."

"Or Lena can do it for you," Mart says, the grin creeping back onto his face. "She won't be happy if you're out of commission. Better rest up and mind yourself, so you can get back in the saddle."

"Jeez, Mart," Cal says, biting back a grin and getting very interested in his toe poking at a chair leg.

"Come on." Under the chair is a towel stiff with dried blood.

When he looks up, he looks into Mart's eyes. He sees Mart think about saying he had a nosebleed, and then think about saying a nameless stranger staggered in with a mysterious wound. In the end he says nothing at all.

"Well," Cal says, after a long while. "Don't I feel like the idiot."

"Ah, no," Mart reassures him charitably. He stoops to pick up the towel, bracing himself on the chair-back and grunting, and stumps unhurriedly across the kitchen to put it in the washing machine. "No need for that. Sure, how would you know the lie of the land, and you a stranger?" He closes the washing machine door and looks up at Cal. "But you know now."

Cal says, "You gonna tell me what happened?"

"Leave it be," Mart says, gently and firmly, in a voice Cal has used a hundred times to tell suspects that they've come to the end, to the place where there's no choice left, no journey and no struggle. "Go home to the child and tell her to leave it be. That's all you need to do."

Cal says, "She wants to know where her brother is."

"Then tell her he's dead and buried. Or tell her he done a runner, if you'd rather. Whatever'll make her leave it."

"I tried that. She wants to know for sure. That's her line. She won't budge off it."

Mart sighs. He pours detergent into the washing-machine drawer and sets it going.

"If you don't give her that," Cal says, "she's gonna keep on coming till you have to kill her. She's thirteen years old."

"Holy God," Mart says disapprovingly, glancing over his shoulder, "you've an awful dark mind on you altogether. No one's got any intention of killing anyone."

"What about Brendan?"

"No one intended to kill him, either. Would you ever sit down there, Sunny Jim, you're giving me the fidgets."

Cal sits at the kitchen table. The house is chilly and smells of damp. The washing machine pulses in a slow, rhythmic trudge. Rain trickles steadily down the windowpane.

The kettle has boiled. Mart pours water into the Dalek and swirls the tea bags with a spoon. He brings over the mugs and the teapot, then the milk and sugar, and then lowers himself into a chair, joint by joint, and pours the tea.

"Brendan Reddy was headed that way anyway," he says, "as fast as he could run. If it hadn't been us that done it, it woulda been someone else."

"P.J. noticed his anhydrous getting swiped," Cal says. "Right?" The walk to Mart's has raised a vicious throbbing in his knee. He feels a weight of dull anger that this should have landed at his feet today, of all days, when he's in no condition to handle it with skill.

Mart shakes his head. He shifts one hip, painfully, and pulls his tobacco out of his pants pocket. "Ah, God, no. P.J.'s an innocent, sure. He's not unfortunate or nothing, but he's got no suspicion in him. That class of carry-on wouldn't even occur to him. I'd say that's why Brendan chose his farm to begin with." He spreads out a cigarette paper on the table and starts carefully sprinkling tobacco along it. "No: P.J. was told."

Cal says, "Donie." Apparently he's been everyone's fool around here, even that fool Donie's. He should have seen it straightaway, back in the fug of body smells and smoke in Donie's room. He knows how the Dublin boys found out that Brendan had been snared, too. Donie understands the ways of trouble well enough to sow plenty of it himself, when he wants to.

"It was. Donie and Brendan never got on, even when they were little lads; I'd say he leaped at the chance to do Brendan a bad turn. Only the feckin' eejit went and told P.J., instead of coming to me, the way he woulda done if he had the brains of an ass. And what did P.J. do only call in the Guards."

"What's wrong with that?" Cal asks, giving Mart something to argue with. "That's what I'da done."

"I've nothing against the Guards," Mart says, "in their place, but I didn't see what they'd contribute to this situation. We'd enough of a mess on our hands already, without them traipsing about the place asking questions and arresting all round them." He rolls the paper into a stingy cigarette, squinting carefully to keep it even. "Lucky enough, they took their time arriving. Enough time that P.J. came up to tell me the news, and I was able to make him see sense. Myself and P.J. sent the Guards off about their business, and I rang another coupla lads—lads that live alone, that wouldn't have to explain themselves to anyone—to get back P.J.'s anhydrous meanwhile." He cocks an eyebrow at Cal over the rollie, as he licks the edge. "You know the place, sure."

"Yep," Cal says. He wonders who was watching him and Trey on that mountain path.

"They found a big loada Sudafed, as well, and a big loada batteries. No surprise there. They took all that away with them, too, for good measure. If you have a cold this winter, Sunny Jim, or if your alarm clock gives up on you, you just let me know and I'll sort you out."

Cal learned a long time back to know when there's nothing he needs to say. He warms his hands on his mug, drinks his tea and listens.

"Mind you," Mart says, pointing with his rollie, "I wasn't taking Donie's word for anything. For all we knew, he robbed that anhydrous himself, then his deal went arseways and he thought he'd take the opportunity to drop Brendan in a bitta shite. But I know a lad whose place looks out over the road to that aul' cottage; he kept an eye out. And sure enough, not long after the Guards came calling, didn't Brendan Reddy go rushing up that road in a terrible hurry altogether. So then we knew for certain."

He clicks his lighter and takes a leisurely, pleasurable drag on the cigarette, turning his head to blow the smoke away from Cal. "Brendan laid low for a few days after that," he says. "Considering his options, I'd say. But we had an eye on him. Sure, he couldn't stay indoors forever; his pals from Dublin were bound to want a word with him. Myself and the lads had no problem with that, but we wanted to get our word in first, so young Brendan'd know where he stood. We were trying to do him a favor; we didn't want him making any foolish commitments to the Dublin boyos. Next time he headed up to that cottage, we were there to meet him."

Cal thinks of how Trey said Brendan went bouncing out the door, chirpy as a cricket, on his way to give Austin the cash to replace what Mart's boys had annexed, get all his plans patched up and back on track. He says, "He wasn't expecting that."

"That he wasn't," Mart says, momentarily diverted from his story to consider this point. "The face on him: like he'd walked into a room fulla hippopotamuses. A lad as sharp as that, you'd think he woulda seen it coming, would you not? But then, you'd think he'd be a step ahead of a thick like Donie, too.

If he'd been a little less sharp when it came to the aul' chemistry and a little sharper when it came to human beings, he'd be alive today."

Cal finds himself with no feelings and no thoughts. He's moved into a place that he knows well from the job: a circle where even the air doesn't move, nothing exists but the story he's hearing and the person telling it, and he himself has dissolved away to nothing but watching and listening and readiness. Even his aches and pains seem like distant things.

"We were intending to explain the situation to him, was all," Mart says. He nods at Cal's beat-up face. "You know the way yourself, sure. Just a bitta clarification. Only this lad didn't want anything clarified. I don't like to speak ill of the dead, but he was a cheeky little fecker, d'you know that? Telling us we didn't know what we were dealing with, if we had any brains we'd fuck off back to our farms and not be sticking our noses into things we didn't understand. I know that fella was dragged up, not brought up, but my mammy would've wore out her wooden spoon on me if I ever talked that way to men old enough to be my grandfather." He reaches for an old jam jar that's become an ashtray and unscrews the lid to tap ash. "We went to put manners on him, but didn't he get rambunctious and try to fight back, and matters got a wee bit outa hand. The blood was up all round, like. The lad landed a few punches, someone lost his temper and caught him a great clatter to the jaw, and he went flying over backwards and hit his head on the edge of one of his own propane tanks."

Mart takes a long drag on his rollie and tilts his head back to blow the smoke at the ceiling. "I thought at first he was only knocked out," he says. "When I looked closer, but, I knew he was bad. I don't know what done it, was it the punch or the fall, but whatever way it happened, his head was twisted round and his eyes were rolling up. He made a bit of a snoring noise and he done a few twitches of his legs, and then he was gone. Quick as that."

In the window behind his head, the fields are a green so soft and deep you could sink into them. Wind blows a whisper of rain against the glass. The washing machine trudges on.

"I seen a man die quick once before," Mart says, "when I was fifteen. The hay baler wasn't clearing right, and he went to see what was wrong, only he left the power running. His hand got caught and the baler pulled him in. By the time I got it turned off, his arm and his head were gone. It shredded him like you'd shred a bitta wet kitchen roll."

He watches his smoke trickle and spread through the air of the kitchen. "My granddad was after dying the month before that, of a stroke. That took him four days. Life seems like a big thing when it takes four days for all of it to leave a man. When it's gone in a few seconds, it looks awful small all of a sudden. We don't like to face up to that, but the animals know it. They've no notions about their dying. It's a little thing, only; you'd get it done in no time. All it takes is one nip from a fox. Or a hay baler, or a propane tank."

Cal says, "What'd you do with the body?"

Mart's eyebrows twitch up. "Sure, we didn't get the chance to do much of anything with it at all; not then, anyway. 'Twas a bit of an action-packed day all round. Before we'd properly got the hang of what was after happening, we got the call from the lad on the lookout, to say that the Dublin boyos were on their way. We put your man on an aul' bedsheet that was in the back room and carried him up the hillside behind the cottage, as far into the trees as we'd time for. When we heard their car—big bull of a black Hummer, they had, I don't know how they got it round the bends in them roads—we laid him down among the bushes and crouched down next to him."

He glances at Cal, through the twists of smoke. "I thought of leaving him in the house for them to find. A message, like. But in the heel of the hunt I decided against it. No point in telling them more than they needed to know, sure. They'd get the gist of things anyway, once he turned up gone."

"What'd they do?" Cal asks.

Mart grins. "They weren't pleased with the situation at all, at all. They went and had a look in the cottage, and then they came out and looked around the yard, and then they went back in and did it all over again. Four of them, there was, and not a one of them could stay still for a bloody second; they were hopping about like they'd fleas. And the language out of them, holy God. We were close enough to hear them— 'twas a grand spring day, not a breath of wind. I'm no prude, but it nearly melted the ears right offa me."

His grin widens. "D'you know what else they did? They rang Brendan. Half a dozen times. I knew they would, so I was after taking the phone outa his pocket, but I couldn't unlock it to turn down the volume. We tried using the lad's fingerprint, but he'd put a code on it. So will I tell you what we did with that phone? I had Bobby sit his great fat arse on it. That'd muffle anything. The face on him when it vibrated, trying not to leap up off it. Red as a big aul' beetroot. The rest of us near burst with trying not to laugh."

He stubs out his rollie in the lid of the jam jar. "In the end they gave up on him," he says, "and off they went back down the mountain. D'you know what one of them was doing, on his way to their lovely shiny Hummer? He was whinging and whining out of him about his good shoes getting all mucky. Like a woman on her way to a fancy ball."

Cal is pretty sure that every word is true. There's no reason it shouldn't be—it's not like he can do anything with any of it—except for Mart's habit of keeping people in the dark on principle. It seems to Cal that they've moved out on the other side of that.

He says, "Where's Brendan now?"

"He's still up the mountains. Buried, now, not just

left there; the child doesn't need to worry that there was crows and rats at him, or nothing like that. We said a few prayers over him and all."

Mart reaches for his packet of cookies and opens it, carefully, so as not to crumble any edges. "And that was the end of that," he says.

"Except for Donie and his messing around with the sheep," Cal says.

Mart blows out a scornful puff of air. "I don't count that, sure. I don't count that feckin' eejit on principle." He offers the packet to Cal. "Go on, get one of those into you. You deserve it. You're a cute hoor, aren't you? Here you were feeling like an eejit yourself, but you'd it all figured out already, sure. You only had the one bit wrong. There's no shame in that."

Cal says, "Donie figured P.J. had to be involved, since it was his anhydrous. How'd he find out you and Bobby and Francie were on board too?"

Mart selects a cookie, taking his time over the decision. "I'd say Donie had an eye on things himself. He musta caught a glimpse of the four of us somewhere along the way and gone running to the Dublin lads—that fella'd make a great double agent, if only he had a brain in his head. And them fine boyos told him to send us a wee message to stay out of their business." He smiles at Cal. "We got the message, anyway. Even if we didn't take it the way they expected."

Cal asks, "Does Bobby still think it was aliens?"

"Ah, God, Bobby," Mart says indulgently, dipping his cookie in his tea. "He's only delighted to have aliens at his sheep. I wouldn't ruin it for him. I couldn't, anyhow; even if I had a video of Donie working away, he still wouldn't believe me. Sure, it doesn't matter what Bobby thinks. Donie knew I'd get the message, after two sheep or three. But he didn't think I'd find out it was him that sent it. He thought I'd take for granted it was the big bold Dublin lads, or someone they sent down from town maybe, and I'd be that petrified of them I wouldn't dare lift a finger. He knows better now."

"Seems to me," Cal says, "if you boys wanted to raise the tone around these parts, the one you oughta have gotten rid of was Donie."

"There's Donies everywhere," Mart says. "They'd do your head in, the little fuckers, but they make no difference in the long run. They're ten a penny, so they are; if you get rid of one, another one'll only pop up in his place. Brendan Reddy was another matter entirely. There's not a lot of those about. And what he was doing woulda made a difference to this townland, all right."

"You've already got drugs round here," Cal says. "Plenty of 'em. It's not like Brendan was bringing 'em into the Garden of Eden."

"We lose enough of our young men," Mart says. It seems to Cal that he should sound like he's defending his actions, but he doesn't. His eyes across the table are steady and his voice is calm and final, underlaid by the quiet patter of rain all around. "The way the world's after changing, it's not made right for them, any more. When I was a young lad, we knew what we could want and how to get it, and we knew we'd have something to show for it at the end of the day. A crop, or a flock, or a house, or a family. There's great strength in that. Now there's too many things you're told to want, there's no way to get them all, and once you're done trying, what have you got to show for it at the end? You've made a buncha phone calls selling electricity plans, maybe, or had a buncha meetings about nothing; you've got your hole offa some bitta fluff you met on the internet, got yourself some likes on the aul' YouTube. Nothing you can put your hands on. The women do be grand anyway; they're adaptable. But the young men don't know what to be doing with themselves at all. There's a few of them, like Fergal O'Connor who you met there, that keep their feet on the ground regardless. The rest are hanging themselves, or they're getting drunk and driving into ditches, or they're overdosing on the aul' heroin, or they're packing their bags. I don't want to see this place a wasteland, every farm looking the way yours did before you came along: falling to wrack and ruin, waiting for some Yank to take a fancy to it and make it into his hobby."

Kojak, smelling the cookies, shambles over and stands by Mart's chair, waiting. Mart holds out the remains of the cookie for him to snap up. He says, "I wasn't going to stand by and watch us lose more of our young men to Brendan Reddy and his notions."

"You lost Brendan," Cal points out.

"I'm only after telling you that wasn't intentional," Mart says, put out. "Besides, if we'd left him at it, we'da lost a lot more than one, one way or another. You can't make an omelet without breaking eggs, isn't that what they say?"

Cal says, "Is that what you were thinking when you went to talk to Sheila Reddy, the other night?" He tries to keep his voice even, but he can hear the rumble of danger rising up.

Mart ignores it. He says, "It needed doing. That's all I was thinking. That's all there was to think."

He gives Kojak a slap on the flank to send him back to the fireside. "And that's what you were thinking when you gave Donie the few skelps, sure. You weren't thinking, 'Ah, sure, what harm?' You were thinking that every now and then there's a thing that needs doing and there's not a lot any man can do to change that, so there's no point in fussing and foostering; you might as well go ahead and get it done. And the pity of it is, you were right."

"Not sure I'd put it that way," Cal says.

Mart laughs. "That's what Theresa Reddy was thinking last night, anyway, when she shot off that rifle. You weren't raising any objections then."

"Whichever one of the guys got hit," Cal says. "How's he doing?"

"He'll be grand. He bled like a stuck pig, but there's no real harm done." Mart takes another cookie and grins at Cal. "Will you look at all the action we've had around here, the last while? I don't want you getting it in your head that the townland's always this exciting. You'll be fierce disappointed when the biggest thrill of the next year is someone's ewe dropping quadruplets."

Cal says, "Were you there last night? At my place?"

Mart laughs, his face creasing up. "Ah, God, no. Me? With my joints, I'm not able for the aul' roola-boola any more."

Or else he didn't want to risk Cal recognizing him. "You're more of an ideas man," Cal says.

"I wish you well, Sunny Jim," Mart says. "I always have. Now drink up your tea, go home and tell the child as much of that story as you like, and tell her it's done now."

"It's not about the story," Cal says. "All's she needs to know is that he's dead, and that it was a fight that went wrong; she doesn't need to know who did it. But she's gonna want proof."

"She can't have everything she wants. She oughta know that by her age."

"I'm not talking about the kind of proof that could get anyone in any shit. But she's had too many people feeding her bullshit. She can't stop unless she gets something solid."

"What kind of something did you have in mind?"

"Brendan had a watch on him. Used to be his granddaddy's."

Mart dips his cookie and watches Cal. He says, "He's been dead six months."

"I'm not asking you to get it for me. You tell me where to look, I'll get it myself."

"Seen worse on the job, hah?"

Cal says, "I've got nothing to do with any job."

"Not any more, maybe. But old habits die hard."

"No maybe about it. And I came here to get away from old habits."

"You're not making a very good job of it, Sunny Jim," Mart points out. "No offense meant."

"Brendan Reddy isn't my problem," Cal says. Even though he understands that in many ways it's the truth, the words don't come out easily. It frightens him that he can't tell whether he's doing the right thing or the wrong one. "I'm not gonna do anything about him. I wish I'd never heard of him. I'm just trying to get a kid some peace of mind, so she can put this down and move on."

Mart thinks this over, savoring his cookie. He says, "And you think she'll do that?"

"Yeah. She's not out for revenge, or justice. All she wants is to leave it."

"Maybe she does now. What about a few years down the line?"

"The kid's got her own code," Cal says. "If she gives her word to let this lie, I believe she'll stick to it."

Mart sucks the last soggy crumb off his finger and watches Cal. His eyes might have been blue once, but the color has faded out of them and they have a watery rim. It gives him a dreamy, almost wistful look. He says, "You know what'll happen, now, if anything comes out of this."

"Yeah," Cal says. "I do."

"And you're willing to risk it."

"Yeah."

"Well, holy God," Mart says, "we'll have to get you in on the card game, because you're some gambler. You've more faith in that child than I would, or anyone else round here would. But then, maybe you know her better."

He pushes back his chair and reaches for the mugs. "I'll tell you what we'll do, now. You're in no fit state to be clambering up mountains; sure, you'd collapse on me halfway, and I'm not carrying you back. You'd squash me flat. You go home and talk to the child. Test the waters. Have a good aul' think about it. After that, if you're still up for the risk, you get a few days' rest, get yourself in fighting form, and then come back to me. And we'll go out digging."

He smiles at Cal over his shoulder, as he puts the mugs in the sink. "Go on, now," he says, the way he'd say it to Kojak. "And get some rest. If you don't get back up and running soon, Lena might get impatient and find herself another fella."

———

While Cal was out, which he feels like he has been for a very long time, Trey gave up on training Nellie. She and Lena have broken out the painting gear and are working on the front-room skirting boards. The iPod is playing the Dixie Chicks, Lena is humming along, Trey is sprawled on her stomach on the floor to get a corner perfect, and Nellie has taken over the armchair. Cal wants to turn around and walk straight out again, taking his knowledge with him.

Trey glances over her shoulder. "Check this," she says. She sits up and spreads her arms. Lena must have somehow convinced her to take that bath; she's noticeably cleaner than she was when Cal left, and she's wearing the new clothes he brought her from town.

"Looking snazzy," Cal says. The clothes are a size too big. They make her look so little it hurts. "Till you get paint all over yourself."

"She was restless," Lena says. "She wanted to be doing something. I figured you wouldn't mind."

"I can just about live with it," Cal says. "The reason those aren't done yet is 'cause I wasn't looking forward to getting down on the floor like that."

"You know what we oughta do," Trey says.

"What's that?" Cal says.

"That wall." She points at the fireplace wall. "In the evenings it goes gold, like, from the sun coming in through that window. Looks good. We oughta paint it that color."

Cal is startled by something rising up inside his chest that might be a laugh or a sob. Mart was right again: here he is, with a woman bringing ideas into his house. "Sounds good to me," he says. "I'll get in a few paint samples, we can pick the one that matches best."

Trey nods. Something in Cal's voice has caught her; she gives him a long look. Then she picks up her paintbrush and goes back to the skirting board.

Lena looks at the two of them. "Right, so," she says. "I'll be off."

"Could you maybe hang around a little longer?" Cal asks.

She shakes her head. "I've things to do."

Cal waits while she puts on her big jacket and packs her accoutrements away in its pockets, and snaps her fingers for Nellie. He walks them out. "Thanks," he says, on the step. "Could you give the kid a ride home, later on?"

Lena nods. "You got things under control," she says, not really asking a question.

"Yeah," Cal says. "I did. Or close enough."

"Right," Lena says. "Good luck." She touches Cal's arm for a second, in something between a pat and a shake. Then she heads off through the rain towards her car, with Nellie lolloping along beside her. It comes to Cal that, while she doesn't know anything for sure and doesn't want to, she's had a pretty fair idea all along.

He closes the door behind them, turns off the Dixie Chicks and goes to Trey. His knee still hurts enough that he has a hard time finding a position he can take up on the floor; he eventually settles for sitting with his leg stretched out at an awkward angle. Trey keeps on painting, but he can feel her stretched taut as a wire, waiting.

He says, "I talked to some people, while I was out."

"Yeah," Trey says. She doesn't look up.

"I'm sorry to tell you this, kid. I got some sad news for you."

After a moment she says, like her throat is tight, "Yeah."

"Your brother died, kid. The same day you last saw him. He met up with some people, they got in a fight. Your brother took a punch, and he fell over and hit his head. No one meant for him to die. Things just went bad that day."

Trey keeps on painting. Her head is down and Cal can't see her face, but he can hear the hard hiss of her breathing.

She says, "Who was it?"

"I don't know who threw the punch," Cal says. "You said all you need is to know for sure what happened, so you can leave it. Did that change?"

Trey says, "Did he die quick?"

"Yeah. The punch knocked him out, and he died just a minute later. He didn't suffer. He never even knew what was happening."

"D'you swear?"

"Yeah. I swear."

Trey's brush scrubs back and forth over the same patch of skirting board. In a little bit she says, "It might not be true."

"I'm gonna get you proof," Cal says. "In a few days' time. I know you need that. But it's true, kid. I'm sorry."

Trey keeps up the painting for another second. Then she lays down the brush, leans back against the wall and starts to cry. At first she cries like a grown adult, sitting there with her head back, her jaw and eyes tight, tears trickling down the sides of her face in silence. Then something breaks and she sobs like a child, with her arm across her knees and her face buried in her elbow, crying her heart out.

Every cell in Cal's body wants to grab his rifle, head back up to Mart's place and march that bastard all the way to town and into the police station. He knows it wouldn't be the slightest bit of use, but he still wants to do it, with such ferocious urgency that he has to stop his muscles from propelling him onto his feet and right out the door.

Instead he gets up and fetches a roll of paper towels. He puts it down by Trey and sits against the wall next to her while she cries. Her arm crooked over her face makes him think of a broken wing. After a while he lays his hand on the back of her neck.

In the end Trey runs out of crying, for now. "Sorry," she says, wiping her face on her sleeve. She's red and blotchy, with her good eye swollen almost as small as her black one and her nose swollen almost as big as Cal's.

"No need," Cal says. He hands her the roll of paper towels.

Trey blows her nose loudly. She says, "Just seems like there oughta be some way to fix it."

Her voice wavers, and for a second Cal thinks she might break down again. "I know," he says. "I've never quite come to terms with that myself."

They sit there, listening to the rain. Trey catches the occasional long shuddering breath.

"Do I still haveta go into Noreen's today?" she asks, after a while. "I'm not having any of them nosy fuckers seeing me like this."

"No," Cal says. "That's taken care of. Those guys won't be bothering any of us any more."

That gets Trey's attention. "You beat 'em up?"

"I look like I could beat anyone up right now?"

The kid manages a watery grin.

"Nah," Cal says. "Just talked to 'em. But it's OK."

Trey refolds her wad of paper towel to find a clean patch and blows her nose again. Cal can see her taking in, piece by piece, the ways things have changed.

"That means you can go home now," he says. "I enjoy having you around, but I think it's time you went home."

Trey nods. "I'll go. Later, just. In a while."

"Fair enough," Cal says. "I can't drive you, but

Miss Lena will, once she's finished work. You want me or her to come in with you? Help you explain things to your mama?"

Trey shakes her head. "I'm not gonna say it to her yet. Not till you get that proof." She glances up from her wad of paper towel. "You said a few days."

"Give or take," Cal says. "But there's one condition. You gotta give me your word of honor that you won't try to do anything about this. Ever. Just put it down and go back to normal, like you said. Put your mind into going to school, hooking back up with your friends. Maybe making it through a few days without pissing off your teachers. Can you do that?"

Trey takes a deep, shaky breath. "Yeah," she says. "I can." She's still slumped against the wall; her hands, holding the paper towel, lie in her lap like she doesn't have the energy to move them. She looks like a long cruel tension is leaching out of her, notch by notch, leaving her whole body slack to the point of helplessness.

"Not just for now. For the rest of your life."

"I know."

"You swear. Word of honor."

Trey looks at him. She says, "I swear."

Cal says, " 'Cause I'm taking a pretty big chance here."

"I took a chance on you last night," Trey points out. "When I let them lads go."

"I guess you did," Cal says. He has that shaky feeling up under his breastbone again. He can't wait for it to be tomorrow, or next week, or whenever he'll have got his strength back enough to react to things like his normal self. "OK. Give me a week. Say two, to be on the safe side. Then come back."

Trey takes another long breath. She says, "What do we do now?"

The idea of a world with no quest in it has left her lost. "You know what I want to do today," Cal says, "is go fishing. That's about all I've got in me. You think us beat-up stray mutts can make it that far?"

Trey makes sandwiches. Cal lends her an extra sweater and his padded winter coat, in which she looks ridiculous. She helps him get into his jacket. Then they walk, taking it slowly, down to the riverbank. They spend the afternoon sitting there, without saying a single word that doesn't relate to fish. When they have enough perch to feed Cal, Trey's family, and Lena, they pack up and go home.

They split up the fish, and Cal finds a plastic bag to hold Trey's old clothes and her pajamas. Lena, on her way back from work, stops by to pick Trey up. She stays in the car, but when Cal comes out to her she rolls down her window to look at him. "Give me a bell when you're through doing stupid things," she says.

Cal nods. Trey gets into the car and Lena rolls up her window, and Cal watches them drive off, with the darkness gathering above the hedges and the headlight beams glittering on the falling rain.

TWENTY-ONE

The rain holds steady, day and night, for more than a week. Cal mostly stays indoors, letting his body heal. His collarbone appears to be only bruised or cracked or something along those lines, rather than broken outright; by the end of the week he can use that arm for small stuff without too much pain, as long as he doesn't try to raise it above shoulder height. His knee, on the other hand, is banged up worse than he thought. The swelling takes its time going down. Cal straps it up with bandages and ices it regularly, which helps some.

The enforced idleness and the misty rain give that week a dreamy, suspended feel. At first Cal finds it strangely easeful. For the first time he can remember, he doesn't have the option of doing anything, whether he wants to or not. All he can do is sit by his windows and look out. He gets accustomed to seeing the mountains soft and blurry with rain, like he could keep walking towards them forever and they would just keep shifting farther away. Tractors trudge back and forth across the fields, and the cows and sheep graze steadily; there's no way to tell whether the rain doesn't bother them, or whether they just endure. The wind has taken the last of the leaves; the rooks' oak tree is bare, exposing the big straggly twig-balls of their nests in the crook of every branch. In the next tree over, there's a lone nest to mark where, sometime along the way, some bird infringed on their mysterious laws and got taught a lesson.

The shaky feeling lingers on for a couple of days, rising up to pierce Cal at random things like a dead wren in his backyard or a nighttime squeal in the hedges. A few good nights' rest gets rid of it. It came out of Cal's body, mainly, not his mind. The beating didn't shock his mind deeply. Men fight sometimes; it's in the natural course of things. What was done to Trey is a different thing, and harder to leave behind.

He knows that his duty is to take what he's learned to Officer Dennis. There are so many reasons why he won't be doing this, all of them so inextricably tangled together, that Cal has no idea which one is the central one and which are just underbrush. The longer he's stuck indoors and idle, the more this question prickles at him. He starts to wish he could spend his days walking, but he needs to rest his knee, so it can heal for the journey up the mountainside. He wishes Lena or Trey would pay him a visit, but he knows that would be a bad idea; right now every-thing needs to be left to settle. He almost wishes he had bought himself a TV.

Once his knee can handle it, he limps down through the rain to Noreen's and explains, over her full range of high-pitched horrified noises, about his fall off the roof. While she's listing home remedies and people who died by falling off things, Fergal O'Connor comes in for a giant bag of potatoes and a giant bottle of some fruit cordial. When Cal nods to him, he ducks his head awkwardly and comes up with a bashful half grin, and then pays for his stuff and leaves fast, before Cal can start asking him questions again.

Cal has thought about Fergal, over the past few days. Of all the people he talked to, sweet dumb loyal Fergal is the one who could have set him on the right track. Brendan may have lacked sense in plenty of ways, but he had enough of it to talk to Fergal, rather than Eugene, when he got the urge to show off his plans. Fergal knew what Brendan was setting up—maybe not in detail, but he knew the gist of things. He knew Brendan had been caught out and was running scared, and he knew that if Brendan wasn't scared of the local guys as well as the boys from Dublin, he should be. The only part that hasn't occurred to Fergal is that things could have gone bad. In Fergal's mind, nature is what turns rogue; people are reliable, or at least reliably themselves. And Brendan, who always was skittish, got spooked at the thought of a beating and took off somewhere, and he'll come back when things settle down.

Cal isn't going to tell him different. He'll come to it in his own time, or he won't, or he doesn't want to. Fergal needs to make his own terms with his home place.

He's not going to tell Caroline, either. She does want to know, but even if he could do it without risk, Caroline can't be his responsibility. She'll have to make her own terms too. Cal would like to at least tell her that it was an accident, just so those terms aren't harsher than need be. If she comes asking someday, he might find a way.

If he's around. The other thing he's thought about, stuck in his house watching the silhouettes of mountains that hold a dead boy folded away somewhere among their dreamy curves, is putting his place on the market and getting on a plane back to Chicago, or Seattle maybe. In a few more days he'll have done what Trey needs from him; there'll be no responsibilities left to hold him here. He could be packed and gone in less than an hour.

He pays for his groceries, and Noreen talks him out the door, promising to send Lena up to him with cabbage poultices and the number of a good roofer. Cal has no way of knowing whether she believes a word he said, but he understands that, as far as she's concerned, that's beside the point.

———

Finally the rain clears. Cal, who the day before would have sworn he was going to start chewing the woodwork if he couldn't get out and get this job done, decides it would be only sensible to let some of the rainwater drain out of the mountainside before he goes digging around in it. He stays home that day, and then the next, to be on the safe side.

He's not shying from Brendan. He doesn't welcome the prospect, but whatever condition the body is in, he's seen worse. He knows what he needs to do there, and he's ready to do it. The part that offers him no such clarity is the part after that.

Any minute now, though, Trey is going to come looking for her proof. Cal has seen nothing of her since Lena took her home. He doesn't like the thought of her up there on the mountainside with no one but Sheila to keep an eye on how she's doing, but he did tell her to give him two weeks, and he figures it's probably a good thing that she's doing it: she needs this time to take in all that's happened, and to ready herself for what comes next. But he also figures that around about now, with the two weeks ticking away and her face hopefully healed up enough that she doesn't flinch from showing herself, she's going to get restless.

It's a Thursday, but late that night Cal sits out on his step and calls Alyssa anyway. He feels dumb doing it, but he's planning to spend the next day heading miles up a deserted mountainside with a man who's already helped kill one person and gotten away with it, and who might reasonably consider Cal to be an unacceptable risk. It would be naïve to ignore the situation's potential, and Cal feels he's been plenty naïve enough already.

She picks up fast. "Hey. Is everything OK?"

"All good," Cal says. "Just felt like checking in. How're you doing?"

"Good. Ben had a second interview for this really great job, so fingers crossed." Her voice has got farther away, and Cal can hear running water and clinking noises. She's put him on speakerphone while she goes back to loading the dishwasher. "What've you been up to?"

"Nothing much. It's been raining all week, but it's cleared up, so I'm planning on going for a walk up the mountains tomorrow. With my neighbor Mart."

Alyssa says something muffled by her hand over the phone, presumably to Ben. "Oh, wow," she says, back to Cal. "Sounds beautiful."

"Yeah, it is. I'll send you photos."

"Yeah, do. It's been raining here, too. Someone at work said it might snow, but I think she made that up."

Cal drags a hand down his face hard enough to hurt his bruises. He remembers how he used to put Alyssa's whole little baby foot in his mouth, and she would laugh till she gave herself hiccups. Above his garden, the sky is a mess of high sharp stars.

"You know what," he says suddenly. "I've run into something you might be able to help me with. You got a minute?"

The noises stop. "Sure," Alyssa says. "What's up?"

"There's a neighbor kid who's been coming round to my place to learn some carpentry. She just found out her big brother died, and she doesn't have what you'd call a good support system: her daddy's run off, and her mama hasn't got much to offer. I want to help her get through this without going off the rails, but I don't know the best way to do it. I figure you might have some ideas."

"OK," Alyssa says. There's a note in her voice like she's rolling up her sleeves to get down to work. "How old is she?"

"Thirteen."

"How did her brother die?"

"Got in a fight and hit his head. He was nineteen. They were pretty close."

"All right," Alyssa says. "So the main thing is to let her know that whatever she's feeling is normal, but direct her away from any action that's destructive or self-destructive. So for example, it's natural for her to be angry at herself, her brother, the person he was fighting with, her parents for not protecting him, whoever—make sure she knows that's fine and she doesn't need to feel guilty about it. But if she's lashing out at other kids, say, she needs to know she can't do that. Help her find another outlet for the anger. Maybe get her into martial arts, or drama. Or running. Hey, you could go running with her."

The mischievous grin in her voice makes Cal grin back, right across half the world. "Hey," he says, mock-offended. "I could run. If I wanted to."

"So do it. Worst case, you'll give her something to laugh at, and she could probably use that. She'll be looking for ways to feel like the world can still be normal. Laughing is good."

All her confidence and competence blow Cal clean away. His baby girl is, somehow, a grown adult who knows how to get shit done and done well; who knows things, and has skills, that he doesn't. Here he was fretting about her like a mama hen, listening every minute for her to fall to pieces, and all the while she was just tired out from the hard work it's taken to grow into this. He listens to her talk about regressive behaviors and modeling healthy emotional expression, and pictures her sitting at ease next to some American equivalent of Trey, deftly and calmly transforming all these words into solid action. It seems to him that he can't have fucked up too badly, if Alyssa turned out like this.

"All of that sounds pretty great," he says, when she finishes up.

"Well, I've had practice. An awful lot of the kids at work, they've lost someone, one way or another."

"They're lucky to have you around."

Alyssa laughs her big wonderful laugh. "Yeah, mostly they think so too. Not always. Is any of that going to be useful?"

"Oh yeah. I'm gonna keep every bit of it in mind. Except maybe the running."

"I can put it in an email, if you want. And if anything specific comes up, like if she starts engaging in risky behaviors or whatever, let me know and I'll give you whatever strategies I've got."

"That'd be great. Thanks, kiddo. I mean it."

"Anytime. You'll be fine. Better than fine. Remember

when Puffle got hit by the car? You drove us all the way out to that forest because I wanted to bury her there. And you carved her a gravestone and everything."

"I remember," Cal says. He wishes he could call Donna and tell her that he thinks he might get what she was talking about, at least some of the time.

"That was exactly what I needed. You'll be fine. Just, Dad . . ."

"Yeah?"

"Your neighbor girl, she really needs consistency right now. Like, the last thing she needs is someone else disappearing on her. So, I mean, if you were planning on coming home any time soon . . . probably you should point her to someone else she can talk to, instead. Maybe another neighbor you trust, or—"

"Yeah," Cal says. "I know." He almost asks her whether she wants him to come back. He stops himself in time; it wouldn't be right to put that on her.

"Yeah, I figured you did. Just checking." In the background, Ben's voice says something. "Dad, I've got to go, we're meeting people for dinner—"

"Go ahead," Cal says. "Say hi to Ben from me. And tell your mama I sent my best. I don't want to hassle her, but I'd like her to know that I'm wishing her well."

"Will do. Talk soon."

"Hey," Cal says, before she can hang up. "I picked up this little toy sheep in town. It reminded me of all those toys you used to have when you were little, the raccoon and all. Can I send it to you? Or don't you want fluffy toys any more, now that you're all grown up?"

"I would totally love a toy sheep," Alyssa says. He can hear her smiling. "He'll get along great with the raccoon. Night."

"Night, sweet pea. You have a good dinner. Don't get to bed too late."

"**Dad,**" she says, laughing, and she's gone. Cal sits on the step for another while, drinking his beer and watching the stars, waiting for the morning.

———

The weather holds; the morning comes in with harsh winter sunshine sliding low across the fields and in at Cal's window. The air of the house has a new, icy edge that the heaters only partly dispel. Cal eats breakfast, re-straps his knee and puts on most of the clothes he owns. When it comes time for Mart's tea break, he heads up that way.

The land has left its luring autumn self behind and put on a new, aloof beauty. The greens and golds have thinned to watercolor; the sky is one scoured sweep of pale blue, and the mountains are so clear it seems like Cal can see each distant clump of browning heather, sharp and distinct. The verges are still soft from the rain, with puddles in the ruts. Cal's breath smokes and spreads. He takes the walk slowly, sparing his knee. He knows he's walking into a hard day, in a hard place.

Kojak is rooting around a corner of Mart's garden, digging for something too interesting to be left. Mart comes to the door. "Long time no see, bucko," he says, smiling up at Cal. "I was starting to wonder should we send in a search party to see were you still with us. But you're looking in fine fettle altogether."

"Doing OK," Cal says. "Well enough to go out digging, now that the rain's stopped."

Mart, peering at Cal's face from various angles, ignores that. "I'd say that nose is just about back to its former glory," he says. "Lena must be pleased, is she? Or is she after ditching you? I haven't seen her car around our way."

"Guess she's been busy," Cal says. "Would you be free to take me for that walk?"

The mischief falls away from Mart's face. He says, "Didja talk to the child?"

"Yeah. She's not gonna do anything."

"You're sure."

"Yeah," Cal says. "I'm sure."

"Your call, Sunny Jim," Mart says. "I hope you're right." He whistles for Kojak. Kojak comes bounding happily over to exchange pleasantries with Cal, but Mart motions him into the house. "We don't want him along for this. Wait there a moment, now; I'll be back to you."

He shuts the door behind him. Cal watches a flock

of starlings billow like a genie against the sky until Mart comes back, wearing his wax jacket and a thick knitted beanie in a startling shade of neon yellow. For an instant Cal has the urge to make some crack about it, call him DJ Cookie Crumble or some such, before he remembers they're no longer on those terms. It catches him with a twist of loneliness. He liked Mart.

Mart is carrying his crook and a straight-edged spade. "That's for you," he says, holding out the spade to Cal. "Will you be able to use it, with that collarbone?"

"I'll figure something out," Cal says. He balances the spade over his good shoulder.

"How about that knee? It's a long aul' walk, and half of it's not on roads. If that knee lets you down on the mountainside, there's nothing I'll be able to do for you."

"Call in P.J. and Francie. They can carry me down."

"I haven't brought them up to speed on this wee expedition," Mart says. "They wouldn't approve. They don't know you as well as I do, sure. You can't hold it against them."

"My knee's fine," Cal says. "Let's go."

The walk is a long one. They start up the same mountain road that Cal took to the Reddy place, but half a mile up Mart points his crook at a side trail, too narrow for them to walk abreast, its entrance almost hidden by scrubby trees and long grass. "You wouldn't have spotted this, now," he says, smiling at Cal. "This mountain's fulla tricks, so it is."

"You know 'em," Cal says. "You go ahead." He doesn't want Mart at his back.

The trail runs over rises and between boulders, among thorny flares of yellow gorse and stretches of leggy heather whose purple bells are fading to brown paper. "All this here," Mart says, stirring a clump of heather with his crook as he passes, "that's ling heather. You'd get the finest honey in the world from that. A fella called Peadar Ruadh that lived up here, he usedta keep bees, when I was a child. My granny'd send us up for a jar of his honey. She did swear by it for the aul' kidney troubles. A spoonful of that morning and evening, and you'd be right as rain in no time."

Cal doesn't answer. He's been keeping an eye out for anyone following them—apart from anything else, he wouldn't put it past Trey to have been watching him again—but nothing moves, anywhere around them. The wet earth of the trail gives under their feet. Mart whistles to himself, a low lonesome tune with a strange cadence to it. Sometimes he sings a line or two, in Irish. In that language his voice takes on a different tone, a husky, absent crooning.

"That's a song about a man who goes to the fair and sells his cow," he informs Cal, over his shoulder, "for five pounds in silver and a yellow guinea of gold. And he says, 'If I drink all the silver and squander the gold, why should any man care, when it's nothing to him?'"

He sings again. The trail slopes upwards. On the flat grassland below, the fields spread out shorn and pale in the sharp sunlight, divided by walls that lie along reasons that were forgotten centuries ago.

"He says, 'If I go to the woods picking berries or nuts, taking apples off branches or herding the cows, and I lie under a tree to take my ease, why should any man care, when it's nothing to him?'"

Cal takes out his phone, turns on the camera and holds it up to the view. "Turn that off," Mart says, breaking off the song in mid-line.

"I told my daughter I was going walking up the mountains," Cal says. "She asked for pictures. She likes the look of the scenery around here."

Mart says, "Tell her you forgot your phone."

He stands on the trail, leaning on his crook, looking at Cal and waiting. After a minute Cal turns the phone off and puts it back in his pocket. Mart nods and turns back to walking. In a little bit he starts his song again.

Ferny plants, like nothing Cal's seen in the grasslands, reach from the verges to brush at his boots. Mart's crook makes a small, rhythmic crunching on the path, underscoring the song. "The man says," he tells Cal, "'People say I'm a useless waster, with no goods or fine clothes, no cattle or wealth. If I'm happy enough to live in a shack, why should any man care, when it's nothing to him?'"

He strikes off the trail and clambers through a gap in a crumbling, lichened stone wall. Cal follows. They cross a patch of land that looks like it was cleared, a long time ago, before being abandoned for tufts of tall fine grass to reclaim. In one corner are the tumbledown remains of a stone cottage, much older than Brendan's. Mart doesn't turn his head to look at it. A wisp of wind shivers the seed-heads on the grass.

As they climb higher the cold sharpens, slicing through Cal's layers and pressing its edge into his skin. Cal knows their route is circling and meandering, doubling back on itself, but one gorse bush or patch of moor grass looks too much like the next for him to be sure exactly how. He glances regularly at the sun and the view, trying to keep his bearings, but he knows he could spend a year looking and never find his way here again. He catches Mart's wry eye on him.

Without his phone, Cal can't be sure how long they've been walking; more than an hour, maybe an hour and a half. The sun is high. He thinks of the four men trudging their slow steady way up these trails, the body in its sheet swaying between them.

Mart takes them through a thick stand of spruce, down into a dip, and out onto another single-file trail where the ridge spreads out into a plateau on either side. Glints of water show among the peat and heather.

"Stay on this path, now," he advises Cal. "Every

year there's a sheep or two that steps into one of them bogs and can't get out again. And twenty-five or thirty year back there was a fella that usedta come down from Galway city—mad as a bag of cats, so he was. He'd walk up and down the mountain barefoot every Good Friday, saying the rosary all the way. He said the Blessed Virgin had told him that some year or other, if he kept at it, she'd appear to him along the way. Maybe she did and she picked a bad spot for it, I couldn't tell you, but one year he didn't come back. The men went looking and found him dead in a bitta bog. Only eight foot from the path, with his arm still stretched out towards the dry ground."

The spade is biting into Cal's shoulder, and his knee throbs at every step. He wonders if Mart is planning to walk him in circles till it gives out, and then leave him to find his own way home. The sun has started to slide down the sky.

"There," Mart says, stopping. He points his crook at a spot in the bog, about twenty feet off the path.

"You sure?" Cal asks.

"I am, of course. Would I bring you all the way up here if I wasn't sure?"

All around them the plateau lies flat and wide. Long grass and heather bend, autumn-bleached. Small shadows drift across them, from wisps of cloud.

Cal says, "Looks a lot like about a dozen other places we've passed."

"To you, maybe. If you want Brendan Reddy, that's where you'll find him."

"And his watch is on him."

"We took nothing off him. If he had his watch on that day, then it's on him now."

They stand side by side, looking at the bog. Patches of water shine here and there with reflected blue. "You told me not to go off the path," Cal says. "If I go in there, what's to stop me from ending up like the rosary guy?"

"That sham was a city lad," Mart says. "Either he couldn't tell dry bog from wet, or he thought the Blessed Virgin would haul his arse outa it. I was cutting turf on this mountain before you were born or thought of, and I'm telling you there's good solid bog from here to that spot. How d'you think we got the lad in there without drowning ourselves?"

Cal can see exactly how this will read, if he's misjudged Mart. A dumbass Yank, out playing back-to-nature in country he didn't understand, put a foot wrong. Maybe Alyssa will remember that he was supposed to go walking with his neighbor; but then, half a dozen men will have spent the whole of today hanging out with Mart.

"If you want to turn around and go home," Mart says, "I'll chalk this up to a nice bitta exercise."

"I was never much of a believer in exercise for its own sake," Cal says. "Too lazy for that. If I've come all the way up here, there might as well be a point to it." He shifts the spade to a less painful position on his shoulder and steps off the path. He hears Mart following behind him, but he doesn't turn round.

The bog gives and rebounds under his feet, as his weight reverberates through the layers deep below, but it holds him. "Step left," Mart says. "Now straight." Far out in front of them, a small bird rises in alarm and vanishes into the sky, its high zipping call coming down to them faintly through all that cold space.

"There," Mart says.

In front of Cal's feet, a man-sized rectangle of the bog is rough-edged and lumpy, against the smooth sweep of grass all around.

"He's not as deep as he should be," Mart says. "But, sure, the government's banned cutting turf on this bitta mountain. He'll be left in peace, once you're done with him."

Cal burrows the edge of the spade into the peat, at the rough line where it's been disturbed, and sinks it with his good foot. The blade goes in smoothly; the peat feels thick and clayey under it. "Cut in around the edges first," Mart says. "Then you can lift out the sod."

Cal jabs the spade down again and again till he's made a rectangle, then levers it up and drops it to one side. It comes out easily, neat-edged. In the gash he's left, the peat is dark and smooth. A deep rich smell comes up to him, bringing back the scent of chimney smoke as he walks to the pub on cold evenings.

"Like you were born to it," Mart says. He pulls out his tobacco packet and starts rolling himself a cigarette.

It takes a long time. Cal can't use his injured arm with any force; all it can do is steady the spade as he drives it down. Within a few minutes his good arm is aching. Mart roots the base of his crook in the bog and rests his free forearm on its head while he smokes.

The heap of cut turf grows, and the hole widens and deepens. Sweat turns cold on Cal's face and neck. He leans on the spade to catch his breath, and for one dizzying second he feels the full tornado force of the strangeness of it, that he should find himself on this mountainside half the world from home, digging for a dead boy.

At first he thinks the reddish tuft sprouting where the blade has been is moss or roots. It takes him a second to realize that the peat has darkened, that the smell coming from the hole has thickened into something rancid, and to understand that what he's seeing is hair.

He lays down the spade. In his coat pocket he has a pair of latex gloves that he bought for working on the house. He puts them on, kneels down at the edge of the hole and leans in to work with his hands.

Brendan's face rises out of the bog scrap by scrap. Whatever strange alchemy the bog has worked on him, he looks like no dead body Cal has ever seen. He's all there, flesh and skin intact, lashes lying on his cheeks like he's sleeping. After almost seven months, he still has enough of himself left that Cal would have recognized the smiling boy in the

Facebook shot. But his skin is a strange leathery reddish-brown, and the weight of the bog on top of him has begun to misshape him like soft wax, sliding his face sideways, squashing his features out of true. It gives him an intent, secretive frown, as if he's concentrating on something only he can see. Trey, frowning unconsciously over her sandpapering, comes to Cal's mind.

The line of his jaw is uneven. Cal puts his fingers to it and probes. The flesh feels thickened and condensed and the bone has a dreadful rubbery give, but Cal can still find the break where the punch hit home. Gently he pulls down Brendan's bottom lip. Two of his teeth on that side are broken.

Cal clears a space around Brendan's head till he can see the back of it. He works slowly and with care; he doesn't know how tightly the body is holding together, what parts of it might come away under his hands if he's rough. Even through the gloves, he can feel the texture of the hair between his fingers, a rough tangle like a network of fine roots spreading. At the base of the skull, a great dent is nothing but give, shards shifting. When Cal parts the hair, he can still see the deep jagged gape of the cut.

"You see, now," Mart says, behind him. "Just like I told you."

Cal doesn't answer him. He starts to scoop away the peat that covers Brendan's torso.

"What would you have done if it wasn't?"

Gradually Brendan's jacket surfaces, a black

bomber with an orange patch still bold on the sleeve, unzipped to show a hoodie that might have been gray before the bog dyed it rust-red. Brendan is lying tilted, half on his back and half on his side, his head twisted at an unnatural angle. The sun lies ruthlessly bright on him.

His arm has fallen across his chest. Cal works his way along its line, deeper into the ground. The peat close to the body has a different feel, wetter. That ripe, clotted smell fills up Cal's nose.

"He's not alone," Mart says. "My daddo found a man in this bog, when he was a young lad, a hundred years ago maybe. He said the man musta been there since before Saint Patrick ran off the snakes. Flat as a pancake, so he was, and sticks twisted all around his neck. My daddo covered him back up and never said a word to the police or anyone. He let the man lie in peace."

Cal takes Brendan's hand from the bog. He's afraid it might rip away from the body when he lifts it, but it holds. It has the same red-brown stain as the face, and it folds and wavers as if it's almost boneless. The bog is transmuting Brendan into something new.

The wrist bends like a twig under its own weight. It's the one Cal needs: when he moves back the water-heavy layers of sleeves, the watch is there. The strap is leather and has fused to the skin. Cal unbuckles it and starts to peel it away as delicately as he can, but the flesh slides and breaks apart into something unthinkable, a slimy whitish mass.

Cal's mind moves outside him. His gloved hands look like things that belong to someone else as they busy themselves with the watch, carefully detaching it and wiping away sodden peat and worse things on the grass, as best they can. He notices very clearly that the grass up here has a harsher texture than the grass in the fields below, and that the shins of his pants are soaked from kneeling.

The watch is an old one, with heft and dignity to it: a gold-rimmed cream face, with slim gold ticks for numbers and slim gold hands. The bog has toughened the leather, but it hasn't changed the gold; that still has its pale, serene luster. There are letters inscribed on the back: **BPB**, in worn, curly lettering; under that, fresh and upright, **BJR**.

Cal cleans his gloves on the grass and gets a Ziploc bag out of his pocket. He would like not to take any scrap of the bog away with him, but for all his cleaning, little shreds and dabbles smear the inside of the bag. He puts it away in his pocket.

He looks down at Brendan and can't imagine how to lay those sods back over him. It goes against every instinct he has, right down to his muscles and bones. His hands want to keep working, clear away the peat and lay the boy bare to the cold sunlight. His throat is full up with the words to say into the phone to set that powerful familiar machine in motion, cameras clicking and evidence bags opening and questions firing, until every truth has been spoken out loud and everyone has been placed where they belong.

He's pretty sure he could drop his phone without Mart noticing. GPS tracking would lead them close enough.

Cal feels that weightlessness again, the bog losing its solidity under his knees as gravity lets go of him. When he looks up, Mart is watching him; steady-eyed, head cocked a little to one side; waiting.

Cal looks back and finds himself not giving much of a shit about Mart. He can make Mart take him back down this mountain, if he needs to. He can protect himself and Trey till he can get her placed in care; she would fight like a bobcat and hate his guts forevermore, but she'd be safe. And in no time flat he would be too far away for her, or anyone else, to put a brick through his window.

What comes into his mind is Alyssa, her voice close to his ear, earnest as when she was a little kid explaining some stuffed animal's problems to him. **Your neighbor girl, she really needs consistency right now. Like, the last thing she needs is someone else disappearing on her.**

Cal can't tell for the life of him what's the right thing to do, or even whether there is one, but he knows what comes closest. He bends down and tucks Brendan back into the earth. He would like to lay him out properly, but even if he was sure he could manage that without causing more damage, he knows why Mart and the rest didn't do it to begin with—if some rogue turf-cutter should happen to come across the boy, it needs to look like he wound up here by accident. Soon enough, the bog will have melted his bones till no one can read his injuries on them.

Instead he places Brendan's arm carefully back across his chest and straightens the collar of his jacket. He scoops up the turf he scraped away and packs it around the contours of Brendan's body and head, covering his face as gently as he can, until piece by piece it's vanished back into the bog. Then he takes up the spade again and lays the cut chunks of turf over the boy. It takes a while; his good arm has started to shake from the strain. He saves the grassy sods for last. He nudges them into place and presses them down, so that the edges match up cleanly and the grass can grow to blur the scars.

"Say a prayer over him," Mart says. "Since you're after disturbing him."

Cal stands up—it takes him a few seconds to get his back straight. He can't remember any prayers. He tries to think what Trey would want said or done as her brother is laid down, but he has no idea. All he can think of to do, with what breath he's got left, is sing the same song he did at his grandpa's funeral.

I am a poor wayfaring stranger
Traveling through this world alone
But there's no sickness, toil or danger

In that bright world to which I go.
I'm going there to see my loved ones
I'm going there, no more to roam
I'm only going over Jordan
I'm only going over home.

His voice evaporates quickly into the vast cold sky. "That'll do," Mart says. He pulls his beanie down more firmly over his ears and uproots his crook from the bog. "Come on, now. I don't want to be up here when it gets dark."

He takes them down the mountain by a different route, one that leads them through plantation after plantation of tall spruce trees, and down slopes steep enough that Cal sometimes finds himself breaking into a half jog that jars savagely in his knee. They pass fragments of old stone-wall field boundaries, and sheep's hoofprints in muddy patches, but they don't see another living creature anywhere on the way. The day has disoriented Cal enough that he finds himself wondering if Mart has somehow warned everyone and everything in the townland to stay hidden today, or if he and Mart have wandered into some time-free zone and they'll come out into a world that's moved on a hundred years without them. He can see how Bobby wound up going a little alien-crazy, if he spent too much time on this mountain.

"So, Sunny Jim," Mart says, breaking a long silence. He hasn't been singing. "You got what you were after."

"Yeah," Cal says. He wonders whether Mart is expecting him to say thank you.

"The child can show that to her mammy, if she likes, and tell her where it came from. No one else."

Cal says, " 'Cause Sheila'll make damn sure the kid keeps her mouth shut."

"Sheila's a smart woman," Mart says. The sun between the spruce branches streaks his face with brightness and shadows. It blurs away the wrinkles and makes him look younger and stronger, at ease. "It's a feckin' shame she ever took up with that eejit Johnny Reddy. There was a dozen fellas that woulda jumped at the chance to get in there, but would she look twice at them? Would she fuck. Sheila coulda had a good house and a farm and all her childer in university. And look at her now."

"You tell her what happened?" Cal asks.

"She already knew the young fella wasn't coming back. There was nothing else she needed to know. What you saw up there, would it do any good, her having that in her head?"

"I'm gonna go up to Sheila Reddy," Cal says, "once I get the use of this arm back. Give her a hand fixing that roof."

"Ah, now," Mart says, with a flinch and a grimace. "Not one of your finest inspirations there, Sunny Jim, if you don't mind me saying."

"You think?"

"You don't want to make a woman like Lena

jealous. Next thing you know, there's a full-on feud breaking out all round you, and I'd say you've caused enough trouble around here for a while, amn't I right? Besides"—he grins at Cal—"who's to say Sheila'd want you? Your reputation for mending roofs isn't the greatest, now."

Cal says nothing. His arm is cramping from carrying the spade.

"D'you know, though," Mart says, struck by something, "you're after putting an idea into my head. Sheila Reddy could do with a bitta looking after, all right. A few bob here and there, maybe, or a few sods of turf, or someone to mend that roof for her. I'll have a chat with the lads and see what we can sort out." He smiles at Cal. "Would you look at that, now. You're after doing some good around here, after all. I don't know why I never thought of it before."

Cal says, " 'Cause she mighta figured out why you were doing it. Now that she knows you were mixed up in this, it can't do any harm, and it'll help keep her quiet. One way or another."

"Let me tell you something, Sunny Jim," Mart says reprovingly. "You've a terrible habit of thinking the worst of people. D'you know what that is? That's that job of yours. It's after warping your mind. That attitude's no use to you now. If you'd only relax a wee bit, look on the bright side, you'd get the good out of the aul' retirement. Get yourself one of them apps that teach you to think positive."

"Speaking of thinking the worst," Cal says, "the kid is gonna keep coming round to my place. I don't expect the townland to give either of us any shit about it."

"I'll have a word," Mart says superbly, holding back branches for Cal as they come out of the spruces onto a trail. "Sure, you'll do the child good. Women who haven't had a dacent man around while they're growing up, they end up marrying wasters. And the last thing this townland needs is whatever you get when you cross a Reddy with a McGrath."

"I'd put him in that bog first," Cal says, before he can stop himself.

Mart bursts out laughing. It's a big, free, happy sound that spreads out, almost shockingly, across the hillside. "I believe you," he says. "You'd be straight back up there with that spade, on the double. Jaysus, man, it's a mad world we live in, hah? You'd never know where it'd take you."

"No shit," Cal says. "Anyway, I thought you thought the kid was gay."

"Well, will you look at that," Mart says, grinning. "We're back on conversational terms. I'm only delighted. And the child can marry a waster whether she's gay or not, can't she? That's what we voted for: the gays can make fools of themselves, same as the rest of us, and no one can stop them."

Cal says, "That kid's no fool."

"We all are, when we're young. The Indians do

have it right: it's the parents that oughta arrange the marriages. They'd make a better job of it than a buncha young people that's only thinking with their wild bits."

"And you'd have been married off to some skinny girl who'd want a poodle and a chandelier," Cal points out.

"I would not," Mart says with an air of victory. "My daddy and mammy never agreed on anything in their lives; there's no chance they'd have agreed on a woman for me. I'd be where I am now, free and single, and without the consequences of Sheila Reddy's foolishness to deal with."

"You'd just find something else to get mixed up in," Cal says. "You'd get bored."

"I might, all right," Mart acknowledges. "How about yourself?" He squints at Cal, evaluating. "I'd say your mammy would have found you a nice cheerful young one with a good steady job. A nurse, maybe, or a teacher; no eejit for you. We're not looking at any Elle Macpherson—she wouldn't want you having the hassle of that—but pretty enough. A girl that was up for a few laughs, but no nonsense about her; no wild streak. And your daddy wouldn't have given a shite one way or another. Am I right or am I right?"

Cal can't help a half smile. "Pretty much," he says.

"And you might be better off. You wouldn't be halfway up a mountain with a banjaxed knee, anyway."

"Who knows," Cal says. "Like you say, it's a mad world." He realizes that Mart is leaning hard on his crook. His steps are jerkier and more lopsided than they were on the way up, or even at the start of the way down, and the lines of his face have tightened up with pain. His joints have paid for the journey.

The path gradually levels off. The heather and moor grass give way to tangles of weeds pushing in from the verges. Birds begin to chirp and rattle.

"There you go," Mart says, stopping where the path leads between hedges into a paved road. "D'you know where you are?"

"Not a clue," Cal says.

Mart laughs. "Head down that way about half a mile," he says, pointing with his crook, "and you'll come to the boreen that goes round the back of Francie Gannon's land. Don't worry if you see Francie; he won't go telling tales on you this time. Just blow him a kiss and he'll be happy."

"You're not heading home?"

"Ah, God, no. I'm off to Seán Óg's for a pint or two or three. I've earned it."

Cal nods. He could use a drink himself, but neither of them has any desire for the other's company right now. "You did the right thing, taking me up there," he says.

"We'll find out, sure," Mart says. "Give Lena an extra squeeze for me." He lifts his crook in a salute and hobbles off, with the low winter sunlight laying his shadow a long way down the road behind him.

The house is cold. In spite of all his layers and all the exercise, Cal is chilled to the marrow; the mountain has burrowed deep inside him. He showers till his hot water runs out, but he can still feel the cold spreading outwards from his bones, and it seems to him that he's still soaked inside and out with the rich smell of peat tainted with death.

That evening he stays indoors and leaves the lights off. He doesn't want Trey to come calling. His mind hasn't come all the way back inside his body yet; he doesn't want her to see him until today has had time to wear off him a little. He puts everything he was wearing in the washing machine and sits in his armchair, looking out the window as the fields dim towards a frosty blue twilight and the mountains lose their detail to become one dark sweep at rest. He thinks about Brendan and Trey somewhere within that unchanging outline, Brendan with the bog slowly working its will on him, Trey with the sweet air healing her wounds. He thinks about how things will grow where his own blood soaked into the soil outside, and about his hands in the earth today, what he harvested and what he sowed.

Trey comes the next day. Cal is doing his ironing on the table when she knocks. Just from that tight tap, he can feel what it's taken for her to stay away this long. Mostly she thumps that door like the whole point is to enjoy the noise.

"Come in," he calls, unplugging the iron.

Trey closes the door carefully behind her and holds out a loaf of fruitcake. She looks a whole lot better. There's still a big scab running down from her lip, but the black eye has cleared to a faint yellowish shadow, and she's not moving like the rib catches her. She looks like she might have grown another half inch.

"Thanks," Cal says. "How're you doing?"

"Grand. Your nose looks better."

"Getting there." Cal puts the cake on the counter and takes the watch from a drawer. "I got you what you need."

He holds the watch out to Trey. It's clean; he put it in boiling water for a while and then left it to dry out on the heater overnight. He knows that probably fucked it up beyond repair, even if the bog hadn't managed that already, but it needed doing.

Trey turns the watch over and looks at the inscription on the back. There are little marks on her hands, pink and shiny, where the scabs have fallen away.

"That's your brother's watch," Cal says. "Right?"

Trey nods. She's breathing like it takes an effort. Her skinny chest rises and falls.

Cal waits, in case there's something she wants to say or ask, but she just stands there, looking at the watch. "I cleaned it," he says. "It's not working, but

I'll find a good watch-repair store somewhere and see if they can get it running for you. If you want to wear it, though, you gotta make sure to tell people Brendan left it behind."

Trey nods. Cal isn't sure how much of that she heard.

"You can tell your mama the real story," he says. No matter what Sheila's done, she deserves that much. "No one else."

She nods again. She rubs the back of the watch with her thumb, like if she rubs hard enough the inscription might have mercy and disappear.

"Whoever gave you this," she says. "They could still have been bullshitting you. About what happened."

"I saw his body, kid," Cal says gently. "The injuries were consistent with the statement I was given."

He hears the hiss of Trey catching a breath. "You sound like a Guard," she says.

"I know."

"Is that where you got this? Off his body?"

"Yeah," Cal says. He has no idea what he ought to do if she asks about the body.

She doesn't. Instead she says, "Where is he?"

"He's buried up in the mountains," Cal says. "I couldn't find the place again if I tried all year. But it's a good place. Peaceful. I never saw a graveyard that was more peaceful."

Trey stands there looking down at the watch in her hands. Then she turns around and walks out the door.

Cal watches her through the windows as she goes around behind the house and down the garden. She climbs over the gate into his back field and keeps walking. He watches till he sees her sit down at the edge of his woods, with her back against a tree. Her parka blends in with the underbrush; the only way he can pick her out is by the red flash of her hoodie.

He finds his phone and texts Lena. **Any chance you still have a pup looking for a home? The kid could do with a dog. She'd take good care of it.**

There's a pause of a few minutes before Lena gets back to him. **Two of them are sorted. Trey can take her pick of the rest.**

Cal texts her, **Could me and her come over sometime and see them? If that runt is still free I should get to know him better before I take him home.**

This time his phone buzzes straightaway. **He's no runt now. He's eating me out of house and home. I hope you're a rich man. Come tomorrow afternoon. I'll be home by 3.**

Cal gives Trey half an hour out by the woods. Then he starts bringing his desk equipment out to the back garden, piece by piece: the drop sheet, the desk, his tool kit, wood filler, scrap wood and brushes and three little cans of wood stain that he picked up in town. He brings out the cake, too: when he was a kid, shouldering the weight of heavy emotions always left him hungry. It's another beautiful wintry day, with wispy brushstrokes of cloud in a thin blue sky. The afternoon sun lies lightly on the fields.

He upends the desk and takes a good look at the broken side. It's not in as bad shape as he thought. He figured he was looking at disassembling the whole thing and replacing the side panel, but while a few pieces of the splintered wood are beyond repair, plenty of it can be slotted back into place and glued. The gaps should be small enough for wood filler. Carefully, kneeling on the drop sheet, he starts picking away the unsalvageable shards. He cleans the dust off the others with a paintbrush and then starts painting glue onto them, one by one, and delicately easing them back where they belong. He keeps his shoulder turned to the woods.

He's clamping a long shard into place when he hears the swish of feet in the grass. "Check this out," he says, without looking up. "Seems to me it's working OK."

"Thought we were going to take it apart and put in a new side," Trey says. Her voice comes out rough around the edges.

"Doesn't look like we'll need to," Cal says. "We can find something else to take apart, if you want. I could use another chair."

Trey squats to take a closer look at the desk. She's stashed the watch away in some pocket. Or maybe she's thrown it away somewhere in the woods, or buried it, but Cal doesn't think so. "Looks good," she says.

"Here," Cal says. He points at the cans of wood stain. "You try these out on some scrap wood, see which one's the best match. You might have to do some mixing to get it right."

"Need a plate or something," Trey says. "For mixing."

"Get that old tin one."

Trey lopes off to the house and comes back with the plate and a mug of water. She arranges herself cross-legged on the drop sheet, lays out her equipment around her and sets to work.

In their tree the rooks are peaceful, tossing scraps of conversation back and forth, occasionally soaring across to a neighboring nest to pay a visit. One skinny young one is hanging upside down from a branch to see what the world looks like that way. Trey mixes stain colors on the plate, paints a neat square of each mixture onto a stray piece of two-by-four and labels it in pencil, in some code of her own. Cal coaxes splinters of wood into place and clamps them there. After a while he opens the cake, and they break off a chunk each and sit on the grass to eat it, listening to the rooks exchange views and watching the shadows of clouds drift across the mountainsides.

ACKNOWLEDGMENTS

I owe huge thanks to Darley Anderson, the most magnificent agent I can imagine, and everyone at the agency, especially Rosanna, Georgia, Mary, Kristina, and Rebeka; my amazing editors, Andrea Schulz and Katy Loftus, who in the middle of a pandemic somehow found the time, focus, and patience to make this book so much better; the wonderful Ben Petrone, Nidhi Pugalia, and everyone at Viking US; the extremely skillful and extremely sound Olivia Mead, Anna Ridley, Georgia Taylor, Ellie Hudson, and everyone at Viking UK; Susanne Halbleib and everyone at Fischer Verlage; Steve Fisher of APA; Jessica Ryan, for being my North Carolina dictionary (any mistakes are mine); Bairbre Ní Chaoimh, for filling in the gaps in my rusty Irish (ditto); Fearghas Ó Cochláin, for making sure I kill people off accurately; Ciara Considine, Clare Ferraro, and Sue Fletcher, who set all this in motion; Kristina Johansen, Alex French, Susan Collins, Noni Stapleton, Paul and Anna Nugent, Oonagh Montague, and Karen Gillece, for the usual priceless combination of laughs, talks, support, creativity, and all the other essentials; David Ryan, clinically proven to cure gout, improve broadband speed, reduce hangovers, and eliminate aphids; my mother, Elena Lombardi; my father, David French; and, as always, the finest man I know and the one I'd pick to be stuck in lockdown with any day, my husband, Anthony Breatnach.

ABOUT THE AUTHOR

Tana French is the author of seven previous books, including **In the Woods, The Likeness,** and **The Witch Elm.** Her novels have sold over three million copies and won numerous awards, including the Edgar, Anthony, Macavity, and Barry awards, the Los Angeles Times Book Prize for Best Mystery/Thriller, and the Irish Book Award for Crime Fiction. She lives in Dublin with her family.

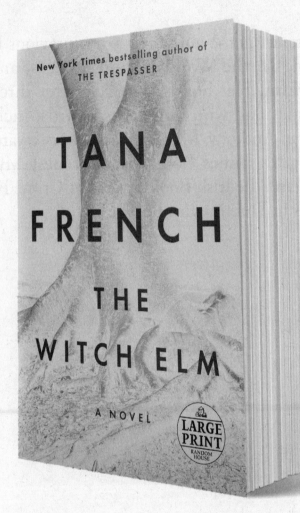